"IMZADI . . . HELP ME . . ."

Riker raced into Deanna's quarters and was horrified by the sight that greeted his eyes. Deanna was lying on the floor, convulsions shaking her. "Riker to sickbay, where's that medunit!" he shouted desperately, and didn't even wait for a reply as he dropped down next to the trembling counselor. His hands moved helplessly over her, and he fought down his own terror as he said, "Shh . . . everything's going to be okay. It's okay, Deanna . . ."

Her eyes were clouding over. He didn't think she could even see him. He had no idea what was happening to her, and even more terrifying . . . neither did she. "Imzadi," she whispered again, her chin shaking. Please . . . help . . . me . . . help . . ."

"I will," he said desperately, "I promise I . . ."

But she didn't hear him. Her breath rattled once more in her chest . . . and she was gone.

A battle for life, love, honor, and the
soul of a woman whom only one man can call
beloved

IMZADI
II

By

Peter David

STAR TREK®

THE NEXT GENERATION™

IMZADI

PETER DAVID

POCKET BOOKS

New York   London   Toronto   Sydney   Tokyo   Singapore

POCKET BOOKS, a division of Simon & Schuster Inc.
1230 Avenue of the Americas, New York, NY 10020

STAR TREK is a Registered Trademark of
Paramount Pictures.

A VIACOM COMPANY

This book is published by Pocket Books, a division of
Simon & Schuster Inc., under exclusive license from
Paramount Pictures.

ISBN: 0-671-02610-0

First Pocket Books paperback printing July 1993

10 9 8 7 6 5 4 3 2 1

POCKET and colophon are registered trademarks of
Simon & Schuster Inc.

This one has to be for Harlan

A Brief Foreword

This novel, the last premise of mine to be approved by Gene Roddenberry, is the first one I've written since his passing. He said, at the time he okayed the idea of a novel exploring the history and depth of the Deanna Troi/William Riker relationship, that he looked forward to reading it. Which he never had the opportunity to do.

The amount of time we have on this sphere to accomplish what we want is always limited, no matter how much we like to pretend otherwise. That's something always to be kept in mind.

Thanks must go especially, once again, to my family. The girls, Shana, Guinevere, and the newest—in case you were wondering—Miss Ariel Leela David. No, she wasn't born on the twenty-fifth anniversary of *Star Trek*. She was born on Labor Day, which is—to be honest—just as good.

And most of all, to my wife, Myra, who naturally didn't invent the term *Imzadi*, but is, to me, the incarnation of it.

THE END

THE END

CHAPTER 1

"Let's get the hell out of here."

A gentle, eerie howling was in the air, which seemed to be permeated with the haunting and lonely cries of souls that had existed or might never exist or might be in some state of limbo in between.

In the distance was the city. Its name was unknown and would forever remain so. The air was dark and filled with a sense that a storm might break at any moment. It was that way all the time. The storm never did break. It just threatened to do so. The very withholding of the actual event implied that, should that storm ever arrive, it might very well bring with it enough power to wash away all vestiges of that remarkable intangible called reality.

None of that mattered to the man who was the leader. The man in the greenish yellow shirt, whose mind was elsewhere and elsewhen. Behind him stood his friends, his crew. They waited patiently. For a moment it appeared that he was wondering just how long they would be capable of waiting. What were the limits of their patience? The limits of their confidence in the man who was their captain?

But it was clear that he was not going to test those limits. A man who had been driven to go out and explore new places, discover new frontiers . . . this man had finally found a place filled with potentially endless vistas of exploration. Anywhere, anywhen. And his response was not to embrace it. No, all he wanted to do was leave it behind, to get as far away from it as possible.

"Let's get the hell out of here." The words hung there a moment, startling in their vehemence, in the longing and resignation and overall sense of *Oh, God, I can't stand it anymore, get me away from here, away to a place where I don't have to think or feel, to a place where I can just be numb.*

The crew took several small steps closer to each other. To a degree it was out of reflex, to make sure that they would be well within range of the transporter effect. But there was something else as well this time. It was an unspoken desire to try to lend support by dint of the fact that they were *there* for him. There was nothing they could say or do. Indeed, they didn't even fully understand what was going through the captain's mind.

They did not yet know the sacrifices their commanding officer had made. Did not know that, in the best tradition of romance, he had found a part of his soul existing in a woman and had been drawn to her. And then had lost that part of his soul, which he hadn't fully realized he was missing in the first place. Lost it beneath the screeching of tires, under a truck's wheels . . .

Not just the wheel of a truck. A wheel of history, an unrelenting, unyielding cog that had ground up his love and his soul and spit them both out, bloodied and battered . . . and broken.

Yes, that was the difference that the crew sensed this time in their captain. Many a time had he been battered . . . but as the old saying went, "Battered but unbowed." This time, though . . . he was bowed.

They got the hell out of there.

And Commodore Data watched them go.

She was simply called Mary Mac. Her last name actually began with a sound approximating "Mac," but the rest was a major tongue twister. As a result, the other scientists addressed her as "Mary Mac."

Mary Mac was extremely peculiar. For one thing, she was an Orion. This in itself was not particularly unusual. She was, however, fully clothed. This *was* unusual, as the vast majority of Orion women existed purely to be the sex toys of men in general and Orion men in particular. They were known as vicious and deadly fighters and radiated sex the way suns radiated heat . . . and indeed, some thought, a bit more intensely.

Mary Mac's skin was green, as was standard for an Orion woman. In every other aspect, however, she was markedly different from the rest of her kind. She wore loose-fitting clothes . . . deliberately loose so as to do nothing that could potentially emphasize the formidable curves of her body. Because she liked her arms unencumbered, her tunic was short sleeved, although an off-the-shoulder cape was draped stylishly around her. She had long, jet-black hair, but rather than hanging saucily around her shoulders, it was delicately and elaborately braided . . . certainly not an ugly hairstyle, but hardly one that would inflame the senses.

Most incredibly . . . she wore glasses. They had a slight tint and huge frames.

Nobody wore glasses. They were considered to be phenomenally out-of-date as well as unattractive.

Which is why she wore them.

Mary Mac regretted, every so often, that she felt a need to "dress down," as it were, so that she could operate within society. She was, however, used to it. There were precious few prejudices that one had to deal with in the day-to-day operations of the United Federation of Planets, but one of the few remaining was that all Orion women were nothing but animalistic sex kittens. It was an understandable notion because that description did indeed fit virtually all Orion women, including most of the ones whom Mary Mac had ever met.

It did not, however, fit her, and if she had to go to extremes to get her point across, well . . . then so be it. Her "look" had gotten her quite far. It had, in fact, been something of a plus. People would be interested and amused by her as she would discuss some involved or arcane bit of scientific lore . . . interested because usually they'd never heard an Orion woman put together a sentence of more than five or so words, and amused because they'd smugly be waiting for her to revert to type any moment. She never did, of course. She'd trained too long and too hard to allow that to happen. As a result she was always a bit of a surprise, and throughout the galaxy, people loved to be surprised.

Which is why Mary Mac had worked her way up through the ranks and eventually landed the assignment of project administrator on Forever World.

The planet did not have an official name. Somehow it had seemed presumptuous for any mere mortal to give it one . . . somewhat like painting a mustache on the face of God. It had simply been nicknamed Forever World, and that was what had stuck.

She passed her associate coordinator, Harry, who didn't seem to notice her. A muscular and dark-hued terran, Harry's attention was fully on a set of equations or some other bit of scientific data on a palm-sized computer padd. "Hi, Harry," she said to him as he walked past. He waved distractedly and continued on his way. He had probably already forgotten that he'd been addressed at all, much less by Mary Mac.

Mary Mac made her way across the compound, nodding or conversing briefly with other scientists on the project. One of the odder aspects of conversation on the Forever World was that one tended to speak in a hushed voice. There was no particular reason for it. It certainly wasn't mandated by law or tradition. But somehow, particularly when one was standing outside and the eerie howling filled one's ears and one's soul, the speaking voice tended to drop to a soft tone that could best be described as "subdued" . . . and perhaps even a bit fearful. Mary had once commented that it always seemed as if the cosmos was hanging on your every word here. It was an assessment that had been generally agreed with.

The gravel crunched under Mary Mac's boots as she got to the other side of the compound and headed toward the reason for the perpetual presence of a half dozen or so scientists on the Forever World.

Just ahead of her was the only other constant noise that existed aside from the mournful sigh of the wind, and that was a steady, constant hum of a force field. She stepped over a rise, and as always, there it was.

As always was not a term used lightly, or incorrectly. As near as anyone could tell, the Guardian of Forever had always been there, and would most likely always be there.

The force field that had been erected around it was ostensibly to protect the unique archaeological discovery from any potential ravagers. But in point of fact, it was there for a subtly different reason. Namely, to protect life (as it was known) from itself.

Erected just outside the force field was a free-standing platform about two meters tall. An array of readouts charted the energy fluxes that surged around the Guardian of Forever within the force field. There were, in addition, two small lights, one brightly glowing red, the other pulsing a very soft green.

To the right of the platform was a large screen. It offered, in essence, a taped delay. When a request for a period was made on the Guardian, it ran so quickly that the best anyone could hope to perceive was fleeting images. But the screen would then capture those images and play specifically requested moments in a more accessible fashion.

At this particular moment, the Guardian had finished yet another run-through of a particular era. It was now silent, displaying nothing, waiting with its infinite patience for the next request from an audience.

Standing outside the field, staring at the Guardian, was an android. Playing out on the screen, having been recorded moments before for replay, was a scene very familiar to Mary Mac.

She stopped and simply took in for a moment the irony of the situation. On one level, what she was seeing was one machine watching another. But neither of them were simple machines. Both of them had sentience, which raised them from the level of machine to the status of . . . something else. Something unclassifiable.

The very thought of something that could not easily be labeled or pigeonholed was anathema to Mary Mac, and yet at the same time the existence of such things was a pleasant reminder that no one could ever fully know every wrinkle that the universe had to offer . . . and that, therefore, a scientist's work would never, ever, be finished.

Her first inclination had been to think of the android, despite the rank of commodore, as an "it." Just as she had thought of the Guardian as an "it" before coming to the Forever World. However, shortly after she'd met Commodore Data, she'd found herself forced to revise her opinion and mentally elevate the commodore to a "he." As for the Guardian, she was still trying to get that sorted out. The best she could come up with at the moment was a "whatever." Or perhaps, more accurately, a "whenever."

Data stood there, his back to Mary Mac, hands draped just below the base of his spine. The stark black and green lines of his uniform, with the silver trim on the arms and trouser cuffs, seemed to shimmer in the perpetual twilight of the horizon. His attention shifted momentarily from the Guardian to the scene being replayed on the screen.

Mary Mac heard a familiar voice, a voice filled with resolve and yet hidden trauma. And the voice said, "Let's get the hell out of here."

She smiled and called out, "That figures."

Data turned and looked at her, his face calm and composed as always. His gold skin glittered in the half light. "Pardon?"

She pointed at the Guardian. "That moment. It's one of the most popular."

Data nodded slowly and looked back. On the screen, the crew of explorers was drawing closer to its leader and then, moments later, shimmered out of existence. "That's not surprising, I suppose," said Data. "Although there are many moments from history that would be far more impressive in their scope, the history of James Kirk and the crew of *Enterprise* would certainly hold some degree of fascination. People would probably feel more empathy toward someone who is closer to their own frame of reference. What I find interesting is how primitive the transporter technology was."

Mary Mac looked at him in surprise. "You know, Commodore, I've seen so many people watch this moment. The story of Kirk's ordeal with the Guardian, and what he sacrificed for the sake of history . . . it's become so well known. One of the few modern-day legends we have. And I've seen so many reactions, ranging from hysterics to mourning. I've never heard anyone just comment on the technology . . . especially not when they're seeing it for the first time."

Data glanced at the screen. "It's not the first time. It's the second."

"When did you see it before?"

"When it was displayed on the Guardian, one point three minutes ago."

She blinked in surprise. "You were able to make out something that played on the Guardian himself?"

"Of course. The image feed may be rapid for you, but for me it's relatively sluggish. Still, I wished to see it on the replay screen in the event that I missed some sort of nuance. But I didn't."

She shook her head. "You are a rather different customer than we usually get around here, Commodore, I must admit. Most people don't quite know how to react when they see their ancestors brought to life, or shadows of life"—she gestured to the Guardian—"before their very eyes."

"Understandable," said Data. "However, the difference is . . . I have no ancestors."

"You were made. Other androids existed before you, even if not in direct lineage. If they're not ancestors, what would you call them?"

He considered it a moment. "Precedents," he decided.

She smiled broadly and clapped him on the back. "Come on. We have dinner up back at the compound. We'd be honored if you joined us."

"I'd like to touch it."

Her hand stayed on his back, but her expression slid into a puzzled frown. "Touch what?"

"The Guardian of Forever."

"Whatever for?"

He looked at her in such a way, with his gold-pupiled eyes, that Mary Mac felt a slight chill. The same sort that she had felt when she first stood in the presence of the Guardian.

As if he had been reading her mind, Data said, "To be honest . . . I'm not entirely sure. The Guardian and I . . . we are rarities in the universe. We are each one of a kind." He shifted his gaze to the

Guardian. "For a brief time I had a brother . . . but he's gone now, although part of him"—he tapped his forehead for a moment—"remains with me. For an even briefer time—forty-two years ago, to be exact—I had a daughter . . . but she was barely here long enough to establish her presence. I sense in the Guardian a kindred spirit." He looked back at Mary Mac. "Would you consider that funny, Doctor? The notion that something inhuman would try to lay claim to something as human as a spirit?"

"No," she said quietly. "No, I wouldn't think that's funny at all. But . . . look. Getting within range of the Guardian . . . it's not exactly regulations. In fact, it's *against* regulations."

"I am very aware of all Starfleet regulations, Dr. Mac. My programming makes me incapable of violating them. What is prohibited is unauthorized use of the Guardian, especially for the intention of altering or changing time lines. I don't wish to use it. I simply want to . . ."

He paused, and for someone as clearly articulate as Data, it seemed very odd for him to be pausing, trying to find the right words. "To connect with it," he said finally.

She studied him for a moment, then showed her white teeth. "All right, Commodore. Although frankly, I'm taking a big chance here of getting my ass handed to me."

Data frowned and looked at her buttocks, but she quickly made a dismissive wave. "Not literally."

She stretched out an arm and placed her palm flat against the control padd that stood outside the Guardian. As she did so, Data looked with curiosity at her upper arm. "How did you acquire that bruise, Doctor? It's very peculiar."

She glanced at where he was looking. Sure enough, there was a small abrasion on her upper right arm, perfectly round and about as large as if one made a circle from the thumb and forefinger. "I don't know," she said in mild surprise. "Must have banged it against something."

She dismissed it mentally and looked back at the control platform. A thin beam of red light shot out from it and scanned her right eye, feeding the retinal pattern into the compound's central data banks. It came back with a Priority Alpha clearance. A moment later the force field faded, the steady hum of the generators disappearing. Now there was nothing but the crying of the wind.

Commodore Data slowly walked forward, approaching the Guardian with as close to trepidation as he could possibly come. He stopped several feet away. "Who are you?" he asked.

The vast, round portal flickered as a voice spoke with a booming, all-encompassing vastness that seemed to come from everywhere at once. "I am the Guardian of Forever."

"Are you a Guardian in the sense of a preserver? Or a Guardian in the sense of a protector?"

"Both . . . and neither."

Data cocked his head slightly. Mary Mac, for her part, had quietly activated her wrist recorder. Any direct communication with the Guardian could result in some unexpected new insight. She had conversed with the vast portal on a number of different occasions, and every time there was some new nuance to its replies.

"How is such a self-contradictory assessment possible?" Data asked.

"Since I am possible . . . then all is possible."

Data considered this a moment. "Are you saying that you are the keeper of time and protect it from trespass . . . but since every man's fate is in his own hands, you really cannot protect it from those who wish to affect it."

"All living beings affect the flow of what is. I am but one portal through time. There is an infinity of others."

This response brought a startled glance from Mary Mac. Data didn't turn his attention from the Guardian.

"Are you saying there are others like yourself?"

"Of course. In every moment of time that there is . . . then I am there. As you exist within all the moments of your lifetime. But you exist in the individual moments. I exist in all."

"Holy Kolker," whispered Mary Mac.

"You transcend all boundaries of time and space?" asked Data.

"No. I do not transcend them."

"What, then?"

"I define them."

Data looked back at Mary Mac. It was a curiously human move.

It was almost as if Data wanted to reassure himself that she was still there. Then he looked again at the Guardian.

"May I touch you?" asked Data.

"You have free will. Do as you wish."

Data paused, then walked up to the rocklike surface of the Guardian. Without hesitation, he placed his gold palm against it.

The lights throbbed beneath his hand. From the chill that cut through the air, he had expected that the Guardian would feel cool, even cold. Instead it pulsed with an odd sort of warmth. Data lifted his hand for a moment and could feel no heat being radiated from the Guardian's surface. But when he placed his hand against it again, there it was, entirely self-contained.

"Very curious," he said.

He stayed that way for a long moment, then stepped back. "I would like to talk again at some other point."

"All will occur," replied the Guardian.

Data turned and walked back to Mary Mac. She watched him with curiosity. Anyone . . . "normal," for want of a better word . . . would have walked away while glancing repeatedly over his shoulder at the Guardian. But Commodore Data, having decided to take his leave, was now completely focused on the next order of business.

"Thank you for the opportunity," said Data.

Mary Mac inclined her chin slightly toward the Guardian. "Did you understand any of that?"

"I have an interpretation that I believe to be fairly accurate. I'd be most interested in comparing my conjectures with those of the other members of your research team."

"Hey, that's what you're here for. To check up on us and keep Starfleet apprised of our progress. The invitation to dinner is still open."

"Thank you. I'll just check with my ship first. . . . Commodore Data to *Enterprise.*"

Mary Mac stood and watched him as he held a conversation with thin air.

"Good. I will be remaining on the planet surface several more hours. Be sure to keep the ship sufficiently outside the range of the temporal distortions, since we're uncertain of the effect long-term exposure could have. . . . I'll want Science Officer Blair joining me. . . . Very well, then, as soon as he's completed them. . . . Thank you, Lieutenant Commander. Commodore out."

He turned and looked back at Mary Mac, who shook her head. "I can't get over that," she said. "That comm-chip implant so that you can hear each other inside your heads."

"A two-second procedure to install. Inserted with a hypo spray. Impossible to lose, so we can remain in touch with each other at all times. Plus increased privacy for communications. Had I wished to, Doctor, I could simply have whispered my replies and you would not have been able to hear any of it. However, there was nothing particularly confidential about this communiqué."

"What's it like?" Mary Mac looked skyward as if she could detect it with the unaided eye. "The *Enterprise*, I mean."

"The *Enterprise?*" Data paused. "In many ways, the *Enterprise* 1701-F is similar to the 1701-D upon which I first served. It is larger, more powerful, more maneuverable. Crew complement of two thousand twenty-three people."

"And you're in command."

He nodded slightly. "There is that, of course. And yet, in some ways . . . I find myself thinking of the past, more and more often. I suppose, as one acquires more memories, that is natural."

"Yes. It is. Certainly—just like yourself—not without precedent."

CHAPTER 2

There was nothing desirable about Starbase 86.

It was far removed from the more frequently traveled space lanes. Visitors were rare, commerce even rarer. The facilities were not exactly top of the line.

Starbases served a variety of functions: ship repair, stopping point, rest and relaxation, observation of the territory around them. At its most basic, a starbase was a signpost of the United Federation of Planets that said, "We are here. We are thinking about you and are here to help you."

Starbase 86 filled all of those requirements . . . adequately. Nothing more than that, and nothing less. It was simply good enough.

Once upon a time, the commanding officer of Starbase 86—and since the term *86* meant something had been killed, the starbase had been nicknamed "Starbase Dead End"—would never have settled for good enough. In fact, he had lived his life by the axiom "Good enough never is."

But that viewpoint had been held a long, long time ago, by a man who was somewhat different from 86's current CO. A lifetime ago, in fact. Someone else's lifetime.

* * *

He stared out the viewport of his office, watching the lights of stars that, because of the time required for light to travel, might have been extinguished years ago. How odd, he mused, to be looking at something that was no longer there. And yet it had reality. Every sense that was available to him told him that the stars were still there. But that didn't mean anything.

"Sometimes," he said to no one in particular, "seeing isn't believing."

There was a chime at the door. He made no move to answer it at first. What was the point? What was the rush? If he didn't respond now, sooner or later the buzz would just sound again. And again. Things happened whether he wanted them to or not. That was a hard lesson that he had also learned.

Sure enough, the chime repeated. This time it was accompanied by a worried "Admiral? Admiral Riker? Are you okay?"

Riker permitted a small smile to tug at the edges of his bearded mouth. The voice was unmistakably that of his second-in-command, Lieutenant Dexter. Dexter always sounded a bit apprehensive, and Riker knew precisely why. Dexter was something of a hypochondriac—not to the point where it interfered with his ability to function, certainly, but he was preoccupied with medical well-being. Not just his own, either, but that of everyone around him.

As a result, Dexter was always clucking after Riker, inquiring after Riker's health, and generally making a polite but determined nuisance of himself. In a way, Riker supposed that it was something of a blessing. Certainly Riker himself didn't care all that much about his well-being. He was seventy-three years old, and although he wouldn't refuse the idea of seventy-four and onward beyond that, neither did he particularly welcome it. It would simply happen or it wouldn't. The rest was of little consequence.

The longer Riker didn't respond, the more apprehensive Dexter would get. Probably the lieutenant was already conjuring up images of an unconscious or even worse, a dead Riker, sprawled out on his desk or under it. He even knew precisely what Dexter would do upon finding a deceased commanding officer. Dexter would undoubtedly drop to his knees and proceed to lecture the corpse.

"I told you you weren't taking good enough care of yourself," he'd say, shaking his thin blond head. "I told you that you should take more of an interest in yourself and the running of the starbase. But would you listen to me? No. You wouldn't. And now look at you, with the average life span being 114 years, and here you are, barely half that, dead as a burned-out star."

"Come in, Lieutenant," said Riker.

Dexter entered before Riker finished the last syllable in *lieutenant*. He coughed nervously. "Did I catch you at a bad time?"

Riker spread his wrinkled hands broadly. "I have nothing but time." Then he pointed off to the side. "See there? Loads of time."

What he was pointing at was virtually the only thing he took any pride in at all: a large, ornate grandfather clock, Swiss construction, made in the early twentieth century. It had been fully restored and was in perfect working order. It stood in one of the corners of Riker's fairly austere office, and its pendulum swung slowly, back and forth, back and forth. Each swing was accompanied by a resonant ticktock.

The sound affected different people in different ways. Riker found the noise calming, even reassuring. Dexter—Riker could tell—thought it was damned distracting. The lieutenant would cast repeated, annoyed glances at the clockpiece whenever he was in Riker's office.

"Yes, sir. Loads of time. As you say, sir." Dexter fingered his thinning hair nervously. "There's some, um, matters to bring to your attention."

Riker sat down behind his desk and half-swiveled the chair so he could stare out at the stars. Rarely did he look at Dexter anymore. He had in the beginning, back when he'd taken on the command of the starbase three years ago. Dexter had been one of the few humans he ever spoke with. He'd considered that a blessing. Now he was bored.

Riker's head settled into his hands. His beard, mostly gray but with a few strands of brown still peppering it, felt brittle against his palms. He raised one hand and ran it experimentally through his gray hair. Strands came out between his fingers, more strands every

16

day, it seemed. He could have treatment done to prevent it, of course. But what was the point? Whom was he trying to impress? Dexter? Surely not. Himself? Hardly.

"The surveying ship *Chance* will be coming in next week," Dexter said, consulting a small computer padd in the palm of his hand. Mostly it was there for security; Dexter's remarkable memory enabled him to recall all information almost instantaneously. But he was anal retentive enough to want to have the printed confirmation in front of him, just in case. "They had a synthesizer malfunction and will be putting in for new supplies and synthesizer repair."

Riker nodded. "Make sure our food stores are adequately stocked to resupply."

It was purely a cosmetic order. He knew damned well that Dexter would already have attended to that. But it was something to do other than just sit and nod his head as if it were going to fall off.

"Yes, sir," said Dexter neutrally, as if Riker's order were a novel idea. "Also, a communiqué from Starfleet. They complained that we were not processing our forms 1021-JKQ rapidly enough."

Riker raised an eyebrow in mild amusement. Amazing how much gravity Dexter could attach to something that Riker considered so utterly trivial. "Not fast enough?"

"No, sir."

"How much faster do they want it?"

Dexter blinked owlishly. "They are supposed to be filed within forty-eight hours of departure of any ship that's Constellation class or larger."

"And we've been taking . . . ?"

Nervously clearing his throat, Dexter tapped his computer padd and said, "We've been averaging three weeks."

Riker stared at Dexter gravely. "My God. This could spell the end of the Federation as we know it. And I'll have to live with that knowledge for the rest of my life."

Dexter blew air impatiently out between his colorless lips. "It's not a laughing matter, Admiral."

"I don't recall hearing laughter, Lieutenant. Not even so much as a mild guffaw. It may have been a while since I laughed, Mr. Dexter, but I do distinctly recall what it sounded like."

"You weren't laughing per se, sir, but you most definitely were making light of the situation."

Riker leaned forward, his fingers interlaced. "If I don't speed up the processing, Dexter . . . what are they going to do to me? Transfer me? To someplace worse than this? We both know there *is* no place worse than this."

Dexter shuddered slightly.

"You know I'm right," Riker said mirthlessly. "And you know what else?" He leaned back in the chair, putting his hands behind his head. "I wouldn't have it any other way. I'm right where I want to be, Dexter. Right where I want to be."

They stared at each other for a few moments. "Anything else?" Riker said.

Dexter cleared his throat again and then said, "There was a communiqué for you of a somewhat personal nature."

At that, Riker frowned. "What was it?"

"Well, sir, I never go prying—"

"Of course you do," said Riker, his voice cracking with impatience. "Don't shadow-dance with me, Dexter. I know damned well you have your finger in every pie that comes through this armpit of the galaxy. Now what's happening?"

"Well, sir . . . the communiqué was from Betazed."

Riker was silent for a long moment. "Betazed?"

"Yes, sir."

Riker drummed for a few seconds on the armrest of his chair. When he spoke, he was looking away from Dexter. "It's from her, isn't it?"

"Yes, sir."

"Is she all right?"

Dexter's lips thinned even more, which one would have thought was impossible. He took a breath and said, "No, sir. She's dying, sir."

Riker said nothing at first. Then, finally: "And?"

"She's calling for you."

"Is she? Yes . . . she would, wouldn't she." He considered it a moment. "There's no way I can get there in time."

"Betazed officials have already spoken with Starfleet command. She is quite influential, you know."

"Yes, I know. Believe me, I know. And what did Starfleet say?"

"The starship *Hood* is in this sector. They had not originally planned to put in here, but we are not significantly out of their way. And Betazed is situated only a few parsecs from *Hood*'s destination."

"How very convenient." Riker frowned for a moment. "*Hood* is Crusher's ship, isn't it?"

"Captain Crusher, yes, sir."

"Um-hmm. Old ghosts, Dexter."

"Pardon?"

"Old ghosts. They're coming back to haunt me." Now Riker shifted his drumming to the desktop. "Old ghosts want to see me. Old ghosts are going to transport me." He paused. "I don't suppose I have the option of not seeing her."

"Of course you have that option, sir," replied Dexter stiffly. "This is merely a request, not an order."

"A request." Once more Riker ran his fingers through his gray hair. "How much time until *Hood* gets here?"

"ETA is fourteen thirty hours, sir."

"All right. Radio Betazed that I'll be there as fast as I can. Tell *Hood* that I'll be ready for them when they get here." Riker rose to his feet and fixed Dexter with a stare. "Anything else?"

"No, sir. It's just that . . ."

Riker could barely contain his impatience. "What? . . . What?"

"I just want to say that I think it's good of you that you're going, sir. You've, um . . ." He harrumphed and continued, "You've spoken of her in the past. It's clear that this will be very difficult for you."

"I've done more difficult things than this, Lieutenant," said Riker stiffly. Then he hesitated and added softly, "But not much more."

He came around his desk and headed for the door. And then Dexter said, "Why do you think she wants to see you, sir?"

Riker paused in the doorway. The door had already slid open, waiting for him. But when he didn't pass through, it slid softly shut again. "Why do *you* think?"

Dexter, after brief consideration, said, "Perhaps, sir, she wants to make amends with you."

"Amends?" Riker said the word with amazement, as if it were the first time he'd ever heard it. "Amends? Lieutenant . . . you don't know her very well."

"It's possible, sir," Dexter persisted. "When people are dying, they tend to see things in a different light."

"You have a lot of personal experience with death, Lieutenant?"

Dexter ignored the verbal jab. "It's possible that she wants to settle loose ends, as it were. Close accounts. It's possible, sir . . . that she wants to forgive you."

Slowly Riker shook his head. "Why should she, Lieutenant . . . when I haven't forgiven myself?"

And Riker walked out of his office, leaving Dexter alone with the steady heartbeat ticking of the grandfather clock.

CHAPTER 3

The structures in which the scientists of the Forever World lived were, at best, functional. But then, these people did not seem to Data the type to care overmuch about physical needs. If what they had served their basic requirements, then they seemed content.

Data looked around the table that served as the communal eating place for the scientists. In every locale on the *Enterprise* that was designed for group consumption of food, Data had always been struck by the steady stream of chatter that had accompanied the act. Indeed, eating a meal seemed as much a social occasion as anything else. Such socializing did not appear to augment the replenishing of the body's stores of nutrition. It was, however, customary. Or so Data had been led to believe.

It was not the case here however. The six scientists who were grouped around the table ate quietly. Talk was at a minimum, and anything said was merely along the lines of some functional request such as "Pass the salt."

Seated next to Data was science officer Blair. Blair was tough to miss in any situation—a head taller than Data, and covered from head to toe with thick, brown fur. His jaw jutted out and his eyes were so small that they were almost impossible to spot. His Starfleet uniform was specially tailored to accommodate his height and bulk.

The others at the table had to crowd a bit closer to each other in order to provide room for Blair.

Thus far there had only been one entrée into conversation. Data had glanced around and said, "My records indicated there were seven of you."

Mary Mac pursed her lips and then sighed. "There were. Recent defection—Mar Loc. He took off the other day—haven't seen him since. You'll have to update your records. To be honest . . . we lose people all the time."

"Why?"

"It's not easy to take this place, Commodore," said Harry as he put food out on the table. Around the table, heads bobbed up and down in agreement. "You have the constant wind. You have the solitude. And with the Guardian out there . . ." He paused, trying to find the words. "You feel . . . you feel like you're staring into a mirror from hell. And it's only so long before you see something staring back out at you. Some reflection that you don't necessarily like. At which point . . . it's time to get out. Or you can lose your mind."

"We've had that happen from time to time as well," said Mary Mac darkly. Again there were nods.

The scientists volunteered no further conversation, and once the food was put out, from then on the only sounds that could be heard were the clinking of eating utensils on plates, soft noises of mastication, and of course, the wind . . . the ever-present, ever-haunting wind.

"Is it always this quiet?" Blair finally asked.

The sound of his hushed question was almost deafening in the relative stillness. The scientists stopped and looked at each other with an air of polite puzzlement.

Mary Mac, who was seated next to Blair, leaned forward on one arm. "It's not just quiet. We're working."

Blair looked at Data. "Working on what?" asked the commodore.

"Our thoughts," said Harry. "Our observations. Every night we record our conclusions in our logs, and every morning we group together and discuss them."

"As part of the Federation's annual evaluation of your work," said Data politely, "I'd be very interested in reading them. If, that is, you wouldn't consider that an intrusion."

The scientists looked at each other and there seemed to be an unspoken, uniform shrug. "No problem with that, Commodore," said Mary Mac.

"What sort of observations do you make?" Blair asked.

Mary Mac glanced around the table. Clearly, both through Federation designation and natural ability, she was the spokesperson for the group. "We make observations on society. On history. Most of us here are social scientists, Commodore . . . Lieutenant," she added, with a polite nod to Blair. "We make studies of the histories of different societies and from that draw conclusions about not only that society's past, but the circumstances that brought them to their present and, most likely, are aiming them toward their future."

Harry now spoke up. "Just an example. Two planets, Gamma Delta and Gamma Origii, had been at war off and on for hundreds of years. Even though they, as a society, had evolved in their perceptions and attitudes, there was still a centuries-old tradition of hatred between the two. Our studies here at the Forever World uncovered the real origins, long forgotten, of the anger between the two worlds."

"That being?" prompted Blair.

Harry endeavored to keep a straight face as he said, "A d'clat belonging to the emperor of Gamma Delta consumed a markill that was much beloved by the empress of Gamma Origii."

Blair looked in confusion from Harry to Data. Data, with just the faintest hint of a smile, said, "A d'clat is a large, caninelike animal, known to be quite fierce and to reach lengths of three meters. A markill is small, somewhat feline, and usually very docile."

Understanding spread across Blair's face. "You mean the guy's dog ate her pet cat?"

"That is essentially correct."

"And *that* led to centuries of hostilities?"

"The incident led to bad feelings," corrected Mary Mac, sounding a bit pedantic. "The bad feelings led to the hostilities. By the time the modern era was reached, the reasons for the hostilities had long been forgotten; only the anger remained."

"How did the two planets react when they learned of the root cause for their antagonism?" asked Data.

Mary Mac could not hide her amusement. "The heads of the two worlds met and with great pomp and circumstance signed into law new, strict regulations about leashing d'clats. A newborn markill was then presented to the present leader of Gamma Origii. Frankly, they were all a bit embarrassed about it and were happy for the opportunity to put it all behind them."

"Well, that's excellent," said Blair. "That's just excellent."

Then he paused, and Mary Mac picked up on the fact that something else was on his mind. "Yes, Lieutenant?" she asked.

"I was just wondering . . . are you ever tempted? To go back, I mean?"

"No," said Mary Mac with such speed and firmness that it was a bit startling.

"What, never?"

"No. Nor are any of us." She looked at her companions for confirmation, and almost as one, they nodded.

"Why wouldn't you want to?"

"Because that is not a responsibility that we would want. It's . . . it's too much. You'd have to be . . . I don't know . . . bigger than life to take on that challenge. I'll pass, thanks."

"If you shun the responsibility, why does anyone have access to the Guardian at all?" asked Data.

"We need access when we want to talk to it," said Mary Mac. "For some reason it won't address us if we speak from outside the force field. The Guardian doesn't acknowledge us unless there're no barriers between us. When we do converse with it directly, we do so with the utmost caution." She put down her eating utensil. "Your conversation was fairly interesting, Commodore. What did you make of it?"

"It would seem to confirm, on the face of it, that which we had always known. That time is fluid. Although"—he paused only a moment, considering the possibilities—"there is another interpretation. And that is that all times coexist."

24

"You mean parallel universes," said Mary Mac. It was clear from the speed with which she picked up on what he was saying that it was something she'd already given thought.

"It's something that has been considered," said Data. "That parallel universes are, in fact, alternative time tracks. There was a fascinating paper done recently, expanding upon a notion ex pressed in, of all things, a newly recovered twentieth-century piece of fiction."

"The Niven Doctrine," Blair said. "I was in the audience when it was presented. Shook up quite a few people."

"Alternative time lines," said Mary Mac, nodding. "The scene you were watching, Commodore—the experiences of Captain Kirk—certainly is one of the better-known instances."

"There have been others documented," said Data. "There was Captain Kirk's experience with an alternative time line that resulted in a parallel universe with an aggressive, warlike Federation. There was another situation that I myself was involved with, the full details of which I didn't learn until some years after the fact."

"You, Commodore?" asked Mary Mac. "What was it?"

"It involved a . . . memorable young woman. Her name was Natasha Yar, although she was more popularly known as Tasha." Data's face, as always, was the picture of composure. But Blair, from his long experience with his commanding officer, could tell that the memory being pulled up was something of great meaning to the android. "It was a . . . unique situation. One of the few instances where an individual or individuals actually crossed over from one parallel universe to another—one being where Captain Kirk and several crewmen, as mentioned earlier, crossed into a parallel universe/time-line with a militaristic Federation. Tasha's experience was another. Unfortunately it . . . did not work out quite as positively as Captain Kirk's did."

Data lapsed into silence and Mary Mac understood immediately that he had said everything he felt needed to be said on the subject. But Data picked up on her expression.

"If you wish to question me further on the incident," Data said quietly, "you may feel free to do so. I won't feel imposed upon."

"Maybe not, but I'll feel like I'm imposing anyway. So I guess I won't." Then Mary Mac paused. "Actually, Commodore . . . I have something of interest to show you. Something along the lines of our discussion. A very intriguing turn of events that our monitoring of the Guardian's playbacks has revealed. And I think"—her green lips drew back into a broad smile—"I think you will find it very interesting."

CHAPTER 4

Riker sat in his guest quarters on the starship *Hood,* watching the stars hurtling by. It had been so long since he was in any sort of real motion that the view outside the port looked . . . *wrong* somehow. As insane as it sounded, he didn't feel as if stars were supposed to move.

"Do you miss it, Admiral?"

He hadn't even heard the door hiss open. He turned to face Capt. Wesley Crusher.

Crusher was standing in the doorway, his arms folded. He was half a head taller than Riker, which was disconcerting enough for the admiral. He sported a Vandyke beard, and his hair—graying ever so slightly at the temples—hung just over his ears. He stepped fully into the quarters upon Riker's silent gesture for him to enter, and Riker noticed with amusement that as he did so, he tugged slightly at the waistline of his black and green uniform jacket. Riker had not seen the gesture for quite a few years—the clothes straightening that had picked up the joking nickname of the Picard Maneuver, wryly named after the famous battle tactic that one Jean-Luc Picard had invented.

He saw Crusher standing and realized that it was in deference to himself. "Please, take a seat, Captain."

27

And Riker was even more amused when Crusher crossed to a chair and, without even thinking about it, reversed it and straddled it. "Pick up any other of my mannerisms, Captain?"

Crusher looked at him askance. "What do you mean, sir?" He looked down at the chair as if seeing it for the first time. "Did you used to sit like this?"

"Used to," said Riker. "Before some sore back muscles decided that they would say otherwise in the matter. In answer to your question of do I miss it, Captain . . . no."

"No?"

"You sound surprised, Captain Crusher."

Once upon a time, Wesley Crusher would have looked down nervously or stammered slightly or cleared his throat as he tried to compose himself. Just yesterday, it seemed to Riker. Now, though, the Starfleet captain merely shrugged slightly. "A little, I admit."

"You can take the man out of space, but you can't take the spacer out of the man, eh?" asked Riker.

"Something like that."

Riker slowly circled the quarters, never taking his gaze off Crusher. "You've carved quite a career for yourself, Mr. Crusher. Your father would have been proud."

"Thank you, sir."

"And what about you . . . Wes." It sounded odd to speak the name out loud. It was as if he were addressing someone who wasn't in the room. "Are you proud?"

"I've done my job. I've done it to the best of my abilities. And"—he paused only a moment—"I had the best teachers."

"The Academy has top people on their faculty."

"That's very true, but I wasn't talking about the Academy, sir . . . and I think you know that."

"We don't have to stand on formality, Wes. You can call me Will."

Crusher considered it for a moment, then said, "Actually . . . no. I'm not sure I can, sir. It would seem . . . presumptuous, some-how."

"Whatever you're comfortable with, then," said Riker easily. He caught a glance of himself in the mirror. Old. So damned old, and he felt older in the presence of the robust captain who sat before him. Robust, even in his fifties.

"What's your opinion of me, Wes?"

Crusher blinked in surprise. "Of you?" For a moment he seemed confused. "I . . . admire you tremendously. You're one of the greatest . . . probably, with all due respect, the second-greatest . . . Starfleet officer it was ever my honor to serve under."

Riker stared at him with a look that bordered on incredulity. "You can't *still* think that, can you?"

"Of course."

With a slow shake of his head, Riker sat down opposite Crusher. He did not, however, straddle the chair. "Wesley . . . everyone has people that they admire in their lives. People who they put on a . . . a heroic pedestal, as it were. But you can't possibly tell me I'm still up there on yours?"

Crusher shifted uncomfortably. "I wouldn't say 'pedestal,' Admiral. But I still admire you a great deal. In many ways . . . I still see you very much the way that I did when I first met you. Strong, decisive, heroic . . . everything a Starfleet officer was supposed to be. It's not unusual for first impressions to be lasting ones, Admiral . . . I mean, admit it"—now he smiled—"you find it just slightly difficult to seriously believe I'm an adult. Captain of a starship. Married twice, father of three. But you look at me and still think of the little kid on Farpoint who, once upon a time, only had two goals: to visit the bridge, and to have to shave more than once a week."

Riker laughed, the boisterousness of his amusement surprising even himself. "You're right, Wes. You're bang-on right. It's just that . . ."

"Just that what, sir?"

"Just that," Riker said soberly, "there comes a time in everyone's life where they start to see their heroes for what they really are: namely, people. Flawed . . . ordinary . . . people."

Crusher didn't say anything at first. Something very unpleasant seemed to be hanging in the cabin . . . an air of self-pity, maybe even a whiff of mortality. "Are you feeling particularly flawed and ordinary today, Admiral?"

"Wes, I haven't felt anything but that for years now. Look at me, Wes. Look at me and tell me that you don't see a broken-down, second-rate starbase commander. Someone who had potential he never fulfilled. Someone who was never everything he should have been. Tell me that you don't look at me and see someone in whom you're bitterly disappointed."

Someone else would have said such things in tones bordering on histrionic. Riker, however, did not. He spoke slowly, succinctly, and in a voice that indicated he had, quite simply, already decided these things about himself and come to terms with them.

Crusher's eyes narrowed, and when he spoke, quiet fire was in his voice. "If that is your opinion of yourself . . . Will . . . then you're certainly entitled to it. But if you're looking for someone to confirm it for you, I'm afraid you're just going to have to keep on looking."

Riker let out a slow sigh, tinged with faint amusement. "Is that your final word, Captain?"

"Yes, it is. And since we're on my ship, and it is my opinion . . . then we'll just have to make it so."

Crusher was about to say something else when suddenly he half-looked away, in that manner that had become so customary with the creation of the minicommunicators. "Excuse me, Admiral. . . . Crusher here." He listened to the voice that only he could hear and then nodded once. "Excellent. We'll be right there. Crusher out." He turned to Riker. "We're five minutes out of Betazed."

"Smooth and uneventful trip, Captain. You're to be commended."

"Thank you, sir."

Crusher rose from his chair and headed for the door. But there he stopped and turned back to Riker. "Do you want me there, Admiral?"

"Oh, I don't think that will be necessary, Captain."

"It's easily justifiable." Crusher took a step back into the cabin. "As a Starfleet captain, it would be eminently politic for me to be present. And as a . . . friend . . . I wouldn't mind being there to lend whatever support I could."

Riker was ready to dismiss the notion out of hand. But then he stopped and considered it—really considered it—and almost to his surprise, he found himself nodding. Feeling some words should accompany the nods, he said, "Very well, Captain. Perhaps it wouldn't be such a bad idea at that."

Crusher nodded. "Five minutes, then. Don't be late. Tardiness is mental slovenliness and is inappropriate for a Starfleet officer."

"Where'd you pick that up? The Academy?"

"No, sir. You told me that—the first time I was late for an astrophysics lesson with Geordi."

"Well, that being the case, I could hardly ignore such sound advice, could I."

"If it's good enough for the captain of the *Hood,*" Wesley Crusher said firmly, "it's good enough for you." He turned and walked out the door.

Through the viewport of his quarters, Riker could now see Betazed, coming up fast.

Help me, he said. *Help me get through this, Imzadi.*

There was, of course, no answer. Nor had there been for quite, quite some time.

CHAPTER 5

Betazed was nothing like he remembered it.

Then again, it had been many years since Riker had set foot on the planet. Not since the days when he had been first officer of the *Enterprise* 1701-D, under the command of Capt. Jean-Luc Picard.

Not since—

He wavered slightly, putting a hand to his head, and he felt Crusher's firm grip on his shoulder. "Are you all right, Admiral?"

All the anger, all the resentment and fury that he had thought he was long past, flashed through him once more with unexpected heat.

"I'm fine!" he practically snarled. "You don't have to sound so damned patronizing!"

Young Wesley Crusher would have taken a couple of steps back. He would have become dead pale, tried to stammer out some sort of a reply—and probably failed.

Capt. Wesley Crusher merely removed his hand from Riker's shoulder, then lanced him with a grim stare. "I was always raised to believe, Admiral, that being concerned over someone's welfare was considered, at the very least, good manners. Hardly patronizing."

Riker met Crusher's stare and said slowly, "Yes. Quite right, Captain. My . . . apologies."

Crusher nodded in a way that indicated that, as far as he was concerned, the minor incident was closed. Instead, he glanced toward the heavens. "Looks like the weather's turning nasty on us, sir."

At that, Riker nodded. It was something that he'd become accustomed to on Betazed. The majority of the time, the weather was calm, pleasant, bordering on the tropical. But when the atmospheric conditions shifted, they did so with startling and almost violent speed. One minute, cloudless and blue skies, and the next minute—bam.

Riker remembered that Lwaxana perpetually carried an umbrella with her when strolling about, particularly in the countryside. She had always prided herself on being ready for anything.

Anything.

"It's this way," said Riker.

They'd materialized on one of the more well-to-do avenues of the city. The homes were far apart and set back . . . but not too far. Betazoids walked a fine line between a desire for privacy and acceptance of its impossibility—for amidst an empathic society, privacy was at best a pretense and it was rude to pretend otherwise.

Crusher could have had them beamed right to their destination, but before he had specified anything, Riker had given specific coordinates that deposited them half a mile from where they wanted to be. It was as if Riker weren't all that anxious to arrive at his goal.

Riker set the pace, which was not especially fast, and Crusher fell into step next to him. The admiral did not seem particularly interested in talking, and they might indeed have gone the entire way in complete silence if an unexpected voice hadn't chimed in behind them.

"It *is* you."

Riker and Crusher stopped and turned, and Riker chuckled low in his throat.

"Wendy Roper. I don't believe it."

The woman who stood behind them seemed a few years younger than Riker. She was small and slim, and her white hair, with a few remaining streaks of black in it, was twisted around in an elaborate braid. A sparkle in her eyes made it seem that a very amused young woman was hiding somewhere in the aged body.

"Will Riker, you old sleaze."

He walked to her and put his arms around her—tentatively, as if afraid that he might break her in half. They separated and he looked at her.

"Don't you dare," she said. "Don't you dare say I haven't aged at all."

"Why shouldn't I?"

"Because the thought that I looked like this half a century ago would be too much to cope with."

His smile widened. "Can I say you look great for a woman your age?"

"With my blessing." She ran fingers across his bearded cheeks. "When did you get so scruffy?"

"About forty years ago."

"Makes you look ancient."

"I feel ancient." He paused, then shook his head. "I can't believe you're still here. I mean, you can't *still* be assigned here with your father . . ."

Her expression saddened slightly. "Daddy died about ten years ago, Will."

"Oh." His face clouded. "I'm sorry. Oh . . . my manners." He stepped back and waved Crusher closer. "Capt. Wesley Crusher, this is Wendy Roper."

She shook Crusher's hand firmly but said, "Wendy Berq, actually."

Riker looked at her in surprise. "Married?"

"That's usually the way."

"When?"

"Actually, about two years after you left. My husband is Betazoid . . . a teacher. That's why I stayed."

"My God . . ."

She patted him on the arm. "Don't worry about it, Will. I know news travels slowly out in space."

He let out a slow breath. "I really am a sleaze. I've been back planetside a few times ... but I never saw you. Never tried to contact you. Not even ..."

"I was at the funeral."

Riker blinked in surprise. "You were? I didn't see you."

"As I recall, you weren't seeing much of anything that day."

To that, Riker said nothing. Then, slowly, he nodded. "That's about right." He paused. "I should have looked you up. I'm sorry."

"It's understandable. If there's one thing that living among Betazoids has taught me, it's to be respectful of people's feelings. If you ask me, the entire Betazoid credo boils down to one word: RaBeem."

Crusher looked momentarily puzzled. "'RaBeem'?"

Riker glanced at him and said, "It means 'I understand.'"

"Very good, Will," said Wendy.

"I had a good teacher."

They stood there for a bit in uneasy silence, then Wendy cleared her throat. "I won't play games or pretend this was coincidence, Will. I knew you'd be coming. I knew she'd asked for you. And I thought—"

"You thought that I could use the moral support," he said, tossing a look at Crusher. "I've heard that quite a bit. Well ... fine, Wendy. I suppose the more the ..." Then he stopped. "I guess that's hardly appropriate to the situation, is it?"

"Hardly," agreed Wendy.

Riker stood there, feeling as if he'd been cut adrift. He felt that way a great deal these days—alone, floating. Unattached to anyone or anything in the galaxy around him. Clumsy with his speech, clumsy with his orders, just ... clumsy. Unable to focus on anything or decide anything.

Make a decision, you idiot.

"Come on, then," he said. "Let's go."

The three of them walked up the small incline that led to the mansion that Riker knew so well. It had been years since he'd been there—a lifetime ago, it seemed—and yet every angle of the house, every aspect of it, had been forever etched into his memory. Tall and graceful, it was constructed on a reduced scale so that, although the upper stories were not abnormally high, they seemed to go on and on, almost touching the sky—the sky that was now darkening with the customary Betazed speed. And yet, somehow, it seemed as if it were holding back. Seemed as if it were waiting for something.

The door was opened before Riker even had the opportunity to knock. And filling the doorway was a figure that momentarily surprised Riker by its appearance . . . and then, he wondered why he had been at all startled. Of course *he* would be here. Where else would he be?

"Mr. Homn," said Riker, bending slightly and formally at the waist.

Wesley Crusher looked up in surprise. He had fleetingly seen Homn from time to time, back in his days on the *Enterprise.* His memory had been that Homn was incredibly tall . . . and yet, in later years, he had wondered how much of that recollection was shaped by the fact that young Ensign Crusher had been that much smaller. Now, as an adult, he found himself no less impressed by Homn's towering presence than he had ever been.

Wendy had never seen the towering manservant before. She just gaped.

And then, Homn did something totally unexpected . . . something that, to Riker's knowledge, he had only done once before.

His voice was low and surprisingly soft for so large a man—and there was even a faint hint of a lisp—as he uttered two simple words: "She's waiting."

The response echoed in Riker's mind—*Waiting for what? Waiting for me? Or waiting to die? Or are the two connected?*

Mr. Homn stepped aside, and Riker entered, Wendy and Crusher following him.

The house, in contrast to its elegant exterior, still smacked of being overdone to Riker, even after all this time. He knew why that was, of course. Lwaxana's late husband had designed the outside and left the actual furnishing to his wife. And furnish it she had . . . with a vengeance.

Every corner, every available bit of space, was crammed with . . .

stuff. Everywhere Riker looked there was furniture or mementos: portraits, trophies, souvenirs, objects of art that ranged from the acceptable to the ghastly. The taste at casa Troi was, to put it mildly, eclectic.

Mr. Homn stood at the bottom of the central stairway and gestured. He remained immobile, like a monument. A living link to days gone by.

Riker started up the stairs. They seemed to stretch on forever. Once, once a very long time ago, he could have charged up these steps, taking them two, even three at a time. And a woman would have been waiting for him up there, her arms outstretched, her face mirthful and loving, her curly black hair cascading about her shoulders.

Back in the old days. Back when he was another person entirely, and the only thing he had in common with the old man who now trudged heavily up the stairs was the name.

He held on to the banister, pulling himself up as he went. He paused for a few moments on a landing to catch his breath before he continued upward. He knew that Crusher and Wendy were directly behind him, but they offered him no support or aid. Nor would he have wanted it.

The stairway opened up onto the second-floor corridor, which seemed to stretch almost to infinity. This effect was aided by the fact that the corridor was illuminated only by flickering lamplight, and also because full-size mirrors were at either end.

Appearances. Once again, appearances. They had always been so important to *her* . . . and now, it would seem that appearances were all she had left.

At first he didn't know which door she was behind . . . but then he realized. It was partly open, and from within he could hear slow, labored breathing. It sounded as if she was just barely hanging on. Hell, she might die any minute.

If he walked slowly enough, if he took enough time . . .

He saw the look in Wesley Crusher's eyes as the captain of the *Hood* stood next to him. He had a feeling that Crusher knew precisely what was going through Riker's mind.

Dammit, Riker, he scolded himself. *Be a man. For crying out loud, get it right!*

His hands curled into fists, and with a stride that indicated a confidence he did not feel, he walked toward the sound of the breathing.

When he was just outside the door . . . it stopped.

The cessation was abrupt; right in the middle of a breath, so it was very noticeable. Riker looked at Crusher as if for confirmation, and it was clear that Crusher had heard it, too. Wendy, feeling tired and labored, had just made it to the top of the stairs and so wasn't there yet.

For just the briefest of moments, relief flooded through Riker. And then it was immediately replaced by anger at his hesitation . . . cowardice, even. Quickly he entered the room.

He was stunned.

He had expected the most ornate of surroundings for this, the master bedroom. But such was not the case. In fact, it was quite the opposite.

Only a bed occupied the room. A canopied bed with black drapes hanging down. There wasn't a stick of furniture anywhere else.

It only took a moment for Riker to realize what had happened. All the furniture had been removed—the different sheen on various parts of the floor indicated that. He did not understand, though, *why* it had been done.

As if reading his mind, Wendy now said softly from behind him, "Betazed tradition. Some feel that you come into the world with virtually nothing. So when you leave, you try not to surround yourself with the things you've acquired. It's . . . excess baggage, for want of a better term."

"Oh."

He walked slowly toward the bed, but now there seemed to be no hurry. There was no doubt in his mind that she was gone. There was still that anger, bordering on contempt, that he felt for himself. *This is what you wanted. This is why you dragged your heels. So why aren't you happy about it?* The reason was, of course, that he also felt tremendously guilty.

Look at her. You owe her that much.

Slowly he parted the black drapery around the bed.

Lwaxana Troi lay there, unmoving. Her skin was taut, conforming uncomfortably closely to the outlines of her skull. Her lips and, incredibly, her hair, were the same parched color as her skin. Her arms and shoulders were bare—she was probably naked, just as was customary for a Betazed wedding, but a sheet was pulled up to just under her arms.

Her eyes were closed. Her chest was not moving.

Riker took a slow breath that seemed incredibly loud to him. The stink of death was heavy in the air, but it didn't stop him from sitting on the edge of the bed. Crusher and Wendy stood a respectful distance.

"I'm sorry," he whispered to her, and he meant it. He really, truly meant it. He knew now that she had really wanted finally to settle things with him. To bury the dead and put the ghosts to rest. And through his trepidation, through the fears and insecurities of an old man, he had allowed that moment to slip away forever.

He leaned over to kiss her on the forehead.

Her withered, clawlike hand shot upward and grabbed him by the throat.

Riker gasped, and the noise was partly cut off by the hand that was closing on his vocal cords with shocking strength. Lwaxana's eyes were open and blazing with pure, unbridled hatred.

"Admiral!" shouted Crusher, acting immediately and instinctively to protect the safety of the senior officer. He ran to Riker's side and was momentarily taken aback by the aura of undiluted fury that radiated from every pore of Lwaxana Troi.

From her ancient lips, as if ripped from the pits of her soul, Lwaxana Troi spat out a condemnation as if it were a curse: *"It's your fault!"* The voice was cracked and aged, not at all like the boisterous, sweeping tones that had once been the woman's staple. But there was still a vitality that would not be daunted by such trivialities as death.

"It's your fault!" she repeated, and the wrath of the woman shook her voice, shook her entire withered body. "You should have saved her! She asked you! She *begged* you! You were *Imzadi,* and you let her die!"

Riker tried to get out a reply, but the pressure was too much on his throat. Wesley tried to yank Lwaxana's hands away from Riker but they dug in. The long fingernails drew thin streams of blood.

"You let her die!" croaked Lwaxana. "It's not right! She was too young . . . too beautiful! And you let it *happen,* and I hope you *burn in hell* . . . it's your fault!"

Crusher tore her hands loose from Riker's throat and pulled the admiral away. Riker was gagging, but through the pain and mortification he still managed to gasp out, "It *wasn't!* I did everything I could! You have to understand!"

"Admiral—" began Wesley.

But Riker was shouting, "Please! It wasn't my fault! Lwaxana, I tried everything . . . it happened too fast! I—"

But Wendy laid a gentle hand on his. "It's too late, Will."

And she was right. Lwaxana's head had slumped back onto her pillow. Her eyes were still wide open, but there was no light in them. Her hand was still in its clawlike grip, frozen in its final gesture.

Wesley Crusher reached over, passing his hand over her eyes and closing them.

And Riker whispered to her, one final time, "It wasn't my fault." But he didn't believe it any more than she had.

CHAPTER 6

The funeral had been surprisingly simple.

Surprisingly so because, considering the larger-than-life manner in which Lwaxana had lived her life, Riker had somehow expected a death that was . . . well . . . larger than death.

Instead, Lwaxana's instructions had been very, very specific. She had wanted only a handful of people there. Only the closest of friends, the one or two most highly placed politicians . . .

. . . and Riker.

Long after the others had left, Riker was left standing there, staring at Lwaxana's body in its clear, sealed entombment.

He kept trying to develop ways to ascribe to Lwaxana more pure motives than those of vengeance or hatred. After all, she hadn't been like that when he first met her. Strong willed, yes. Stubborn and meddlesome and—again—bigger than life. But anger? Vituperation? That hadn't been part of her makeup. Or so, at least, it had seemed.

Then again . . . the years have a way of changing people. Years, and unpleasant experiences that can harden the heart and blacken the soul.

Perhaps . . . perhaps she had wanted him there because she was genuinely trying to heal the rifts. Perhaps she had wanted him at her side in her final moments because she really did want to make amends—and it was only in the last, momentary panic, with icy death upon her, that hidden resentments had boiled over. Perhaps she had wanted him at her funeral not because she wanted to rub his nose in the notion of *See? See how your shortcomings have deprived me of happiness in life?* but rather because, ultimately, she wanted some sort of connection to her daughter to be present at her last rites. And he was, after all, Imzadi to her daughter.

Riker stood there in the chill air of the Troi mausoleum. They were somewhat rare items on Betazed—the more frequent modern method of disposal was cremation and then to be scattered on the winds; the northern cliffs in the Valley of Song were a popular point of such activity.

But the older families—and few were older than that of the Fifth House of Betazed—clung to the traditional method. The method was dictated by the notion that the best way to have a sense of who one's ancestors were was to have a perpetual reminder at hand.

Which was why Riker was now standing alone in the mausoleum, staring at Lwaxana's shrouded body, but being even more painfully aware of who was lying in the next room.

What, dammit. Not who. She hasn't been a who since . . .

. . . since you let her . . .

Riker tried to force away that line of thought. Blast it, he hadn't *let* it happen. It had just happened.

He couldn't go in and look at her.

He turned to head for the door, and that was when the uncommonly slow storm front chose finally to act. There had been a few passing drizzles earlier, and he had hoped that that would be the end of it. But now the full fury of the storm cut loose. Lightning ribboned across the sky, and rain began to fall in blinding cascades. Far in the distance, the Troi mansion was silhouetted against the stormy sky, something out of an ancient horror movie.

Riker stepped back into the mausoleum, turned and looked at Lwaxana.

"You arranged this, didn't you," he said with just the faintest hint of irony. "You're up there less than twelve hours, and already you're telling them how to run things."

Lwaxana made no reply. She didn't have to. The thunder did it for her.

Riker sighed. "All right."

He walked past Lwaxana and even rapped a quick knuckle on the clear encasement with just a flash of the old irreverence. He walked into the next room . . .

And there she was.

He approached her slowly, and for the millionth time in as many imaginings of this scene, he envisioned removing the clear covering over her body. Envisioned leaning over, kissing her, and her large, luminous eyes would flutter and open.

He placed his hands on the covering. He was amazed at his ability to remember things, for Deanna was even more beautiful than his recollection had been able to retain.

She was as her mother presently lay—nude but heavily swathed in pure, white shrouds. But unlike Lwaxana, the ravages of time had been spared her. Spared at a hideous price, but spared.

She was perfectly preserved. The black hair still thick and full, the perfect lips formed into a small, round O shape. Her chiseled features were immaculate—perfectly formed, perfectly preserved. Cut down in the prime of life, she had at least retained the look of that primacy.

He wanted to remove the spherical cover over her, to take her in his arms. But that would have been the worst move he could have made. The preservative atmosphere within the clear coffin would be compromised—her body would be subjected to the ravages of time. Besides, it wouldn't be holding *her* . . . no amount of preservation could put the warmth back into the soft skin, breathe the life back into her, open the eyes and put the soul back into place.

She could not be made whole. She could not open those eyes and drink in his presence. She could not open that lovely mouth and say—

"Will?"

Riker jumped at least three feet in the air, letting out a yell of shock. He twisted around and slammed his back into Deanna's coffin, turning to face an equally startled Capt. Wesley Crusher, who was holding his chest and seemed to have developed trouble breathing. When he found the air, he gasped out, "I'm sorry . . . did I startle you?"

Riker paused a moment to allow his heartbeat to approach somewhere near its normal rate. "Where in hell did you come from?"

Crusher was soaked to the skin. He pointed. "Out there. Beamed down. You said you hadn't wanted me at the funeral, and I respected that . . . but I thought now that it's over and all . . ."

"That I'd be ready to come back."

Crusher nodded, sending droplets of water spattering to the floor. Riker looked at him with mild amusement. "You look completely waterlogged. How long were you out in the rain?"

"About two seconds. It just seemed disrespectful somehow to beam directly into a—" He looked around. "Into here. Didn't think I'd get this drenched in such a short time, though."

"Typical Betazed storm," said Riker. "You're right, Captain. I'm ready to leave."

"Very well. Crusher to *Hood*—"

"However—"

"Cancel," said Wesley without missing a beat. He looked expectantly at Riker and waited.

"However," continued Riker, "it's not quite that simple. Lwaxana's will had an odd stipulation—she wants me to go through her memorabilia and catalogue it."

Crusher blinked. "I beg your pardon?"

"You heard me, Captain."

"But why in the world would she want you to do that?"

Riker lightly rested his hands on Deanna's coffin; Crusher wasn't even sure that Riker was aware that he was doing it. It was as if he were trying to draw strength from her. "Ostensibly because she feels I'm best qualified—which is nonsense. Mr. Homn is. The real reason, Wes, is because she wants me to relive it. Relive and remember all of it."

"But . . . but why?"

"Because," he said with a sigh, "I imagine that a day didn't pass where she didn't dwell on it. And perhaps she's under the impression that I was somehow able to put it past me. She credited me for more than she herself could accomplish—which is a compliment of sorts, I suppose. So she wanted one last opportunity to put me through what she's put herself through all these years."

"You don't have to do it, Admiral," said Crusher reasonably. "Tell them you simply can't take the additional time from your station. Tell them what you just said—that Mr. Homn is more qualified. Tell them—"

"Tell them whatever it takes to get me off the hook?"

Crusher shrugged. "That's one way to put it."

"Maybe. But it's not a way that I can subscribe to." He shook his head and stepped away from the coffin as he said, "I'm not going to deprive Lwaxana of her last shot at me. I was gutless enough to try and delay my coming to her until the last minute. I owe her this . . . I owe her something. I—"

He stopped as he realized that Crusher wasn't looking at him anymore. Instead Wesley's gaze was focused on Deanna's body, which Riker had partly been blocking from view. Riker said nothing for a moment, but instead simply watched the starship captain. Eventually Crusher rubbed the bridge of his nose, as if something stinging had lodged in his eyes.

"You had a crush on her, didn't you?" said Riker.

Wesley glanced at him. "Was it that obvious?"

Riker shrugged. "Teenage boys are very good at thinking they've got their feelings completely hidden. It helps to compensate for the fact that, more often than not, they're wearing them on their sleeves."

Crusher let out a slow breath as if a great weight had been lifted off him. "She was . . . the most exotic woman I'd ever seen. And you didn't have to pretend with her. No games, no posturing . . . she just accepted you as you were. All us guys had a thing for her, really. We'd sit around and—"

And then Crusher flushed slightly and cleared his throat.

Before he could continue, Riker said, "And wonder what it would be like to—"

"Yeah," admitted Crusher. Then, sounding slightly and amusingly defensive, considering his age and the years that had passed, he added, "We were just kids."

"We were all just kids. You, me, her . . . all of us. We just didn't know it at the time." Riker smiled. "Remember that blue-green outfit of hers?"

"Ohhh, yes. That was my favorite."

"Mine, too. Every so often, when I was feeling frivolous, I'd put it on and romp around the holodeck."

Crusher stared at Riker's deadpan expression. "You . . . ?"

"I'm kidding, Wesley."

"Oh." He laughed uncertainly. "Oh."

"Gave you a strange mental picture there for a second, though, didn't it?"

"Yes, sir. It did, sir."

Riker walked slowly across to the door, looking out at the thundering rain. "What else did you and the guys discuss?"

Crusher was looking at Deanna's coffin. "Truthfully?"

"That's usually the best way."

"We talked about how dumb you were to be just friends with her when you could have been so much more."

Riker looked at him askance. "Was the nature of my personal life such public knowledge on the *Enterprise?*"

Crusher shrugged. "A thousand people in an enclosed community for years on end . . . I'm sorry, Admiral, but there just weren't all that many secrets around."

"I see." Letting out a heavy breath, Riker said, "For what it's worth, Captain Crusher . . . we *were* 'so much more.' If we made any mistake . . . or if I made any mistake . . . it was allowing myself to take too much for granted. Like that she would always be there, like Old Reliable. Like that, if I wanted the nature of our relationship to change, I could do so anytime. That was probably my biggest presumption."

They were quiet for a time, listening to the rain falling on the structure. Every so often the thunder would crash, and they would involuntarily jump. Crusher could, of course, have beamed up to his ship anytime, but instead it was clear to Riker that Wesley had unilaterally placed himself at Riker's disposal for however long the admiral needed him . . . or however long Crusher believed he was needed.

Riker wondered obliquely how many strings Crusher had pulled, and how many noses he had put out of joint, to delay whatever missions the *Hood* might have in the hopper. Whatever it was that Crusher had done, Riker found himself extremely grateful.

"How did it happen, sir?"

"How did what happen, Mr. Crusher?"

For a moment, Wesley seemed reluctant to put it into words. "I read about it . . . about how she died. I read the formal reports. I know what my mom told me, but at the time she was so broken up about it that she really couldn't talk about it much. And somehow she never wanted to discuss it, even in later years. It hurt too much for her . . . for all of us, really. But now, I thought maybe—"

"You'd like to know what, precisely, was happening at the time."

"Well . . . I wasn't there," Crusher reminded him. "I was off at the Academy doing my extra year. And when I heard the news, I felt so removed, and I . . ."

"Wanted answers."

"Yes, sir. I remember, I just sat there in my quarters, shaking my head . . . I was too stunned even to cry . . . and I just kept saying, 'Why? Why?'"

"And now you're hoping I might have a few whys and wherefores."

"That's right, sir."

Riker shook his head. Then he walked toward the door and stepped just outside, allowing the rain to spatter on his face. The thunder cracked once more, and over its sound, Riker called out, "I have no answers for you, Wesley! None! But if you want to know what happened . . . I'll tell you. You're entitled to that. God knows we all are."

THE END
OF THE
BEGINNING

As if it were an old-fashioned campfire, or perhaps stories being traded in a haunted house, Adm. William Riker sat on the floor of the mausoleum and—holding nothing back—spoke to Wesley Crusher of those last days. . . .

CHAPTER 7

"**C**ome."

Comdr. William Riker, upon the command/invitation of his superior officer, entered the captain's ready room. Jean-Luc Picard, seated behind his desk, was studying his computer screen and gestured for Riker to sit in front of him. Riker did so, swinging the chair around and straddling it, then waiting patiently for Picard to conclude what he was doing.

He knew that Picard's first expression when he looked away from the computer screen would determine the thrust of the discussion. So Riker breathed an inward sigh of relief when Picard turned the computer display away and smiled up at Riker. Apparently there wasn't going to be any problem.

Still, it never hurt to be cautious. "You wanted to see me, Captain?"

"Merely to touch base, Number One. How are the delegates settling in?"

"Excellently, sir. I'd say the mood was even somewhat jovial. The Byfrexian, Luss, and Cordian ambassadors, and their aides, have absolutely no complaints with their accommodations . . . although the Byfrexians did request the atmosphere in their cabin be somewhat chilled. I've attended to that."

"How amazingly minor," said Picard, looking pleasantly surprised. "No problems at all?"

"Well . . . one small embarrassing moment, I suppose," admitted Riker. "One of the younger children stopped the Cordian ambassador in the hallway and said . . ."

Picard raised an eyebrow. "Said what?"

"He, um . . . well, the child seemed to be under the confused impression that the Cordian was, in fact, an accordion. He asked the ambassador to play 'Twinkle Twinkle, Little Star' on himself."

Picard moaned softly. "How did the ambassador react?"

"He took it in stride, actually. He said it's happened to him on several occasions in the past and suggested that it might be time, and I quote, 'to learn how to play the smegging thing.'"

"Good." Picard sat back in his chair in relief. "These sorts of missions are always delicate, Number One. Considering that ambassadors and delegates are supposed to promote interstellar harmony, it's amazing how often these things can degenerate into acrimony and emotional free-for-alls."

"True enough, but I don't think that's going to happen in this instance, sir. Everyone is just so relieved that the Sindareen are willing to put an end to decades of warfare."

"I'm not surprised. I was just updating myself on the conflict, Number One." Picard tapped the computer screen. "Truly amazing. The warlike attitude of the Sindareen is certainly on par with anything the Klingons or the Kreel ever had to offer. What is amazing is not only the aggressiveness with which they fought, and the zealousness with which they pursued every dispute, no matter how trivial . . . all of that, Number One, is secondary to the fact that they were able to keep it going for so long."

"From everything I read of them," said Riker, "they paid no attention to the fact that their economy was falling apart around their ears."

"Quite right. They kept telling themselves that whatever difficulties they had would disappear once they had conquered their enemies. Except even when they did achieve victories, the results were so devastating that there was nothing left to gain from the conquest—not riches, not any useful goods . . . nothing."

"A series of Pyrrhic victories."

"Precisely. Until the Sindareen reached a point in their war efforts at which they—to use the old-style vernacular—ran out of gas."

"Suing for peace was the first smart thing that the Sindareen have done in close to a century," said Riker. "They're just damned lucky that their closest enemies—the Cordians, the Byfrexians, and the Luss—were willing to listen. They could have put the screws to them."

"Yes. They could. Hopefully it's a lesson in tolerance and acceptance from which the Sindareen will learn. Nothing would better suit interstellar harmony than to have the Sindareen act in a civilized manner. At the same time, Will"—Picard leaned forward, steepling his fingers—"we have to make sure that whatever resentment the Sindareen might feel with the situation doesn't feed whatever fires of self-satisfaction the ambassadors might have burning in them. They are accomplished, intelligent individuals—but at the same time, in a situation like this, there can be a tendency towards smugness. We'll have to watch that.

"By the same token," Picard continued, "we'll have to keep a wary eye on the Sindareen. Yes, they've sued for peace. But we'll have to make sure they're sincere."

"That certainly sounds like it's right up the counselor's alley."

"I've already spoken with Counselor Troi," said Picard. "She had said that the Sindareen were not always easy to read; that their natural aggression could screen her empathic abilities to some degree."

"I know. But on the other hand, if she's with specific members of the Sindareen long enough, she can 'punch through' that resistance and get a very clear feeling for them."

Picard did not attempt to hide his surprise. "That's right. That's exactly what she said."

His captain's expression informed Riker that an explanation was anticipated. Riker simply shrugged. "Deanna had some experience with the Sindareen some time ago."

"And she told you about it?"

"Something like that."

"Is there something that's preventing you from volunteering more information about the counselor's Sindareen experience than you are currently doing?"

"Yes, sir."

"And that would be . . . ?"

Riker smiled. "My innate modesty, sir."

"I see," said Picard, and he harrumphed slightly. "Very well, Commander. Far be it from me to compromise your sense of modesty."

"Thank you, sir. Will there be anything else?"

Picard hesitated a moment and then said, "Let's watch ourselves on this one, Will. I agree that everything would appear to be going smoothly. On the other hand, we haven't reached Sindar yet. Once they get here, things could change very drastically. And we have to keep alert for anything vaguely out of the ordinary."

"If there's one thing I've learned, Captain, it's always to watch out for anything out of the ordinary."

"So have we both, Number One. And we've learned it through trial and error . . . sometimes costly error. And whenever possible —I'd like to avoid more costliness."

"Sometimes, sir, no matter how cautious we are . . . things happen."

Slowly Picard nodded. "That, Number One, is also something that we must both, reluctantly, agree upon."

CHAPTER 8

After touching base with Worf to make sure that all security requirements were met, Riker headed down to Deanna Troi's quarters. It was, he felt, a reasonable thing to do—he had already spoken to her about her feelings vis-à-vis the state of mind of the various ambassadors, and because of her report, he had told the captain all was well. Still, it couldn't hurt to confer with her once more and see whether she had picked up on any second thoughts, hidden hostilities—anything that could conceivably interfere with the successful completion of the mission.

He walked up to the door of her quarters and rang the chime. "Deanna?"

At first there was no sound from within and Riker thought that he might have missed her. He tapped his communicator and said, "Computer, locate Counselor Troi."

"Counselor Troi is in her quarters," the computer calmly informed him.

This confused the hell out of Riker, and small alarms began to sound in his head. Was there a problem? Was she in danger? Why wasn't she answering?

More insistently now, he rang the door chime and said, "Deanna? Are you all right? It's Will."

The door slid open and Deanna was standing there, wrapped in a gold dressing gown that hung half off her bare shoulder. A naked leg was also visible through the folds, which she pulled shut as an afterthought. She appeared slightly out of breath, and her visible skin was slick and glistening, as if from perspiration—or perhaps some sort of skin moisturizing oil.

"I know it's you, Will."

"Is everything okay? I wanted to talk to you about—"

And then he saw him.

A man—a member of the Luss delegation, if Riker was remembering correctly—was seated on the bed. He was clearly naked and was self-consciously holding a pillow on his lap. Riker noted that the sheet was on the floor, out of reach.

The man's orange skin was likewise tinted with some sort of moisture, and his ears—normally elegantly pointed—were drooping somewhat, as if in disappointment or letdown.

Riker waited for the sixteen-ton weight that he was sure would momentarily show up to land squarely on his head.

"You're busy," he said lamely.

"I *was,*" was Troi's pointed reply.

Riker was trying to get himself to move, but his feet had apparently turned into large blocks of granite. Blowing air impatiently out between her lips, Deanna took him by the arm and yanked him into her cabin. The door hissed mercifully shut behind him.

Deanna brushed stray strands out of her face and said, with something remotely approaching civility, "Will Riker, this is Dann Lendann—aide to the ambassador of the Luss. Dann is an old . . . friend. Dann, this is Commander Riker."

"I know." Dann shifted his legs in a vain attempt to look casual. "He welcomed us when we came aboard."

"Yes, although . . . not as enthusiastically as you apparently did, Counselor," said Riker.

Deanna's dark eyes shot him a look that could have dented the deflector screens. And to Riker's surprise—since she did it so infrequently—her voice sounded in his head: *That was a cheap shot, Commander.*

"It was just a joke, Counselor," Riker said. "Just . . . to leaven the moment."

Dann looked from one to the other, sensing that something had just passed between them but unable to discern what it was.

"I think, Commander," said Deanna, readjusting the robe around herself as she held it shut, "that the moment would be sufficiently leavened if you left my cabin."

"Of course. Yes, I'll . . . I'll just be going." Riker backed up, feeling completely lost inside his own body. "Good seeing you, Dann . . . I mean, not that I expected to see this much of you—"

Deanna stared at him witheringly. Riker chucked a thumb in the direction of the door and she nodded. He turned, and mustering what few shreds of dignity he had left—which weren't much—he went back out into the hallway. The door closed with a very decisive hiss.

He leaned against a wall of the corridor. "Perfect."

Riker sat at his customary table in Ten-Forward, nursing his customary drink. A couple of times, crewmen started to wander in his direction. But when they got close enough to him to pick up on the unspoken body language that said *Leave me alone,* they would invariably back off.

Everyone, of course, except Guinan.

The Ten-Forward hostess glided up to the table and simply stood there until Riker looked up.

"The problem is the weather," she said succinctly.

He stared at her. "I beg your pardon?"

"A traditional entrée into conversation has always been to discuss something utterly inconsequential; something that no one can do anything about. The weather has always filled the bill. Saying things like 'I think it's clouding up' was always a good way to ease yourself into talking about something a bit more uncomfortable." Guinan inclined her head slightly toward the viewport. "But look at that. Not much to say, is there? 'Hmm . . . looks like a vacuum today. And they predict more of the same for tomorrow.' You see the difficulty."

"It's a formidable obstacle to casual chitchat," said Riker gravely.

She remained standing opposite him. "So is sending out waves of frustration."

"Have I been doing that?"

"Look around you, Riker. There were twice as many people in here when you came in. Half of them left to do something more fun than be near you—like shoot themselves out the photon torpedo tube."

"Bad as all that, am I?"

She waggled her head slightly. "Not *that* bad. People overreact sometimes. If you were an ensign on custodial detail, that would be one thing. But when the second-in-command looks like he lost his best friend, well . . . crewmen get a little unnerved by that."

"I'll try to be more sensitive to people's needs."

"Have you?"

"Been more sensitive?"

"No. Lost your best friend."

He stared into the contents of the glass. "I don't know. I acted like an idiot with her."

"I see. And were your actions unforgivable? Did you hit her?"

Riker looked shocked. "Of course not!"

"Rough her up a little?"

"No!"

"Call her obscene names?"

"Of course not, Guinan. I'd never do that, and she'd never tolerate it."

"How about beating up one of her friends? Would she tolerate that?"

"No. She wouldn't."

"Well, then," said Guinan, "how do you think she'd react to your beating up on yourself?"

Riker opened his mouth to reply and then closed it again without doing so.

"Uh-huh," said Guinan.

Then she looked behind her in that way she had, reacting to something before she'd even seen it. Riker craned his neck to see around her, already suspecting what would be there.

Sure enough, there was Deanna. She had entered Ten-Forward

and was simply standing there, her arms folded across the top of her gray uniform with the purple V-neck. She was looking at Riker with an arched eyebrow. Her face was unreadable.

Guinan drifted over to her and Deanna glanced at her. "He's all yours," Guinan said. "If you want him, that is."

"I don't know," said Deanna with just the faintest hint of amused tolerance in her voice. "He looks pretty pathetic."

"Looks can be deceiving," said Guinan sagely. Then she looked to Riker, and back to Troi. "On the other hand, sometimes looks can be right on target."

"Thank you, Guinan."

"Don't mention it."

Deanna walked across the Ten-Forward with her usual purposeful stride. And then, in deliberate emulation of Riker, she spun the chair around on the opposite side of the table from him and straddled it.

"I am . . ." Riker tried to find the words, and nothing better than the obvious occurred to him. "So sorry."

He waited for Deanna to say something. All she did was stare at him before finally saying simply, "And . . . ?"

He looked at the drink again. "I handled it very badly. It was an embarrassing situation under any circumstances. Walking in on someone when they're . . . involved with someone . . . can be very disconcerting. And it's even more disconcerting when that person is someone you have . . . had . . ."

"Have and had?"

"Feelings for," he finished. "Feelings that you always think you've sorted out, but then every time you think you have a handle on them, something happens."

Again he paused, and again she simply said, "And . . . ?"

Now he was starting to get just a bit annoyed. "Well, I mean, Deanna—you're the counselor, after all . . . the one who's spent years getting in touch with her feelings. Can you say to me that you wouldn't feel the least little bit thrown off if you walked in on . . . I don't know . . ."

"Ensign Ro?" she said helpfully.

His face fell. "Bad example." But then he brightened slightly.

"Actually . . . you know, I had this odd feeling of reverse déjà vu when I walked in on you, because if you remember, you didn't handle it particularly well on Betazed when—"

She waved it off quickly, saying, "Youth excuses a great deal," but Riker knew that he'd hit home with that reminder of times past. And she knew it, too. When she looked up at him again, it was with an expression that he'd come to know extremely well—understanding.

"Will," she said slowly, "we have a lot of history between us. A lot of reasons why our relationship is precisely where it is. Partly because we're serving on the same ship. Partly because . . . well, partly a lot of things. One thing that we both agree on, though, is that neither of us is interested in leading a celibate life."

"I know, Deanna. I don't deny that. I don't deny your right to be involved with whomever you want. In fact, I'm happy for you." He smiled sincerely, which wasn't difficult because he really was sincere. "You're entitled to every happiness that life has to offer you. And I understand that, since we've decided that our relationship is best served by remaining simply close friends—"

"There's nothing 'simple' about our relationship, Will," she said with her usual sparkle.

"Granted. What I'm saying is that I understand . . . hell, I *know* . . . that relationships of a more—physical—nature than we're pursuing with each other are natural. Expected."

Guinan appeared without saying a word, placed a drink at Deanna's right, and moved away as silent as a ghost. Deanna picked up the drink almost unconsciously, dropped in a small stirrer, and mixed it absently. "We've made no claims on each other otherwise," she pointed out.

"Right. And naturally we're going to be involved with other people."

"You keep saying that, Will. Do you repeat it because you want to emphasize it . . . or because you want to convince yourself of it?"

He smiled lopsidedly. "A little of both, I guess. What I'm saying is that I understand it intellectually. In the abstract. But being put face-to-face, unexpectedly, with the reality of it . . . it just caught me a little off guard, that's all. I felt surprise, and maybe . . . just maybe"—he brought his thumb and forefinger together to measure out a minuscule amount of space—"just a smidgen of jealousy."

"Just a smidgen."

"Nothing significant. I mean, after all, Deanna"—he spread his hands helplessly—"I'm only human."

"I've tried never to hold that against you," she said somberly.

And they clinked glasses.

CHAPTER 9

In a time-honored tradition for getting attention, Captain Picard clinked his knife several times against his glass.

All around the banquet table, the delegates ceased their amiable chatter, putting down their utensils or drinks and giving their full attention to the captain.

Around the table were grouped the ambassadors from the Cordians, the Byfrexians, and the Luss. Also seated there were Data, Worf, Riker, and Troi.

Riker was not seated next to Deanna but instead several spaces down. That had not been the original seating arrangement, but when Deanna had arrived, she had been mildly surprised to find Dann next to her.

"Commander Riker insisted," said Dann, sounding just a bit puzzled. "I thought I was supposed to be sitting with my delegation, but . . ." And he shrugged.

Deanna had turned and looked at Riker, who was sitting next to the Lussian ambassador and speaking with him animatedly. The Luss was nodding his bald head thoughtfully, and giving that enigmatic half-smile that was so typical of the elders of his race.

As if sensing Deanna's gaze on him, Riker continued to talk to the ambassador but glanced in Deanna's direction. Her smile said it all—*The seating rearrangement wasn't necessary, but it's a sweet gesture. Thank you.* He cocked his head slightly in unspoken response and then turned his full attention back to the ambassador.

The evening had progressed quite smoothly as the *Enterprise* continued in its stately orbit around Sindar, the home planet of the Sindareen. Their arrival had been uneventful, which in and of itself was unusual. Once upon a time, anyone getting within a parsec of Sindareen space, much less the home world of Sindar, was met with challenges and hostilities . . . even if they were expected.

But the *Enterprise* had sailed through with nary a whisper from the Sindareen and had settled into orbit around Sindar while attracting nothing more than a muted greeting from the planetary government and an assurance that delegates would shortly be prepared to beam up to the *Enterprise* to begin the hammering out of a peace settlement between the Sindareen and their longtime opponents.

Those delegates were now seated at the head of the table and were paying polite attention to Picard as he rapped for silence.

When all was silent, Picard spoke. "The Federation is, at its heart, an organization dedicated to peace. So a mission such as this one is always particularly gratifying, since we are fulfilling the most fundamental function of the United Federation of Planets. I extend welcome once more to the delegates of the Cordians, the Luss, and the Byfrexians." As he mentioned each one, he raised his glass and moved it slightly in the direction of each in acknowledgment. "And now, it is my honor to welcome the delegates from the Sindareen . . . Ambassador Nici, and her retainer, Eza."

Nici slowly rose. She was tall, with her coal-black hair swept up and back, exposing her long, narrow throat. Her mouth barely moved when she spoke—instead, the sound issued predominantly from the nictating membranes that fluttered at the base of her neck.

"It is . . . *our* honor," she said carefully, "to meet with our . . . associates . . . in a place other than the battlefield. I have advocated the putting aside of hostilities for many years now. Our leaders have finally accepted the inevitability of . . . ."

She paused, and immediately Picard knew why. She was waiting for one of the delegates to be classless enough to finish the sentence with the word *defeat*.

No one said anything, but simply waited expectantly and courteously.

". . . compromise," Nici concluded after a respectable pause.

Picard was pleased that the initial thrust from the Sindareen had worked out so smoothly, as they all raised their glasses and drank. He, along with the other delegates, knew perfectly well that the Sindareen used language as yet another weapon—to probe, prod, and generally to try to trip up potential opponents and reveal their true mind-sets. So no one at the table had any desire or intention of falling into one of the renowned Sindareen verbal traps.

Seated next to Nici, and just to Deanna's right, was Eza, Nici's aide. Eza was darker complexioned than Nici—perhaps a resident of another province, Riker figured. Eza had a dark scowl on his face and seemed even less enthused with the proceedings than Nici. But at least he properly kept his own counsel, and Riker hoped that Eza would not serve as any sort of impediment to the proceedings.

Also, Eza did seem capable of being swayed—the only times he smiled during the meal were when Deanna would engage him in conversation. He seemed grateful for the attention, and several times throughout the course of the meal he actually laughed rather boisterously, his nictating membranes flapping with furious speed. It seemed quite a positive sign. Clearly, Riker thought, the counselor's ability to charm people was not limited solely to Riker himself.

By the end of the dinner, everyone seemed in high spirits. It was as upbeat a beginning as anyone could have hoped.

Still, Riker and Picard managed to sidle up to Deanna during a leisurely time afterward, when the delegates had broken up into smaller groups and were chatting informally with each other. The full meetings were scheduled to begin the next day.

"Any feeling on the Sindareen?" Picard asked in a low voice. He kept his smile firmly fixed in place, though, and even nodded in the direction of Nici when she glanced at him from a corner of the room.

"On a surface level, Captain, their motives seem to be precisely what they say they are: they want peace."

"Any agenda beyond that?" Riker said.

Deanna paused, giving the question full weight. "I cannot say for sure. As I told you, Captain—and as Commander Riker knows— the Sindareen can be a challenge to read. Through continued exposure, however, as I gain a feeling for the individual's psyche, I might be able to tell you more."

"You'll do your best, I'm certain, Counselor," said Picard. "At least we're off on the right foot."

A hand rested on Deanna's shoulder and she turned to look into Dann's smiling face. "Are you about finished here, Deanna?" he asked, and then looked to Picard and Riker. "Sorry, gentlemen . . . I didn't mean to interrupt."

"That's all right, Dann," said Deanna. "We were finished." Then she looked to Picard for confirmation. "Weren't we, Captain?"

"By all means." But Picard's eyes narrowed slightly, and he watched as Dann led Deanna out of the room, an arm around her waist in a most familiar fashion. Deanna was laughing lightly at some comment he had just whispered to her.

Picard turned to Riker and noted that the muscles of his jaw were working under his cheeks. "Problem, Number One?"

"No problem, Captain," said Riker neutrally.

Picard took a step closer to his second-in-command and observed, "She seems rather friendly with him. That's not going to present a difficulty for you, is it, Number One?"

Riker regarded Picard with an arched eyebrow. "I already said there's no problem, Captain. I hope you don't think I'm lying to you."

"Number One, never in a million years would I believe that you would lie to me."

"Thank you, sir."

Picard paused only a moment before he added, "However . . . lying to yourself would be another matter entirely."

Riker had been turning away, but now he looked back at Picard with some surprise. "Deanna's happiness is my happiness," Riker said firmly, and then deciding that his tone sounded just a bit too aggressive for a statement directed to his commanding officer, quickly added a respectful, "Sir."

Picard nodded slightly. "A very commendable and adult attitude, Number One. If you are satisfied with the situation, then I certainly am—especially seeing as it isn't any of my business."

"As you say, sir."

One of the Byfrexians came up at that moment and engaged Picard in a discussion of Prime Directive ethics that had been a bone of contention in a seminar the ambassador had taught. Riker listened for a few moments before drifting over to Nici and striking up a polite and, he hoped, informative conversation with her.

But his gaze kept shifting over to the doors of the banquet room—the doors through which Counselor Troi had exited moments earlier with Dann. And Riker had taken note not only of the arm around her waist but also that Deanna had placed a hand over his as if she wanted to make sure he didn't remove that arm.

"I'm happy for you," he said to no one in particular.

CHAPTER 10

Riker lay on his back, staring up into the darkness of his quarters.

His hands were interlaced behind his head, the pillow soft under him. He had been that way for over an hour as sleep refused to come.

Sorting out his feelings was rapidly becoming something of a royal pain. He still remembered that time a couple of years ago, in Deanna's quarters . . . Both he and Deanna had been in an extremely mellow mood, and he had also been allowing the more relaxing qualities of the Synthehol he'd consumed to have sway over his actions. A friendly good-night kiss had turned into something far more passionate, and for a moment they had been kissing each other eagerly, hungrily, and it had been just like the old days.

And then Deanna had whispered, pleaded, telling him that they shouldn't, reminding him of the difficulties of involvement while both served on the same ship. Yet even as she spoke, she would have let him . . .

But he pulled back. Her words had penetrated the Syntheholic haze on his brain and washed it away, bringing with it instant sobriety and a reminder of the line that they had drawn for themselves.

And nothing had happened.

Not that he hadn't wanted it . . . they had both wanted it . . .

But what had they wanted? Momentary gratification? Or something more . . . a rekindling of something that they had thought they'd left behind them?

Perhaps they'd been kidding themselves. Here he was someone accustomed to command situations, and here she was someone who was always in touch with feelings. So it was only natural that they would decide they could control their feelings, dictate their relationship. Turn their emotions on and off like an old-style light switch.

How realistic was that, though? Lying there in the darkness, imagining Deanna at that moment, wrapped in the arms of Dann, laughing or saying things softly . . .

Did she say the same things to Dann that she had to Riker?

For a moment there he had actually been drifting off, his feelings about Deanna lulling his brain and convincing him that everything would seem more clear in the morning. And then something, some impulse, made him sit bolt upright in bed, moving so swiftly that he had a momentary sense of disorientation.

Someone was there. He didn't know how, he didn't know why . . . but someone was there, hiding in a corner, lurking in the darkness.

He called out, "Lights!"

Obediently his quarters filled with light. And there he saw—

Nothing.

The doors had not opened. No one had entered. Except for himself, no one was there.

He had no way of describing the feeling that was cutting through him. What was the old saying? *Someone just stepped on my grave.*

"Hello?" said Riker tentatively, not having the faintest idea why he was saying it.

The ship's computer, aware that the room was unoccupied except for Riker, interpreted the salutation as an oddly variant, but no less legitimate, means of address to itself. "Working," replied the computer. It then waited patiently for further instructions.

He didn't know why he was asking, but he said, "Computer—who's in this room?"

"William Thelonius Riker."

"Anyone else?"

"No."

Slowly he nodded. "Lights off," he said after a moment.

He lay back down as the lights faded, wondering whether he wasn't making himself a little crazy over the situation.

At first he felt wide-awake, but then gradually the fatigue settled in, and slowly, gradually, he drifted off to sleep.

She filled his dreams. She was smiling at him, walking toward him, her arms outstretched, and somehow everything seemed to make so much more sense when she was there. Without her, there was no—

"IMZADI!"

The word screamed in his mind, throughout every part of his body, and he snapped to full wakefulness in a split instant. He didn't know how much time had passed since he had fallen back to sleep, and it didn't matter.

All that mattered was the voice, was the word, and it had been unmistakably no dream. Definitely, it was Deanna, and whatever was happening, it was utterly terrifying to her.

"Deanna!" shouted Riker.

The computer said helpfully, "William Thelonius Riker is the only occupant of—"

"Shut up! Lights!"

The lights immediately snapped on. He winced against it momentarily, but it didn't slow him as he ran to his closet and grabbed his robe. "Riker to Counselor Troi!" he called out in the more recognizable comm command that would, ordinarily, patch him through the ship's intercom to Deanna.

There was no response. She wasn't acknowledging—but he could still feel that cold, dark terror invading him. Whatever was happening, she was replying in a far more primal manner than via a ship's communication system.

Immediately switching gears as he yanked on his robe, he said, "Riker to Dr. Crusher!"

This time there was a response. Beverly sounded groggy—obviously he'd woken her up. But there was no hesitation to her voice because late-night interruptions were hardly unusual in her line of work. "Crusher here."

"Something's wrong with Deanna! Get a medunit to her quarters now!"

To her credit, Beverly Crusher wasted no time with confused questions such as "How do you know?" or "Why didn't you call sickbay directly?" To the latter question, she obviously, and correctly, reasoned that Riker had instinctively contacted the person he most trusted in a medical emergency. To the former question, when it came to matters of Riker and Troi, she was more than willing to accept a great deal on faith.

All she said was a stark "Acknowledged."

Riker didn't even hear her reply. He was already out the door.

He barreled down the corridor, attracting curious glances from passersby due to his state of extremely casual dress that contrasted with his air of barely controlled panic. Ensign Chafin had the poor luck to turn a corner without watching where he was going, which was directly into Riker's path, and Riker plowed into him like a linebacker. Chafin went flying and smacked into the far wall. Riker barely lost a step and kept on going, not even registering until sometime later that he had decked a crewman without so much as a word of apology.

Deanna's quarters were just ahead and he raced into them, heedless of his safety. After all, he had no idea what threat Deanna might be subjected to—for all he knew, berserk Sindareen were skinning her alive and were ready to turn on him next. Nothing mattered except helping her.

He entered her quarters and was horrified by the sight that greeted his eyes.

Deanna was lying on the floor, convulsions shaking her. She was nude except for a sheet that had been tossed over her, like a shroud. Dann was standing over her, having pulled on trousers, but otherwise looking confused and helpless.

"Deanna!" shouted Riker.

Dann looked at him, and his skin had gone a shade or two lighter. "I . . . I don't know what happened! She just—"

"Why the hell didn't you summon help!" shouted Riker.

"I don't know how!" said Dann. "I've never been on a starship before! Is there something I press or—"

Riker shoved him aside, unnecessarily hard, and called out desperately, "Riker to sickbay! Where the hell's that medunit!" He didn't even wait for a reply as he dropped down next to the trembling counselor.

Her skin was dead white. He took her hand in his and it was clammy. His hands moved helplessly over her, and he fought down his terror as he said, "Shh . . . everything's going to be okay. It's okay, Deanna."

Her eyes were clouding over. He didn't even think she could see him. He had no idea what was happening to her, and even more terrifying . . . neither did she.

"Imzadi," she whispered, voicing the word that had lanced through his mind and soul. "Please . . . help me . . . help."

He scooped her up into his arms urgently and was out the door, heading toward the sickbay. He was by nature a strong man, and now, driven by adrenaline and fear, he was so worked up that he hardly even felt her weight. He kept whispering to her, talking frantically, as if afraid that the only thing keeping her attached to the world was the sound of his voice.

He encountered the medunit partway. Beverly Crusher had not even bothered to toss on a robe—in her nightgown, she was guiding the techs with the antigrav crash cart. "Quickly! Quickly!"

Deanna's hand still gripped Riker's robe as he laid her down on the cart and ran alongside it. And again, she said, "Help me . . . please . . . so cold . . ." Her body was shaking faster.

"Stabilize her!" shouted Crusher, and Dr. Selar, who had been on duty when the call came in, jammed a hypo into her arm.

"I'll help you," Riker told Deanna, and the fear that ran through her leaped into him and clamped around his heart. He felt as if his world were disintegrating. "I promise, Imzadi. I'll do anything . . . everything. I . . ."

But she didn't hear him.

Her breath rattled once more in her chest . . . and by the time she was rolled into sickbay mere moments later . . .

. . . she was gone.

Thousands of light-years away, Lwaxana Troi woke up And she began screaming.

She did not stop for two solid hours.

She was never the same after that.

EPILOGUE

Admiral Riker stared at Captain Crusher, who was stony faced. "Your mother blamed herself for quite some time afterwards," Riker said. "It was so unnecessary . . . she did everything she could. She worked on Deanna for . . . I don't know . . . it seemed forever, trying to bring her back. But nothing helped. Nothing . . . helped." And he added silently, *Not even me.*

"She blamed herself but she didn't have to, that's what you're saying?" asked Captain Crusher.

"That's right."

Wesley stared out at the rain, which had tapered off to a mere trickle. Within a minute or two, it would stop altogether. "And I guess another reason it wasn't necessary . . . was that you pretty much had a lock on the self-blame category."

Riker nodded slowly. "I guess the difference is that your mother did everything she could . . . and didn't succeed. And I kept feeling as if . . . as if I should have done something. Somehow, someway . . . I should have done *more*. And it was always a great frustration to me that I never figured out what that more should have been. All I knew is that I promised to help her . . . and I didn't do much except be by her side when she died."

"Maybe that was all she wanted."

Riker said nothing.

Crusher considered a moment and then said, "And Mom never found the cause?"

"Never," said Riker, shaking his head. "That's the most agonizing thing about a situation like that. You find yourself wanting answers, some sort of answers. And there were none to be had. Beverly couldn't find any cause for Deanna's . . . passing. It was just as if her body simply . . . stopped. Massive cardiovascular collapse, but there seemed no physiological reason for it. Beverly ran a full trace of all known foreign substances, for the purpose of ruling out foul play—which was pretty farfetched, but your mom covered all the bases—and there was nothing. Deanna just . . ." He struggled with the word and then exhaled it: "Died." He paused.

"And what happened then?"

Riker shrugged. "It all went downhill. The ship; my life . . . just . . ." And again he shrugged, this time a bit more fatalistically. "Sometimes you just don't really appreciate how key someone is to your world until they're gone. And then, of course, it's too late."

They sat there for a few moments longer, and then Wesley suddenly cocked his head slightly in that gesture that Riker had come to know so well. "Crusher here."

Riker didn't bother to stand by and watch Captain Crusher have a conversation with thin air. Instead he walked back into the other room where Deanna's body lay in a perfectly preserved state and rested a hand on the covering.

"I'm sorry, Imzadi," he said softly. "I tried."

He heard Wesley's soft footfall, and then the captain said, "I have to go. Sudden groundquake on Cygnia III. Code One disaster situation." He paused. "You're welcome to come along, Admiral. There's . . . well, I'm sorry, sir, but there's nothing here for you except fairly unpleasant memories."

"That may very well be, Captain, but as I mentioned to you, Lwaxana Troi's wishes in the disposition of her things were quite specific. And Lwaxana was always a tough woman to say no to."

"All right, Admiral. Whatever you say." Crusher paused. "It

stopped raining. If you'd like, I'll walk you back to the house before I go."

Riker nodded.

They walked out of the mausoleum together, their feet squishing softly into the now spongelike ground. The clouds were passing and hints of sunlight were already streaming through. As they approached the house, the admiral turned to Crusher and took him by the shoulders.

"It's been a pleasure seeing you again, Wes."

Crusher grimaced. "I just wish it could have been under more pleasant circumstances."

"So do I. Maybe next time it will be."

Then, in a rather nonregulation but perfectly understandable move, Riker embraced Crusher firmly, patting him on the back. Then he took a few steps back, and both of them, without any intention of doing so, simultaneously tugged on their respective uniform jackets, straightening them. Each saw the other making the gesture, and they both laughed.

"Good sailing, Captain Crusher. The *Hood* is a good ship. I served on one of her predecessors. Fortunately she has a fine captain at the helm."

"Good luck in your future endeavors, Admiral Riker. I hope you find happiness . . . and some peace." Then Crusher tilted his head and said, "Crusher to *Hood*. One to beam up."

Wesley Crusher's body shimmered out, and Riker was alone.

He found the Holy Rings of Betazed. They were, for no reason Riker could determine, in Lwaxana's closet. He shrugged and put them with the pile of other materials, trinkets, and mementos that he was organizing in the living room.

Mr. Homn had vanished. There had been no word of explanation. No good-byes. When Riker had returned to the mansion, Homn simply wasn't there. It was as if he'd done his job to its conclusion and, once having reached that conclusion, had no reason to remain. And so he had left. Left Riker with a huge pile of material to go through.

Betazed had an excellent museum of antiquities, and Lwaxana

Troi's collection was going to be a considerable and valuable addition. Riker had made the arrangements for it to be taken away, and they had only asked that he go through everything first to remove any possessions that might simply be considered personal and of no interest to the general Betazed public.

Lwaxana had left no family behind. The furniture had already been cleared out, donated to a local charity. All that were left were the keepsakes that Riker was now sorting through.

Having gone through all the other rooms in the house, he now approached the one he least looked forward to: Deanna's.

He opened the door, and sure enough, it was what he had anticipated. Lwaxana had left everything exactly as it was, like a shrine to her daughter. The room was decorated in large splashes of purple, with various small statues—the type that Deanna had liked to stare at for hours on end.

And in Deanna's closet, he found a box.

It had a lock on it, but the lock wasn't closed. Riker opened the lid, curious as to what he would find.

He recognized everything that was in the box.

Everything had been perfectly preserved, no matter how arcane or trivial. There was a piece of vine from the Jalara Jungle. There was the headband that she had been wearing at Chandra's wedding. There was her study disk on "Human Dysfunctions." There was . . .

"Good lord." He reached down and picked up a small but sharp rock. It had a discoloration on it that was quite clearly blood. "She even kept this."

He looked further and found the poem.

He read it over, separated by decades from the youthful exuberance with which he'd penned it. Phrases that he could remember sounding so clever to himself when he'd come up with them now sounded trite, facile. A kid who knew nothing, trying to sum up in a few lines of poetry feelings that even now, as an old man, he couldn't completely frame for himself.

"This is terrible. I can't believe I wrote this." And then he picked up the headband, fingering it. "And I can't believe you liked it. I can't believe you—"

He was surprised to find that his face was wet. He wiped the tears with the headband and felt the softness of it against his face and started to cry harder.

He had thought he'd finished with the grief. He'd thought he'd been able to move on. But there, sitting on the floor of a room once belonging to a young, vital woman, he realized that he had never moved on. Never put it behind him. His entire life reeked of unfinished business. And he would never be able to finish it. There had been so much he had wanted to say—and would never be able to because time had outsped him before he'd even fully grasped the notion that he was in a race.

It was never going to get better. Despite all his accomplishments, his great failure—the failure that everyone had told him he'd had no reason for shouldering—would always be with him. Always.

He clutched the headband even tighter and tried to remember a time when he felt no pain.

THE BEGINNING

CHAPTER 11

Lieutenant William T. Riker punched the bulkhead and managed to bruise his hand rather badly. The bulkhead, for its part, didn't seem to care all that much.

He stared once more, with utter hatred, at the packed suitcase that sat in the middle of his bed, as if angry the thing even existed. "This really stinks," he informed the case, and went on to add, "I can't believe you're doing this." The suitcase showed as much interest in Riker's anger as had the bulkhead.

"Lieutenant Riker to the bridge," came his captain's voice through his communicator.

He tapped it with his hand, which made it feel sore all over again: "On my way." He cast one last angry glance at the suitcase and the bulkhead, which had obviously conspired to make his life just that much more miserable, before heading out the door and up to the bridge.

He drummed impatiently on the railing grip of the turbolift. Everything about the ship seemed slow and frustrating. For that matter, everything about his *life* seemed slow and frustrating. He had places to go, a career to forge . . . and the fates had conspired to slow that career to an agonizing, frustrating crawl.

The 'lift door opened out onto the cramped bridge of the *Fortuna,* and Riker stepped out. He nodded a brisk acknowledgment to Captain Lansing and took his place at the survey station.

Lansing, middle-aged and content with the relatively low point in the pecking order that he had reached in his career, swiveled in his chair to face Riker. "I thought you might want to know, Lieutenant, that we'll be arriving at Betazed in . . ." Lansing paused and glanced at the helmsman.

"Twenty-seven minutes," said the helmsman.

Riker noticed that everyone on the bridge seemed to be staring at him.

"And we thought that you might want to spend your last half hour aboard our vessel with our small but sturdy bridge crew," continued Lansing.

Riker frowned. "That's very kind of you, sir."

Lansing rose, drawing his portly frame out of the command chair. "You did make it quite clear that you did not want any sort of going-away function."

"Yes, sir. And I appreciate your honoring my request."

"You know the wonderful thing about being in command, Mr. Riker?" Without waiting for Riker to respond, Lansing continued, "You get to ignore the wishes of your junior officers whenever it suits you. Mr. Li, if you don't mind."

Navigator Kathy Li rose from her chair and brought her hands around. Riker saw that she was holding something, and he fought down a grin when he saw what it was: a large cupcake with a sparking candle lodged serenely in the top. And the words *So Long, Cupcake*—Li's nickname for him—were scrawled across the top of it in pink icing.

Captain Lansing said, "Computer. Run 'Riker Farewell Program One-A.'"

The bridge was promptly filled with the sound of Dixieland music, and now Riker laughed out loud in spite of himself.

Over the music, Lansing called out, "We decided to compromise, Mr. Riker—a send-off, but with a very proscribed time limit, namely twenty-seven—excuse me, twenty-six now—minutes."

Riker made the round of the bridge crew, shaking hands and

laughing and nodding, accepting with good grace their best wishes for his new assignment. Kathy Li kissed him rather passionately— they had made some minor effort to be discreet over their relationship while serving together. They had, of course, fooled absolutely no one, and with his imminent departure she saw no need to pussyfoot around. They broke for air and she patted him on the face. "It's been a lot of laughs, cupcake."

"No more than that?" he said mischievously.

She looked at him, feigning total astonishment. *"More* than that? With Will-the-Thrill, I-Never-Met-a-Woman-I-Didn't-Like Riker? Oh, come on, Lieutenant. You wouldn't *want* more than that. Doesn't fit in with your game plan."

"Are you saying the good lieutenant isn't the type to commit to one woman?" said Lansing in mock horror.

"I'm really enjoying discussing my psychological profile in a public forum," Riker said.

As if Riker hadn't even spoken, Li said cheerfully, "Remember the old days of space travel, Captain? Where every single article had to be carefully measured and accounted for because of fuel consumption? If you had weight that you didn't allow for, it could cost the early astronauts their lives. Well"—she squeezed Riker's shoulder—"the lieutenant operates on the same principle. A real, solid romance—true love and everything—would amount to additional weight in his travels through space. Our Mr. Riker doesn't like to deal with excess baggage."

Riker looked at her. "Kathy, are you mad at me?"

She blinked in surprise. "No. Not at all. I just know how you are. Or am I wrong?"

He thought about it and said, "No, you're probably right."

"See there?" said Lansing. "Mr. Li is probably right. And that is good enough for me. Mr. Riker, do you have any final things you'd like to say before you embark on your new and exciting assignment?"

Science Officer Sara Paul was going around from person to person, holding a bottle of champagne. Glasses had been produced and she was filling each of them up about halfway.

"Anything I'd like to say? Truthfully?"

"The truth is preferred aboard the science exploration vessel *Fortuna,*" said Lansing.

Riker stared at his cupcake. "Well . . . to be honest . . . I wish I weren't leaving."

This caused a fairly surprised reaction from the others. "But Lieutenant," said Lansing, "being promoted to first officer on the *Hood* . . . it's a sizable step up. And—"

"If I were going to the *Hood,* sir, I'd be ecstatic. But I'm not. I'm going to be cooling my heels planetside for the next few months. I could be far more use remaining on the *Fortuna.*"

"Lieutenant," said Lansing understandingly, "it's an unfortunate piece of luck, I'll admit. But let's try being unselfish, shall we? We can just thank the stars that the *Hood* is still in one piece. From what I've heard, those Sindareen raiders gave her quite a shellacking. It's a testament to the *Hood,* her capabilities and her crew, that she not only survived the sneak attack but destroyed the raiders. Still, she's going to be in dry dock for the next two to three months, undergoing repairs and overhauls which were past due anyway. Look at it this way—you'll be getting a ship that's better than new."

"But to be planetside . . ." Riker shook his head ruefully. "I feel like I'll lose my space legs. The timing is so lousy."

"True enough," admitted Lansing. "But what are we supposed to do? Your transfer to the *Hood* was arranged a month ago. Who expected a Sindareen attack on her? And the same time your transfer was arranged, so was the transfer of your replacement. We rendezvous with him in eighteen hours. We don't need the both of you here, and when the vacancy in the Betazed embassy opened up—"

"So why not let *him* stew on Betazed for a few months?" said Riker, hoping he wasn't sounding too whiny.

"Because Starfleet wanted the more experienced officer there, Lieutenant, and that's you. Face it, Mr. Riker . . . you're just too popular. Everyone wants you."

Riker shook his head. "It's been years since I've been planetside for more than seventy-two hours."

"You'll get the hang of it," said Lansing consolingly. Then he raised his glass. "Lt. William T. Riker: Here's wishing you all the success in the galaxy, and hoping for a great and glorious future. To your future."

"To your future," chorused the crew of the *Fortuna*.

Riker nodded and smiled. "To the future," he said, and drank the champagne.

CHAPTER 12

Riker's first view of Mark Roper, the man who headed the Federation embassy of Betazed, was what would become a fairly typical view of him—behind his desk, looking utterly besieged. Roper, for his part, didn't seem to notice Riker at all.

Roper was heavyset, with graying hair and a thick, red nose that God seemed to have slapped on one day while He was in one of His more puckish moods. Roper had two computer screens on his desk and was going from one to the other, tapping notes into a small padd in front of him and muttering to himself much of the time.

Riker cleared his throat. Roper glanced up at him, nodded briskly in acknowledgment, and then promptly, and rather obviously, forgot Riker was standing there. Instead Roper continued with his work, saying things like, "Unbelievable. Can't expect me to be everywhere. They want me to . . . ? That's two conflicting appointments. *Now* the Rigelian ambassador wants to come through? *And* he expects me to set up a reception. Lord . . . Grace!"

The last word was shouted, and for a moment Riker thought that Roper was loudly calling for divine intervention. But then the harried but determined young woman who had greeted Riker when he first arrived outside Roper's office barreled in in response. She sidled past Riker, who had the distinct feeling that he had been thrown into the middle of carefully, but barely, controlled chaos.

"Grace," Roper said, "get me Harras at the catering facility. I have to meet with him as soon as possible. Also with Counsel Head Timbor—"

"You just met with him yesterday," Grace reminded him, sounding slightly confused.

"Yes, but I didn't know about the Rigelian ambassador yesterday," replied Roper in exasperation. "Utterly paranoid people. Never like to give anyone more than forty-eight hours notice. And he probably won't even show up! Cancel at the last minute. Typical. Typical."

Riker wasn't sure precisely whom Roper was talking to—Grace, Riker, or himself . . . or some combination of the three.

"When's the earliest I can see Harras? Tonight," he said, answering his own question. "It has to be tonight."

"You have the Xerx wedding tonight."

Roper held his face in his hands. "Perfect. Just perfect."

He was silent for a long moment, and Riker seized the break in the steady flow of conversation. "Mr. Roper? I'm Lieutenant Riker. I presume you were told about me?"

Roper stared at him through his fingers. "When was our appointment?"

"Appoint—?" Riker looked from Roper to the woman who'd been addressed as Grace. "Is *anyone* here expecting me?"

Grace said to her boss with a gentle, prodding tone, "Starfleet? Remember, Mark?"

Roper still looked blank for a moment, and then understanding flooded through his face. "Riker! William Riker!"

"Yes, sir," said Riker with a sigh of relief.

"The new Starfleet liaison! My boy, please accept my apologies." Roper circled around his desk and took Riker's hand, pumping it furiously.

"I'm sorry if I came at a bad time."

"Daytime is generally a bad time," said Roper. "The second worst time is nighttime. Nevertheless, it's good to have you aboard.

As you can see by my perpetually discombobulated state, the more help we have here, the better."

"Whatever I can do to help, sir."

"Yes, well, the first thing you can do is take a load off." Roper gestured to the chair opposite him. "And have patience with my natterings and ramblings. Would you like some coffee?"

"That would be great, thanks."

Roper started to head for the door, but Grace stopped him. "It's okay, Mark. I'll get it." She looked to Riker and said, "Cream?"

"Black."

"Coming up." She smiled and flashed two rows of clean white teeth at him before walking out.

Roper looked at Riker with what appeared to be newfound respect. "I admit, I'm impressed, Captain."

Riker looked at him with mild confusion. "It's 'lieutenant.' And why are you impressed, sir?"

"Because Grace has been my assistant for three years and she rarely sees fit to bring me coffee . . . and she never volunteers. But you—" Roper paused. "Have a way with the females, do you, Captain?"

A slow smile spread across Riker's face. "Women seem to . . . appreciate me. Why do you keep calling me captain?"

"Starfleet forwarded me your file. Very impressive body of work. The word on you is that you're an aggressive, hotshot, up-and-coming young officer, with a flair and aptitude for some of the finer points of diplomacy. The general poop—do you Starfleet types still use nautical terms like *poop?*"

"On occasion." At first put off by Roper's style—if such a term could be applied to it—Riker was slowly finding himself amused by, and even liking, this somewhat harried diplomat.

"Okay. The general poop is that you're on a fast track, my young friend. Some even believe you might beat out Jim Kirk's record for youngest captain . . . and that's stood firm for close to a century."

"That's the poop, is it?"

"And nothing but the poop. So I figure I'll start calling you captain now and beat the rush." Roper leaned forward. "Unless you'd like me to just skip straight to 'admiral'?"

"That's quite all right, sir, you run the embassy. You can address me however you want . . . although I would appreciate it if, in the presence of other Starfleet personnel, you addressed me by my proper rank. Genuine captains might not consider it amusing."

"Whatever," said Roper with a casual air.

Grace came back in with a cup of black coffee, which Riker took carefully from her. She stood over him and said, "Anything else I can get for you?"

"This will be fine."

"Grace, see that we're not disturbed."

"All right, Mark," she said, but her smile and gaze were directed to Riker. Then she turned and walked out.

Roper shook his head. "Oh, yes. *Very* impressive. So . . ." His tone changed to a more businesslike timbre. "What have they told you?"

"About this assignment? Well . . . Betazed is supposed to be environmentally quite lovely." Riker turned his attention to a large window that opened out onto a dazzling vista. The sky was dazzling blue with pink clouds hanging against it as if they'd been painted there. They were on the twentieth floor of the building, and Riker had an overview of the city. Rather than being a combination of a variety of styles, as in so many cities, the buildings seemed to flow seamlessly one into the other. Either the city had been meticulously planned from the beginning or else the growth of it had been consistently smooth and organic. Far, far in the distance, Riker could see the barest hints of a mountain range. "In that," he continued, "I would have to say the word *understatement* comes to mind."

"It is a lovely world. A lovely people," confirmed Roper. "Sensitive to a great degree. Thoughtful and caring, and utterly cooperative. A people steeped in tradition, and a world filled with great thinkers. I am not—it pains me to admit—a great thinker, Captain. How about you?"

"For the moment, I'm happy to be a quick thinker. I presume the rest will take care of itself."

"A very mature attitude. What else do you know?"

"Betazed is a long-standing Federation ally, and quite valued."

Then Riker's face darkened. "I also understand there have been some recent difficulties with the Sindareen."

"Quite correct," said Roper gravely. "The Sindareen have a history of belligerence. They also seem to operate in shifts."

"Shifts?" Riker didn't quite understand.

"They have a number of planets and peoples with whom they have disputes, or just perceive as being ripe pickings. But they don't attack them steadily. They go after them for periods of time until they've reached the point where they're almost crossing the line from nuisance and threat to genuine menace . . . and then they pull back. They won't be heard from for months, even years at a time . . . until they've been pretty much forgotten about. At which point they start their assaults and raids all over again."

"And right now they're picking on Betazed."

"That's right. There have been three attacks in as many months at various points throughout the city."

"What about the outlying cities?"

"Small. Primarily agricultural. A lot of farmland on Betazed, or cities that are devoted primarily to philosophical studies. Here is where the real economic action of Betazed occurs—almost all of the trading, the commerce, funnels through here."

"Not the smartest way to arrange things," said Riker grimly. "Apparently they've never heard about putting all the eggs in one basket."

Roper shrugged. "It's their planet, Captain. We can't tell them how to run things. We can, however, take steps. A squad of Starfleet security has been stationed here. As the ranking Starfleet officer, you'll be in charge of them."

Riker nodded. He was familiar with ground-based Starfleet security men—essentially, they were security guards without a ship. They would be dispatched by the UFP to situations where a Federation presence was going to be required for an extended period of time. You couldn't leave a starship in orbit around a planet for weeks, even months—but you could send in a squad of Starfleet security men and leave them there for however long it took to solve the problem.

Riker had encountered ground security teams on a couple of

occasions. They were generally tough, strong headed, sometimes contemptuous and even distrustful of officers who spent their careers in "fancified starships," as one ground security man had put it. They were also, Riker knew, extremely formidable.

"Anything else I should know, Mr. Roper?"

Roper nodded and leaned forward. "Don't try to con these people, Riker. Their sensitivity to thought processes is second to none."

"I wouldn't try to 'con' anyone, sir," said Riker, feeling a bit indignant.

"Oh, come on, Captain, we all do it. For example—you run into a woman at a party and she's wearing a dress so ugly it looks like a Klingon Targ vomited on it. Do you say to her, 'Hello, how are you—why are you wearing such a god-awful dress?' Or do you say, 'Hello, my dear, you look lovely tonight.'"

"Well . . . the second, I suppose. I mean, just to be sociable."

"Save it. On Betazed they know precisely what you're thinking. The fortunate thing is that, because of that, these people are hard to offend just on the basis of pure unspoken opinions. They've had to develop a high tolerance for unexpurgated thought . . . it was either that or kill each other. The only thing they have little tolerance for is prevarication. They'd consider that to be insulting. Be straightforward and honest with the Betazoids and they'll appreciate and respect you for it."

The door to the office hissed open and Roper looked up in irritation. "Grace, I thought I said I didn't want to be disturbed."

A young, cheery-eyed woman with straight black hair and a bit of the devil in her eye flounced into the office. "Hello, Daddy."

"Oh! Wendy!" He gestured to Riker, who got to his feet. "Lieutenant Riker, this is my daughter, Wendy. Wendy, this is William Riker."

"Nice to meet you," said Riker, taking mental note of the fact that Roper had introduced him using his correct rank. For that he was most appreciative.

Wendy pumped his hand in much the same manner that Roper had. "We have the same initials," she observed. "W.R." She was looking at him with a frank, appraising attitude.

"So we have," agreed Riker.

"Good." She grinned impishly. "When we get married, we can have identical monograms on our towels."

Riker blinked in surprise and looked at Roper, who shrugged. "Wendy's been here with me the past three years. She's gotten into the habit of stating her mind . . . even with those people who can't read it."

"Saves time," she said. She released Riker's hand but continued to smile. "If you could read my mind, though, Lieutenant, you'd know I was just joking."

"Oh." Riker felt a little foolish. "Of course you were."

"You're cute, though. I like your eyes. They look like they've seen a lot . . . a lot of amazing things, and a lot of nasty stuff."

Riker was beginning to find her forthrightness somewhat refreshing. The idea of an entire planet where people said what was on their minds began to seem a little less daunting. Since when was the notion of honesty something to be concerned over?

"You're right," he said. "I'll be happy to fill you in on some of it."

"I'll be happy to listen."

"And I'm happy everyone's happy. Oh, happy happiness," Roper put in, sounding a bit curmudgeonly. "Wendy, was there something in particular you wanted to discuss?"

"Yes." She turned to her father. "I just wanted to know, which do you think would be better to wear to the Xerx wedding tonight? The blue dress with the ruffles, or the green dress that's cut low?"

"What difference does it make?" asked Roper. He looked at Riker. "Yet another one of the social engagements that this office is expected to participate in. Chandra Xerx, a daughter of the third house of Betazed, is getting married tonight. The Federation is to send a representative. Guess who."

"Well, *I'm* looking forward to it," said Wendy.

"What third house?" asked Riker.

"Oh, that. Well, Betazed society has a number of families that are considered founding families, tracing ancestry back all the way to the earliest writings of Betazed history and culture. There are twenty of these senior 'houses,' as they're called. The house of Xerx is the third oldest, hence the designation 'third house.' Chandra is the eldest daughter of Gart Xerx, and as Wendy mentioned, the wedding is tonight. I hate Betazoid weddings," he added darkly. "And the timing of this one in particular . . . when in hell am I going to meet with Harras to discuss this sudden reception I have to pull together?"

"Look, sir, if it's too much of an inconvenience for you, I have a simple solution," said Riker. "I'll go."

Roper looked up. "You?"

"If," said Riker, and he turned smilingly to Wendy, "it wouldn't bother you to have me as your escort instead of your father."

She looked him up and down in an even more appraising manner than before, and Riker couldn't understand why she was grinning so widely. "That sounds great."

"You really wouldn't mind, Lieutenant Riker?" said Roper. "You'd be doing me a tremendous service—clearing up some free time for me to attend to other matters, and sparing me yet another one of those ceremonies."

"I don't see what the problem would be," said Riker. "I'm glad to pitch in and help wherever I can."

"That's settled, then," said Wendy cheerfully.

"Good," said Roper, slapping his ample belly. "I must admit, I think that you'll present a much more dignified presence for the Federation than I usually do."

Riker smiled politely, not completely understanding what Roper meant.

But later, he would.

CHAPTER 13

The wedding chapel was small and sedate, a one-story building shaped like a trapezoid.

It was a crisp, cool evening, and Riker in full dress uniform had called on Wendy at her home to pick her up. He saw that she had indeed decided on the low-cut green dress, and he felt somewhat appreciative of that. The cleavage it revealed was most attractive, and she had a long and slender neck that was nicely accentuated as well.

She smiled at him and said, "Very chic, Lieutenant."

"I wanted to make a good first impression on all concerned. And please, call me Will."

"Try and stop me." She inclined her head slightly. "The chapel's less than a kilometer away, and it's a lovely night. Feel like walking?"

"That sounds charming." He proffered his elbow and she took it.

They headed down the street, keeping up a pleasant and enjoyable string of chitchat between them. Riker found out that Wendy was a sociologist; that her mother had passed away some years previously; and that she preferred new age music.

Riker feigned being wounded. "I *must* introduce you to the joys of real music. This new age stuff is just noise."

"So what's real music, then?"

He grinned. "Dixieland. Swing. The big-band era."

"Big band?" she said, sounding puzzled. "You mean they're excessively tall?"

"I'll explain it later," he said, for he had spotted the chapel just up ahead.

He saw a number of Betazoids filing in through the doors, smiling and greeting one another. It was his first opportunity to see a large number of them together, and he was struck by the feeling that something seemed a bit wrong. Then he immediately realized what it was.

There was hardly any talking.

People would nod, smile to each other, tilt their heads as if they were listening intently to one another. But except for the occasional stray word of exclamation, or some random laughter here and there, not a word was spoken.

"They're communicating telepathically, aren't they?" said Riker in realization as they approached.

"Of course."

"Then this is liable to be a fairly dull ceremony. Everyone standing around thinking things at each other and we can't hear them."

"Oh"—Wendy waved off the concern and laughed—"that won't happen. Weddings are always done out loud, in consideration of any offworlders who might be in the audience."

"That's a relief." He thought about it a moment. "Will I be able to communicate with any of them? Mentally, I mean? I've never met a Betazoid . . . I'm not sure what's involved."

"You won't be able to, no. Oh, they'll be able to pick up on what's going through your mind easily enough. But for you to send and receive projections, well . . . it's a technique. It's something that you have to learn, involving mental discipline and learning how to clear your mind. Unless, of course, you're dealing with a really strong telepath."

He looked surprised. "You mean they're not all equally adept?"

"Of course not. Are all humans equally intelligent? Equally athletic? Equally eloquent? No. All Betazoids are telepathic to some degree. Most can read minds without too much difficulty. But only a small percentage are really so powerful, so . . . formidable," she said, for want of a better word, "and they're the ones you have to watch out for. They're the toughest."

"Toughest?"

"To know how to act around. They're so casual about their abilities, it's hard to feel like anyplace inside you is . . . I don't know . . . safe."

"I'll watch out for that."

They entered the chapel. The air inside was cool and fresh. They entered a large room where everyone seemed to be milling about, just conversing . . . or whatever one would call it . . . with each other.

Riker looked slowly around the room. It was fairly plain, although inscriptions written in Betazed lined parts of the wall. What was also odd were the recesses all along the side, and dangling from the recesses were what appeared to be clothes hangers of some sort. On the floor was a series of small boxes. Riker idly tapped one with his toe and the hollow sound confirmed that it was empty.

Hangers and empty boxes. Probably for days when the weather was inclement and people brought coats and such.

At the far end of the room was a set of ornate doors, closed. Riker presumed that the actual ceremony would be through there, but they probably weren't ready yet.

Several of the Betazoids seemed to pick up on Riker's presence. They looked in his direction, smiled and nodded. It was as if to say, *We know you're here. Welcome.* And then they went back to their own communications.

Riker had once been to a world where none of the occupants had standard auditory or verbal equipment. They communicated entirely through hand movements. Riker had been to a party there, and the silence was positively eerie. The only sound that had broken the quiet was the slap of skin on skin as their hands would come together to form certain words.

This wasn't quite as bad as that . . . but still, it was rather disconcerting.

"A little difficult to deal with, isn't it," said a voice from behind him.

Riker turned and saw a thin but pleasant-looking Betazoid smiling at him. "Pardon?" asked Riker.

The Betazoid gestured. "All this. The quiet communion. You are from Earth, are you not?"

Riker realized the man knew the answer to the question already, but was doing Riker the courtesy of allowing him to answer it. "That's right. Lt. William Riker."

"Gart Xerx, your host."

"Ah. Congratulations, Mr. Xerx."

"'Gart' will do." Xerx nodded at Riker's companion. "Good to see you again, Wendy."

"You too, Gart. I'm very happy for you and Chandra."

"Thank you, Wendy." Xerx indicated the closed doors with a nod of his head and said, "They should be ready to start in just a moment or two. Chandra's quite nervous, of course. She wants everything about her appearance to be perfect."

"I know how it is," said Riker. "The bride wants to make sure the dress looks just right."

Gart Xerx smiled politely. "Well . . . that might be true in *your* culture, Lieutenant. We don't have that problem, actually."

"Then you're very fortunate," said Riker.

The edges of Xerx's mouth turned upward slightly. "You don't know, do you." It wasn't a question.

"Know what?"

At that moment, the doors at the far end opened. They moved very slowly and ponderously, and Riker watched them, interested to catch a glimpse of the wedding sanctuary within.

It was dazzling, filled from ceiling to floor with flowers, all exotic and tropical. It seemed as if a small jungle had been grown inside the sanctuary specifically for the purpose of the marriage. Riker caught a whiff of moist air—obviously the climate was carefully maintained in order to preserve the flowers to their maximum advantage.

He turned back to Gart Xerx to compliment him on the

arrangement and was astounded to see that Xerx had removed his shirt, revealing a bare chest that was amazingly smooth.

"Excuse me . . . what are you doing?" asked Riker, trying to keep the astonishment out of his voice. He turned to Wendy to see her reaction.

What he saw was Wendy's low-cut green dress even lower than it was before . . . namely on the floor. She was stepping out of it, and Riker was seeing a lot more of her cleavage than had been displayed previously . . . to be specific, all of it that there was to see.

His now-nude escort looked up at him with innocent doe eyes. "What are you waiting for, Will? Musical accompaniment?"

She laughed lightly, turned, and headed toward the hangers, her dimpled backside swaying cheerfully back and forth. And now Riker saw, to his utter shock, that all of the guests were stripping off their clothes and placing them on the hangers provided.

Gart, who was naked and holding his clothes draped over one arm, looked at Riker sympathetically. "I'm very sorry, Lieutenant. They should have told you. Perhaps Mark Roper was concerned that, if you knew, you wouldn't be interested in attending."

Riker's mouth was working, but at first he couldn't get any words to come out. Finally he managed to stammer, "Is this . . . *standard?*"

"Oh, yes," said Gart calmly. "At a Betazed wedding, the bride, groom, wedding party, and guests all attend nude."

"Why?"

"To symbolize that, physically and spiritually, there is nothing to hide. That all are sharing in complete cooperation in the spirit of harmony and unity."

Riker had a feeling that all the blood had drained from his face. "Well . . ." He cleared his throat, unsure of what he should do. Starfleet protocol required cooperation with local mores and customs wherever possible, so long as no violation of the Prime Directive was involved. There was nothing in the Prime Directive about getting naked in front of over one hundred strangers, so he was clear on that score. But even so . . .

"Lieutenant," said Gart, trying not to show as much amusement as he was clearly experiencing. "If you don't go naked, I assure you, no one will think the less of you. We believe in not asking more of an individual than he is capable of giving. This is a time of celebration, not embarrassment. Attend the wedding in whatever manner you will feel the most comfortable."

"I don't want to insult anyone . . . ," said Riker uncertainly.

"Nor will anyone take offense. Now, if you'll excuse me . . . I have guests to attend to." Gart walked to the hangers, leaving Riker alone in the middle of a room of stripping people.

Wendy walked back up to Riker and looked at him reprovingly. She placed her hands on her hips in a fashion that was probably chosen to look especially provocative. "What's this, Will? Having trouble? Here . . . I'll help." She reached up to the fastenings on his uniform.

He grabbed her wrists, though not particularly hard. Through a tight smile he said, "You could have told me beforehand, you know."

"What?" She looked shocked. "And miss the opportunity to see your expression?"

"You've seen it. How did it rate?"

"I think you'd look at a firing squad of Klingons with less trepidation than you're looking at a bunch of naked people."

"At least with the firing squad, I'd have a bit of warning."

"Oh, Will." Now she was grinning widely. "Come on. You have nothing to be ashamed of." Then she paused and raised an eyebrow thoughtfully. "Do you?"

"No!" said Riker a bit too loudly, so he repeated, "No," but more softly this time.

'Well then . . . ?"

"Well, to be honest . . ." He put his fingers to his forehead, trying to figure the best way to put it. "I've never been in a position where I'm trying to maintain my dignity and status as a Starfleet officer without benefit of the uniform . . . or anything else."

"Then don't worry about your position. Worry about joining in the celebration. Look . . . if you don't want to strip, then don't. Come in anyway."

"Okay. Fine. Thanks for understanding."

He went in with her to the chapel, and the full fragrance of the flowers wafted through the air. It was as if he'd stepped out from the city and straight into the jungle.

Wendy guided him to an aisle seat about halfway down. He looked around.

Naked people to the right of him, and to the left. In front and behind.

Everyone seemed utterly casual, even oblivious of their nudity. No one was tense or embarrassed. In fact, they seemed even more relaxed than they had been outside. Even men and women who, by the standards of the human ideal, would have been far better served wearing clothes (if not pup tents) weren't the least bit bothered by their nudity.

He felt as if everyone were staring at him. Riker knew they weren't, of course . . . but he felt that way.

Turning to Wendy, he said, "Excuse me . . . be right back," and he got up and walked out before she could ask him where he was going.

She sat there, staring at his empty chair, nodding and smiling to the other people, and wondering where in hell Riker had gone off to. Then she heard him say, "Thanks for saving my seat."

She looked up and grinned. "So you decided to join the party after all."

He sat down next to her, not precisely sure how to place his bare legs. He wound up just sitting with them flat, his hands on his thighs. He noted for the first time that the seats were nicely cushioned, for which he was grateful. Cold metal would not have been especially appreciated right about then.

Wendy leaned over and said softly into his ear, "You were right, by the way . . . you have nothing to be ashamed of."

He liked the tone of her voice as she said it . . . it had a certain degree of promise to it. "Thank you. You're very kind."

She sat back and said, "I'm not sure why you were so nervous. I mean, what did you think was going to happen? Women were going to point and laugh?"

"I don't know. It's just a different situation for me, that's all. I thought people might say things that made me feel self-conscious."

"Oh, don't be silly. Like what?"

An older Betazoid woman was being guided toward the front by Gart Xerx. Riker assumed that it was probably his mother, or perhaps a great-aunt. She stopped, looked at Riker, and frowned. "You human men are very hairy. Why is that?"

Xerx rolled his eyes in mild mortification. Wendy put her hand over her mouth to cover her grin.

But Riker, nonplussed, merely said, "Traction."

Wendy emitted a quick burst of laughter, which she just as quickly stifled. Xerx was grinning openly. The old woman looked at Riker through narrowed eyes and then allowed herself to be led away.

"Traction?" whispered Wendy.

"I had to say something."

"Well, what you said was wonderful. You see? And you were worried that you wouldn't be able to maintain your dignity while naked. You handled that in a very dignified manner."

"Thank you."

Wendy appeared to be sizing him up for a moment, and then she coyly fingered a strand of his chest hair.

Riker crossed his legs.

At that moment, the ceremony started . . . a moment marked by the sound of a very loud gong.

The lieutenant focused his attention toward the front of the wedding sanctuary.

The wedding party was entering, and yes, they were naked as well. From one side of the sanctuary entered the groom, in the lead, followed by his mother.

To Riker's surprise, the mother was pulling on his arm, trying to stop him. He ignored her, taking one implacable step after the other, toward the middle of the room. Into his path stepped a man whom Riker assumed to be his father. The father raised a hand, putting his palm up, signaling the groom to stop. The groom took his father by the forearm and shoved him aside . . . not roughly, and in fact, Riker saw that the groom was taking care not to make the action too violent, for fear of actually causing the older man to stumble.

"Symbolic, I take it," Riker said in a low voice to Wendy. She nodded confirmation.

The groom stopped in front of a clergyman (presumably), who stood dead center of the room with a long scroll between his hands. They looked off to the right, and now the parents of the bride entered—the bride's mother sobbing loudly onto the shoulder of Gart Xerx. Too loudly—clearly more symbolism, but Riker thought the mother might be playing it up just a bit too much even for something that was supposed to be representational.

And then the bride walked in. The bride . . .

Walked . . .

Riker blinked in that way people do when they're not entirely sure they're seeing what their eyes are telling them they're seeing.

She was gorgeous.

Her eyes were the most luminous that Riker had ever seen. She held her pointed chin in an almost aristocratic manner, and her dark hair hung in thick ringlets around her head. Her neck was slender, and her figure . . . well, as they said in old detective novels, her body had the kind of curves that, if you were a car, made you want to hug the road.

Thoughts of what he would like to do with that body ran rampant through his imaginings, but he had to tell himself that, for crying out loud, she was taken. She was the bride. She was about to get married. She—

She stepped aside and gestured to a young woman who was seated in the front row.

"I summon you to the place of marriage," she said. Her voice was low and musical and had an exotic accent that Riker had never heard before. It sound vaguely like a combination of three Middle European intonations, and yet a bit different.

The young woman rose. She had blond hair, tied back in a white band. She took the hand of the woman who had "summoned" her and stepped up to the side of the groom. They took each other's hands and turned to face the clergyman . . .

And that was when, belatedly, it hit Riker. The brunette wasn't the bride. She was some sort of equivalent of the maid of honor.

Unbidden, uncensored, thoughts about getting to know the maid of honor on a variety of levels stampeded back through his mind. His eyes drank her in hungrily as she stood with her back to him. The sumptuous lines of her hips, the elegant arch of her spine, and the way her shoulder blades played against the skin . . . and the way the light shined off that skin . . . the richness of her smile . . .

Her smile.

Her back was to him but he could see her smile . . .

Because she'd turned her head.

And she was looking at him.

Right at him.

At him. And smiling.

Oh, my God, he thought, *she knows what I'm thinking. She knows what I'd . . .*

Wendy looked at him and saw that his face had gone several shades of red. "Will . . . are you okay?"

"I'm fine." His voice was thick and hoarse. It didn't even sound remotely like his. "Just fine."

"You sure? You're sweating."

"It's hot in here. That's all. Just hot."

She was still smiling at him, for what seemed to Riker to be an eternity. Her bosom *(God, her bosom)* shook slightly in what he took to be (correctly) silent laughter. And then, mercifully, she turned away from him and put her attention back on the ceremony.

Riker didn't hear a word of the rest of the proceedings. He had his own proceedings in mind. The only question was how best to proceed with the proceedings.

A reception had been arranged out in a garden behind the chapel. Large lights had been set up that flooded the evening with illumination.

Riker paid absolutely no attention to the types of food he was eating or how much . . . indeed, he would pay for it later that night with a major bellyache. For now, though, he popped various hors d'oeuvres into his mouth, one after the other, but his mind was elsewhere.

The guests were now all clothed, and the fact that Riker had his uniform back on was something of a blessing. It enabled him to—to a degree—put his mind on autopilot, speaking pleasantly and adroitly to all those who approached him in his capacity as representative of the UFP. He wondered if they were aware that his thoughts were only partly on his surroundings.

His eyes kept scanning the crowd for some sign of the maid of honor. The bride and groom hadn't materialized either—apparently there was ceremony and delay involved in this, too.

He couldn't get her out of his mind. He had encountered so many women in his lifetime, and yet when he had seen her, there had been something . . . something he couldn't put his finger on. It was almost as if he *knew* her somehow, from somewhere.

But he had never seen her before. He was sure that he hadn't. Hell, she wasn't even the kind of female that he usually considered his "type." But there was *something* about her that—

A burst of applause brought his attention back to focus, and there she was. She had emerged from the chapel with the bride and groom, and several other friends of the newlywed couple were crowding around them, congratulating them, laughing and smiling.

He waited for the maid of honor to look his way, to catch his gaze. But she didn't. In fact, she seemed to look everywhere except in his direction. He wasn't sure if this was intentional or not. Whatever it was, it was damned frustrating.

There was a tap on his shoulder. He turned and Wendy was looking up at him with those large doe eyes of hers. "Is there some problem, Will? You seem to have time for everyone except me, and I'm supposed to be your date."

"No problem. No problem at all." He draped an arm around her and kept her close to him the remainder of the time. Almost as if she were a shield; a reminder that there were plenty of other women in the galaxy.

Almost as if he were a little afraid of the way that the young Betazoid maid of honor had gotten to him.

It was crazy. He didn't know her . . . not at all. Oh, sure, he knew she looked good naked—okay, great naked—okay, spectacular beyond belief naked—but even so, nothing about her could account for this feeling of urgency he had whenever he looked at her. This feeling that he had to get to know her better.

"Do you believe in love at first sight?" he asked Wendy.

"Nope. I think you can look at someone and be attracted on a physical level. That's easy. But true, genuine love? No. You can even be attracted to someone and fall in love with them subsequently. That doesn't make it love at first sight though. That just makes it . . . I don't know . . . fortuitous infatuation."

"Absolutely right." He even felt a measure of relief. Here was someone to throw a bucket of cold reality into an unreal situation. "I feel the same way. You find something, you study it, you draw conclusions, and you proceed. You don't just leap into something on blind faith."

"Will," Wendy said, smiling coyly, "is this your way of telling me that you find me attractive? I mean . . . what are you saying? That you think you might be falling in love with me at first sight?"

"Of course not. I thought we agreed . . . there's no such thing. Don't you remember?"

'Ooooh, yes. So we did."

All the young women were clustering together now, including the maid of honor. Riker watched with curiosity and Wendy said, "You know the old Earth custom of the bride throwing the bouquet?"

"Yes."

"Well, there's something similar here. Except it's not a bouquet. The bride wears a white band in her hair, and she tosses that."

"Oh."

Chandra, the bride, stood with her back to the young women and after a moment of hesitation tossed the headband over her right shoulder. It fluttered through the air toward the throng of grasping hands, and one pair of hands snatched it from its flight. There was a burst of applause as the maid of honor came up with it triumphantly.

"Oh, how nice! Deanna caught it," said Wendy. "She and Chandra have been friends for years."

"Deanna?"

"Deanna Troi. She was the maid of honor."

"Was she?" said Riker with very carefully cultivated neutrality in his voice.

So carefully, in fact, that it drew a strange look from Wendy. "Yes, that's right. I'm surprised you don't remember."

"Well, you know how it is . . . all naked bodies tend to blend in with each other. So what does catching the white cloth signify? That she's the next to get married?"

"No. What it means is that the great love of her life is at this gathering."

"How romantic." Riker found himself turning the full force of his gaze, of his every thought, directly at the young woman who he now knew was called Deanna Troi.

She did not so much as glance his way the rest of the evening.

CHAPTER 14

"**Y**ou could have told me, you know."

Mark Roper looked up at Lieutenant Riker and grinned. "Good morning, Captain."

"Don't call me that." Riker's stomach felt achy, which matched the condition of his head. "Why didn't you tell me that no one wore clothes at the wedding?"

Roper sat back in his chair and looked with mild scorn in Riker's direction. "Oh, come now, Captain. All throughout Starfleet they teach you how to adapt and deal with the unexpected. I'd have thought that you wouldn't be phased for a moment by the situation."

"They didn't cover stripping in Starfleet Academy." Riker sagged into the chair opposite Roper.

"Maybe you should suggest it be added to the curriculum," Roper said helpfully.

"I'll do that," lied Riker.

"Wendy was, I take it, an excellent companion?"

"Very socially adept."

"Did you take her to bed with you?"

Riker's jaw dropped as he stared at Roper's mirthful expression.

"What *is* it with this planet?" said Riker incredulously. "Casual nudity. Fathers inquiring about the sexual activities of their daughters first thing in the morning . . ."

"Would you prefer I wait until midafternoon?"

"Mr. Roper," Riker said after a moment, "I really don't think it's any of your business."

"Riker, Riker, Riker. You don't understand. I'll find out anyway. My daughter and I have a very open relationship. We've learned that technique from our stay here on Betazed. Honesty—that's the key whenever possible. And if you and my daughter enjoyed each other, then I'll take pleasure in that enjoyment."

Riker stared at him. "You know . . . I never thought of myself as a prude, by any stretch of the imagination. But in comparison to what goes on with you people here . . . I feel positively archaic."

"You'll get used to freedom. Everyone does after a while. Sometimes it just takes a bit of adjusting, is all."

"All right, then. For the record . . . no, I did not take your daughter to bed. Nor did she take me. It was late, we were tired . . ."

And I couldn't get Deanna Troi out of my mind. But he didn't say that part, though.

"Whatever," said Roper casually. "My daughter is a perfectly capable young woman. I trust her decisions whenever she makes them, and whomever she makes them with." He paused. "That Chandra Xerx was quite a lovely bride, I'll wager."

"Yes. Yes, she was." This was the perfect opportunity to bring up what he was really thinking about. "So was her maid of honor . . . what was her name? Donna? Dena?"

"Deanna? Deanna Troi?"

"That's right," said Riker, hoping that his affected casual air was remotely convincing. "That was the name I heard mentioned. Deanna Troi."

"Lovely girl. Just lovely. Now what is she up to these days?" Roper glanced outside for a long moment, as if the answers he sought were in the clouds. Perhaps they in fact were, because he turned back to Riker and said, "Psychology student. That's it. Over at the university. Near the top of her class . . . I should remember that since Lwaxana's always boasting about her."

"Lwaxana is her mother?"

"Ohhhh, yes. Quite a character, that one. You know the old axiom about how, if you want to get a feeling for what the daughter will be like twenty, thirty years down the road . . . all you have to do is look at the mother?"

"Yes."

"Case in point."

Riker looked surprised. "What, is she that ugly?"

"Lwaxana? Oh, not by any means. In fact, she's a very striking woman. Quite attractive, and she knows how to use her appearance to her advantage. But she can be very . . . overpowering."

"Overpowering in what sense?" But before Roper could respond, Riker added, "Wait . . . Wendy was talking about a small percentage of Betazoids who are, telepathically, pretty formidable."

"She may have been speaking specifically about Lwaxana," Roper affirmed. "I think 'formidable' is a perfectly apt description. For that matter, according to what Wendy's told me . . . and believe me, that girl is up on all the latest scuttlebutt . . . if you happen to be a suitor, then Lwaxana can be downright intimidating. Poor Deanna doesn't see much in the way of a social life."

"What a waste."

His tone of voice had slipped more than he'd have liked. Roper looked at him with a cunning expression. "You're interested in her, aren't you."

"Mark, I don't even know her."

"You're dodging the question."

"No, I'm not. How can I possibly decide if I'm interested in someone if I haven't even exchanged ten words with her."

Roper looked wistful. "Other than my marriage, the most memorable relationship I had in my life involved a young woman and an exchange of less than five words." He regarded Riker. "That, of course, was when I was a very young man. Vital, alive, and feeling my oats. Much as you are now."

"My oats are reined in, thank you, Mark," Riker told him firmly. He stood and said, "If you'll excuse me, I have a meeting with the commanding officer of the security team."

"Sergeant Tang? Good man. He knows his stuff." Roper swiveled the computer screen around to check his itinerary for the day. "Give him my regards."

"I will."

"And I hope I didn't offend you with my observations about young Troi."

"Not at all," said Riker, heading for the door. "But to be perfectly honest, I have far more on my mind right now than Deanna Troi."

"I'm sure you do. You know where the university is?"

"No, but it shouldn't be hard to find . . ." And then Riker's voice trailed off as he realized what he was saying. He turned back to Roper and said, "That is, of course, if I were interested in finding it."

"Of course," said Roper calmly. "If you were interested. Which you're not."

"Not at all."

"Glad to hear it."

CHAPTER 15

Deanna Troi walked across the campus, her thoughts still on the topics they'd been discussing so forcefully in her psychological ethics class. So she paid no attention whatsoever to the young, dashing Starfleet officer who ever so casually, ever so coincidentally, strolled past her.

But then a voice called out, *"I remember you."*

She stopped in her tracks. She couldn't place the voice at all, but the *sense* of the person behind her was damned familiar. Then she smiled . . . inwardly. *I should have expected this,* she thought, and turned slowly.

He walked toward her, making a great show of trying to place precisely where he recollected her from. "The wedding yesterday. You were at the wedding, weren't you."

Slowly she nodded, making sure to maintain a very carefully constructed air of disinterest.

He stuck out a hand. "Lt. William T. Riker, at your service."

She looked at his proffered hand for a moment. Then extremely carefully, as if handling a specimen, she took the tips of his fingers in hers and shook his hand very lightly. "What does the *T* stand for?"

"Terrific." He waggled his eyebrows slightly to put across, just in case she didn't get it, that he was making a joke.

She got it. But her expression made it quite clear that she didn't care for it.

Or him.

"I'm new here . . . to the planet, I mean . . . and I'm just trying to get to know as many of the residents here as I can."

"I see." She had been holding a computer padd under her arm. Now she crossed her arms over her breasts, holding the padd over them as if it were a shield. She was dressed in flowing blue, a loose-sleeved tunic and a long blue skirt that the wind was swishing about her legs. "So you're going around and introducing yourself, one person at a time. That could take quite a while."

"It'll take even longer when the people I'm introducing myself to don't even tell me their names."

She angled her head slightly, regarding him with that outthrust jaw of hers. "Why should I bother? You know my name."

Now he folded his arms. "You know . . . it's going to be very difficult being at ease with a population that considers my mind an open book."

"I didn't read your mind. I hazarded a guess. All you did was confirm it."

"Oh. I . . . just assumed . . ."

"Assumptions can lead to great embarrassments, Lieutenant. As I'm sure you can attest."

She turned and walked away from him.

He stood there for a moment and watched her go.

Don't give up.

The thought entered his head, and he wasn't entirely sure where it came from. Was it his own mind . . . or was the source elsewhere? Was there a remote chance that the encouragement had come from her . . . either consciously or unconsciously?

A remote chance, yes. Remote. Very, very slim. Pathetically thin, as a matter of fact. So thin as to be virtually nonexistent.

But still worth a shot.

He kicked into high gear and trotted after her. It was surprising how quickly she moved, with brisk, rapid steps. His quick pace brought him alongside her and he said, "You used to do some geology, didn't you."

That brought her up short and she stared at him.

"A lot of fieldwork," he continued.

"When I was a teenager, yes."

"Why did you give it up?"

"My true talents lay elsewhere. How in the world did you know?"

"The way you walk. I had a friend, she was also a geologist, except she made her life's work out of it. She walked the same way . . . a very precise, measured stride. And she knew exactly how much space each of her strides covered. That way she could always measure off distances even if she didn't have an instrument handy to measure them."

Slowly she nodded her head. "Very good, Lieutenant. I'm impressed."

"And I'm impressed that I impressed you." Once more he stuck out a hand. "I'm Lt. William T. Riker. And you are . . . ?"

She sighed. "We've been through this, haven't we?"

"I have. You haven't."

This time she took his hand and shook it firmly. "Deanna Troi. The answer is no."

He wished he could get more than a handful of sentences out of her at a time. He loved listening to her voice. "The answer to what?"

"The answer, I would presume, to just about any question you'd care to pose." She folded her arms once more. "Look, Lieutenant . . . I really don't mean to be rude here . . . but I don't have the slightest intention of leading you on. I know you saw me at the wedding last night. In fact, we both know you saw me, and we both know what was going through your mind."

He took a step closer to her, sounding as suave as he possibly could. "Then we're not exactly on even footing. I don't know what was going through your mind."

"Then I'll tell you now. I'm very flattered by your intentions,

Lieutenant. I'm vain enough to be pleased that I could provoke such . . . strong feelings from you . . . merely by the display of my body. Your reaction, however, would indicate an obsession for surface attributes only."

"That's hardly my sole interest," he said defensively.

"No, but it's a driving one."

He drew yet another step closer, trying to discern whether his growing nearer was having any sort of effect on her. She wasn't stepping back, which either meant that she wanted him near her, or else she just figured it wasn't worth the trouble to back away from him. "Even if it is . . . it doesn't mean that I wouldn't want to get to know you better on a variety of levels."

"That might be. But it's the order of the levels that I have difficulty with. I also have difficulty with the transient nature of your personality."

That stopped him. "Transient?"

She looked down and seemed almost reluctant to speak. "I don't wish to say things that will upset you."

His voice took on a deeper, somewhat annoyed air. "You won't upset me, I assure you."

"Very well." She looked him in the eyes. Other students passing by afforded them quick glances before going on about their business. Her voice took on a clinical air as she said, "I sense that you're someone who thrives on quick encounters. Who enjoys the physicality of relationships without the deeper emotional attachments those relationships can and should bring with them. And that natural tendency of yours is heightened by the fact that you're only going to be on Betazed a few months. That's much more incentive, then, to engage in passing romantic assignations without any concern of long-term relations since, by definition, you won't be here long enough. Well? Am I close?"

His lips thinned almost to nonexistence. "I suppose you feel you have me pegged pretty well."

"Well enough for my purposes. Good day, Lieutenant."

She turned and walked away, and this time there was no additional beckoning in Riker's mind, leaving him totally in the dark about where his mind was at, where her mind was at, and what precisely he should do next . . .

. . . if anything.

I'm home.

Deanna nodded to Mr. Homn, who stepped back away from the front door of the mansion as she entered.

In her head, her mother's voice replied, *I'm up here, Little One.*

Deanna looked in the direction of the upstairs bedroom. *What's wrong, Mother?* It was very unusual for Lwaxana Troi to be upstairs at this time of day . . . usually she was bustling around, tending to this, that, and the other, or perhaps entertaining some head of state. Her absence was reason for curiosity.

Deanna trotted upstairs and into her mother's bedroom. Lwaxana lay in her bed, looking utterly spent. She blew her nose loudly into a cloth.

"Oh, Mother, what happened?"

It snuck up on me, replied her mother, responding to Deanna's verbal expression of concern. *One minute I was fine, and the next minute my head felt ready to explode. Treasure your health, Little One. You never appreciate it until it's gone.*

Is there anything I can do, Mother?

Lwaxana sneezed loudly, then thought, *Yes, there is. Substitute for me.*

Where?

The Federation embassy is hosting a reception for the Rigelian ambassador tonight. As a daughter of the fifth house, it's my responsibility to be there. Obviously I can't go when I'm in this shape.

Deanna sat on the edge of the bed and fidgeted with her hands. Out loud she said, "I'd really rather not, Mother. I was out late yesterday with Chandra's wedding. I've been working late hours on my studies. I—"

Lwaxana sat up, but her expression had changed from self-directed misery to a puzzled frown. "Who's Lieutenant Riker?"

With a loud sigh of annoyance, Deanna said, "He's no one, Mother. And you know, after all this time, I still hate it when you do that. If I wanted to discuss him with you, I'd discuss him."

"You would have sooner or later." But then the draining of Lwaxana's sinuses prompted her to lie back down, and as she blew her nose again, she thought, *So who is he?*

I told you, he's no one. Just some Starfleet officer who can't keep his . . . more base thoughts . . . under control. He's of no consequence to me.

He's of enough consequence, Little One, to be the primary factor in why you don't want to go to the embassy tonight.

Deanna made an irritated noise. *I'll go, Mother. All right? I'll go. I'll be charming and wonderful and I assure you I'll have absolutely no trouble with Lieutenant Riker. All right?*

Her mother reached up and patted her affectionately on the cheek. *That's my girl.*

And deep enough down in her psyche that she hoped even her mother wouldn't be able to discern it, Deanna thought, *Great. Just great.*

CHAPTER 16

The Federation embassy was fully lit up that evening and was alive with the boisterousness and frivolity of the gathering.

Unlike the wedding ceremony, which was almost entirely attended by Betazoids and hence was rather quiet, protocol required that conversation at embassy gatherings be primarily verbal, in order to accommodate offworlders. So it was that Riker found himself eminently more relaxed this time out.

He watched Mark Roper working the crowd, overseeing the catering functions, and doing everything he could to make the Rigelian ambassador feel at home. Considering that up until that point Riker's sole exposure to Roper had been watching him fuss and bother over the details of his job, it was somewhat comforting to observe that Roper was indeed a perfectly talented diplomat when in the proper circumstances.

Riker was no slouch at such activities himself. He had his charm cranked up to all burners and continually made all the right moves and said all the correct things. At one point Roper drifted over to him and said, "You ask me, Captain, I think you've missed your calling. You have a real flair for this line of work."

"I'm just a gifted amateur, sir."

"Oh, now don't be modest."

But Riker hadn't heard the last thing Roper had said because his attention had been distracted when Deanna Troi came through the door. He watched as she looked around, trying to spot someone she might know. She attracted the attention of one of the older counsels and immediately went off with him.

Roper watched the entire thing and his mouth twitched in amusement. "Your mind seems to be elsewhere, Captain."

"Hmm? Oh." Riker looked down, slightly abashed that he'd allowed his attention to be so easily diverted. What the hell kind of training was that? "Sorry, sir."

"Once again your famed noninterest in Deanna Troi appears to rear its head."

"Frankly, Mark . . . she's not a particularly friendly person."

"Really?" Roper seemed genuinely shocked. "She's been nothing but friendly to me, and everyone who's gotten to know her. Are you quite sure?"

"Well, she was extremely standoffish with me."

"When was this?"

"I . . . happened to run into her. In the city."

"I see. And how do you think you behaved?"

Riker stared at him. "I was fine. Polite." Then he paused and admitted, "Frankly, I was damned uncomfortable."

"Why, in heaven's name?"

"Well . . . I had a hard time becoming totally at ease with a woman who can read my every thought."

Roper looked from the young lieutenant to Deanna, who was across the room, and back to Riker once more. "Who? Deanna? She can't read your every thought."

"What? But—" Now Riker was clearly confused. "I thought that . . . I mean, I just figured . . . and you said her mother was so—"

"That's her mother. But Deanna isn't anywhere near the telepath that her mother is. To be specific, she's half the telepath her mother is. Deanna's father was human."

"Human?" Riker was astounded. Here he couldn't figure out how to come to terms with even *talking* to a Betazoid, and some man had actually found a way to marry one. And a powerful one, at that.

"That's right. Deanna's no mind reader. She's an empath. She senses moods, emotions, feelings. She can sense honesty, duplicity, sexual desire . . ." Roper paused after saying that, waited for Riker's expression of surprise, and when he got it, continued, "She's very, very adept at that . . . but only in a general sense."

"I see." Then Riker nodded and grinned. "Well . . . perhaps I'd better try and rectify the situation."

He took a step forward and suddenly Wendy was in the way. She was holding a drink and looked extremely mellow.

"Will, have you been avoiding me?" She placed a hand on his shoulder and assumed a distinctly pouty air. "I'd be very hurt if you were."

Riker tried to come up with a smooth response that would ease him through the situation, but now Roper stepped in and said, "Wendy . . . there's someone I'd like you to meet. The Rigelian ambassador."

"Really?" she chirped. It was becoming rapidly clear that the drink she was holding was hardly her first of the evening.

"Yes, really. He's right over this way." Roper took his daughter by the arm and guided her away into the crowd, leaving Riker alone. Roper slowed only long enough to toss a wink in Riker's direction.

Riker immediately seized the opportunity and cut his way through the crowd like a shark. Within moments he had drawn up behind Deanna and simply stood there, waiting for her to turn around.

He knew that she was aware of him almost immediately, but for what seemed an eternity she only presented her back. The diplomat she was talking to was suddenly distracted by someone else clamoring for his attention, and he allowed himself to be pulled away with an apologetic nod to Deanna. Then she sighed and her shoulders slumped just a bit.

"Why are you just hovering, Lieutenant?"

"How did you know?"

"I could feel you breathing down my neck."

"No, not that. I mean how did you know that I was only going to be assigned to Betazed for a few months?"

Slowly she turned to face him, an amused expression on her face.

"I mean," continued Riker, "I had assumed you'd just picked it out of my thoughts. But someone who's an empath wouldn't be able to focus that tightly, would she?"

"No. She wouldn't."

"Well? I'm waiting." He even made a show of tapping the toe of his boot with impatience.

She studied her fingernails as she said, "I asked around. All right?"

"Now why did you do that?"

"I was curious. Are you satisfied, Lieutenant?"

"Call me Will."

"For the moment, I believe I prefer 'Lieutenant.'"

"For the moment?" He smiled ingratiatingly. "Does that mean you anticipate that there will be opportunities in the future to address me?"

"Right now, Lieutenant, I'd like to address you to Vulcan and send you out with the next batch of communiqués."

He mimed being stabbed to the heart. "Oh! How you sting, Miss Troi! To be at the receiving end of your rapier wit . . ."

"Lieutenant," she said with a heavy sigh, "what do you want from me? No . . ." She put her hands palm up in a don't-move gesture. "No, strike that. I know what you want. The question is, what will it take to get through to you that I'm not interested?"

He set his jaw determinedly. "Go out with me."

"Go out with you?" She laughed. "You feel the best way to *dis*courage you is to *en*courage you? Now that is truly a unique piece of logic."

"I didn't say it was logical."

"That's a relief."

"What I do say is that it gives you a chance to make a decision based on something other than first impressions. If we spend some time together and you decide that you're not interested . . . then fine. I'll accept that. Believe me . . . I don't go where I'm not wanted."

She couldn't resist. "You must not get around much, then."

His eyes narrowed, then slowly he nodded. "Fine." He put up his hands. "Fine. Have it your way."

He started to turn away from her; then to his surprise she placed a hand lightly on his arm. He turned and looked back at her.

"Tomorrow's terrible for me," she said. "The day after. Pick me up around midday, at my home. We'll go on a picnic. I'll pack it."

"I don't want you to feel like you have to do me any favors, Miss Troi. I mean, don't go to any trouble, or—"

"Lieutenant, don't push your luck."

"Midday it is."

"Good." Then she paused. "Tell me, Lieutenant. There are any number of women around . . . and quite a few might be much more inclined to be impressed by your—peculiar—brand of charm than I would. Why so interested in me?"

"Because, I like a challenge."

"Well, that's splendid. In that case, when you come by to pick me up, the two of you will probably hit it right off."

"The two of us?"

"You and my mother. You see, she likes challenges, too." Deanna smirked in a way that made Riker extremely uncomfortable. "And I have a feeling she's just going to *adore* you."

CHAPTER 17

Sergeant Roger Tang, grizzled veteran and squad commander of the security unit assigned to Betazed, caught a glimpse of Riker as he headed for the door. "Lieutenant," he said, and snapped to a salute.

Inwardly, Riker shook his head. Salutes hadn't been in style for two centuries now, but Tang was retro enough to harken back to those days of extreme discipline. Riker waved his hand in close approximation of a salute and said, "At ease, Sergeant."

Tang stroked his round, stubbled chin. The large phaser he always wore was clipped to his waist and slapped against his thick leg. Riker was willing to bet he wore it to sleep. "Lovely day today, Lieutenant. Where you off to . . . if you don't mind my asking," he added quickly.

"Out."

"Yes, sir, I can see that. The general direction of your path would seem to be leading you out the door. I was just curious as to where, sir. Security reasons. Can't be too careful, you know."

Riker sauntered over to Tang and draped his hands behind his back. "If you *must* know, Sergeant, I have a date."

Tang appeared to consider that for a moment. "Local girl, sir?"

"That's right. A local girl. I tried to bring a girl with me from the *Fortuna,* but she didn't fit in my suitcase."

"Damn shame," commiserated Tang. He lowered his voice to confidential tones. "You don't mind a piece of advice, sir?"

Riker shook his head.

"These people can ruin you."

At that, Riker blinked. "Pardon?"

"They're soft. They're pleasant." He tapped the side of his head. "They're always philosophizing about things, dwelling on things, pondering things. They think too damned much, if you ask me."

"Thinking about things is a good habit, Sergeant."

"Oh, of course. But not to the point where it's *all* you do. Not to the point of overintellectualizing. They don't fight . . . they'd rather talk about the reasons for disputes. I told one of them that the only thing the Sindareen understand is force, and the guy looked at me like I'd just dropped down from outer space."

"Well . . . in all fairness . . . you did."

Tang emitted a short laugh that sounded like a bark. "Yeah, I suppose I did at that. Look, Lieutenant . . . all I'm saying is, remember who you are. And who they are. Getting to know different cultures is fine and all that . . . but just remember that the galaxy is divided into two types."

"Those being?"

"Starfleet . . . and everyone else." Tang put a finger to his lips and then added, "Enough said."

"Thank you, Sergeant."

Tang tossed off one more salute and said, "All part of the service." Then he turned and walked off, the phaser continuing to slap comfortingly against his thigh.

Riker stood outside the mansion that was the home of Deanna Troi. Impressed by the structure, he hesitated a moment before rapping on the door.

He heard no footsteps, but then slowly the door opened.

Riker looked up.

And up.

A towering man loomed over him. He didn't look precisely Betazoid. He didn't look precisely anything. He stared down at Riker impassively.

"I'm Lieutenant Riker. I'm here to pick up Deanna Troi." Then Riker hesitated. "This is the Troi residence, isn't it?"

The man nodded slowly and stepped back, providing space for Riker to enter. He did so, looking around the opulent setting in curiosity.

"Where should I wait?"

The giant closed the front door, but did not answer Riker's question. He studied the looming figure, utterly perplexed, and then a voice behind him said, "So I see you've met Mr. Homn."

Riker turned and saw an attractive woman with long dark brown hair, and a very aristocratic bearing. She came sweeping toward him in a pink and gray gown that set off her dark eyes and rosy-complexioned face. "And you're Mrs. Homn?" he asked.

She laughed lightly. "No, no. I'm Deanna's mother."

He took her extended hand and bowed slightly at the waist. "Lt. William Riker. But please, feel free to call me Will. Or William, whichever you prefer. And I should call you . . . ?"

"Mrs. Troi."

"Oh." He smiled gamely. "All right, Mrs. Troi. Um . . . Deanna and I have an appointment."

"Yes, I know." She took him by the arm and led him into the spacious living room. "She'll be with you in a moment. She's just getting ready . . . and I thought it would be nice if we had a few moments to chat."

"That sounds very nice."

He sat down on a couch, sinking unexpectedly deeply into the cushions. Lwaxana took a seat nearby that bore a striking resemblance to a throne. "Now . . . tell me all about yourself."

He stroked his chin and said, "Why don't you tell me about myself?"

She chuckled at that. "Oh, that's very good, Lieutenant. Instead of voicing statements that you know I can puncture, you instead ask me to take the first step so that you know what you're in for. All right." Suddenly the sound of her voice changed just a bit. "You're aggressive, hardworking, dedicated, cautious. You're someone who's guarded, and so finds himself ill at ease in an environment where your only option is forthrightness. Oh, and you are extremely attracted to my daughter and have had a variety of sexual fantasies about her. In fact, you are hoping that this outing will be in a romantic enough setting that you can employ your considerable charm to break through Deanna's defenses and introduce her to the full joys of your masculinity. Your preferred position for intercourse is—"

"Mrs. Troi!" said Riker, more sharply than he would have liked. "And what's this about lime-flavored oil rubs?"

He got to his feet. "Mrs. Troi, I must admit, I'm shocked."

"You're shocked?" She looked up at him with overwhelming innocence. "Lieutenant, they're *your* thoughts."

"That may very well be, but it was my understanding that Betazoids prided themselves on courtesy. By my definition, your treatment of me here is not particularly courteous."

Her expression was stricken. "You're right. Where in the world are my manners? I haven't offered you anything to drink. Mr. Homn!" She clapped her hands together briskly. "A drink for our guest."

"That's not what I'm referring to. You're speaking . . . like I'm the enemy."

"That's your interpretation, Lieutenant. I don't think of you as an enemy. No, not at all. At most, I think of you as . . ." She paused, considering. "As an experience. A transient, passing experience that Deanna will encounter, learn from, and grow from. That's all. *Enemy* is much too strong a word. As for the things I'm saying, Lieutenant—my assessment of your nature and thoughts—you invited me to comment. You can hardly take me to task just because I took you up on your offer."

Mr. Homn appeared at Riker's side with a drink, balanced perfectly on a gleaming silver tray. Riker took it without even really noticing.

"You have to understand, Lieutenant. There are certain responsibilities that come with being who I am. I am a daughter of the Fifth House. Holder of the Sacred Chalice of Riix. Heir to the Holy Rings of Betazed. I am accustomed to speaking my mind, and I am also accustomed to watching out for the best interests of my daughter. She is an attentive, intelligent young lady. She will inherit from me the tremendous responsibilities that are presently all on my shoulders. Unlike you, whose life in Starfleet means that endless vistas are open to you . . . Deanna does not have that luxury. There are certain dictates upon her that come with who she is. She accepts that. She welcomes that. I want you to be considerate of those dictates. And I want you to do nothing that will interfere with her destiny or sense of purpose."

"Nothing meaning . . . ?"

"Nothing," said Lwaxana firmly, "meaning *nothing.*"

"Mrs. Troi," Riker said slowly and deliberately, "I understand what you're saying. I appreciate your position. But with all due respect . . . you can't give me orders."

"Quite true," she replied with utter calm. "But Starfleet can. And believe me, Lieutenant . . . if a daughter of the Fifth House complains to Starfleet, there will certainly be those who listen. Do we understand each other?"

She gestured that he should take a drink. He stared at the contents of the glass and for just a moment tried to see any telltale residue that indicated poison.

"It's perfectly safe, Lieutenant."

He looked up and once again realized that his thoughts were completely open to her.

"I never seriously thought it wasn't."

She smiled sweetly.

Deanna chose that moment to make her entrance. Riker felt a flash of disappointment—her long, thick hair was tied up in a small, tight knot. The lines of her shapely figure were hidden under a loose-fitting, caftanlike outfit. In front of her she held a small basket. "Hello, Will," she said genially.

He got to his feet. "Deanna, you look lovely."

"Aside from the fact that he hates the dress and the way you're wearing your hair," said Lwaxana.

Riker fired her a poisonous glance, and Deanna said, sounding a bit confused, "Mother . . . you suggested the hairstyle and dress."

"Did I?" She smiled disingenuously. "So I did. Not too fond of my taste, Lieutenant?"

Gamely, he replied, "It wouldn't matter if she shaved her head and wore sackcloth and ashes. Deanna would still look lovely."

Mother and daughter exchanged a glance, and Lwaxana looked back to Riker. "Very smooth, Lieutenant," she said.

"Thank you."

He went to Deanna and gestured toward the front door. She continued to clutch the picnic basket in both hands, but smiled at her mother as they went out.

Lwaxana did not smile back.

"I hope she wasn't too hard on you."

Deanna and Riker were seated up on a grassy knoll overlooking a particularly lovely stretch of Betazed countryside. The picnic basket sat open next to them, the contents scattered about the ground around them.

Much of the time they had eaten in silence. Every so often Deanna would look up at Riker and either frown or smile. He had the distinct feeling that they were having a conversation without a word being spoken, or for that matter, without him even being fully aware of what was being said.

The statement she had now uttered was just about the longest of the afternoon.

"Nothing I couldn't handle," he said easily. When he said that, she laughed in a manner that he found very peculiar. "Why did you laugh that way?"

"Well, it's the way you responded. I asked you a question about how something made you feel. And your basic response was to make it clear that the situation was something within your control."

He stared at her uncomprehendingly. "So?"

"So, not everything has to be defined in terms of whether you can handle it or not. Sometimes it's enough to acknowledge that a situation has occurred and that you're aware of it."

"That doesn't seem like it would accomplish all that much."

"Why not?"

He lowered himself onto the grass, propping up his head with one hand. "Just acknowledging that a situation exists is rarely enough in my line of work. You have to deal with it."

"That's not true. What about your Prime Directive? Doesn't that tell you that you're not to get involved?"

"What it tells us is the preferred way of handling a particular type of situation . . . namely one involving interference with cultural development. But it still boils down to the idea that every situation must be dealt with in some way . . . even if occasionally the method of dealing with the situation is to keep your hands off."

"I see." She lifted the napkin off her lap and folded it carefully, replacing it in the picnic basket. "Is control very important for you, Lieutenant?"

"Not letting things get out of control is very important. There's a difference."

"And what might that be?"

"The difference is that you can have a specific situation with specific parameters . . . and as long as the elements within that situation don't go beyond those parameters, then everything is fine. You don't have to do much beyond sitting back and letting things run their course. This is as opposed to having to be in control, where you are handling every element personally every step of the way. It's a bad way to command. Shows a lack of ability to delegate."

She cocked her head slightly. "Do you think of everything in terms of Starfleet?"

"Not everything."

They looked at each other for a long moment, and Riker saw something in her eyes . . . something that beckoned to him.

He reached across, grabbed her by the arm, and pulled her to him. She fell to the ground with a startled cry of exclamation. For a moment he felt her body go limp against him, and he brought her face to his, pressed his mouth against hers. He felt something electric pass between them. . . .

And then he felt her knee in the pit of his stomach.

Riker gasped and rolled away, clutching his belly and moaning softly. He came up, gasping, and saw Deanna smoothing out her dress and looking utterly composed.

He sucked in air gratefully and tried to force the pain to go away. Deanna, for her part, reached into the basket and pulled out a brown pastry. "Dessert?" she asked innocently.

"Wh . . . why did you do that?" he managed to get out.

"Will, why are you asking obvious questions?" She held out the pastry to him. "I mean, I'm not asking you why you mauled me just now. I think it's fairly self-evident. I think my reason for stopping you is equally self-evident. So tell me . . . do you still feel in control?"

"Not . . . particularly." The soreness was just starting to recede.

"Now you see . . . that's just how I felt a moment ago. Lovemaking, Will, is when two people voluntarily decide to give control over to the partner. I wasn't voluntarily relinquishing anything. So I needed to reclaim it, quickly."

"You . . . could simply have said no."

She frowned at him. "I did."

"No, you didn't."

"I distinctly remember—"

"You didn't. If you'd have said no, I'd have stopped." Slowly he sat up, still rubbing his sore middle. "That I can assure you."

Her eyebrows knitted together, a puzzled expression on her face. "I was quite sure that I—"

"You know what?" said Riker, pointing at her. "You may have thought you said it . . . but you didn't. And maybe that's because you didn't really want to. For a moment there, you weren't resisting. As a matter of fact, you were pretty damned encouraging. I'll tell you something—you're so certain that you know my mind. Well, I don't even think you know your own."

"Is that a fact?"

"Yes."

"Well, then, just answer me this. . . ."

He waited for the question. "Yeah?"

"Do you want the dessert or not?"

He shook his head in confusion. "That's the question?"

Even she looked puzzled by it. "Yes."

"No. No dessert, thanks. Between the filling meal and your knee, my stomach's pretty much finished for the afternoon."

"Okay. Fine, then." Never taking her eyes off Riker, and regarding him with a very suspicious air . . . probably because she wasn't sure herself how he was making her feel . . . Deanna Troi ate Riker's dessert along with her own. Riker said nothing as he watched her do it.

Finally he asked, "Have you met a lot of humans?"

"A few. Mostly friends of my father."

"Formed an opinion?"

"Not especially. They're people, just like anyone else. Sweeping generalizations are rarely much use. I prefer a case-by-case diagnosis."

"Spoken like a true student of psychology. So . . . what are you going to do with your degree once you've gotten it?"

"Do with it?" She shrugged. "I don't know. Probably nothing."

He stared at her. *"Nothing?"*

"Well . . . knowing how the mind operates, and being able to talk to people . . these skills will certainly be helpful to me in my societal responsibilities. Far more so than geology would have been."

"But . . . but don't you want to forge a career?"

"My life is my career. My responsibilities that are part and parcel of Betazed tradition. I'm not like you, Will. Many aspects of my life are already set."

"You know, I've had this conversation before," said Riker grimly. "With your mother. It's a shame you haven't got a mind of your own."

"I have a mind of my own," shot back Deanna hotly. "It's hardly my fault if my opinion concurs with that of my mother, now, is it?"

"You're right, you're right. I'm the poor dumb human who barely understands what's going through his own head, and you're the all-wise Betazoid who knows everything. Does that pretty much cover it?"

Making a sound of great frustration, Deanna began shoving all the picnic materials back into the basket. "This was stupid," she muttered partly to herself. "I don't know why I let myself be talked into this."

"Because you wanted to be talked into it."

"Oh, nonsense."

"You know what your problem is, Deanna?"

"Yes. My problem is you."

"No." He drew himself closer to her and hunkered down in front of her. When she wouldn't look at him, he took her pointed chin in his hands and brought her around to face him. "Your problem is that you overanalyze everything. You are so damned used to studying feelings, and thinking about feelings, and contemplating feelings, that you have no idea of how to just *go* with feelings."

"And you," she shot back, pushing his hand away, "can *only* go with feelings. You're going to make *some* Starfleet officer, Lieutenant. Someone who's incapable of studying a situation and deciding what to do about it calmly and rationally. I bet you'll never ask anyone for their opinions. I bet you'll never look for suggestions. You'll just do what you want, when you want, on impulse, because your feelings tell you to do so, and you'll just drag the rest of the crew along with you. And heaven help them if you're wrong."

He sat back on his heels. And looking somewhat stupid, he grinned. "You must really like me if you get that worked up over me."

"Oh, you're intolerable."

She picked up the picnic basket and started to walk, her large caftan swishing around her. Riker got to his feet and walked along next to her.

"And I bet you don't believe in love at first sight," he said challengingly.

She didn't even glance at him. "Now you're saying you love me?"

"No, I'm not saying that. I'm asking about the idea in principle. Do you believe in love at first sight?"

He fully expected that she would say no, just as Wendy had. So he was surprised when she slowly came to a halt and turned to look at him full in the face, her eyes large and thoughtful.

Then she turned and walked off in another direction. Puzzled, he followed her.

The terrain got more steep and hilly, and she put down the picnic

133

basket and used her hands to help pull herself up. He followed her, unsure of what was happening, but reluctant to say or do anything that would possibly stop her. He wanted to see what she was up to.

Eventually Deanna reached what appeared to be a peak, and she sat down carefully, meticulously arranging her caftan. Riker climbed up next to her, and his breath caught in his throat.

It was a stunning vista. The view earlier paled in comparison. The sky was now pale orange, and hundreds of feet below a river ribboned between two high banks. Long, untamed blades of grass sprouted here and there, on the one hand appearing random, but on the other, adding to the overall look and feel of the place as if it had been carefully planned.

"I like to come here to think. It's one of my favorite places."

"What do you think about?"

"Love at first sight." She paused. "Yes. I do believe in it."

"Well, now, I must admit, I'm surprised. That's hardly the sign of a rational, nonimpulsive mind. Love at first sight is the ultimate leap of faith."

"Nothing about it is particularly rational," she admitted. "I'd suppose you'd say my rationale is more romantic than anything else."

"And what's your rationale, may I ask?"

At first she said nothing, as if trying to figure out the best way to put her thoughts. "I think that, to some degree, all of us are fractured souls. Cut in half. And we wander through life looking for the rest of ourselves. And sometimes we're fortunate enough to meet someone who possesses, in themselves, the part of ourselves that we've been missing. We may not realize it on a conscious level, but definitely on a subconscious level. We see in someone else . . . something of ourselves."

She held her hands up in front of her, palms facing each other. "That's why sometimes you meet someone and you just immediately feel comfortable with them. You feel like you've known them all your life. The reason is that they're a part of you, and you're a part of them. You're soul mates. You . . . fit." She interlaced her fingers. "And once you've fit together, nothing can pull you apart unless you let go." She released her grip, drawing her hands apart.

"And how did you develop this . . ." He coughed politely. "This theory?"

She smiled gamely. "It seemed the most reasonable explanation for why my parents came together. I mean, no rational being would have seen them as any sort of workable couple. Yet my mother claimed that the moment they met they just . . . just knew." She shrugged. "So who knows?"

"But that's kind of sad, really."

"Why?" she asked, puzzled.

"Because, since you're such a rational type, if you ever met your 'soul mate,' you'd probably intellectualize it to death. How could any sort of pure romantic notion stand up to being rationally disemboweled? You'd never follow your impulse."

"Love at first sight is hardly the sort of thing that happens all the time. My attitude is different from yours. You always follow your impulse. And you have good impulses, I'm sure, by and large. You're very confident, and that's a requirement in your career. But it's not the kind of mind-set I'm used to. I doubt there's any sort of future for us."

He slid closer to her and then said, "Change me."

She stared at him. "What?"

"You're studying to be a psychologist. The entire point of that is to help people. If you think I have some sort of emotional shortcomings, then you can try and do something about it."

"I'm hardly a fully trained therapist, Will. I'm not qualified. You'd be . . . you'd be little more than a guinea pig. It wouldn't be ethical."

"Why not? It's only unethical if you pass yourself off as something you're not. And I'm perfectly willing to be a guinea pig. Believe me, I doubt if anything you'd say or do could be any more grueling than officer training at Starfleet."

He stuck out a hand. "What do you say? Deal?"

She stared at him for a moment. "You're just hoping that this will afford you an opportunity down the road to make love to me."

"That's right," he said without hesitation. "And you're hoping it will, too. Secretly, you're grateful for the chance to bring me 'up' to your level so that you can then feel better about allowing yourself to come 'down' to the more basic altitude of *my* level."

He spoke with such conviction and such certainty that Deanna actually felt an unusual sensation . . . her cheeks were burning.

Riker noticed the flush in an instant and then said, using precisely the tone she had the other day, "I didn't read your mind. I hazarded a guess. All you did was confirm it."

And he looked at her with such challenge in his eyes that she took his hand and squeezed it firmly . . . so firmly that it left him numb for a few minutes as she said, "It's a deal. Prepare to be a guinea pig, Lieutenant Riker."

"Miss Troi, point me to the maze."

CHAPTER 18

In a café just outside the Federation embassy, Mark Roper sat down for breakfast. He studied the menu, then thought about what he'd like to have. Moments later, it arrived, courtesy of a smiling waitress, who knew that he would want nothing else, knew the name on his credit account, and went off to deduct from it not only the cost of his breakfast but how much he would want to tip her.

To Mark Roper, it eliminated a lot of the fuss and bother of meals.

A rap on the window of the café next to Roper made him look up. Outside was Lieutenant Riker, looking pleasant and refreshed. Roper gestured for Riker to join him, and the youthful officer entered the café and sat down across from him.

"So how did it go with young Deanna yesterday?" asked Roper.

"Very nicely. Very nicely."

"Lwaxana was something else, I'll bet."

"Oh, yes."

"So tell me . . . did you do it with Deanna?"

Riker's whole body sagged in disbelief. "Mark . . . what is this obsession with my sex life?"

"I have none of my own," replied Roper a bit sadly. "I have to get my enjoyment vicariously."

"May I suggest you find someone, and quickly. This is becoming a bit obsessive. Besides, aren't you concerned about how your daughter will react if I take up with Deanna?" And then Riker's eyes narrowed. "Wait a minute. That's it, isn't it."

"That's what?"

"You'd *prefer* if I became involved with Deanna because then you figure I'd stay away from your daughter."

At that, Roper laughed loudly, so loudly that he started to cough. Finally, upon composing himself, he said, "Captain . . . you're giving me motives that are far too Machiavellian. Whatever my daughter and you do is fine by me. Whatever you do with Deanna is fine by me. To be honest, whatever my daughter and Deanna did with each other would be fine by me. Although, I must admit, it'd be surprising as hell. I'm just curious, that's all."

"Well, to satisfy your curiosity . . ."

"Nothing happened."

"Right."

"As a matter of fact," said Roper, leaning forward and pointing at Riker, "I'll bet that you put some moves on her, and you were shot down cold."

"Well . . ." Riker coughed politely. "As a matter of fact, yes."

"Thought so."

Riker looked puzzled at that. "Why did you think so?"

"You're not Deanna's type. I know her, I know the kind of background she comes from. Her taste would run towards someone more intellectual—no offense."

"None taken," said Riker, although he wasn't entirely sure how to react. "But I'm hardly a mental midget."

"Oh, I didn't say that you were. Far from it. You're an extremely bright fellow. But you just don't think along the same lines she does. She's a gentle rainstorm, and you're lightning in a bottle. I doubt either of you would have the patience with the other to get anything going."

"Actually, we're going to be seeing each other again. Tomorrow, in fact."

"No!"

"That's right."

"Up to you, Captain. I just hope that you're not counting on Deanna to be the one who breaks your streak of celibacy while on this fair planet."

"I have no intention of being celibate, Mark," said Riker, leaning forward and dropping his voice. "And if you absolutely *must* know . . . she definitely wants me."

"Nonsense."

"It's true. She just hasn't admitted it yet. But she'll come around."

"When? On her deathbed?"

"A lot sooner than that."

"Never happen."

"It will, Mark. Bet on it."

Roper looked at him with mischief in his eyes. "All right. One hundred credits says you never 'become intimate' with her."

Riker laughed in disbelief. "Mark! I'd never bet on anything like that! It's . . . it's crass, it's tasteless, it's . . ."

"Two hundred credits."

"It's a bet."

Roper raised a warning finger. "And no funny stuff. No getting her drunk. Has to be utterly mutual. You can't force her."

"Force her! Mark, I've never 'forced' a woman in my life. Honestly, now. What do you take me for?"

Roper patted the top of Riker's hand. "Captain . . . I believe I've taken you for two hundred credits."

CHAPTER 19

The Betazed museum of art was a tall, impressive building, and extremely ornate. Deanna and Will stood outside as she explained to him the history of the structure, the design work and theory that had gone into it. She spoke at length for some minutes.

Riker, for his part, was happy that she was once again wearing her hair down, and that the outfit she was wearing was more flattering to her figure. Much of what she said barely registered until finally she turned to him and said, "Why am I bothering?"

"What?"

"You don't seem at all interested in what I'm saying, Will. I'm trying to explain to you why this building is, in and of itself, a work of art."

"And I'm trying to explain to *you*, Deanna, that I can only appreciate one work of art at a time."

"And right now you're still appreciating me."

"I guess so, yes."

She sighed, took him by the hand, and said, "Come on." She pulled him toward the building and through the large columned doors.

Inside there was music playing, loud and sonorous, and it sounded somewhat like organ music.

It was coming from a large, multiple-piped instrument in the middle of a great rotunda. Seated in circles around the musician were various Betazoids, who were listening to the music, their eyes closed, their faces blissful. Riker looked around and tried to get a feeling for what was going on. The music sounded okay to him, but nothing particularly special. He couldn't understand why it seemed to be affecting the listeners so deeply.

He looked at Deanna, and she, too, appeared to be totally taken by it. Her eyes were half-lidded, and she was swaying slightly to the tones. Riker whispered, "Are you all right?"

She opened her eyes and looked at him. Her stare was almost incredulous, as if she couldn't believe that he was still capable of speech. "This is soul music," she whispered. "Listen to it. Let it pervade you. What does it say to you?"

He listened. He let it pervade him.

"What is it supposed to say?" he asked.

With an irritated noise, she pulled at him and dragged him off down a large corridor.

The air in the cavernous building was cool. Riker looked around, trying to take things in. His eyes adjusted to the dimness, and he kept trying to find something that would be startling and revolutionary to him. Something that would give his innermost thoughts a voice and fill him with understanding. Nothing in particular seemed to leap out at him, however.

Deanna led him into a room and made a sweeping gesture.

Paintings hung on the walls. All of them appeared to be what Riker would term "abstract" . . . that is, they didn't seem to be pictures of anything in particular. In front of every single painting was a small bench, and in a number of instances, Betazoids were seated on the benches staring intently at the works.

"I come here once a week," whispered Deanna. Her voice, although it was as low as she could possibly make it, still attracted glances from the occupants of the room. Silent communion was the norm here. People looked from her to Riker and then back to her, and their expressions changed from mild irritation to understanding tolerance . . . and even, in a couple of cases, a degree of pity—much to Riker's annoyance.

"Once a week? Why?"

She led him over to one work in particular, which was concentric splashes of red, blue, green, white, black, and a couple of colors that Riker didn't recognize. Here, in one of the more far-off sections of the room, no one else was sitting nearby at the moment.

"Because, Will," she said quietly, "it's one of the methods I use to stay in touch with myself." At his blank expression, she continued gamely, "In order to fully understand others, you must learn to understand yourself. Only by being in touch with what motivates you can you then grasp what motivates others."

"I studied this in the Academy. The course was called Dynamics of Command."

"Commanding who?"

"Other officers. Crewmen."

"Yes, well, you see . . . here the only person you're trying to command is yourself. Now . . . I want you to look at the painting and tell me what it says to you."

"This is supposed to talk to me, too? Can't anything on this planet keep its mouth shut?"

His comment came out sounding a bit more sarcastic than he would have liked, but Troi appeared undeterred. "On Betazed, we believe in full communion. Communion with each other. Communion with our world. But before any of that can occur, we must have communion with ourselves."

"What's the painting called?"

She stared at him in confusion. "What?"

"What's it called? What's the name of the painting? At least I'll have *some* clue to what the artist was trying to put across if I know what he called the damned thing."

"The 'damned thing' doesn't have a name. That would be presumptuous . . . it would be as if the artist were trying to impose his own worldview upon the viewer."

"Terrific. Look, maybe we can start with another painting? Something that *looks* like something?"

He started to rise and she pulled him back down again. "Will, you're not even trying. You said you were going to cooperate."

"I'm sorry," he sighed. "I'll try, all right?"

The problem was, every time he looked at her, he kept thinking about trying to get her clothes off. But he knew that such unguarded thoughts were only going to get him into trouble again. So, gamely, he focused on the picture again.

It was swirls. Splashes of color. No matter how long or how intently he looked at it, it still looked like jumbled paints and nothing more.

"You're trying too hard."

He blew air through his lips in exasperation. "First you tell me I'm not trying at all, and now you tell me I'm trying too hard. Now which is it?" He looked at the painting. "Would you mind telling me what it is you want of me?"

Then he felt two strong fingers at the base of his skull, squeezing together and massaging him. Deanna's arm moved in a steady, circular motion.

He started to feel tension that he didn't even know he had ebb from him. He was glad that he couldn't see his face because he had the distinct, detached feeling that he had a rather goofy expression at the moment.

"Now," she said softly, "while you're relaxing . . . look at the painting and tell me what you see. Learn to look below the surface, beyond the superficial. What is there to learn from the painting . . . and what can we learn from ourselves?"

His head swayed back and forth in gentle rocking motions. He stared at the painting for what seemed an eternity.

"I see . . ."

"Yes?"

He was silent for a moment and then said, "I see . . . paint swirls."

She stopped the rubbing. "That's it?" she said with flat disgust.

"That's it. I'm sorry." He turned to her, not sure whether to be more irritated with himself or with her. "You wouldn't want me to lie to you . . . and I doubt I could, even if I wanted to. I see paint swirls. Big, goopy paint swirls."

"Goopy? This is a word? *Goopy?*"

"I don't have much taste for abstract art. When I look at something, I like it to look *like* something."

She paused, her hands carefully arranged on her lap. "Tell me, Lieutenant. As you further explore the galaxy, you will inevitably run into things that don't look like anything you've ever imagined that anything could look. What are you going to do in those instances? Are you going to decide that they're inferior somehow? Or that there's something wrong with them? How are you going to judge? By their degree of goopiness?"

"In those instances, when encountering new life-forms beyond my experience, I'll have instrumentation to help me. Sensor arrays. Medical scans. Instantaneous translators and communications devices. I won't have to—"

"You won't have to depend on yourself."

"Now I didn't say that."

"No, you didn't. But that's what it boils down to, Lieutenant. And believe me, you're going to find yourself in situations where all the instrumentation in the world isn't going to do you a bit of good. They can guide you, but you're going to have to rely on something beyond that. As a matter of fact, I'll wager that there will be times when you have to act in ways that are contrary to what instrumentation is telling you . . . that are contrary to what *people* are telling you, for that matter. And you have to be fully conversant in *why* you think what you think, because otherwise you're going to find yourself heading down the wrong road."

"Thank you for your opinions, Miss Troi . . . drawn, no doubt, from your many years of experience with Starfleet."

"I don't have to be experienced with Starfleet, Lieutenant, in order to be aware of the importance of knowing your own mind."

"Really?" He took her hand in his and squeezed it firmly. "And what does your mind tell you about your feelings for me? Hmmm?"

She met his gaze levelly. "It tells me that perhaps we have to begin with something a bit more fundamental than this." She stood. "Come on. We're getting out of here."

"Where are we going?"

"Back to basics."

The tree towered over them, its trunk brown and gnarled. There were no leaves on it, and its branches seemed to stretch up forever.

The trunk was so twisted that climbing up it was easy. Deanna did so and gestured for Riker to follow. He climbed, relieved that this was at least something that was mildly entertaining . . . particularly because he liked watching the play of Deanna's muscles under her tight clothes.

She stopped at a point about ten feet above the ground. Large branches stuck out in either direction. She sidled out onto one, and when Riker started to follow her, she shook her head and indicated that he should go in the other direction. With a shrug he did as instructed.

"Your problem, Lieutenant, is that the demands of your body have too much sway on your mind," she said once they were both perched on their opposite branches.

"What do you mean?"

"Your attraction to me, for example. Indeed, your attraction to most women, I would think. It's purely hormonal. It's being fueled entirely by your sex drive, which is biological, not intellectual. But you are more than willing to turn your intellect over to the requirements of your biology."

"What about what you were saying before? About love at first sight being something you believe in? Where does biology figure into that?"

"It doesn't. Love at first sight is spiritual. You're too primal for that."

"You're saying"—he smirked slightly as he spoke—"that I'm incapable of falling in love with someone at first sight because I think with my glands and that automatically pushes out all higher emotions?"

"That's correct."

"Well, thanks a lot, Miss Troi."

"It wasn't a compliment," she said primly. "Higher emotions are what separate us from the lower orders of life."

"Is that all?"

"Higher emotions, and table manners."

"Tell me, Deanna, have you ever had really good sex? Or is that just a theory to you?"

She actually laughed at that. "You really can't figure me out, can you, Lieutenant. You think that all you have to do is smile at me, wink devilishly, overpower me with your charm and strength, and I will willingly succumb to your overwhelming manliness."

"Something like that."

"Commander, welcome to the twenty-fourth century. I don't know what goes on on Earth, or even aboard starships . . . but on Betazed, a woman wants more from a man than for him to simply be a strong hero figure. Someone who is going to carry the helpless damsel off in his big, muscular arms, causing her to swoon and give herself over to him in hot and sweaty throes of passion. Women aren't like that here. *I'm* not like that."

"No, of course not. You're much too busy doing precisely what Mommy tells you, and being precisely what she wants you to be, to let yourself be influenced by anyone as down-and-dirty as me."

Her expression was not a particularly pleasant one. "Listen, do you want to do this or not?"

"Sure. Sure. You were going to show me how to separate the needs of my mind from the needs of my body."

"All right. It's very simple, really. I want you to get a solid grip on the branch, just like I'm doing." He followed her demonstration and she continued, "Then we're going to just drop off from the branch and hang on for as long as possible."

"This is a test of muscular strength . . . which seems kind of silly, since obviously I'm stronger than you. So if this is some sort of competition . . ."

"The only one you're going to compete with, Lieutenant, is yourself. And furthermore, it has nothing to do with muscular strength because muscles, and the body, invariably have limits, no matter how well trained they are. You reach a point that can't be surpassed. But the properly trained mind, on the other hand, has no limits. Ready? And . . . go."

Deanna dropped down off the branch and hung there, her feet suspended more than a meter above the ground. Riker did likewise.

He stared at her, noticing that her toes were not pointed downward, but rather were straight out. Her eyes were fluttering closed as she said in a low, melodious tone, "Now . . . sooner or later, your fingers will want to release. Your instinct will be to fight

146

this impulse. Do not fight it. Instead . . . simply ignore it. Banish it to the inner core of your being, and instead focus on something else."

"Like what?"

"Like anything. Anything that will take your mind away from your body—the sky. The clouds. Birds in flight. The creation of a star. Anything to disassociate yourself from the demands of the physical. Now do what I'm doing—bring an image to mind, a focal image. Close your eyes. Breathe slowly and steadily, in through your nose, out through your mouth, like this," and she demonstrated. "Slowly, steadily, gradually . . . that's it."

Riker had closed his eyes, but now he turned and peered again through narrowed lids at Deanna.

She seemed perfectly at ease. Her breasts were rising and falling so slowly that the motion was almost imperceptible.

Clear his mind. Think about something else other than the fact that his fingers were starting to ache a bit, and his upper arms were feeling a tad numb.

He thought about Deanna.

He pictured her as he had first seen her at the wedding—naked and smiling.

She stood on a beach, having just come out of the water, her body covered with thin rivulets of moisture. She shook her head in slow motion, water spraying out in all directions from her thick hair. Then she came toward him slowly, smiling, her arms outstretched toward him, her fingers gesturing for him to approach her . . .

Her fingers waving . . . her arms outstretched . . .

He felt an ache growing beyond his ability to ignore it. He opened his eyes and found that his fingers were covered with perspiration and were slipping, losing their grip. He tried desperately to readjust, but now his fingers felt nerveless. He had no idea how long he had been hanging there, for he had lost track of time . . . but however long it was, it was enough for him to have lost all feeling above the elbows.

With a low, muttered curse, he dropped from the branch and landed with a hard thud.

He sat there, dusting himself off, and looked up.

Deanna was still hanging there. Serenely. Calmly. Looking as if she had all the time in the world. Her eyes were still closed, her breasts still rising and falling at the exact same pace as before . . . no. As a matter of fact, they were moving even more slowly.

He sat there and watched her, shaking his arms to try to restore circulation.

Deanna hung there.

As blood began to return to Riker's upper arms, he felt a fierce pain, and he winced as he touched the abraded skin on his palms. He looked back to his teacher.

Deanna hung there.

And hung there.

He had no idea how long it was . . . ten, maybe fifteen minutes. Maybe longer. Her slim body continued to display no ill effects whatsoever.

After what seemed an interminable length of time, Deanna began to rock back and forth, slowly and gently. Her eyes remained closed. She gained enough momentum to swing upward like a gymnast, wrapping her legs up and around the branch and bringing herself back to sitting.

"What are you doing down there?"

"What are you doing up there?" he countered. "Finally get tired?"

"No. I could have continued that way for quite some time. A shame that you couldn't. Maybe the weight of all those muscles dragged you down. What an inconvenience, being so much stronger than little me."

He stood, brushing himself off, and walked toward the base of the trunk. As he did so, Deanna clambered upward, standing on the branch as if she were a tightrope walker. She looked completely at ease.

"All right, you've proven your point," he said, trying to keep the disgust out of his voice. "You can climb down now."

Deanna took a step toward the trunk so that she could get a grip and descend . . .

And her foot slipped.

Her arms pinwheeling, and with a startled shriek, Deanna lost her balance and tumbled off.

Riker, still a short distance away, moved like lightning. His arms outstretched, he skidded in and caught Deanna before she hit. But he hadn't had time to brace himself, and the weight of her carried him down. He dropped to his knees, the shock rattling his teeth, but he still held on to her.

Reflexively her arms had gone around his neck. She tried to compose herself, automatically doing the breathing exercise to regain her equilibrium. Riker, meantime, shook his head briskly. Then he looked at her . . . and grinned ear to ear.

He got to his feet, still holding her in his arms. "You okay?"

"I'm fine. You can put me down—"

Their faces had been mere inches from each other, and Riker now seized the initiative. He kissed her full on the lips.

They held like that for a long time, and he felt her body go limp. And then she just seemed to melt against him, and reflexively her hands squeezed his shoulder blades, as if afraid he might vanish, or the moment might end.

But ultimately it was she who ended it, breaking off with an audible popping sound. "Put me down," she whispered.

He grinned and said, "But we were just getting—"

Put me down NOW!

He dropped her.

He hadn't intended to do it. But the imperative was so startling and so overwhelming that it caught him completely unawares. She fell at his feet and, quickly scrambling to hers, backed away from him.

"I heard you," he said, "in my head. That must mean I'm getting better at this. Right?"

"You couldn't have heard me in your head."

"I know I—"

"You *couldn't* have!" she said with an infuriated stomp of her foot.

She turned away from him in an obvious attempt to compose herself. He made no move toward her, stayed as far from her as he could.

She was in pain. My God, she was in pain over him.

At that moment, he cleared his mind because instinctively, he didn't want to think or even feel anything that she might pick up on and cause her more distress. Just like that, he was suddenly thinking about nothing at all. And he felt totally relaxed.

"Deanna—"

She said nothing. Her hands were pressed against each other, palm to palm, and she had slowed her breathing down. When she did turn back to face him, all the confusion was gone. Instead she was lit with inner calm.

"Your problem earlier," she said, sounding very clinical, "was that you were once again entertaining erotic thoughts about me. All that did was focus you on the needs of your body. You can't put yourself beyond those needs if you use that as your focal point. You should watch out for that, Lieutenant."

"Really." He took a step toward her. "Well, you know what I think, Miss Troi. I think your body and mind aren't quite as synchronized as you like to think. I think your body wanted to fall into my arms, contrary to what your mind might think of me. And so your ever-so-sure feet deliberately betrayed you."

"I subconsciously threw myself at you, is what you're saying?" She laughed lightly.

"It's possible, yes."

Again she laughed. "No, Lieutenant. It's not possible. For your information, a piece of bark broke off, and that's what caused me to slip. That's all. If you look around on the ground, I'm sure you'll find where it fell. Now, if you'll excuse me . . ."

She turned and walked off. He called after her, "When is our next lesson?" But she didn't respond.

He spent the next twenty minutes searching every inch of the ground, trying to find the stray piece of bark.

But he never did.

CHAPTER 20

Dinner that night in the Troi household was subdued. The only sound was a persistent and gentle chiming as Mr. Homn stood at the middle of the table repeatedly striking the small instrument that gave thanks to the gods of Betazed for the food being eaten.

Lwaxana kept glancing up at Deanna. Her daughter seemed preoccupied this evening, her gaze and thoughts focused entirely toward herself. When, out of habit, Lwaxana sent a gentle and subtle probe into her daughter's mind to find out what was troubling her, she was astounded to find that her mental inquiry was turned aside. She could have, of course, immediately pushed more deeply and with more force, but that would have been utterly out of line. Casual mind brushing was one thing; shoving one's way in after meeting initial resistance was quite another thing entirely.

Deanna . . . ?

There was no response, and with an annoyed air, Lwaxana resorted to the far more inconvenient, since it meant she had to disrupt her eating, verbal "Deanna."

Deanna looked up. "Yes, Mother?"

"What is troubling you, Little One?"

Her daughter smiled gamely. "Nothing, Mother."

"Casual lies?" Lwaxana looked disapproving. "First you thwart a mind brush, and then you resort to telling me that nothing is bothering you when something clearly is. I thought we were more open with each other than that, Deanna. Frankly . . . I'm a little hurt."

"There's no reason to be hurt, Mother, just because I don't want to share every intimate detail of my life every moment."

Lwaxana raised an eyebrow. "Intimate?"

"Mother, I don't want to get into it."

Lwaxana let a rather crude response float from her mind into Deanna's, and it got the expected reaction. Deanna flushed slightly and said, "Mother, that was uncalled for."

"Perhaps. But how accurate was it?"

"Mo-ther . . ."

"It's him, isn't it. That Starfleet officer, Striker."

"Riker."

"Him." Lwaxana carefully arranged her napkin in front of her and turned to her manservant. "Mr. Homn, I'll want to send a communiqué to Starfleet."

Deanna slapped the table impatiently and said, "Don't you dare!"

She might just as easily have spit into Lwaxana's food and gotten the same response as she received. Slowly, with an air of complete and utter shock, Lwaxana turned and openly gaped at her child. " 'Don't you *dare'?"* she repeated incredulously. Deanna looked down, her mouth moving but no sound coming. "You're telling *me,"* continued Lwaxana, "what *I,* the keeper of the Sacred Chalice of Riix, should and should not *dare?* May I ask you, young lady, who in the Great Fire you think you're talking to?"

"Mother, please, I'm sorry—"

"I will *not* be addressed in that . . . that cavalier, offhand manner. I am *not* one of your 'pals,' Deanna. I am not one of your casual acquaintances. I am certainly not one of your Starfleet friends."

"He's not a friend! He's not even . . . Mother, I don't even *like* him!"

"Then what is he?" demanded Lwaxana. "What is he to you?"

"A frustration. A big frustration, that's all. He's a . . . a case study in surface arrogance. He's . . . he's nothing. *Nothing*. Not on a personal level."

"Need I remind you," said Lwaxana stiffly, "of your commitment to Wyatt?"

"I know about that, Mother. But frankly, I can't believe that you're really going to hold me to that . . . that agreement."

"Little One, *I'm* not holding you to anything! This is tradition and custom we're talking about. I don't just fabricate things to inconvenience you and make your life more difficult. I simply teach you what they are and expect you to abide by them. And you, knowing your place in society and the responsibilities that place entails, are going to abide by them. Aren't you." The last was not a question.

Deanna looked down.

"Aren't you." This time there was even a bit more of an edge than before.

"Yes, Mother," said Deanna automatically, a phrase she had repeated any number of times before on a variety of occasions.

"Good, because frankly . . . and I'm only giving you my surface interpretation here, since you seem uncomfortable with allowing me to probe more deeply on this . . . you're making it quite clear that you can't exactly control yourself when it comes to this lieutenant."

Now Deanna looked up, her jaw set. "I can control myself just fine, Mother. I'm not some . . . some animal in heat."

"I never said you were."

"No, but you implied it."

"I didn't—"

"You *did.*"

"All right, maybe I did," said Lwaxana, putting her hands up. "But it's understandable. You don't seem yourself when it comes to thoughts of him. Perhaps I should have a talk with the people at the university. If this lieutenant is merely a case study for you, then I think that the university is doing a pretty shabby job of teaching you something as simple as clinical detachment."

"They're doing a fine job, Mother. Please . . . stay out of it. I can handle Lieutenant Riker just fine."

Lwaxana stared at her piercingly. "And how do you define 'just fine'?"

"I define it as being capable of rising to a situation without your help."

Lwaxana appeared to consider this a moment, then speared another piece of fish with her prong. And then she said simply, "See that you do."

Mr. Homn hit his chime and Deanna winced slightly. Funny how, after all these years, she'd never realized just how damned annoying that persistent chiming was.

Riker lay in his quarters at the embassy, reading a primer on Betazed philosophy that Deanna had recommended.

It was puzzling to him. In example after example, situations were presented and the reader was asked, basically, "What would you do or say in such a situation?" And Riker was consistently getting it wrong.

He went on to the next example and read it out loud to see if it would make more sense: "A friend tells you that she is very upset. Her immediate supervisor has said several overly critical things in regards to her work, and she feels frustrated and hurt over the situation. How do you respond?"

Riker thought about it and then said out loud, "All right. I tell her one of two things: either she can analyze her work habits, see where she's being remiss, and improve her performance, or, if she firmly believes that the criticism by her supervisor is unwarranted, she can tell her supervisor that and demonstrate why. If he continues to be overly critical, she can inform him that if he does not cease and desist in his unreasonable demands, then she will go to the next level in the chain of command and file a grievance."

He pondered that for a moment, decided that it was a good, solid, reasonable response, and moved on to what the text claimed was the proper way to handle it.

He read it out loud without understanding it.

"'Tell your friend'"—and there was incredulity in Riker's voice—"'that you understand her frustration. That you know she's in a difficult situation, but have confidence she'll work it through.

Cite an instance in your own life where you experienced similar feelings of anxiety. Let her know that she's not alone and that she can count on you as a source of emotional support.'"

He stared at the words floating there on the screen and shook his head. "But what's that going to solve?" he asked in frustration. "Sitting there and commiserating about how difficult life is? That's not going to do anything to address the problem! It's not going to make things better. I mean, why would she come to me with this problem if she didn't want me to try and come up with ways to solve it?"

He pushed the screen away in annoyance, shutting it off. This was ridiculous. Tang had been absolutely right about these people. They seemed to dwell endlessly on how everyone felt.

He resolved to ask Deanna about it the next time he saw her.

Which was not the next day.

Or the day after that.

Or the day after that.

By the end of the week, the silence on the part of his "tutor" had become somewhat puzzling, if not downright irritating. He made several calls over to the mansion and was repeatedly told that Deanna wasn't there or wasn't available. He asked that she return his calls, but she never did.

He was starting to become irritated, and his irritability showed through when Sergeant Tang happened to stop by to chat about a new piece of ordnance. Riker was short-tempered with him and then immediately regretted his tone.

"Sorry, Sergeant. That was uncalled for."

Tang stared at him and rubbed his beard stubble thoughtfully. Riker wondered for a moment how in hell Tang perpetually managed to look as if he needed a shave. Did he just scrape along the edges of the stubble, cutting it to a particular disheveled length?

In a manner that was a bit too overfamiliar for a sergeant to deal with a lieutenant—but nevertheless seemed utterly in keeping with Tang's personality—the veteran spacer slapped Riker on the forearm and said, "C'mon with me, Lieutenant. I got something set up downstairs that you look like you could use."

Riker followed Tang to the lower sections of the embassy, to rarely used storage facilities. At the moment, the facilities were relatively empty, particularly because the reception for the Rigelian ambassador had depleted much of the stock. Riker knew there would not be a ship along to restock for several weeks.

Riker was surprised—but not *too* surprised—to see that Tang and his men had converted the large facilities into a makeshift armory. "We're good at making do with what we have," said Tang. "Every so often, though, we fall into a bit of luck."

"Good lord." Riker was looking at one of the most massive pieces of armament he'd ever seen. It hung on the wall and was almost as large as Riker himself. He looked around to Tang and said, "May I?"

Tang waved toward it. "You're the CO. Be my guest."

Riker lifted the long, cylindrical weapon down and staggered under the weight of it. He had trouble placing his hands correctly and felt it slipping off his shoulder. But then Tang was there, steadying him, although actually he seemed a bit more concerned about the weapon's safety than Riker's.

"Here, you take it," said Riker, handing it off to Tang. Although Tang was a head shorter than Riker, he hefted the weapon as if it weighed a fraction of what it actually did. Riker tried to suppress his astonishment at the display of strength and was only partially successful. "What *is* that?"

"This," said Tang, patting it proudly with his free hand, "is the latest in mobile ground-to-air defense. The portable Level 10, shoulder-mounted phaser cannon, Model II."

"Makes you wonder what Model I was like."

"Model I blew up during field testing and destroyed half of Pluto. No one cared—it was a boring planet, anyway." Then, when he saw Riker's expression, he grinned, showing slightly irregular teeth. "I'm kidding, Lieutenant."

"I knew you were," Riker lied. "How powerful is that thing?"

"On full strength, I'd probably have a shot at knocking one of Betazed's moons out of orbit."

"You're kidding again."

Tang looked at him, his face inscrutable. "I didn't say I'd have a *good* shot at it."

He placed the gun back on the wall and took a couple of small target-practice phasers out of their mountings. "Come on. I'll show you what we got set up."

He led Riker over to another area, which was somewhat darkened, and handed him one of the phasers. Then from his belt he unclipped a couple of small, diamond-shaped devices. "Standard issue for ground security," he said. "Keeps us from getting stale no matter where we are."

He tossed them into the air, and on their own, they started hurtling around the chamber. "Pick your shot and start firing, Lieutenant."

Back to back, Riker and Tang began firing at the diamonds, trying to nail them in midflight. They glistened as they darted about the room, bobbing and weaving in no particular pattern. Riker managed to land a couple of shots; Tang landed far more.

And as if the tricky piece of firing only required part of his attention, Tang said, "It's a woman, isn't it."

"Pardon?"

"One of the local girls, like you said you were going to be going out with. She's got you hooked . . . no disrespect intended."

"I'm not *hooked,* Sergeant. They have interesting philosophies. I'm trying to understand them."

"How much philosophy do you need to get through life? If something attacks you, shoot it. If it doesn't attack you, leave it alone. Everything else is just window dressing."

"That's a very narrow mind-set, Sergeant."

"That mind-set is what keeps you alive, Lieutenant Riker. I'm still here. My men share my mind-set. They're still here. That's all that matters."

"Hello, Will."

The two men stopped and turned, and there stood Wendy Roper. She was wearing a white jumpsuit that clung to her like a second skin. "Hi, Sergeant."

"Ma'am," acknowledged Tang.

She turned back to Riker and wasn't able to hide the disappointment in her face. "Will . . . I haven't seen you around much."

"I, um . . . I've been very busy lately, Wendy."

"Really?" she said with a pert angle of her head. "Doing what?"

"I've . . ."

"The lieutenant has mostly been preoccupied with perimeter inspections, ma'am," Tang said stiffly. "Word on the line is that we're ripe for an attack at any time."

"Yes, anytime," echoed Riker.

"A great deal of time being spent in security procedures. All out of concern for your safety, ma'am."

"I see. Well . . . when you do have some free moments, Lieutenant . . . it'd be nice to get together. I thought we were hitting it off rather well." She nodded to Tang. "Good seeing you, Sergeant." And she walked off. Riker could hear her light footsteps receding up the stairs.

"She's a nice girl," Tang observed. "Very pleasant companion, I'd think. And best of all—no offense intended—not overly intellectual, if you catch my drift."

"I'd have to agree."

"But I take it she's not the young lady . . . ?"

"No. She's not."

"Never burned the candle at both ends, Lieutenant?"

Riker looked at him askance. "You mean juggled more than one relationship at a time?"

"If you want to put it that way, sir, yes."

"To be honest . . . yes. But somehow, until I get things sorted out with Deanna—"

"Deanna's the local girl?"

"Yes. I don't know how to put it, Sergeant, but it wouldn't seem . . . I don't know . . . *right* somehow."

Tang made a disapproving clucking noise. "Bad sign, Lieutenant. Very bad sign. Shields up, proceed with caution."

"Noted and logged, Sergeant. Oh, by the way." Riker started targeting the flying diamonds again. "You didn't have to lie for me to Wendy."

"I know, sir. On the other hand, I'm rather experienced with laying down covering fire. Just consider it all part of the service."

"Well . . . it's appreciated. I didn't exactly know how to tell her about Deanna . . . especially when I'm not even sure if there's anything to tell."

"No problem, Lieutenant."

"I haven't even seen her in close to a week. Maybe I should head over to the university where she's got classes . . ."

Tang shook his head violently, although it did nothing to spoil his shot. "Big mistake, sir. Very big mistake. Keep in mind that she hasn't heard from you either. Now either that's weighing on her mind, in which case you should just let it simmer until she can't stand it anymore, or else she's not thinking about you at all, in which case you certainly don't need her. But you go pursuing her, you're giving her the strategic advantage. Not a good maneuver at all."

"You make it sound like a military campaign."

Tang looked at him. "Well, sir . . . they *do* call it the war of the sexes. Wars are wars. Strategies are strategies. And winning"— Tang fired again, in rapid succession, and this time nailed both floating diamonds dead center, disengaging them. They clattered to the floor—"is what counts."

"Winning isn't everything, Sergeant."

"Winning isn't everything, sir . . . but losing isn't anything."

Riker tried to come up with a response to that, but couldn't. "That's true, I suppose."

"Can't claim credit for it, sir. I was told a twentieth-century philosopher came up with that. They sure knew their stuff back then."

"What philosopher?"

Tang paused and frowned. "Can't say I rec—wait. I do remember. His name was Charlie Brown."

Riker considered it and nodded. "This Charlie Brown must have been a very wise man."

"I expect he was, sir. I expect he was."

CHAPTER 21

Mark Roper was chuckling. "So when do I get my two hundred credits?"

They were seated across from each other at the café, where meeting for breakfast had evolved into a morning ritual. Riker looked up at Roper innocently while buttering a piece of rye toast. "What do you mean?"

"The two hundred credits you owe me over the bet about Deanna."

"I've got considerably more time on that, don't you think, Mark?" said Riker evenly.

"Time?" Roper laughed. "Captain, time doesn't make any difference. She's cut ties with you. Now or doomsday won't make any difference. It's not going to happen. Lwaxana told me—"

"She told you what?" demanded Riker, his eyes turning keen and a bit angry. "When did you speak to her?"

"Casual conversation a week or so ago."

"Why didn't you tell me?" He crunched down on the toast.

"I *am* telling you. Frankly, you weren't even the topic of conversation. We were comparing notes about the difficulties of raising daughters. And Lwaxana was boasting about how Deanna

160

listens to, and does, everything Lwaxana tells her to do because she has Deanna so well trained in her responsibilities as a daughter of the Fifth House. And an example she gave was how she shut down the relationship between Deanna and 'that Starfleet fellow' because it wasn't appropriate."

"Oh, she did," said Riker icily. "Odd. That's not how I see it."

"I don't imagine you would see it that way," was Roper's calm response. He speared a piece of egg and said, "But then again . . . I suppose how *you* see it doesn't matter all that much, does it, Captain?"

Riker looked daggers at Roper, but the older man was the picture of tranquillity. And why shouldn't he be? As far as he was concerned, he'd won a two-hundred-credit bet.

But Riker saw it a bit differently.

The problem was, Sergeant Tang had made a valid point. Running in pursuit of Deanna, making calls to the mansion, trying to start things up when she was clearly so intimidated by her mother . . . it didn't sound like a pleasant experience. The question was, which was the potentially more humiliating? Throwing himself at Deanna? Or losing the bet?

He kept hearing Tang's voice in his head, warning him about strategy. Warning him . . .

. . . his voice in his head.

That's when it hit him.

The next day, after an early-morning meeting with Tang to review the latest Starfleet reports about raider activity, Riker headed over to the university. He staked out a place for himself, seated on the edge of a large, ornate sculpture in the middle of the campus. And he simply waited. Sooner or later, Deanna was going to have to pass by.

He spent half a day there, watching the sun pass over in the sky, watching the shadows shift position. They were simple, meaningless things. But he stared at them, focused on them, practicing. And as he did so, he slowed down his breathing, drawing out each breath. In through the nose, out through the mouth.

He did so with more than just an interest in finding his calm, inner self. He had a purpose, a drive to his actions. He used the urgency and determination to focus his thoughts, focus everything he did.

He had completely lost track of time, but something made him look up.

There she was.

She was walking across the campus, chatting with a couple of friends. She was laughing at something, and for a flash of an unreasonable instant, Riker felt tremendous resentment. Why should she be cheerful when he was feeling so much mental clutter?

But that wasn't what this was about. He couldn't submit to that clutter; he had to brush away the confusion, concentrate fully on the matter at hand.

He didn't look at her. Instead he was staring at the lengthening shadows, once again performing the steady in-and-out breathing. He reached down into himself, down into that determination that fueled the drive of his career. Except now that core of energy was going to fuel something else.

He felt it welling up inside him, felt—or at least hoped he felt—the ability, the potential, there for him to tap. And now he sought out Deanna.

There she was, her measured strides having taken her only a couple of meters beyond where she had been before. And she was looking his way. Apparently she had just noticed him, and she gently elbowed one of her girlfriends and nodded in Riker's direction. The other girl looked, too, and all three of them seemed to be sizing him up for a moment before putting their heads together and giggling.

And Riker took Deanna's image, took a mental snapshot, and imprinted it onto his mind. And then he cut loose in an undisciplined, inelegant burst.

You're afraid of me, he informed her.

The reward to his herculean effort was immediate. Deanna was thrown off-step, and her head snapped around in astonishment. She looked right at him, and on her face was utter shock.

To her credit, she recovered immediately. She fell back into step and made every effort to act as if nothing unusual had happened.

But Riker knew, dammit, *he knew*.

He tried to send again, but now his thoughts were cluttered, whirling and flushed with the excitement of his success. He couldn't pull himself together again fast enough—he hadn't developed nearly enough discipline.

He realized that he'd had the equivalent of beginner's luck. That didn't change the fact, though, that he had let Deanna know precisely what he was thinking. He had, in essence, thrown down the gauntlet right on her own turf of the mind.

She studiously looked away from him as she and her friends made their way across the campus. Deanna had, in fact, picked up the pace. It was clear to Riker why: she was concerned that he was going to come running after her.

However, he had no intention of doing that. In fact, when Deanna was almost out of sight, she risked a quick glance behind her. All she saw was Riker sitting precisely where he had been before, his legs crossed, looking like a smug Buddha.

Riker was sound asleep when an insistent rapping came at his door. He sat up in confusion, checking his chronometer. It was the middle of the night.

The first thought he had was that there was some sort of attack. He tossed the blanket around himself and ran to the door.

Deanna was standing there, her arms folded, her eyes bright.

"I am *not* afraid of you."

It took a moment for Riker to shift gears and realize that there was no danger from imminent alien assaults. Still, he composed himself quickly. "You could have fooled me."

"Obviously you're not all that difficult to fool. On what grounds do you say that I'm afraid of you?"

"On the grounds that you cut off all communication with me. On the grounds that you're steering clear of me."

"I cut off communication with you because, as far as I was concerned, I had better things to do with my time than devote it to someone who couldn't possibly understand the subtleties of our philosophies."

"Well, obviously I'm understanding something," he said, leaning against the doorframe, "because I projected thoughts to you."

"A fluke. Pure happenstance. Besides, you didn't do it for the satisfaction of opening up your mind. You did it so that you could get my attention; maybe even get back at me, in some crude way. As for steering clear of you, my presence here should be enough to show how ridiculous that is. On what grounds can you—?"

"On the grounds," Riker interrupted remorselessly, "that every time you're close to me you start to lose control. Your body starts sending you signals that your brain doesn't want to accept. Face it, Deanna . . . I'm upsetting your nice little intellectual applecart."

Her gaze was steady and unrelenting. "Get dressed."

"Where are we going?"

"Out."

"Where? Why should I go with you if you won't tell me where it is we're going."

She looked at him defiantly. "What's the matter, Lieutenant, afraid of me?"

"All right," he said after a moment. "Give me a couple of minutes."

"Take all the time you want."

It was a fairly warm night. Where Deanna stood, she was framed in the moonlight reflecting off a large lake, providing some degree of illumination. Her arms were crossed as if she were cold.

Riker stood behind her, waiting patiently. "Lovely area," he said tentatively. "You come here often?"

"Yes." She sounded distracted. "From time to time."

"It's pretty remote."

"That's deliberate."

They were at the edge of a forest. Riker glanced up at the trees with their outstretched branches, like fingers that wanted to drag him into the darkness of the woods. "So now what? We hang from branches some more?"

She turned to face him. "Take your clothes off."

He stared at her. "I beg your pardon?"

"It's a therapy technique I learned in class a couple of days ago. Take your clothes off. All of them."

He grinned lopsidedly. "Okay. What's the joke? One of your girlfriends hiding in the woods here? I get naked, you guys grab my clothes and run off. I have to make my way back to town, show up at the door of the embassy, and explain why I'm seriously out of uniform. Big laugh on the human. Right?"

Deanna gave a loud sigh and reached back around to the back of her tunic, undoing some fastenings. Within seconds she stood naked in front of Riker and tossed her outfit to him. It landed in a small bundle at his feet.

"Take your clothes off."

Riker did so.

They stood nude in the moonlight, facing each other, and then Deanna walked toward him. Riker's body was trembling inwardly, but he tried not to show it.

"Lie down." Her voice was firm, but Riker wondered if she was just as nervous inside as he was.

Now why in hell was he nervous? It certainly wasn't as if she were his first.

Deanna saw him standing there, unmoving. "If you want, and if you still think this is some sort of prank, you can keep your hands on your uniform so no 'accomplice' can grab it."

Slowly Riker lay down on the ground.

"On your side. Your back towards me."

Completely puzzled, Riker did as she asked. He tucked his legs up slightly, looking slightly fetal and feeling slightly foolish.

He heard motion behind him and then Deanna was lying next to him. She curled up against him in the manner that humans still called spoons, for the way that spoons fit together when stacked. She slid one arm under him and brought the other over, wrapping herself around him.

He felt her chin against his shoulder, and that particular connection was easily the least incendiary that occurred to him. The rest of her front was pressed against his back, and his pulse and mind were racing. She felt incredibly warm against him. Every muscle was aching; he felt as if his entire body had too much blood in it . . . that it didn't know where to go, and any moment he was going to explode out every pore.

"Now," she said softly, "we're going to talk."

His voice was strangled. "T-talk?"

"Yes. You see . . . you still have to develop mental discipline. You still have to learn control. You have to be able to deal with me without thinking about me on a physical level."

"And *this* is supposed to make me stop thinking about you physically!" He wanted to flip over and face her, to grab her, to turn her over and—

"That's right." She sounded inhumanly calm. "We are going to chat about whatever you want and just stay like this. You are going to become comfortable with the notion of my sexuality and yours, and that way you'll be able to move beyond it to more spiritual matters."

"I can—" But his voice had gone up an octave. He cleared his throat, trying to ignore the horses galloping through his brain, and started over. "I can think of a far better way to get comfortable with sexuality—and it'll be a lot more fun than the way I'm feeling right now."

"How are you feeling right now?"

"My body hurts, and I want to bay at the moons."

To his surprise, this actually prompted a soft laugh. But then she said, "To give in to those impulses, Will, only undercuts everything I've said. The desires of the body must be secondary to the desires of the mind."

Riker was ready to kill her. "Why in hell are you doing this?" he grated. "Why are you making me feel like I want to jump out of my skin? I mean, obviously it has no effect on you, but it's making me crazy!"

She said something so softly that he didn't hear it at all. "What?"

"I said," she repeated, not without effort, "that it is definitely having an effect on me."

"It is? What . . . um . . . what sort?"

One of her hands moved across his chest, and she said, sounding somewhat frustrated, "Well, now, what do *you* think?"

Doing the best he could to control his voice and keep the tremble out of it, he said, "Deanna . . . if both of us are feeling this way . . . then maybe it would make sense if we . . . ?"

"Will." For the first time she actually sounded pleading. "Will, I can't. Don't you see? First and foremost, two people have to connect on an intellectual and spiritual level. If they make love purely because of the physical attraction, then it's just . . . just a sex act. It would be a mistake."

"Deanna . . . how could giving in to what we both want be a mistake?"

"I don't want to, Will."

"But you said . . . ?"

"I don't want to give in to the impulses that I'm feeling. How can you not understand? It would undercut everything that I believe in. I don't feel a connection to you on a spiritual level. I don't feel *comfortable* with you. I can't just give myself over, I . . ."

"You're afraid of me." This time when he said it, there was no challenge in his voice, no mockery. This time he said it and there was . . . sympathy? Understanding? He wasn't sure what it was, but all he knew was that he wanted to comfort her. He wanted her to feel better.

He held her arms tightly against himself, and there was nothing sexual about it. It was as if he were trying to send some of his strength into her.

"A little," she said in a voice so small he had to strain to hear it. "I feel a little afraid. When you live by a certain philosophy, and then you meet someone who disrupts that philosophy . . ." She paused a moment. "It goes back to what we were talking about . . . about love at first sight. I can accept love at first sight. I can accept lust at first sight. But the latter is something I don't feel I want to be a part of."

"There's something to be said for just giving yourself over to the pleasure of the moment."

"I'm sure you'd be the expert on that, Will."

They were silent for a long time after that. He still felt the heat from her, and the slow in and out of her breathing. But it wasn't affecting him quite the same way.

"So . . . so what do we do now?" he asked.

"We talk."

"About what?"

"About anything you want . . . anything except sex. The whole point of this is—"

"To rise above the impulses of our bodies. Yeah, I know." He thought about it a moment. "Okay. Okay, I've got something to talk about."

"What?" She sounded almost eager.

He tried to ignore the musical way her voice seemed to float, and the soft feel of her breath against the back of his ear. "This stuff I was reading about Betazed philosophy . . . the one you recommended to me."

"Yes?"

"I don't get it."

"What don't you get?"

"Well, for instance . . . there was this example about a woman being criticized unduly by her supervisor. And she comes and tells me about it."

"Yes, I know the scenario. And let me guess: you came up with ways to solve her problem."

"Right."

"And the text informed you this was the wrong approach."

"Right."

"And you don't know why."

"Right. So what can possibly be wrong about wanting to solve her problem, instead of just moaning and wailing about it."

"There's nothing wrong with it, if that's what she wanted. But that's not what she wanted. The problem is that you're insensitive to her desires."

"Insensitive?" Riker propped himself up on his elbow. "How was I being insensitive? I listened to her difficulties and tried to make her life better for her."

"She wasn't asking you to do that."

"But if she—look, let's make up a name for her . . . 'Jane' . . ."

"Catchy name," said Deanna dryly.

"If Jane came to me with her problem, obviously she was coming for help in solving it. That's a given."

"No, it's not."

"Yes it is," he insisted. "Look . . . if a technician goes to the chief engineer and says there's trouble with the warp core, the chief engineer isn't going to say, 'Oh, what a shame, that's too bad, I know how difficult this must be for you.' He's going to say, 'We've got to get that fixed!' A busted engine, an abusive boss . . . it all boils down to the same thing. Namely, a bad situation that needs to be repaired."

"You're missing the point, Will."

"No, I'm not missing the point." He turned over to face her. Their bodies were now pressed up against each other, flesh to flesh. And incredibly, Riker wasn't paying attention. "You're just being obstinate."

"And you're in command mode, Will. The universe isn't Starfleet. Emotions aren't regulated. And Jane, as you call her, wasn't looking for you to solve the problem."

"Then why in hell did she come to me!" demanded Riker.

"She came to you because she was looking for emotional support," said Deanna patiently. "She knew she had a problem. She knew it had to be solved; or perhaps she wasn't going to solve it but simply live with it. Either way, though, she had to deal with it in her own way because *it was her problem*. What Jane was looking for from you was an augmentation of her emotional strength. She needed you to say that you were sympathetic to her difficulties and were supportive of her. This is the philosophy of RaBeem, which, simply translated, means 'I understand.' An even better way to handle it is to tell her of a time when you faced a similar situation—"

"And describe how I solved it?"

"And describe how it *made you feel*. So she knows that whatever frustration and embarrassment she might be encountering is not unique to her. When you're unhappy or discouraged, it's very easy to believe that you're the only person in the world who has ever felt this way. Teenagers experience that feeling most sharply, but adults do also. And what Jane was simply looking for was a sense that she was not alone."

"But . . . but then how does the problem get solved?"

"It gets solved by her, in whatever manner she chooses. And she's also looking to you to say that whatever she does, you will support her because it's the action that she has decided to take."

"I'm still not sure I get it."

"Oh, you're starting to." Deanna smiled. "You just haven't admitted it."

"What you're saying is that I'm faced with a problem and I shouldn't make the slightest effort to solve it."

"That's not such a bizarre notion for you to have to deal with, Will. Isn't that what the Prime Directive is all about?"

"Not at all. We talked about that, it's completely different."

"Only in scope, not in practice. Just because the problem involves a close friend rather than a civilization of strangers, it doesn't make the theory any less valid."

He was about to reply but realized that he couldn't think of anything to say. Smiling sympathetically, she ran the back of her fingers across his face. "I know it's difficult for you, Will. Your impulse is to take command. It's what you were trained for. It's what you long to do. But command isn't the be-all and end-all of life."

"It is to me. I hope that doesn't sound egotistical, but . . . it's all I want to do. It's what I'm aiming for. I want to beat Kirk's record."

She frowned politely. "Pardon?"

"Youngest starship commander in Starfleet history. That's my goal. I want my own command . . . and I guess my mind-set sometimes shapes all of that, and makes me . . ."

"Want to command every situation? Every person you meet?"

He saw the slightly mocking way she raised her eyebrow. "Not exactly . . . but maybe a little," he admitted.

"Well, who knows? Someday you might find yourself in a situation where you find that you enjoy following someone more than you would commanding."

"Never happen. Every person I serve under is just a means of learning more and more so I can have my own command."

"You can't see yourself serving with someone simply for the sheer joy of serving with them? Or with the others on board the ship?"

"Never happen. No matter how much I liked the ship or crew, if I was then offered my own command, I'd be out of there in a heartbeat. Trust me on this." Then he paused. "You probably don't understand."

"You're wrong, Will. I do understand. I may not agree. But I understand. So," she said after a moment's thought, "tell me what other things about Betazoid philosophy puzzle you."

And they remained that way, naked, wrapped around each other, talking. Just talking, until the early-morning hours, when the first rays of the sun stole across the treetops. They dressed, Riker feeling extremely self-conscious, Troi feeling . . . he didn't know how she felt.

"Thank you for an . . . interesting evening," he said.

"I think we've made some progress."

"When can we get together again?"

"Why do you want to get together again?"

"I . . . well . . ." He smiled. "A lot of reasons."

"In that case, I think we've made even more progress than I thought," said Deanna teasingly. "I'll be in touch with you, Will." And she turned and walked off.

When she snuck into the mansion, Lwaxana was waiting for her.

Her mother was standing there, hands on hips, lips thinned virtually to nonexistence. "Would you mind telling me where you were?"

Deanna looked downward. "Yes, I would."

"Deanna, we've never kept things from each other."

"Not quite, Mother. I've never kept anything from you. I've never had much choice."

Lwaxana pointed to the stairs. "Go up to your room, Little One. We'll speak of this later . . . maybe."

"Mother, I'd rather—"

"*I don't care!*" Lwaxana's voice was filled with more fury than Deanna had ever heard, and it occurred to the young Betazoid that now would probably not be the best time to discuss matters in more detail . . . particularly considering the details.

Nevertheless, though, she felt she had to say something.

"Mother," she said very quietly, "don't you trust me?"

The muscles under Lwaxana's face worked for a moment, flexing and unflexing. And then, softly, she said, "Of course I trust you, Little One."

"Well, then . . . ?"

"It's others that I don't trust. Deanna"—she took her daughter's face in her hands—"you have a purpose in life. A higher purpose. And I distrust anyone and anything that seems as if it will dissuade you from that purpose."

"But don't I owe an obligation to myself to—"

"Your obligations," said Lwaxana sadly, "are far greater than those to yourself. You have history to protect. You have tradition to uphold. People who died years, even centuries ago did so with a sense of comfort. Even completion. Because they knew that they were part of a larger tapestry; that they were part of something greater than themselves. It is not easy, Deanna, to sublimate your interests and desires to those long gone and those to come. But the happenstance of your birth and lineage means that you owe it, not only to those who preceded you, but to those who will follow. Please, Deanna . . . tell me that you won't let me down."

In her face was more of a pleading expression than Deanna had ever seen. At that moment, as they had so often before, her own interests and willpower wilted before the needs and demands of the woman who had so shaped her life.

"Of course, Mother. I won't let you down."

"Are you certain?"

"Yes."

Lwaxana drew herself up, almost looking embarrassed about her heartfelt plea. "Well . . . that's . . . that's good to hear. Um . . . it's early, but . . . how would some hot chocolate sound to you about now?"

Deanna had to smile at that. Chocolate was one of the few tangible reminders—aside from Deanna's presence, of course—of her father. He had absolutely adored chocolate, and it was a craving that he had imprinted on his wife and, apparently, passed on to his daughter. She licked her lips at the thought and said, "That would be wonderful . . . but I wouldn't want you to go to any trouble."

"Oh!" Lwaxana waved dismissively. "It won't be any trouble at all." She turned, cupped her mouth, and bellowed in a voice that shook the rafters, *"Homn! Wake up! Deanna wants some hot chocolate!"*

"Mother! I thought you were—" And then she saw Lwaxana's stunned expression and amended, *"I* could have made it."

"Oh, nonsense. A daughter of the Fifth House? What an absurd notion."

"But why did you have to yell?"

"Because Mr. Homn has an annoying habit of sleeping through my thought-castings. Amazing. The only other person I ever met who could do that was your father."

Mr. Homn appeared moments later. To Deanna's surprise, the towering manservant was fully dressed. She wondered if he was simply a fast dresser, or whether he just slept that way in the event that Lwaxana needed him for something. Actually, for all she knew, he never slept. Certainly life with Lwaxana would seem to preclude the opportunities for such mundane activities.

"Deanna wants some hot chocolate," Lwaxana informed him.

Mr. Homn looked at Deanna impassively, and Deanna gestured in a manner that silently said, *I'm sorry about all this.* Homn merely inclined his head slightly and headed off toward the kitchen.

"Now you see, Little One?" said Lwaxana, looping her arm through Deanna's. "There are still some people who know how to give proper respect to those who are entitled to it. I suggest that you keep that in mind . . . particularly in the way that it applies to Lieutenant Riker."

Deanna looked at her nervously. "You're not going to contact Starfleet, are you? We're just friends, Mother."

"Just friends because of your actions, my dear, not his. But no . . . I doubt I'll really speak to Starfleet about him. After all, Little One"—Lwaxana patted Deanna's cheek—"you do want me to trust you, don't you?"

173

CHAPTER 22

Breakfasting at their customary café, Riker and Roper looked up in surprise when Gart Xerx appeared next to them. "So here's where you're hiding, Roper," he said in mock annoyance to the Federation ambassador.

Roper shrugged. "This is where I am every morning. Ask Mr. Riker here."

"He is," said Riker solemnly. "I can vouch for him."

"Although actually," said Roper, putting his napkin down, "I hate to say this, but I have to cut our usual morning ritual short. I have an early meeting this morning."

He started to rise, and Riker automatically started to put his own food aside, even though he hadn't finished it. But Roper quickly stopped him. "Just because I have to abort breakfast, Captain, doesn't mean you do. Stay. Chat with our great friend Xerx."

"Great friend," said Xerx with an exaggerated *harrumph*. "Didn't come to my daughter's wedding weeks ago."

Roper shrugged. "My daughter and the captain here attended on my behalf. And I did send a lovely gift, didn't I?"

"Quite true," said Xerx diplomatically.

"So there you are then," said Roper with satisfaction. He

gestured to the now empty chair. "Sit. Order something and charge it to me."

"As you wish, Mark." Xerx sat and then waited patiently until Roper departed. "He'll regret that," Xerx told Riker.

"Why?"

A moment later, the waitress walked up with a steaming plate of food and placed it in front of Xerx. Riker stared at it and said, "That's the most expensive thing on the menu."

"Yes, I know," said Xerx cheerily. "Want some?"

"No thanks."

Xerx looked at him quizzically. "By the way . . . 'captain'? I thought you were a lieutenant?"

"That's right. It's a . . . well, a sort of running joke between myself and Mark."

"Yes. He does have a peculiar sense of humor."

"So," said Riker, taking a sip of coffee before continuing, "how is your daughter doing?"

"You know how it is with young marrieds," said Xerx with a small laugh. "They live in a world of their own making. At the moment they're still doting on virtually everything that the other one does. The way each of them walks, talks, breathes. We had them over the other night, and it was amusing to see how Chandra simply sat and adored the way her new husband chewed his food."

"Chewed his food?"

"Newlyweds. What can I say?" Xerx shrugged, and then his eyes narrowed slightly. "And how goes it with you and young Miss Troi?"

Riker raised an eyebrow. "Reading my mind, Gart?"

"Merely enough to confirm what I already knew. I noticed the way you were staring at her at the wedding and reception. And I also know that you've been seeing her socially. I've overheard Deanna and her friends discussing it at the university."

"What were you doing at the university, if you don't mind my asking?"

Xerx took another forkful of food. "I'm a professor of psychology. Where else would I be?"

175

"Oh. I didn't know that."

"Somehow it never came up. I even have Deanna in one of my classes."

"Is it the class where they teach about nude therapy?"

Xerx stared at him. Gart had been about to eat another forkful, but now it remained suspended several inches from his mouth. "I beg your pardon?"

"I'd heard there was this . . . technique . . . where a patient and his or her therapist take off their clothes and lie next to each other . . . even . . ." He cleared his throat. "Even pressing up against each other."

"I'd think that would probably lead to sex," said Xerx, looking amused.

"Well, no. It's done in order to move past physical considerations and deal with each other in a purely intellectual manner. But . . . why am I explaining this to you? I mean, certainly you know about . . . ?"

Xerx was trying not to laugh. "Lieutenant . . . I've been teaching, and practicing, psychology for going on thirty years now. And I can assure you I've *never* heard of any 'technique' that has therapist and patient removing their clothes and lying against each other . . . except in those cases specifically involving sexual dysfunctions and therapy for those dysfunctions. Was this a case involving dysfunctions?"

"N-no," stammered Riker, looking utterly befuddled.

"In that case," said Xerx, spreading his hands, "I would see little purpose for that sort of contact beyond the obvious gratification." Then he leaned forward. "Who told you about this 'technique'?"

"No one," said Riker quickly. "I just . . . just heard it around."

"Well, it sounds to me as if such actions would be extremely pleasurable, but other than that, I wouldn't attach much psychological value to them."

Riker sat back in his chair, and then a slow grin spread across his face.

"Lieutenant, is there something you'd care to discuss with me?"

"No," replied Riker, unable to wipe the smile off his face. "No, nothing at all. I just find the entire thing . . . funny."

"I see."

At that moment, Riker's communicator beeped. He was mildly startled. Whereas the page was certainly common enough on board a ship, here in the more leisurely surroundings of Betazed, it was extremely unusual. So much so, in fact, that Riker had a dim sense of worry even as he reached up to tap it. "Riker here."

"Lieutenant, this is Tang," came the sergeant's voice.

"What is it, T—"

Tang didn't even give Riker a chance to get out the entire question. "Planetary sensors detect incoming ship moving extremely quickly, ignoring all attempts at hailing it. General shape would indicate Sindareen origins."

Immediately Riker was on his feet. "Planetary defense systems—"

"Too late, Lieutenant. These Betazoids are so damn peaceful, they hardly have anything anyway. And what they do have is too little, too late."

Xerx was looking up at Riker with tremendous worry reflected in his eyes, but Riker had no time to try to quell fears. "Scramble the squad."

"Already done."

"And track the vessel's likely destination, based on trajectory."

"Already done, sir. Our calculations have them making planetfall right in the heart of this city."

Riker was ecstatic. "Right where we'll be waiting for them. Their overconfidence is their first and last mistake. I'll be right there. Riker out."

All in the café were now looking at Riker with tremendous worry on their faces. Even though no one was saying anything, he could almost sense the anxiety level skyrocketing. He started to head for the door, but for a moment, Xerx stopped him.

"An open area makes them easy targets," said Xerx. "But densely populated as we are here, means that you have to worry about innocents. Don't let your determination to capture your targets be *your* first and last mistake."

Riker regarded him for a moment, then nodded briefly.

"Understood," he said, and then ran out of the café.

CHAPTER 23

Deanna and Chandra stared at the painting. They had stared at this particular painting once a week, every week, for the last ten years. Every time they did, they saw something new . . . although whether it was something new in the painting or in themselves, neither of them could have said for sure.

Deanna crisscrossed her arms and ran her hands up and down as if to shake off a chill. Chandra noticed the gesture and said, "Are you okay?"

"I'm fine. I just . . ."

Her voice trailed off, and gently Chandra said, "It's that Riker, isn't it? The one from the wedding."

Deanna nodded hesitantly.

Chandra turned away from the painting. "What is it about him, anyway?"

"I don't know. He's not at all like any of the men I . . . I mean, he's so *un*intellectual."

"You mean he's stupid?"

"No! No, not at all. He's very bright. Very quick. Very intelligent, really. He's just so . . ." She tried to think of the best way to put it. "So primal. His actions seem governed as much by instinct as any sort of rational thought."

178

"What's wrong with that? There are few things in the world more natural than instinct. When I met Teb," Chandra continued, referring to her new husband, "there was a sort of instinctive attraction."

"But at least you two were compatible. Riker and I, we're . . ."

"You're what?"

Deanna shivered slightly again. "Every single bit of rational thought tells me that Will Riker is completely wrong for me."

"And your irrational thought?"

"My irrational thought," she admitted, "makes my skin tingle."

"Well!" Chandra smirked. "And what does your mother say to that?"

"Ohhhh, don't ask. You think *I* have trepidation about him? He's not at *all* the type of man my mother wants me with. No social standing. No ties to Betazed or Betazoid society. No . . ."

And suddenly her voice trailed off, and her dark eyes went wide. Her face took on the color of paste.

"Deanna," said Chandra in alarm. "What's the matter with . . . ?"

Then she sensed it, too. "Oh, Gods," she muttered.

Deanna grabbed her arm and grated, *"Come on!* Let's get *out* of here! Before we—"

Other Betazoids were reacting as well. They were already in motion in response to the strong and frightened thoughts that were affecting the crowd to various degrees.

But their actions weren't fast enough.

All over the gallery, doors burst inward. At one end, a powerful ray blast blew in a chunk of the wall. The hurtling fragments flattened a man, pinning him writhing on the ground.

Sindareen warriors entered, dressed in glittering armor, cradling pulse blasters under their arms. One of them fired in the air, and the deafening noise froze a number of people in their tracks.

Deanna and Chandra spun and dashed toward one exit that remained clear. They were several steps short of it when it slid open, and the open space seemed to be completely filled with a massive and extremely formidable-looking Sindareen.

His lips pulled back, and his entire face was cast in a death's-head glow. He leveled his weapon at the two women and said, in a deceptively pleasant voice, "Step back."

Chandra whimpered slightly as Deanna guided her back. In a low voice Deanna advised, "Don't show them you're afraid." She was no less frightened, but she found it easier to ignore her fear by focusing on calming her friend.

She sensed the terror running rampant through the mind of her friend. Newly married, her main concern was that she was never going to see her husband again. Deanna, for her part, hadn't taken it quite that far; she hadn't really accepted the notion that she might die here, pointlessly and unexpectedly. Her main concern was survival.

As the Sindareen prodded and herded the thirty-plus Betazoids together into a small circle in the middle of the room, Deanna's mind was racing with thoughts of rescue. She was certain that the Sindareen's presence here could not possibly have gone undetected. She knew that, even now, steps were certainly being taken to rescue them.

And somehow, beyond any shadow of doubt, she knew that it would be Lt. William T. Riker who would be spearheading that rescue operation. For no rational reason, she derived great comfort from that, and a certainty that everything would work out.

She felt that way up to the point where the barrel of one of the Sindareen blasters was shoved into her mouth.

"What have we got?"

Riker was standing next to Tang, about a hundred yards away from the art building. Betazoids were trying to get near, sensing as one the terror emanating from the building and instinctively wanting to help and soothe those who were trapped within. But Tang had ordered his people to keep everyone back, and they were busy shooing the concerned citizens away from the immediate area. Tang was stroking his perpetually grizzled chin.

"There's the ship they came in." Tang pointed. Sure enough, situated on top of the building was a small Sindareen vessel, of the style commonly called a Spider, so nicknamed for its odd sectional style and eight leglike extensions.

"Can you pick it off from here? Disable it?"

Tang studied Riker for a moment and said, "Yes. Do you want us to?"

Riker pondered that. "No. It wouldn't be a good idea. Then they'll be trapped, and desperate. The first thing we have to do is secure the safety of whoever's inside."

Tang nodded briskly and Riker realized that the veteran spacer had already come to the same conclusion. For some reason, Riker felt a brief flash of pride. But his mind was already racing ahead. "Who's your communications expert?"

"Hirsch," said Tang, and before Riker could say anything further, Tang tapped his communicator and said, "Hirsch—haul your butt over here."

Riker studied the building as they waited for Hirsch to show up. "Do we know how many people are in there?"

"Not for certain, sir. Some people on the lower floors managed to get out. One of the more sensitive mind-types said she detected about thirty or so locals, and about nine Sindareen—which would be consistent with the known crew complement of ten for a Spider."

Hirsch, a stocky brunette woman, ran up to them. She was cradling a small phaser rifle, but also had with her a portable comm unit. Of greater power and range than the standard portable communicators, it was also capable of more functions.

"Yes, Sergeant?"

Tang merely pointed to Riker, and she turned to face him, waiting.

"I want to talk to the Sindareen," said Riker. "The odds are that they left someone behind in the ship with whom they're in communication, to be their eyes and ears outside."

"You want me to find the frequency they're talking on and break in so you can come on?"

"That's right. Keep in mind their communications might be scrambled."

Hirsch's contemptuous expression showed precisely what she thought of Sindareen scrambling capabilities. "No disrespect, Lieutenant, but I thought you were going to give me something hard to do." She dropped down to one knee, removing the large comm unit from her equipment pack and studying the frequencies registering over it. Her fingers flew over the touch padds.

"Got it, Lieutenant," she announced after less than thirty seconds. "Just need a few more moments to unscramble." She smirked. "Apparently they think we can't do it."

"Enlighten them, Hirsch," said Riker, "as to the error of their ways."

The Sindareen who had cut off Deanna and Chandra's escape was apparently the leader of the group. As was mostly the case with the Sindareen, his hair was tightly swept back and coal black. His skin was pale, virtually to the point of the chalk white shade of an albino. Although he possessed a mouth, it existed exclusively for eating. Speech issued from the nictating membranes on his long throat.

"Baytzah!" he snapped to others of his group. "Zroah! What are you standing around for? Charoset, you and Chazeret get to the other room and clear that out. And you others—move! We don't have all day!"

The Sindareen were moving through the great museum, carrying with them large cases. They hurriedly pulled paintings off the wall, shoved glittering sculptures into the cases. Each action was greeted by gasps and audible protestations by the Betazoids—which were quickly silenced by the leader's subtle movement of his weapon in the direction of the prisoners.

"My dear Betazoids," he said, sounding unexpectedly reasonable. "I am called Maror. If you would be so kind as to cooperate, we can do this briskly and without serious difficulty for any of you."

"But why!"

The uncontrolled outburst had originated from Deanna, who had said it without thinking. Chandra tried to pull her back into the relative obscurity of the crowd, but it was too late. She had attracted Maror's attention. Somehow, though, surviving the emotional trauma of being shoved, courtesy of a blaster in her mouth, had emboldened her.

Maror's gaze wandered along the lines of her body in a manner that made Deanna suddenly feel dirty. She derived the feeling purely from the surface, however. She found that she couldn't get an empathic lock on any of them, which was unusual and frustrating for her. The uncontrolled, and unwise, question had been a manifestation of that small but aggravating defeat.

"But why what?" asked Maror. Behind him the rest of his men continued with their task. "Why should you not interfere with our little procedure?"

Deanna, keep quiet! Chandra's voice rang in Deanna's head. But she knew that wasn't possible. Her outburst had already attracted the Sindareen's attention. Besides . . . some part of her genuinely wanted to understand what in the world could be motivating these beings into these destructive acts.

She called on the image of her mother, who had never seemed intimidated by any situation. She squared her shoulders and firming up her voice, demanded, "Why are you stealing our art treasures? They can't hold any meaning for you. They're works that spring from the hearts and minds of Betazoid artists."

Maror made a noise that must have been the Sindareen equivalent of laughter—it was a more rapid fluttering of the membranes, unaccompanied by any noise other than the flapping sound. "Are you really under the impression," he asked when he had recovered himself, "that we are going to sit around and look at the pretty pictures? Don't be ridiculous. What we have is a client who is a very avid collector, with a taste for one-of-a-kind pieces. And he is very wealthy, and very willing to pay whatever it takes to obtain those things that have struck his fancy. You should be flattered that your work has attracted his attention—he's very discriminating."

And now whatever fears Deanna might have had were overwhelmed by a fundamental sense of indignation. "You would deprive a people of their cultural heritage just to satisfy the greed of an individual? What sort of beings *are* you?"

His mouth turned up slightly as he replied, "Entrepreneurs." Then he stepped back, clearly ending the discussion, or at least his interest in it. He tapped his wrist comm unit and said, "Karpas. Report."

Over the comm unit came back a voice, saying, "There's a fairly large assemblage on the street. Typical bunch of Betazoids—

everyone standing around, trying to understand how everyone else feels about the situation, and nobody doing anything about it."

"Yes, that *is* typical," grunted Maror. "Anything else?"

"Yeah. What appears to be a squad of Starfleet security men. Apparently they're taking charge of the situation."

"Let them. I know their regs. As long as we've got the hostages in here, they won't dare make a move against us. Keep the engines primed. I estimate we have another three to four—"

But before Maror could complete the instruction, another voice broke in on the comm unit. "Attention, Sindareen raiders. You are completely surrounded and cannot escape. Surrender is your only alternative."

Deanna's dark eyes widened and she looked at Chandra, who immediately knew what was going through Deanna's mind. For the briefest of moments, Deanna wanted to shout out, "Will! I'm trapped in here with them! Do something!" But fortunately, and wisely, she held her tongue. Riker certainly did not need personal involvement dragged into the middle of all this.

Maror, for his part, bubbled in fury. "Who is this!" he demanded.

"Lieutenant Riker, of Starfleet," came the stern reply. "Who is this?"

"Maror of the Sindareen. So tell me, Starfleet man . . . where's your ship? We didn't see it coming in, and there's none within light-years of here. We checked."

"A ship isn't necessary to deal with this situation."

"You flatter me," said Maror sarcastically.

"No. I warn you. I have an entire squad of men, with more on the way. The entire area has been sealed off. You cannot escape. If you surrender now, your cooperation will be noted."

"'Noted.' How nice. That will make a lovely tombstone: 'Here lies Maror. He cooperated.' I think I'll take my chances, Lieutenant, thank you. Now if *you're* interested in taking chances, then I invite you to try and impede our departure." Then Maror's voice grew cold and harsh. "And you can explain the three dozen Betazoid corpses to your superiors! Do we understand each other, Lieutenant?"

Riker's reply was firm and unyielding. "You will not escape."

"You will not stop me," shot back Maror. "Now get off my comm unit."

"We are scrambling your transmissions. You will not be able to communicate with your ship for as long as you refuse to cooperate."

"Oh, really." Without hesitation, Maror swung his weapon around and squeezed off a shot.

The blast struck Chandra in the upper thigh. She went down with a shriek that echoed throughout the museum and certainly was audible over the comm unit. Deanna dropped to the floor with her, Chandra clutching her leg and whimpering. An ugly carbon-scored gash was across her thigh.

"Did you hear that?" demanded Maror. "I could have killed her just then! That is the extent of the cooperation you'll have from me, Lieutenant! The next time I fire it's going to be at somebody's heart, and I assure you, Riker, I hit what I aim at! Now unclutter my transmission or somebody dies in the next ten seconds—and that's on your head, Lieutenant Riker. *Yours!*"

There was only the briefest of pauses before Riker's voice came back. "In the interest of cooperation, I'll put you back in touch with your ship. I anticipate you'll extend further good-faith courtesies in the future."

A moment later, Karpas's concerned voice was back on the air. "They're going to give us trouble, Maror! Did you hear what they—"

"Of course I heard, you idiot," snapped Maror. "And what's more, they're going to hear. Namely, they'll hear everything that's being said over this frequency. I don't need them eavesdropping! Maintain radio silence except in case of extreme emergency! Maror out!"

He lowered his comm unit and turned to the Betazoids. Deanna had ripped a length of cloth from her sleeve and wrapped it around the burn that was blistering the skin on Chandra's leg. She looked up at Maror with anger and defiance flashing in her eyes. Maror, for his part, looked utterly calm, and again Deanna met frustration in being unable to get any sort of feeling for what was going through his mind. Something in his psychological makeup—in the makeup of all of them, in fact—rendered them impervious to Deanna's empathy. Or at least, for the moment it did.

"Your rescuers," said Maror, "are only going to make matters worse for you. I suggest you pray to whatever gods you believe in that the Starfleet security and their noble lieutenant are less effective than they think they are. Because their effectiveness will be measured entirely in the number of deaths that arise because of them."

CHAPTER 24

Riker turned away from Hirsch and looked at Tang with frustration. "That could have gone better," Riker said.

"It could have gone worse," replied Tang. "At least nobody's dead."

"We have to determine what they want. What their demands are."

"No, we don't. We know what they want," said Tang reasonably. "It's whatever is in this building. We know what their demands are—they demand we let them get away with it. The only question becomes, do we let them?"

Riker's face was set. "No. We don't."

"Even if people die?"

"We try to avoid that at all costs," Riker said slowly. "But the bottom line is that if we let them get away, we simply invite them to continue their activities at the expense and lives of other innocent people. It has to stop here and now."

At that moment, Gart Xerx appeared at Riker's side, his huffing and puffing indicating that he had been running the entire way. "Sindareen raiders!" he gasped out.

Riker glanced at him and said, "Yes, sir, we know. We're handling this. Now if you'll just—"

"Chandra's in there!"

"What?" Riker turned back to him. "How do you . . ." And then he caught himself, remembering with whom he was dealing. "Yes, of course you'd know, wouldn't you. Is she all right?"

"She's been hurt. The bastard shot her in the leg."

Riker's face darkened, thinking of the sweet, eager bride he'd seen all those weeks back. "Is she all right?"

"As all right as can be expected, considering she's been shot," said Xerx evenly. Clearly he was trying to fight down the panic that threatened to overwhelm him. He was obviously searching for that place of central calm that Deanna had told Riker about. And then, almost as an afterthought, Xerx added, "Deanna's with her. She's bandaging the wound as best she can."

Riker tried not to show his reaction to this latest bit of information. In fact, instead of acknowledging the news, he merely said, "Good." But the way Xerx looked up at him spoke volumes to Riker; Xerx must have immediately intuited precisely what was going through Riker's mind, and what his true feelings about learning of Deanna's presence were.

Riker was determined to remain all business. "Can you communicate with her? Find out information?"

"What do you want to know?"

"Everything."

Deanna dabbed at the wound with the cloth, the bleeding having slowed down significantly. She looked up at Chandra, ready to offer some words of comfort, but she saw from Chandra's expression that her friend's mind was not on the trouble at hand. At first she assumed that Chandra had merely separated herself in order to spare herself the pain. But then she realized precisely what was going on: Chandra was communicating with someone outside. Chandra took a moment to glance at Deanna and nod slowly in confirmation.

Maror came up behind them and looked at them once before nodding brisk approval. "Good. No whimpering. Keeping things to yourself. That's what we like to see. You're making this much easier on all of us." Then he raised his comm unit to get a very brief assessment from Karpas as to the movements of the Federation personnel . . . brief since he was perfectly aware that Riker was doubtlessly monitoring every word.

"Precisely thirty-two of our people in there," said Xerx to Riker. He wasn't looking at Riker, but instead seemed to be staring off into thin air. "There are nine of the Sindareen. This Maror you spoke to is definitely the leader. They aren't threatening the hostages beyond telling them to keep out of trouble. They seem intent on stripping the museum of its works for the purpose of selling them to some private collector." Xerx shuddered slightly. "What a barbaric idea."

"Compared to some of the things I've heard about the Sindareen doing, that's positively civilized," replied Riker. "They're probably the only race in the galaxy that the Ferengii actually enjoy dealing with. All right, Gart . . . tell her that she should let us know the moment that the Sindareen start moving for their ship. Tang, I want your people deployed—"

"Already done, sir." Tang pointed to several different locations.

Riker looked around and smiled grimly. The security personnel gathered in the street served as a distraction. In the meantime, more of them had been deployed to strategic points in surrounding buildings, crouched on rooftops or poised in windows. They had phasers armed and targeted on the rooftop where the Spider perched like an oversize predator.

"Problem is," continued Tang, "the Sindareen may not look it, but they're pretty tough. Phaser blasts can stop them, but not on lower settings. Ranges that stun the Sindareen can severely injure, even kill other humanoids."

"Humanoids such as Betazoids," said Riker slowly.

"Right. Which means if they bring any of the hostages along as potential shields . . ."

"You'll have to work around it, Sergeant. Alert your marksmen to take extreme care. We're not going to lose these raiders, under any circumstances."

"Yes, sir. And just in case they do make it to their ship . . ." Tang gestured to one of his security team. He was lugging a large case, and he staggered over with it to Tang and placed it at his feet. Tang snapped it open and Riker saw within the case the formidable Level 10, shoulder-mounted phaser cannon, Model II. Tang hefted it out of the case, and Riker was impressed again by the display of strength on the part of the smaller man. As he had before, he patted it affectionately and said, "Believe me, Lieutenant . . . they're not going to get away."

"That's good to hear. All right, Sergeant. Apprise your people that we definitely have nine Sindareen in there. I don't want any, repeat, *any* shots fired until we've counted nine of them emerging and approaching the ship. As soon as the last one is out, which means the hostages are unguarded—start firing. If they manage to get airborne, I'll be counting on you to bring them down. I do *not,*" he reiterated, "want to see them get away. We're going to be sending a message to them and all of their kind, and we're sending it now."

"Understood, Lieutenant."

"Good. Oh . . . and watch your aim, Sergeant," Riker cautioned. "You miss them and hit the Betazed moon, and we'd have a problem on our hands."

"I won't miss, Lieutenant. Count on it."

The cases were loaded and the other Sindareen were bringing them up toward the roof. Maror stood in front of the Betazoids, studying them apprisingly for a moment.

"As charming as this has been," he said, "we really have to take leave of you now. However . . . it's my concern that the Federation men might decide to give us problems upon our departure. And so, just for some added protection, I'd like one of you to accompany me. Ideally, I'd bring all of you . . . but our ship is small, and we're heavily loaded already. So it's going to have to be one. Now, let's see . . ." He scanned them briefly, and then, tucking his weapon under one arm, he said firmly, "You. You're wounded anyway, so you won't give any trouble." And he reached for Chandra.

"No! Leave her *alone!"* shouted Deanna as Maror grabbed the frantic Chandra by the arm. Deanna leaped forward, her fingernails raking across Maror's face, and Maror howled in fury as lines of

blood welled up on his pale cheek. His face contorted with rage, he hurled Chandra to the parquet floor, and her head cracked with explosive force against it.

Deanna instinctively turned toward her friend, but Maror grabbed her and swung her around. He yanked her forward and snarled in her face, "You know, I thought you had nerve. And intelligence. Out of respect for that, I was going to leave you be. But you weren't intelligent enough to know when you were getting off lucky. So now, foolish little Betazoid . . . it's going to be you."

Xerx actually gasped in fright and staggered slightly. Riker put a hand behind him to steady him and was almost afraid to ask what had happened.

He didn't have to ask as Xerx said, "I've lost contact. Chandra's unconscious." Riker waited for Xerx to pull himself together sufficiently to provide more information, and Xerx did so. "There was something . . . they—the Sindareen—were going to take one of the hostages with them. For a shield. And they were taking Chandra. And she struggled and fell . . . and now I have no sense of her. Lieutenant . . ." And there was pure terror in his voice.

Tang's comm unit crackled to life. "This is Sommers at Gamma Point," snapped a voice. "I have a visual. They're coming out, sir!"

"All units are to wait for my signal!" barked Tang. "Repeat, not a shot is to be fired until you have the clearance from central command!" He looked to Riker. "You're the CO, Lieutenant. Gonna be your call."

"We stick with the plan. When all nine are exposed, we open fire," said Riker firmly.

"My daughter! Gods, Lieutenant . . . you can't shoot my child!"

"They'll shoot clear of her, Gart," Riker said, looking to Tang for confirmation.

Tang nodded his head in agreement. Then from his supplies belt, he removed a small pair of electronic sensor binos and, putting them to his eyes, studied the rooftop.

"Get me one of those," ordered Riker.

"Binos for the lieutenant!" snapped Tang, not removing his gaze from the rooftop. Moments later, Hirsch reappeared and handed a pair of the instruments to Riker. Now he had the roof under close scrutiny as well.

At first there was no movement at all, and for a moment Riker toyed with the notion that this was all some sort of scam—that, in fact, another means of escape was all set up, and the ship was simply there as a distraction. But then he saw the door to the roof slide open and the first of the Sindareen appeared—two of them, lugging a large crate between them.

"Hold fire," said Riker softly, and the order was repeated by Tang. It wasn't necessary, really. Everyone knew what their orders were and what they were supposed to do.

There was an eerie silence over the area. When Tang had been in similar situations, the buzz of the crowd was positively deafening, and sometimes came close to interfering with the job. Whatever was going through the minds and hearts of the Betazoids, they were having the exquisite courtesy to do it quietly.

More of the Sindareen appeared, lugging more crates. Riker counted them off softly to himself . . . five . . . six . . . and then he said, "Have we got them targeted, Tang?"

"Target report," said Tang into his comm unit.

"Alpha Point, target acquired," came the first reply. The snipers had chosen their targets in order of appearance based on their designation: Alpha took the first target to appear, Beta took the second, and so on.

One by one the rest of the snipers reported in. All of them had targets in their sights.

Eight of the Sindareen had made themselves visible. Riker muttered a low curse. The lead two were approaching the confines of the ship. Sure enough, a second later one of the snipers reported, "This is Alpha Point. About to lose target acquisition. Awaiting instructions."

Riker could envision the finger of the sniper, poised over the trigger. He wanted to give the order to cut loose, and he could feel Tang's gaze upon him. But there was no way that he could give the clearance . . . not when the ninth raider was still unaccounted for.

Then there was more movement, and the final member of the Sindareen raiding party made his appearance.

In his right hand, he was cradling a blaster. His head was turning slowly, clearly trying to spot whatever Federation people might be trying to target him. His left arm was curled around the throat of a woman.

"Deanna," breathed Riker.

He zoomed in on her face. Her jaw was set, her eyes unblinking. If she was afraid, she was making a great show of keeping her feelings to herself.

"That's nine," said Tang. "Lieutenant—?"

"They have a hostage," Riker said tonelessly.

"I know that, sir."

Riker was silent. "Who's your best marksman?"

Tang anticipated the request and tapped his comm unit. "Sommers. Shift target to the Sindareen in the rear. Lorie, pick up Gamma's target."

"Acquired," came Lorie's voice from Alpha Point.

This was immediately followed by Sommers saying, "Got him in my sights."

"Clear shot?"

"Negative," replied Sommers, "repeat, that's a negative. Target's moving too much."

Riker saw immediately that Sommers was correct. Maror was too experienced at this. He kept shifting his position, swinging Deanna around so that she was constantly in the way.

Riker pressed the binos so hard against his eyes that he thought they were going to come out the back of his head. He knew what he should do. The vast majority of the hostages were already in the clear. Only one was left . . . one who might still survive if everything fell right. But if they made no move, then the raiders would escape, and more people would pay down the line.

Deanna, he thought bleakly.

At that moment, Deanna was swung directly into Riker's sight line . . .

And she looked straight at him. Straight and proud and unafraid.

Two words rang in his head.

I understand.

"Take them," said Riker.

"Take 'em," Tang ordered. "Take 'em."

Deanna flinched.

From all around, phasers blasted outward, enveloping the surprised Sindareen in coronas of energy. Several staggered and went down. One of them managed to survive the blasts and tumbled into the ship.

Sommers missed Maror. Deanna's instinctive, uncontrollable shiver, anticipating the barrage that was about to occur, had been enough to warn the Sindareen leader that something was about to happen. As a result he'd dropped to a crouch, dragging Deanna down with him. Sommers had been aiming high anyway, banking on Maror's exposing his head for the brief moment that Sommers would need. But it didn't happen, and now Maror dashed for the ship, dragging Deanna with him. The marksmen shot around him, steering clear of the trapped Betazoid.

For a split instant, Maror's back was exposed, and Sommers fired. The high-power phaser beam, which would have severely burned and possibly even crushed Deanna Troi, staggered Maror. It caused him to stumble forward, almost falling atop his prisoner, but then he recovered and reached the inside of the ship, shoving Deanna inside ahead of him. The hatch rampway closed, with several crates of Betazoid art treasures—along with five of the Sindareen—left lying on the rooftop.

"Dammit!" shouted Riker. "Dammit!" It was a totally un-Starfleet response. It was also understandable.

With a roar of impulse engines, the Spider swayed into the air. Obviously whoever was piloting the ship was doing so in a god-awful hurry, not taking time to engage in proper navigational procedures, but instead concentrating only on getting the hell out of there.

Riker didn't even have to look behind him to know what Tang was doing. The hard-bitten sergeant had swung the phaser cannon onto his shoulder and activated it. "Can you bring them down?" said Riker without turning.

"I can blow them out of the sky. Quick and fast."

"Can you cripple them?"

"Trickier. Not as sure. And," Tang added quietly, "there's no guarantee she'll survive the crash. You may not be doing her any favors."

"I know."

The Spider had now gained the skies and was heading west, angling upward. In a moment it would pick up even greater speed and hurl itself far, far away from Betazed.

"Cripple them," said Riker.

Tang made an adjustment on the power and fired.

The intensity of the phaser blast was beyond anything Riker had ever experienced directly. The air crackled around him, and he thought he was going to choke.

The blast took out the starboard engine and the navigational instrumentation of the Spider. The ship lurched wildly, tried to regain control, and failed. It spiraled downward, leaving a trail of thick black smoke behind it miles long.

"Where's it going to come down?" said Riker tonelessly.

"Judging from the speed and trajectory," Tang replied, "somewhere in the region known as the Jalara Jungle."

There was silence for a moment, and then Gart Xerx said, "If she makes it through the crash, she has a good chance. The jungle has its dangers . . . mud pits and such . . . but there are few really dangerous animals to contend with."

Riker turned and stared at him. "You're forgetting the most dangerous animals. They're the ones steering the ship."

CHAPTER 25

Maror didn't know what he was running from, or what he was running to.

No. That wasn't precisely right. He knew what he was running to. He was running straight to hell. But if there was one thing of which he was resolved, it was that he was going to take the damned Betazoid woman with him.

She sat on a rock nearby, and to his frustration she looked exactly as she had the day before, and the day before that. Even though her clothes were ripped and dirty, her face filthy, her hair hanging in stringy ringlets that had lost all their bounce in the moisture of the jungle. Even with her shoes gone, her prospects slim.

Still, she had composure.

He couldn't take it anymore. He wanted her to be like other women he had captured. He wanted her to beg or plead. He wanted her to whimper or moan. He wanted her to . . . to *something*.

He swung his gun up and aimed at her. "Ask for your life."

With a small shrug of her slim shoulders, she said evenly, "Please do not kill me."

He stared at her in disbelief. "You call that begging?"

"No. I call that asking. To be honest, it's pointless. You'll kill me

196

or not. I can't stop you. Begging will demean me and accomplish nothing. I see no advantage to it, and I won't do it."

With a roar of unbridled fury, he stalked over to her and grabbed her by the back of her head. He yanked down hard, and the angle in which he pulled her skull made her mouth open involuntarily. He shoved the barrel of the gun into her mouth, angling it so that the ray blast would be certain to blow her brain up through the top of her skull.

"I said beg," he repeated.

Her eyes rolled up to regard him for the briefest of moments, and then up into the top of her head. Her breathing slowed, and her entire body went limp.

For an instant he thought she'd passed out, but then he realized what she had done. She'd put herself into a trance, or into some sort of deep meditative state. When she was like that, nothing he could say or do would bring her out of it until she was ready to be brought out. He could blow her brains out and she would never know or feel it.

So there he was, feeling like something of a fool. You couldn't threaten someone who wasn't aware of you. Which meant either he should kill her or not. If he killed her, he had a corpse and nothing to hold over any of the Fed men should they catch up with him. There was no point to it. Hell, there was no point to any of it.

With a curse he released her and took some small measure of satisfaction in watching her thud to the ground like a bag of stones. Then he perched himself on the rock that she had occupied moments before and stared down at her, waiting for her to come out of it.

Slowly, after some minutes, she did. She lay there, staring up at him.

"You wonder why I haven't killed you yet?"

She tilted her head slightly and said, "You hope that I will serve some purpose in the near future."

The membranes on his neck fluttered a bit faster as he asked, "And have you wondered why I haven't raped you?"

"You're not a rapist. A thief, yes. A killer as needed. But not a rapist."

Maror studied her. "You're that certain?"

"I wasn't at first." She drew her knees up under her chin. "At first I was terrified that you might do that. When the two of us were the only survivors of the crash, I was certain you might take that course. But as time has passed, I have begun to have a sense of you. Prolonged exposure to you has enabled me to get an empathic feel for you that I didn't have before."

"Keep your empathic feelings to yourself." He walked toward her and yanked her rudely to her feet, as if to try to make up for the fact that he wasn't the type to assault a woman sexually. "I still can't believe," he grumbled, "that you survived the crash when others of my men didn't."

"I was not tense," she said simply. "I had relaxed myself. Your men were tense. The stiffness resulted in the internal injuries that killed them."

"Thank you for that diagnosis," he snarled.

He led her through the jungle, watching carefully all about him for any sign of pursuit.

Deanna, for her part, took the opportunity to expand her senses and get a feel for the life that throbbed all about her in the jungle. It was rare that anyone really ventured any real distance into the Jalara, and rarer still for anyone to be out this far. In a way she found it exciting. She just wished that that excitement wasn't coming at the expense of those who loved her.

She was certain that her mother must be frantic by now, and not for the first time she silently cursed the fate that had made her half-human. Had she been full Betazoid, there was a great likelihood that she would be able to send free-ranging thought broadcasts as far back as the city. Summon help right to the spot where she presently was. It wouldn't matter that geographically she didn't have a clue as to her whereabouts. They would simply be able to sense her.

But her ability to send and receive was diluted by her human heritage. She needed greater proximity to be at all reliable. And out here, in the middle of nowhere, proximity was not exactly easy to come by.

Birds fluttered past her, and she had to step carefully to avoid treading on a small serpent that slid past her. It was not poisonous, but she had no desire to injure something innocent. The thing she found most heartening was that she had sensed the creature's presence rather than seen it.

The vegetation around them was thinning out, and ahead of them was a cleared area that prompted Maror to let out a sigh of relief. It was a watering hole.

He turned to Troi. "Even you have to be thirsty. You're made of ice, but ice requires water."

"I'm hardly made of ice," she said, brushing strands out of her face and trying not to let the fatigue she felt be betrayed in her voice. "That water will taste as good to me as it does to you."

"That's very comforting." He gestured with the gun. "You first."

"Thank you."

She went to the water and knelt down before it. The rips in her dress exposed more skin than she would have liked, but at this point there was no use getting overly concerned about such things. She cupped her hands, scooped up water and brought it to her lips, sipping gingerly and being careful not to take the big gulps that her impulses urged.

He frowned as he watched her. "You drink like a bird."

"There's no point in overdoing it," she replied evenly. "If I overindulge, the result will simply be stomach cramps. I see no advantage to that."

"Fine. Fine. Do what you want."

She looked at her reflection in the water and moaned softly. Then she shoved her hands in once more, wetting them thoroughly, and brought them up to her face, making an effort to wash away as much of the dirt as possible. After a few moments she studied the result and decided that, while it wasn't perfect, at least it was an improvement.

"You realize," she said, "that you're not heading anywhere in particular. You're just marking time. You have no one waiting to pick you up. No rendezvous. No secret hideout."

"I've never been caught. I take tremendous pride in that. I'm not about to get caught now, no matter what. Besides, I'm betting that they stop looking for us. They've probably found the ship by now.

They found the bodies of the others. Maybe they'll even continue the search for a couple of days. But sooner or later, they'll conclude that we couldn't have survived—that we probably fell into a . . . what did you call it?"

"Mud pit," she said evenly.

"Right. Mud pit. Or maybe a ravine. Or maybe even got eaten by some huge animal they didn't even know hung about in these woods. They won't search for us forever."

"Oh, yes, they will," she replied with quiet confidence. "I don't believe they'll ever stop. And neither, in all honesty, do you."

"Really? Then why am I going to all this trouble if it's so certain that I'll be caught?"

She turned and looked at him with her ebony eyes. "You are afraid. You are afraid of whatever actions might be taken against you by Starfleet. Afraid of giving up some measure of your freedom. So afraid, in fact, that you would much rather live a handful of days fighting for survival, but free . . . than you would live many days, or months or even years, in captivity or under the supervision of the Federation."

His eyes narrowed, but he said nothing.

After one more brief pass of the water over her face, she rose and pointed to the water. "All yours."

He nodded and gestured for her to step away from the water. "You know, I was just tired of you before. But now I'm really, really sick of you. All you're doing is slowing me down." He crouched in front of the water and scooped some up. He was able to bring it to his mouth and continue to converse at the same time. "You yammer at me. You analyze me. You try to make me feel like some sort of coward. I'm starting to think that whatever minimal use you might have had as a hostage would pale next to the sheer, selfish pleasure I'd feel at blasting the top right off of your pretty little—"

She kicked him in the small of the back.

With a yell, Maror stumbled forward, wet soil slipping beneath him, and he fell headfirst into the water. He floundered around and was about to pull his upper body out when some inquisitive water snakes, which Deanna had sensed were in the area, came to investigate and did so by wrapping themselves around Maror's throat.

Deanna, for her part, bolted.

For a moment she had considered the idea of making a grab for the gun, but a tentative step she had taken toward it quickly dissuaded her of that notion. Maror's hand was firmly on the grip, and she had a feeling that if she'd pulled at the gun, it would simply have told him, without any shadow of doubt, precisely where his target was located.

And right now she did not want to be a target. That was why she had chosen that moment to make a bid for freedom. For she had sensed, beyond any doubt, that Maror really had had enough. That he was beginning to realize that his flight was hopeless and was becoming angry enough and frustrated enough to take that realization out on anyone who happened to be near.

In other words, he was genuinely ready to kill her as the likelihood for her serving any purpose faded.

So she ran.

Maror sputtered in indignation as he lurched to his feet, pulling at the snakes. The snakes, for their part, were uniformly startled to be removed so unceremoniously from their natural watery habitat. The shock caused them to lose their grip on Maror, and he was able to yank them free. He threw them back down into the water with loud splashes, spun, and roared Deanna's name in a frenzy. He even fired blindly into the jungle with his weapon and by blind luck came within two feet of blasting Deanna's head off.

There was no rational reason for him to pursue her at that point. Dashing pell-mell through the jungle the way she was, the odds were that she was just going to get even more lost and maybe even run headlong into something that was lethal. Whatever pleasure that knowledge might have brought him, however, was diluted by the fact that she had royally embarrassed him. And that was something that he was simply not going to tolerate.

With a howl of vexation he lashed his weapon around himself and took off after her.

It wasn't difficult to track her. Her rush through the jungle left a series of broken branches and crushed shrubbery in her wake. He could have followed the trail if he were blindfolded.

Deanna hadn't been sure if he would try to chase her, or whether he would be happy just to be rid of her. She was banking to some degree on the latter. When she heard the crashing of the jungle underbrush behind her, her heart sank.

She looked around desperately, trying to find some sort of weapon, or perhaps some place to hide so that he would run past her. But no place seemed to be sufficient shelter.

She dodged to the right and stumbled on an outstretched root. She fell forward, catching herself by hitting her palms against the ground, and she felt pain stab through her forearms. She lifted her right hand and found a small, pointed rock, which she wrapped her fingers around for reasons she didn't even fully understand. Then she scrambled to her feet and kept going.

She heard his pursuit getting closer and closer. Between the noise of shoving shrubbery aside, and his loud and constant string of profanity, it was hard to miss him.

His blaster roared behind her and she could feel the heat. He must have used it, she realized, to clear away some underbrush so that he could make better time. She would have given anything to have some sort of weapon or tool like that.

For one insane moment, she envisioned Will Riker coming to her rescue. Striding forward like some great hero, showing up out of nowhere at the penultimate moment, drawn there by fate, happenstance, and that incredible timing that always seemed to accompany such last-minute saves. She wanted it more than anything, to believe that such things could occur in real life. Because it would mean that in real life people really could be drawn together not because it was the intelligent or smart thing to do, but simply because *not* to be together would be completely wrong. It would mean that in real life there were greater things than that which her mind could grasp, analyze, and study.

She wanted him. Gods, she knew that, had known that all along, and she had been such an idiot to fight it for all sorts of reasons that had made sense then but now seemed pointless. If only she had that time back. If only she could see him again.

But she knew, in her heart, that that wasn't going to happen. It was up to her; live or die, it was up to her, and there would be no rescue, and the chances were extremely good that in a few minutes, there would be no Deanna Troi either.

Abruptly the ground in front of her angled upward sharply. She'd come to the base of some sort of small slope. It would take her more time to make her way up it, but backtracking wasn't possible. She took a deep breath and started upward. Roots and small outcroppings of rock provided her with handholds that sped her on her way.

But they did not speed her nearly enough, and suddenly she heard a triumphant yell from behind her. She tried to climb higher, but a hand wrapped around her foot.

"Got you, you Betazoid bitch!" growled Maror.

She screamed, her fingers clawing for purchase, but he dragged her down toward him and spun her around so that his face was mere inches from hers. "You have been far more trouble than you could possibly be worth," he snarled, "and I'm going to . . ."

In her palm she felt the hardness and sharpness of the rock she'd grabbed mere moments before. She didn't hesitate as she brought the pointed end around and slammed it squarely into Maror's forehead.

The Sindareen raider shrieked, a high-pitched sound emanating from the sides of his throat, as blood trickled down his face. Deanna, animalistic, fighting for her life, twisted the rock around and tried to drive it farther into his forehead. But the Sindareen was far too strong. With a roar he shoved Deanna back, but she maintained her grip on the rock as she fell and it tore loose from his forehead. More blood poured freely down his face.

He shoved one hand against it to staunch the wound as he approached her, his gun trembling because of the sheer fury filling him. "You—!" And his rage was beyond his ability to articulate, so he stammered out again, "You—!"

He dropped down on top of her, pressing his full body weight against her. She squirmed under him but couldn't dislodge him as he pressed the gun squarely against her stomach and snarled, "Belly wound. Very slow, very painful, and you'll die anyway. It's what you deserve. You've ruined everything—"

"I didn't—"

"Shut up! You never *shut up!* But I'm going to shut you up! I'm going to blow a hole in your—"

And from above them, a voice spoke in a tone that was deliberately cool and controlled. "Back away from her."

Maror looked up and his already pale face went one shade lighter. Deanna twisted her head around, her eyes wanting to confirm what her ears and her mind had already told her but she still couldn't quite believe.

Riker was standing about ten feet higher up on the slope. He held a phaser, aimed squarely at Maror. He was dressed in survival gear, with a utility jacket, and a supply belt strapped around his middle containing food rations, a patch holster for the phaser, and other miscellanea in small pouches.

His emotions flooded over Deanna, he being open to her in a way that no one outside of her closest friends or her mother ever was. Relief mixed with fear, all carefully bottled up so that he could present an image of utter composure to the frazzled and desperate Sindareen.

"I said back away from her." Riker's phaser wasn't wavering. "Put your hands over your head."

"No, Federation man!" snapped Maror. He twisted his body around, his legs wrapped around Deanna's middle and exposing no part of himself to a clear shot. "No, you're going to put your phaser down! You're going to put your hands over your head! You got that? Just do it! Or I swear I'll kill her. I swear!"

Don't listen to him, Will, he heard in his head. *Don't do what he wants. He'll kill you.*

"Kill her," said Riker evenly, "and you'll have nothing to bargain with."

"I don't *care* whether she lives or dies!" shot back Maror. "If you don't care either, then that's that. So I kill her, put my hands over my head, and surrender. You won't be able to do a damned thing except turn me over to the authorities. And she'll be dead. Now if that little scenario doesn't bother you, then fine! Or maybe you just want to take a whack at shooting the both of us. But I don't stun easy, Lieutenant! You'll probably fry her while you're trying to knock me out. And if you fail to stun me, then I'll kill her anyway. From where I sit, you don't have a hell of a lot of choices!"

"I have plenty of choices."

"No, you don't! I know that and you know that!" His voice went up in register, his barely restrained panic starting to overwhelm him. "Now throw down the weapon! Come on! Do it! Throw it down or I'll kill her, I swear I will, now do it, throw it down, *throw it down now or she's dead right now!*"

"All right!" And Riker tossed the phaser to one side. It clattered away, out of sight.

Deanna sagged against Maror, her thoughts black.

"The jacket, too! You might have some weapons hidden. And the belt! Slowly! Keep your hands in sight! So much as one twitch and she's dead. Her life's in your hands now, Lieutenant. Yours!"

Carefully, making no sudden moves, Riker slid the jacket off. Then he reached around and undid the fastening on the belt. He ran it slowly through his hands, saying, "See? Nothing on it. I don't have any other weapons." Then he dropped the belt to the ground.

Grinning, Maror raised his weapon and took dead aim at Riker. But to Maror's surprise, Riker remained as calm as if he had the upper hand and said, "Now lay down your weapon and no one will hurt you."

"You've got to be kidding me."

"No, I'm not kidding you. You see . . . you're surrounded."

For the briefest of moments, Maror seemed confused. Then, firming up his convictions, he said defiantly, "You're lying! This is just some . . . some pathetic bluff!"

"No bluff. There are Starfleet people on either side of you. And although they're trained to give innocents priorities, they're also trained to protect ranking officers. Put down your weapon now, and you won't be injured. But if you take any offensive action against me, my men will shoot. Even if it means injuring or killing your hostage. They will endeavor to save my life over hers."

"You can't fool me. That's against Starfleet policy," Maror snarled.

"True. But security men sometimes follow their own dictates. And frankly, you're not in a position right now to question their priorities."

Maror was silent for a long moment. Then he stood and hauled Deanna to her feet, shoving the blaster against her.

"I think," he said slowly, "that you are bluffing. I think that all of you split up in order to cover more ground. This is a very, very big jungle. Oh, you may be in communication with them, but there's no way that they can possibly be close enough to make any sort of difference. In fact, it'd probably take you a couple of days to rendezvous with them, seeing how much time has gone by. And so I'm calling your bluff, Lieutenant. Tell them to shoot. Go ahead."

"This is your last warning," said Riker sternly.

"I know. I'll chance it."

Riker looked bleakly at Deanna and said, "I'm sorry." And then, suddenly, he spread his hands wide and shouted, "All right, men! Fire!"

For a second there was nothing, and then, to his shock, Maror caught movement out of the corner of his eye, to his right. He snapped his weapon around and fired, and then he saw something over to his left. He spun, not sure where to look first. He had been so certain that Riker was alone, and now there was movement behind—

The distraction was all that Riker had wanted, all that he had time for. Without hesitation he took two quick steps and leaped off the slope, arms outstretched, directly toward Maror.

Maror looked up in alarm, realized his error, swung his blaster around, and fired. Deanna chose that moment to shove upward and back, and the sudden movement sent Maror's shot wide, just missing the fast-moving Riker.

Riker plowed into Maror, pushing Deanna clear with one hand while grabbing at Maror with his other. The two of them went down, rolling and shoving, struggling desperately, each of them trying to get leverage.

"Will!" shouted Deanna, for Maror had temporarily gotten the upper hand and was now trying to bring his weapon to bear on the Starfleet officer.

She ran toward them and grabbed at Maror, trying to yank him off Riker. Maror rammed the stock of his blaster back, slamming Deanna in the stomach. She went down, gasping and retching, the agony threatening to overwhelm her.

It was all the delay Riker needed. He swung his hands up and boxed Maror on either side of the throat, at the base of the nictating membranes that served as his vocal apparatus. It was the equivalent of slamming a punch to the Adam's apple in a humanoid.

Maror gagged, his breath momentarily cut off, but his strength was still far superior to Riker's. So when Riker got his hands on the blaster, Maror was still able to hold on to it as his injured membranes fought to regain their equilibrium.

The combatants shoved against one another, pitting their full weight and strength, grunting and growling low and incomprehensible noises. A twist, a turn, jockeying for position, and Riker managed to get his feet planted. With a quick twist of his hip he slammed Maror up against a tree with a bone-jarring jolt.

Maror lost his grip on his blaster, and it clattered to the ground at his feet. Riker had a split instant to make a decision. He released his grip on Maror, gambling on his speed and the damage he'd inflicted on the Sindareen thus far, and lunged for the blaster.

It was the wrong move. Maror's foot lashed out, kicking the blaster away into the underbrush. Riker was off-balance, and Maror drove his foot up into Riker's face.

Riker went down, rolling, tasting his blood welling up in his mouth. Maror came after him, kicking furiously, Riker just barely staying ahead of him.

Riker managed to scramble to his feet, and Maror came in fast. Riker braced to meet the charge, his back against a tree, and only at the last moment did he see the knife flashing in Maror's hand. Where he'd pulled it from, Riker hadn't a clue . . . probably he'd kept it secreted up his sleeve.

Riker immediately switched tactics, twisting and just barely avoiding the slashing attack. The blade sank into the tree trunk. Riker's hands swept up and he slammed his head forward, his forehead cracking against Maror's face.

Maror fell back toward some brush . . .

And his questing hand came up with the blaster that had been knocked over there.

Riker dove for cover as the blaster bolt sizzled over his head. Maror pivoted, dodging to the right to try to get a clear shot at Riker.

And Riker saw where Maror was heading.

"Wait!" shouted Riker. "Stop! Don't go there! Don't move!"

Maror, his voice returning, cackled, "Why not, Federation man? Because this will give me the best angle to turn you into a sack of boneless skin? Or maybe security men lie in wait for me? I'm tired of your bluffs, Lieutenant! I'm tired of you!"

Maror leaped to his right, landing with an odd squishing noise, and aimed his blaster at Riker, whose hiding place was now fully exposed.

Incredibly, Riker had not given up the apparent pretense that he somehow had the upper hand. In what seemed a masterpiece of acting, Riker shouted, "Move! Before it's too late!" and he waved his hands wildly.

"The one who it's too late for is—"

And that was when Maror realized that he was getting shorter.

He looked down.

He was standing squarely in one of the infamous Jalara Jungle mud pits.

He knew what they looked like. Yesterday a small animal he'd been chasing for food ran headlong into one and had sunk from sight in a little under two seconds.

From the speed with which Maror was vanishing into the dark, pasty nonsoil, it appeared that larger creatures, such as humanoids, took a bit longer. Like, five seconds.

He looked back up and finished the sentence with slow realization. "Is me," he said as the mud crept up to his shoulders.

Riker scurried forward, arm outstretched, watching for the edges of the mud pit so that he didn't slip in. "Hold on!" he shouted.

Maror actually seemed amused. "To what?"

That was the last thing he was able to say as the mud covered his throat. Riker got to the edge of the pit, which he could discern by the dark rim, and reached out, trying to grab at Maror's hair. But Maror was just beyond Riker's grasp, and then five seconds were gone . . . and so was Maror. He vanished beneath the surface of the mud pit without a trace.

And insanely, Maror's final expression had been one of quiet triumph.

CHAPTER 26

Riker went to Deanna and saw how she was staring at the center of the mud pit. In a low whisper, she said, "He won. He was never caught."

"Are you all right?" asked Riker, taking her by the shoulders. "Did he hurt you?"

"I'm fine." She got to her feet, pausing only to nurse the dull ache in her stomach. "I'm fine. I want to get out of here."

"All right. Let's just wait a few minutes until—"

"No. Now." There was an urgency in her voice, a desperation to try to distance herself as much as possible from the site of these events.

"Okay. Let me just get my equipment together."

She nodded, her gaze never wavering from the mud pit.

Riker quickly got his jacket and belt and retrieved his phaser from where he'd tossed it. Then he tapped a small button on one of the belt compartments, and Deanna blinked in surprise as two small diamond-shaped objects shot past her. "What are those?"

"Target-practice devices. Standard issue for ground-based security personnel. They're what I used to distract Maror."

"Oh." She nodded, and her voice sounded very distant. "That was quite clever, Will. Quite clever."

He stared at her. "Are you sure you're all right?"

"Positive. Let's go."

Riker didn't say anything further, but simply guided her gently away from the mud pit site. He studied her bedraggled condition and, insanely, still couldn't help but think how good she looked despite her ordeal. She seemed to have an endless reserve of inner strength.

Once they began walking, Riker contacted Tang. Maror had indeed been correct in his guess. Riker and the various members of the security crew had split up, the better to cover the vast distances of the jungle. It had been Riker who was fortunate enough, after several days of searching, to detect the life readings of Deanna and Maror using his tricorder.

He informed Tang that Deanna had indeed been recovered (he avoided using the word *rescued* . . . it sounded melodramatic somehow) and that they would now be heading toward the rendezvous point. It would take a few days to get there, but Riker was still well stocked with provisions, and no abnormal delays were anticipated.

Riker had been preoccupied with his mission throughout the past few days and had not paid all that much attention to the jungle, other than to avoid its pitfalls or obstructions. His judicious use of a phaser to carve himself a path now served him in good stead, making it that much easier for him to make his way back . . . even if the tricorder weren't capable of enabling him to retrace his steps.

With the pressure off, he was really able to take notice of the true beauty of the Jalara Jungle. He realized now that the flowers and vines that had decorated the interior of the wedding chapel must have been taken from the jungle. The flowers and growths were exotic combinations of colors. The air was warm, even steamy, without being irritatingly humid. It was filled with a scented mist that was invigorating, or perhaps simply smelled all the sweeter with Deanna's freedom now a reality.

He turned and looked to Deanna, who had been extremely silent for the past half hour.

She was shivering. Her arms were wrapped around herself, and there, in the midst of a warm jungle, she was shivering. Her teeth were chattering.

Immediately he knew what was happening. All during the time when she was in danger, she had managed to keep everything bottled up. She had detached herself from the fear and uncertainty, from the terror that must have accompanied every moment. Such feelings could be repressed or ignored for the duration of a crisis. But sooner or later they would come roaring back and would have to be dealt with.

He went to her and put his arms around her, settling her into a seated position. "Shh. It's okay. Let it out, Deanna. That's all right."

She trembled more violently, staring not at Riker but straight ahead, as if she expected someone or something to come at her from the underbrush. Her hand clamped onto his upper arm, her fingernails digging into the skin with such fierceness that Riker had to stifle the impulse to push her hand away. As it was, he kept his mouth shut, not letting on that it hurt like hell.

He stroked her face, continuing to make soft, comforting noises. Letting her know that it was okay to be frightened. Reminding her that she wasn't alone. Telling her that everything was going to be all right, that she was out of danger and soon all of this would just be a distant, bad dream.

As he spoke, she drew herself closer to him, pressing against him and readjusting his arms so that he completely enveloped her. The quaking still convulsed her body, and her lower lip trembled. Tears rolled down her face, but she did not cry out loud. Her complete silence was almost eerie.

He didn't say anything further. He merely rocked with her, back and forth, gently, letting his mere presence be something from which she could draw reassurance. And slowly, ever so slowly, the trembling diminished and eventually stopped. The tears ceased, and then she brought her hand up and wiped away the remainder of the moisture.

Then she looked up at Riker. He smiled down at her and, wondering if she was prepared to move on, said, "Ready?"

She nodded. "Yes. Yes, I am." She reached up, wrapped her hand around the back of his head, and drew his face to hers.

The kiss was very long and very sweet and filled with promise. Their lips parted and he looked at her, the jungle air making him feel giddy. There was an unreality to it all. *Going native* was the old phrase.

"Deanna," he said, his voice low. "This . . . this isn't right. This isn't the time. You aren't thinking straight, you've been through a lot, you—"

"Let me"—she held his face in her hands—"let me put this to you in a way that I know you'll understand."

He waited. With her eyes wide, her lips mere inches from his, she whispered, "Shut up and kiss me, Riker."

He did.

Moments later, all the perfectly logical reasons why this was wrong, inappropriate, completely incorrect behavior for a Starfleet officer . . . all those blessed reasons flew completely out of Riker's mind. Instead all there was was *her,* was the moistness of the jungle combined with the sweat of her. The rustling of trees mixed with the rustling of clothes, and this time when their nude bodies pressed against each other, there was no intellectualizing, no deep discussions that required anything beyond soft, whispered words, punctuated by faint, occasional gasps.

In that moment they knew all there was to know of each other . . . body and soul, flesh and spirit, all combined and permeating every inch of both of them. Instead of moving away from each other, instead of resisting the pull, they gave in to it completely. They complemented each other, became each other, filling out each other's needs and rejoicing as pressures built in them. Throughout the Jalara Jungle it seemed that all noise had ceased. That there was nothing in the jungle, nothing in the planet, nothing in the universe except the two of them and their discovery, their admission, of their mutual need and hunger.

The pressure built beyond their ability to contain and they released, clutching each other, as if hoping they could meld their bodies into one as seamlessly as they had with their souls. And somewhere, somewhere deep within Riker's mind, merged with his spirit, a word echoed. A word that he had never heard before. A word filled with mystery and promise and a future . . .

And the word was *Imzadi*.

They lay next to each other, Deanna's head against his shoulder. She ran her fingers idly across his chest hair.

"I hear that's for traction." It was the longest sentence she had uttered in half an hour . . . the first sentence since their lovemaking. Their most recent lovemaking, to be precise, although how many times they had engaged in their mutual sexual calisthenics was a bit of a mystery to both of them. Things had blurred one into the other; had just finished and begun again with hardly a word passing between them. It was as if, having decided upon a course of action, they were both afraid to speak after that for fear of botching it up somehow.

They had not moved from the spot where it had all first begun untold hours ago, and Riker had a feeling that impressions had been dug into the ground that would probably mystify future geologists.

"You heard about that, did you?" he asked.

She nodded. "Chandra's father told her. She told me."

"Oh. Well . . . yes. Traction." Riker paused, trying to find something to say.

She said it for him. "So where do we go from here?"

"To the rendezvous point. But I have a feeling we're going to be pretty late."

"That's not what I meant."

"I know." He turned over, propping himself up on his elbow, and ran his fingers through her hair. He picked out a length of vine that had become tangled up in it and was about to toss it aside. But she took it from him.

"No. I want to keep that. As a souvenir."

"A piece of vine?" he asked incredulously.

She shrugged.

"In answer to your question . . . I don't know. I know how you make me feel. I think I know how I make you feel. But I . . . I don't

214

have any answers. I'm still getting this all sorted out. I mean . . . you're the expert on feelings. What do *you* think?"

She sighed. She felt slightly chilled, even in the warm jungle air, and she drew her naked body tightly against his. "I don't know. That's . . . that's what I find appealing about you, Will. When I'm with you . . . I don't think."

He raised an amused eyebrow. "I'm not sure how to take that."

"When I'm with you . . . when I think about you . . . all my training, all my . . . my overintellectualizing, as you put it . . . just vanishes. I've never felt this way about anyone and I . . . I finally decided I wanted to give in to it. To fully experience it. How can I be any sort of complete person if I'm not willing to go where my . . . where my spirit wants to take me."

He brushed back a lock of her hair. "I think you have a very beautiful spirit."

"Why thank you, Lieutenant. It's nice of you to notice it. And so do you."

He paused. "This is going to sound so . . . so trite, but believe me when I say . . . I've never felt like this with anyone. More than just the physical part . . . which was great, don't get me wrong," he added hurriedly. "But there was . . ." He felt tongue-tied. "I really don't have words to express it."

"There are none. There don't have to be."

"There was . . . when we were . . ." He cleared his throat. "There was a word. You thought it at me . . . at least, I presume it was you. I don't think there was anyone else rattling around in there. 'Imzi' or something?"

Now she propped herself up as well and faced him fully.

"Imzadi," she said softly. When she said it, there was a musical, loving tone to her voice such as he had never heard.

"That's it. Imzadi. What does that mean?"

"Well . . . it has several meanings. The surface level is simply 'beloved' or 'dear one.' But when used with certain people, under certain circumstances . . . well, you need to know the further nuance to it to understand its full meaning."

"So what is its full meaning?"

She smiled shyly, which was a direct contrast to the casualness of her nudity. "It means . . . the first."

"The . . . the first?" He wasn't sure he had heard correctly, or perhaps didn't want to.

"Yes. No matter what happens from here on . . . we will always be true Imzadi. We will forever be each other's 'first.'"

She looked up at him with those large, dark eyes, and he felt like a total cretin.

"You mean . . . you mean I'm the first man that you . . . that you ever . . ."

She nodded.

"Had sex with?" he managed to finish.

She nodded again.

"Oh, my God."

"You seem surprised," she said, looking quite amused. "Is it so difficult to believe?"

"Well, I mean . . ." He couldn't remember when he'd felt quite this embarrassed. "I mean, you're such an open society and all . . . and you're so gorgeous . . ."

"Thank you," she said demurely.

"That I'm . . . I mean, it never occurred to me that no man had ever . . ."

"Bagged me?" she asked, her eyes twinkling slightly.

He winced. "That's one term that's occasionally used . . . although not by me."

"Oh, of course not. Never by you."

"And . . . um . . . look. Deanna. I . . . I don't know if I said or did anything to give you the impression otherwise, but . . . but you're not my first. I mean . . . I've been with other women."

"No, you haven't," she said serenely.

"Yes, I have. I mean, I was there. I think I'd know."

"Oh, I understand. You mean you've had sex before."

"Well . . . well, yes. I thought that's what we were talking about."

"You still don't understand, Will. The physical part, as pleasurable as it was . . . and as exciting as it was for me, I must admit . . ." She hesitated and suddenly looked vulnerable. "Did I do all right?"

"Oh, yes! Yes. You did . . . you did great. I'd never have known if you hadn't told me that . . ." He gestured, trying to sum up his conflicting feelings.

"All right, then. But you see . . . the concept of Imzadi goes beyond the physical. You've had other women physically. I know that. And even though I haven't had other men before you, that's almost incidental. To be Imzadi is to go far deeper than that. Don't you understand, Will? Other women may have had your body"— she smiled—"but I'm the first who's ever touched your soul."

And he realized, with a dim astonishment, that she was right. Sex for him had always been directed toward the pleasurable aspects. Even when he had thought he was in love, it had turned out to be purely superficial . . . an excuse to add some additional excitement to the physical gratification.

Was he in love now? Thoughts were tumbling around far too fiercely for him to assimilate fully. It was the kind of sensation that he had always wanted to avoid. He liked knowing precisely what he was doing at all times. He liked being in control. But to be in love was to surrender some degree of that control, and he had never been willing or able to do that.

And now, here with Deanna Troi, he still wasn't sure if he was able. But for the first time in his life, he realized that he was genuinely willing.

"Imzadi," he said, and smiled.

She returned the smile and nodded. "I understand."

He sat up and saw that the sun was setting. It hung low, streaks of pink and orange dancing like liquid fingers across the Betazed sky.

"You know," he said slowly, "I've been looking at stars in space for so long . . . that I completely forgot how utterly beautiful a star can be when it's setting. And you know what else? Those clouds right there"—he pointed—"the way they're coming together . . . they look like two dragons battling."

"You see conflict in the sky. That's understandable. When you launch yourself into space, then to a very large degree, it's you against the vacuum."

"It's like the painting, isn't it."

"To some degree," she acknowledged. "When you look at any sort of tableaux, be it hanging on a wall or hanging in the sky . . . you see in it a reflection of your innermost wants and desires. That is, if you look at it in the right frame of mind."

"You want to watch the sunset and wax philosophical?"

"By all means."

She drew her body next to his and they sat there, staring up at the setting sun and seeing in it all sorts of aspects of their souls that they had never before examined.

Riker was thoroughly enraptured.

But after about thirty seconds, Deanna turned to him and said, "Right, then. That's enough of that. Come here, Imzadi." She pressed against him and bore him tenderly to the ground.

The sun set the rest of the way without them.

CHAPTER **27**

Riker stared at the paper, shaking his head. What could he possibly have been thinking?

He started to shove it back into the supplies belt when he heard Deanna's soft footfall behind him. Her unexpectedly fast return from her morning ablutions had caught him by surprise. As a result he fumbled slightly, and the sheet fluttered to the ground.

Deanna picked it up, staring at it in surprise. "Paper. Now here's something you don't see every day."

"Federation security men believe in being prepared for any eventuality—even leaving a message stuck to a tree. Give it here."

She looked at him, her head slightly tilted. "Will, we've been traveling together through this jungle for five days now . . . covering distance that we could have covered in three days, if we weren't always . . . interrupting ourselves."

At that he had to laugh. Deanna's enthusiasm and positive lustiness for the newly developed physical part of their relationship was almost overwhelming. Apparently Deanna Troi didn't do things in half measures. When she was being cerebral, she was totally cerebral. But now that her attention had been drawn to the pleasures of the flesh, all of her enthusiasm was directed toward exploring all the various possibilities and extremes to which such pleasure seeking could be taken.

"We have to watch out for those interruptions," Riker said dryly. Then he reached for the paper again and she snatched it away.

"The point is," she continued, "that even if we hadn't been drawn so close through our physical activities . . . and even if my empathic feelings for you weren't so strong . . . it would still be obvious to me that you've written something on here that you're embarrassed about."

"All right, I agree with that," said Riker evenly. "And don't you think that's something that you should respect?"

"You're right. I *should.*" Grinning mischievously, she unfolded the paper and started to read it.

Riker moaned softly. "I really wish you wouldn't. I wasn't going to show it to you until it was finished. Hell, it'll probably never be finished. I'm terrible at things like that. I never even tried before. It's lousy. I—"

"Shhh!" She looked up at him with genuine irritation on her face. Then she returned to reading the paper, her lips moving silently to the words.

Riker made no further attempt to interrupt. Instead he made a great show of nonchalantly checking his chronometer and tricorder, and then nodding in satisfaction. He was, in fact, satisfied. They were late, that much was true . . . but within an hour they'd be at the rendezvous point, and from there it was only a short ride back to the city.

He worked up the nerve to look at her. She was studying him frankly, her lustrous eyes seeming to take in the whole of him. Just as she had taught him—and just as he had perfected over the past several days—he took in and let out a slow breath, clearing his mind with facility.

This is beautiful, Imzadi, she told him.

He smiled, inwardly and outwardly. *Do you really like it?*

You'd know if I were lying.

She studied the paper and read out loud:

"I hold you close to me.
Feel the breath of you, and the wonder of you
And remember a time
Without you
But only as one would remember
A bleak and distant nightmare
And you shudder against me in your sleep
Do you share the memory with me of dark times past?
And you smile
Do you share the memory of times to come?
The future holds such promise
And just as I cannot imagine how I survived the past
Without you
I cannot imagine a future
Without you."

"I don't know," Riker said, trying to keep the pride of authorship out of his voice. "I thought maybe it was a little syrupy."

"Oh, you thought no such thing," admonished Deanna. "You thought it was a perfect statement of how you felt. You were proud of it. In fact, you still are."

He grinned. "I should have known better than to try false modesty with an empath."

"Absolutely right. That will get you nothing except embarrassment."

"Speaking of embarrassment, we better get moving. We're already so late that that, in itself, is pretty damned embarrassing. Sergeant Tang's been in touch with me four times in the past two days, just to make sure that I'm still alive."

"It's nice that he's so concerned about you." She folded up the paper and tucked it in her bodice, and Riker looked at her in surprise.

"Aren't you giving it back to me?"

"Please don't make me. I'd like to keep it."

He sighed. "Only if you promise not to show it to anyone."

"Deal."

Forcing themselves not to yield to temptation, they went the rest

221

of the way without any more impromptu interruptions. They held each other's hand tightly, their fingers intertwined, and it was only when they were within sight of the encampment that they released their hold on each other, mutually deciding that it would probably look better if they didn't arrive at the rendezvous with the flush of new love upon them.

Tang and several other security people were waiting for them. The recovered art treasures of Betazed had already been sent on ahead back to the city and were safely ensconced back in the museum. Tang had also arranged for the bodies of the Sindareen raiders to be shipped back—without comment—to the Sindareen homeworld.

"Good work, Sergeant," said Riker approvingly. He turned and extended a hand to Deanna, who took it while maintaining as neutral an expression as she could. "This is Deanna Troi."

"Ma'am," Tang greeted her with a slight inclination of his head. Then he exchanged looks with Riker. If Tang had any inkling as to what had gone on in the Jalara Jungle, he gave no indication whatsoever. He was far too much of a veteran, in every sense of the word, to be that open with whatever was going through his mind. "You're certain that the leader of the raiders was attended to?"

"Oh, yes," said Riker. "It's not the most pleasant thing I've ever witnessed . . . but he's definitely attended to."

"Very well then, sir. Shall we go?"

"By all means, Sergeant."

The journey back to the city took relatively little time. All the way back, Deanna and Will exchanged only the most minimal of conversation, most of it carefully polite inquiries into the health and well-being of the other. But then, as they approached the outskirts of the city, Riker heard in his mind . . .

Why don't you come over to the house tonight.

Are you sure your mother wouldn't mind?

Mind? Deanna's voice sounded almost scoffing. *How could she mind? I imagine that she'll want to thank you for saving me. I'd like to have her more kindly disposed towards you.*

That would be nice. The thought of her being less kindly disposed towards me is a really chilling one.

"I want details."

Riker stared across Roper's desk at the senior Federation representative. "Details on what?" asked Riker politely.

"On what?" Roper looked incredulous. "The entire thing! What do you think?" He gestured toward the chair for Riker to sit down. "And don't hold anything back!"

With a shrug, Riker started to sit . . . and then, just on impulse, he swung the chair around and straddled it. "It was a fairly straightforward operation. We searched the jungle. I was fortunate enough to come upon the Sindareen raider before he had the chance to injure Deanna. He resisted my attempts to capture him and died in a mud pit. I brought Deanna to the rendezvous and she is, at this moment, safe and sound at home. End of story."

"No," said Roper, waggling a finger. "No, not end of story. You and her, out in the jungle. The steamy, romantic Jalara Jungle. You having just saved her life, her incredibly grateful. The atmosphere, the mood. Our bet. Our *bet,* dammit. You're not going to tell me that with all that falling your way, you didn't take the opportunity to . . . ?"

Riker sighed and said, "All right, Mark. I have to admit it."

Eagerly Roper clapped his hands together. "Tell me. Go on. Give an old man his vicarious thrills."

"I'm afraid I can't do that," said Riker slowly. "What I can give you is your two hundred credits."

Roper's face fell. "You're telling me that—"

"Pure as driven snow, Mark. And I grew up in Alaska, so believe me, I know what I'm talking about."

Roper sat back, his expression that of a child having just been informed that Santa's existence was, at best, a dubious proposition. "I can't believe it."

"Believe it, Mark. To use the old baseball parlance, no one bats a thousand. I gave it my best moves, but I'm afraid that it just didn't happen. And I'm tired of bruising my ego trying."

"I must admit," said Roper, shaking his head, "I'm just a bit disappointed. I generally can get a feeling about people, Captain. And despite my posturing to the contrary, I just had this gut instinct that you and Deanna would make a good couple. I've generally learned to trust that instinct. I hate to find out that I was that much off target."

"It happens to the best of us, Mark. As far as Deanna and I go, I'm afraid I just wasn't in her league. But look at the bright side. Sure, we both feel frustrated. But at least you're frustrated and got two hundred credits out of the deal."

"Is that supposed to make me feel better?"

"It's supposed to make one of us feel better."

Roper studied him for a moment, with Riker maintaining a carefully neutral expression. "You know what I think?" said Roper after a time.

"No, Mark. What?"

"I think that you are the most self-satisfied-looking 'loser' I've ever seen."

Riker smiled enigmatically.

CHAPTER 28

Riker stood at the entrance of the Troi mansion, waiting patiently for the door to open. But he waited for what seemed an extraordinarily long time before it finally did.

Mr. Homn wasn't standing there. Lwaxana was.

Riker smiled graciously. "Mrs. Troi," he said by way of greeting. She forced a smile, but did not step aside to allow him admission.

"Lieutenant," she said slowly, "I want you to believe me when I tell you this is not easy for me."

"What isn't easy, Mrs. Troi?"

"First, I have a moral obligation to thank you. You rescued my daughter from a very dangerous situation. You have, for that, my eternal gratitude and sense of obligation. I will always keep your heroism in mind whenever I think of you in the future."

"Thank you."

But she had clearly not finished. "Because of that, I am not using my considerable influence with Starfleet to see that you're severely reprimanded."

"I . . . I beg your pardon?" But even as he said it, the thought flashed through his mind in bleakest fashion: *She knows.*

Of that, Lwaxana promptly left no doubt. "Your subsequent

actions with my daughter were completely out of line. You took advantage of a very incendiary situation."

"What happened between Deanna and myself, Mrs. Troi," said Riker hotly, doing everything he could not to lose his temper, "was entirely mutual and entirely our business. I want to see Deanna." He started to step past Lwaxana.

She put her arms out rigidly and her voice was iron. "So help me, Lieutenant, no matter what obligation I have to you, if you set foot in here without my permission I will have you up on charges for criminal trespass. *Is that clear?*"

He halted in his tracks.

"I want to see Deanna," he repeated in a low but forceful tone.

"And do what? And say what? What do you have to offer her, Lieutenant? What, except a further dilution of her purpose."

"Further . . . ?"

She stamped her foot in anger. "Don't you understand anything? *Anything?* Do you have *any* comprehension of what you've shoved your way into the middle of? A line of obligation that stretches back centuries! Tradition that was already old at a time when your ancestors were still discovering the mysteries of footwear! Blast it, Lieutenant! Deanna isn't like the others! She isn't like the other women you've known! She isn't even like other Betazoids!" Lwaxana slapped one hand against her palm for emphasis. "Every step of her life has been mapped out for her! Her education, her career, her place in Betazoid society—all of it!"

"By you," he said tonelessly.

"Yes, by me. Of course by me. You think I'm eager to shoulder that responsibility? No, Lieutenant. No, I'm not. But I do it because it's my obligation and I accept it. And Deanna has accepted hers, and her obligation and her future. And I'm telling you, Lieutenant, right here, right now, that it's a future in which you don't figure."

His gaze ice, he said, "That's for Deanna and me to decide."

"Oh, really," Lwaxana said, making no effort to keep the sarcasm out of her voice. "And where's that decision going to lead? Are you going to give up your career exploring the galaxy? Pass it up for a permanent position here on Betazed? Clip your star-faring wings? Trade in your space legs for walking shoes?"

"I want to see Deanna—"

"And where's that going to lead, Lieutenant?" Lwaxana continued relentlessly. "Are you really prepared to give all that up for Deanna? And if you do, then how long, Lieutenant? How long before the prospect of one planet wears thin on you? How long before the sight of the same old sun, rising and setting, day after day after day, weighs on you, chokes and suffocates you? How long before you blame Deanna for making you give it all up? A year? Two? Five? When the first rush of unbridled romance is faded, Lieutenant, and the fires don't burn anywhere near as hot as the stars that were once your home . . . what's going to happen then? Answer me."

Cold fury choked him and at first he couldn't reply. But then, in the hallway behind Lwaxana, he spotted her. She was standing there, near the bottom of the stairway, a haunted look on her face.

"Deanna!" he shouted to her.

Her hands moved in small, vague circles.

Lwaxana looked from one to the other, and then she said firmly, "Tell him, Deanna."

Deanna looked down, unable to put words together.

"Deanna," said Riker, and then he said, "Imzadi."

Lwaxana fired him a look that could have extinguished one of those blazing stars to which she'd referred moments before.

And Deanna now looked him square in the face. She stood mere yards away, but her tone and words made her seem much, much further.

"She's right, Will," said Deanna tonelessly.

"She's not right! She—"

"Sooner or later," continued Deanna, as if Riker hadn't even spoken, "you're going to want to leave. Your place is out there. Mine's here." She hesitated, then said, "I have to be adult about this. We both do. It's never going to get any better for us than it was in the jungle, Will. That was it. That was the high point. I . . . I want to remember it that way. Before your nature leads you to other places, other women . . ."

"Deanna," he said hopelessly, feeling as if she were fading from sight even as she stood there.

"Let it end on a high note, Will. Not in the downward spiral of a relationship gone wrong. Think about what we had. That's what's important. Because there's really nothing for us in the future. Nothing."

She turned on her heel without another word.

Imzadi, he hurled at her bleakly.

She didn't even slow down as she walked . . . no, ran from him . . . up the stairs and out of sight.

Lwaxana regarded him steadily. There seemed no triumph in her eyes, he thought, which was odd.

"No, it's not odd, Lieutenant," she replied to his unspoken thoughts. "I'm not some ogress. Believe it or not . . . all I want is what's best for Deanna. Perhaps if you have children someday, you will realize that watching out for what's best is not something that brings a great deal of pleasure. Sometimes—at times such as this one—it's a responsibility filled with much pain. As a Starfleet officer . . . William . . . this should not be a particularly alien concept to you. You've promised to assume responsibilities that are not always going to be gratifying: obeying the orders of a superior, even when you disagree. Or staying your hand in the name of the Prime Directive, even when your sense of morals would have you do otherwise. Well, you don't have to be in Starfleet to face such difficult moments. Deanna's facing one such now . . . and so am I. And believe it or not, I take no joy in it. Because it's causing my daughter sorrow, and I hate having to do that. But we all face our responsibilities, Lieutenant. We do what we have to do. I know and accept that, as does Deanna. And now I think it's time that you faced up to that as well. Good day, Lieutenant."

The door closed in his face.

CHAPTER 29

The Scotch burned as it went down Riker's throat.

He had gotten it from Tang. The sergeant had seen Riker's bleak mood when the young Starfleet officer had returned from the Troi homestead and without a word had extracted the bottle from his private stock, offering it to Riker with the contention that it could make everything go down more smoothly . . . frustration, pain, hurt, whatever.

Riker stared at the bottle, then gripped it firmly by the neck. He had looked at Tang and asked, "Are you interested in joining me?"

Tang had placed his hands behind his back and rocked on his heels thoughtfully. "Frankly, sir," he had said after a moment's thought, "I don't think you'd want me there. There are times when a man just wants to get stinking drunk on his own."

Riker had nodded. "Sergeant, you're wise beyond your rank."

"Thank you, sir. All part—"

"—of the service," Riker had finished along with him.

Now Riker, alone in his quarters, poured himself another glass. He resisted the impulse to just swig it directly from the bottle. Somehow such action didn't seem remotely in keeping with Starfleet decorum. He was sure that somewhere, in some regula-

229

tions book, he had read that rule one of being an officer was that an officer always drank from a glass.

He tossed back another shot and tried to remember what in hell had gotten him so upset in the first place.   ‥

"Deanna," he said out loud, and consequently reminded himself.

What in hell had he been thinking of, anyway? Getting involved with a local that way. That kind of thing never led to anything but trouble. And not just involved, no. He'd actually had to go and get . . . *feelings* for her.

"Not feelings," he muttered to himself, and tried to take consolation in that. Yes, that had to be it. He hadn't *really* felt anything for her. Not really. It had all been . . . been self-delusion. An attempt to convince himself that there was some sort of genuine love for her rattling around in that brain of his, because that was the only emotion that *her* type would accept before they would get to the really *worthwhile* part of a relationship. Yes, the worthwhile part, which was . . . which was . . .

He frowned. "What was the worthwhile part again?" he said.

The door chimed.

Riker tapped his communicator. "Riker here." He waited for a response.

The door chimed again.

Again Riker tapped his comm unit. "Riker here," he said with growing irritation.

"Will?" came the voice of Wendy Roper through the door.

"Speak up, Wendy," he told the communicator. "We have a lousy connection."

"Will, I want to see you."

He shrugged. "Sure. Come on over."

The door slid open and Wendy entered. Riker blinked in surprise. "That was fast."

Wendy didn't quite understand what he was talking about, but didn't pretend to. "I heard you were upset about something, Will."

"Nonsense!" he declared, rising slowly to his feet. "Do I sound upset?"

"No. Actually, you sound drunk."

"Drunk!" said Riker indignantly. "That, young woman, is an ugly rumor, spread by people I've tripped over."

She giggled slightly at that. "Well, if you are drunk, at least you're funny about it. Daddy sticks mostly to Synthehol when he drinks."

"Synthehol!" sniffed Riker. "That stuff's for infants! You'll never catch me drinking that Ferengii garbage."

He circled his room, taking slow and steady steps that were a bit exaggerated. Without any preamble, he turned to Wendy and said, "She wasn't even that good-looking!"

"Who?"

"Her! Her . . . her nose was too long. And her mouth was too wide. And . . . and her cheekbones were too high. Frankly . . . she was ugly."

"Her who?"

"Someone I knew. Or thought I knew." He dropped down onto the edge of the bed and stared off into space for a moment. Wendy sat next to him, waiting for him to say something else.

"You know," he said after a time, "you get in your head this . . . this picture of the way you think things are going to go. And they never match up. Nothing ever turns out the way you think it's going to."

"I know how that is."

He looked at her. "You do?"

"Of course I do. Fate's always kicking you in the teeth."

"But why me?"

"Not just you." She almost laughed at the persecuted look on his face. "Everyone. I've had my share of busted romances. And my dad—well, how do you think he took it when my mom died?"

"Not well?"

"Not well at all. He was wrecked up about it. But just because fate kicks you in the teeth doesn't mean you have to grin and give him more targets. You fight back, that's all. You just let him know that you're not going to take it. You're just not."

"She didn't understand," said Riker bleakly. "I thought she did, but she didn't. She can't see anything beyond this . . . this lousy little planet. A whole galaxy of opportunity, and she's got her head buried in the sands of Betazed. . . ."

"Not me," said Wendy firmly. "I'm not living out my life here, you can bet on that. Not on this overphilosophized ball of rock. Uh-uh."

"No?"

"No. No attachments for me. No strings. I want my freedom," Wendy said with fire in her voice. "Another year or two here, tops. Then I'm gone. Diplomatic corps, maybe. An attaché or something. Or who knows? Maybe I'll just hitch. See the galaxy. Grab rides on star freighters, doing odd jobs for passage."

"No attachments."

"No strings."

He stared at her. "Has anyone told you," he said, feeling an extremely pleasant buzz in his head, "how terrific you look?"

She grinned. "Not for a long time."

"And"—he paused—"has anyone *done* anything about how terrific you look?"

"Not for an even longer time."

He kissed her, feeling giddy. She was warm and supple against him. Undemanding. Yielding. Wanting nothing more from him than he was capable of giving.

He broke from her for a moment. "What do you think of art?"

"Boring."

"Thank God," he said, and they sank down onto the bed.

Lwaxana sat in her favorite chair in the study, reading and feeling totally relaxed. Deanna sat at a desk nearby, surrounded by texts for various psychology courses.

"What are you studying, Little One?" Lwaxana called to her.

Deanna did not respond.

Lwaxana turned to look at her and saw that Deanna was staring off into space. *Deanna,* she tossed into her daughter's head. Deanna looked up, and Lwaxana continued, *What are you studying?*

"Oh." Deanna looked blankly at the texts in front of her. She held one up. "Human dysfunctions."

"Well," Lwaxana said with a faint smile, "we've certainly had our up-close-and-personal study of that for today, haven't we."

"Mother, that's not nice," said Deanna tightly.

"You know," Lwaxana said with a thought, "you might be able to get some genuine use out of your extended contact with him— purely on a clinical basis. He's a fascinating study in obsessive behavior, don't you th—"

Deanna rose from her chair and started across the study. "I'm going out."

Immediately Lwaxana frowned, getting up from her chair. She didn't precisely block Deanna's way, but Deanna was definitely going to have to go around her. "It's late," Lwaxana said.

"I think I'm a little old for a curfew, Mother."

"Maybe. But not too old to exercise common sense. You're going to see him, and don't bother trying to lie to me."

"It was too abrupt, Mother. It—"

Lwaxana raised a stern finger. "It was exactly as abrupt as it needed to be. It's what you both needed. Simply dragging things out would have done neither of you any good. It's over. It's finished. That's it. Now go back and study."

"Mother, I don't want to. I can't. I—"

I don't care what you want, Lwaxana's voice echoed sharply in Deanna's head for emphasis. *Do as I tell you!*

Deanna took a step back, a physical reaction to the mental rebuffing. Then her eyes narrowed, her fingers rolled up into tightly clenched fists.

"You don't, do you," said Deanna carefully. "You don't care what I want."

"I care about what's best for you—"

And with such force that it seemed as if the air molecules crackled, Deanna hurtled a blistering, *NO YOU DON'T, MOTHER!* right at Lwaxana.

Lwaxana staggered, paling under her makeup. "How dare you think at me that way! To imply that I—"

"I'm not implying it, Mother! I'm saying it outright!" For a moment Deanna felt as if her courage were going to falter, and then she realized that if she'd been able to face up to the fear that had pervaded her in the jungle, then this should be easy in comparison.

It all burst from her at once. "For years, Mother—*for years*— while you've done whatever you wanted, wherever and whenever you wanted, you've told me what I'm *supposed* to do, what I *have* to do. And you keep telling me it's for me, all me. But it's not for me, Mother! It's for you! It's to satisfy *your* needs and *your* desires and *your* decisions. You've never asked me whether I care about any of these so-called responsibilities! You've never cared! You just . . . just assumed that I would embrace them because they were important to you. Well, they're not important to me, Mother! I'm sorry! I don't want to hold the sacred chalice! It's all yours! Make wind chimes of the Holy Rings for all I care!"

"Deanna—!" Words could not begin to express the shock flooding through Lwaxana. "I'd have sooner died than talk to *my* mother this way!"

Deanna didn't stop. She was afraid that if she did stop, she'd never have the nerve to start again. "I want my own priorities, Mother!" She thudded her fists against her own bosom for emphasis. "I want to make my decisions! My choices! Not yours. Not hundreds of years worth of tradition. Mine! I'm entitled to that! Every single thing I've done, I've done because you've made that decision for me! So when do I get a chance, Mother? When do *I* get to make decisions about careers and opportunities and marriages? *When?*"

"When you have a daughter! Just the same way that I did!"

Deanna gaped at her mother, appalled. "I can't believe you said that."

Lwaxana was silent.

"I cannot believe that you said that," repeated Deanna. "Generation after generation, women not being allowed to think for themselves . . . perpetuating that pattern, child after child . . ." Deanna drew herself up. "It stops here, Mother."

"It's that Riker," Lwaxana said angrily. "He put these thoughts in your mind."

"No, Mother. The thoughts were always there. I just never had the nerve to say them. And what's worst of all is, you knew they were there. You must have known. You knew that I was unhappy, and that didn't stop you from doing whatever you pleased with my life, counting on my obedience and 'dutiful daughter' mind-set."

"I knew that when you were older, you'd understand—"

IMZADI

"Well, you were wrong, Mother."

Deanna walked around Lwaxana and headed for the door. Her mother turned and called out, "You'd take him over me!"

Deanna spun and shouted back defiantly, *"Yes!"*

"You can't do this! You have studies . . . duties . . . a destiny!"

"I want to be with him, Mother! I was wrong to let you intimidate me into submission again. I was wrong to let him just walk away. We can't go back to the way it used to be, Mother. It's not going to happen. It would be a lie, and I won't live a lie!"

Lwaxana placed her hands on her hips and said sarcastically, "And what are you going to do? Quit your studies?"

"Probably."

"Marry him?"

"Maybe. Maybe not. Maybe I'll just go with him, be happy to be near him. When he ships out for his next assignment, I'll try to sign on. Some sort of job, I don't care what. Chief cook and bottle washer—it doesn't matter as long as we're together."

"You on a starship?" Lwaxana said, appalled. "A beautiful, free creature like you, cooped up in a ship for years? Millions of light-years away from home? It's insanity!"

"I've thought about Starfleet for years. A life of adventure, of experiencing minds and philosophies beyond what I have here. But I never really considered it as an option. Now, though, I understand. There's a galaxy of possibilities out there—even for a daughter of the Fifth House, if she simply has the nerve to take them. And who knows? Maybe I won't join Starfleet. Maybe I'll go back to geology. Maybe I'll paint myself blue and become a naked dancing girl in the Zetli system. But whatever I do, it will be *my* choice, not yours."

Deanna headed for the door, and in her head she heard, *If you go out that door, don't come back.*

Deanna went out the door.

CHAPTER 30

Deanna entered the embassy, which was quiet since it was after hours. But she stumbled upon several security men, whom she remembered from having met them in the jungle at the rendezvous point.

"Evening, miss," said Sommers, nodding slightly.

"Hello. I'm . . . I'm here to see Lieutenant Riker."

"Yes, miss. I'm sure you are," Sommers said. "You know the way?"

"Oh, yes."

He waved her past and Deanna disappeared down the hall. Sommers whistled softly to himself. "The officers get all the women."

Deanna went straight to Riker's quarters, her heart pounding. She had envisioned what he would say, what he would do. He was going to be so proud of her. The way that she had stood up to her mother, the way that she had taken control of her life. He would congratulate her, he would be thrilled at her love for him, he would take her in his arms . . .

She walked into his quarters and stopped dead in her tracks.

The room was only partly lit, but she could see Riker was lying in bed, naked. His uniform was tossed in several places around the room. He was asleep . . . and curled around the naked form of a woman whom Deanna immediately recognized as Wendy Roper.

Deanna made no sound, but her mind screamed in embarrassment and mortification.

It was more than enough to awaken Riker.

He sat up, confused and disoriented. He also sat up much too quickly because he was solidly hung over, and for a moment he thought his head was going to ricochet across the room. He sputtered uncomprehendingly . . . and then he saw Deanna, standing in the doorway, backlit by the hall light.

It took him a moment to reach the full realization that this wasn't a dream, or for that matter, a nightmare. "Deanna?" he said in a voice that sounded distant and ill.

She wanted to run shrieking down the hallway, but there was no way that she was going to retreat in that manner. "My apologies, Lieutenant. I seem to have come at a bad time. Perhaps if I'd called ahead, you might have been able to fit me into your schedule."

Her tone made Riker's hair hurt. "Deanna," he said again, and started forward. But his coordination was way off and instead he crashed to the floor.

The noise awakened the stone-cold-sober Wendy, who sat up in confusion and looked around. She saw Deanna, blinked in mild chagrin, and pulled the blanket around herself.

"Deanna," Riker began again. He grabbed at his uniform and started to pull it on.

"How nice. You have a thorough command of my name," she said, her arms folded.

"This isn't what it seems." Then Riker looked at Wendy, and the rumpled bed, and back to Deanna. "All right, it is what it seems. But I . . . you said you didn't want to see me anymore. You said we were finished and—"

"And it had been less than twenty-four hours since you'd had female companionship, so naturally you got over me. In fact, not only did you *get* over me, you practically *vaulted* over me," Deanna said, her voice getting louder.

Riker made shushing noises, which only prompted her to raise her voice more. "Are you afraid someone will hear?" she demanded.

"No," he whispered. "It's just . . . my head hurts."

"I'm sorry about your head," she said, not sounding remotely sorry. "I won't burden it further."

She spun on her heel and walked away. Riker, his uniform disheveled, nevertheless ran after her. He caught up with her halfway down the hallway and spun her around.

"You said—" he began.

"I know what I said. And would you like to know what I said to my mother? I told her I'd been wrong to toss you away. That it was time for me to find my own path. And that I wanted that path to be with you." Hot tears welled in her eyes and she fought them down. "But I foolishly assumed that you wanted that as well."

"I do—"

"No, you don't. I crawled out on a limb for you, and you chopped it off behind me."

"It wasn't like that. I wasn't thinking straight, and Wendy showed up, and—"

"And it was an opportunity."

"Yes."

"And it didn't really mean anything."

"That's right."

"And how do I know," she said icily, "that our time together didn't fall into the same categories?"

He took her by the shoulders. "You know that it didn't."

"I thought I knew that. But now I'm not sure. And what's worse, you're not sure either. Will . . . I thought we had something special. The physical and the spiritual. But for me, one hinges on the other. For you, it doesn't. And I don't think that's ever going to change for you."

Riker felt something slipping away from him, something very important—more important than he could have guessed—and suddenly, desperately, he wanted to save it. "I can change," he said. "I can—"

"Not overnight. Maybe someday, but maybe not ever. It may be, for you, something that can only come with maturity. I can't hinge my life on maybes. Because you're going to go away and I have to make decisions, and I can't base those decisions on uncertainties."

For a moment he bristled. "You sound so damned holier-than-thou. How do you know how it's going to be for you? Maybe as you mature, *you'll* change. Maybe you'll decide that you don't have to be heels over head in love in order to be intimate with someone. Maybe you'll discover that the physical side can have its own rewards, now that you've allowed yourself to experience it."

"Perhaps," she said evenly. "But there's one thing of which I'm reasonably sure at this point."

"Oh, really? What?"

"That you're not going to be there to find out."

He tried to think of a response to that, but before he could, she put a hand to his cheek and said, sounding not angry, but simply sad, "I'm sorry, Will. I just don't think there's a future for us."

And she turned and walked away.

Riker stood there, unmoving, watching her go. Wanting to say something, but unable to. Perhaps it was the drink still buzzing in his head, or perhaps there simply were no words . . . or even thoughts.

He turned and there was Sergeant Tang, leaning against a wall and regarding him thoughtfully.

"You were right to let her go, sir," said Tang. "Mark me, there's a twinkling star for every broken heart that a Starfleet man leaves—"

"Shut up, Tang," said Riker, and walked past him, heading back to his quarters.

Tang, unruffled, merely nodded. "Shutting up, sir. All part of the service."

Deanna Troi peeked into the study, sensing that her mother was still there.

Lwaxana was staring at a small holograph. She said nothing to Deanna, but Deanna sensed that her mother was not mentally wishing her to stay away. Tentatively, she entered the study and peered over her mother's shoulder.

"That's Grandmother, isn't it," said Deanna.

Lwaxana merely nodded.

There was a long silence, and then Deanna said, "I just came to get some of my things."

Her mother stared at the holograph for a time longer and then said, "You know . . . when I said that if you went out the door, you couldn't return . . . the words sounded familiar somehow. I racked my brain trying to remember where I'd heard them."

"And did you?"

"Mm-hmm. My mother"—Lwaxana waved the holograph slightly—"said it to me. When I told her I wanted to marry your father."

"She had her own plans for you?"

"Of course. Just as you are promised to Wyatt, I was promised to . . . what was his name?" She paused, and then remembered. "Stahly. That was it. But when we were of the proper age, we met for the first time, and . . . well, things just didn't . . . work out."

Deanna hunkered down next to her mother, fascinated. Lwaxana had never spoken of this before. "Why not? Didn't you like each other?"

"Oh, we got on quite well. I liked him, he liked me. But . . . I knew moments after we were introduced that it was hopeless. For one thing . . . he was in love with someone else."

"Another woman?"

Lwaxana looked at her bleakly. "Another man."

All Deanna could say was, "Oh."

"The hell of it was," admitted Lwaxana, "they made a cuter couple than we did."

Deanna tried not to smile. "It must have been very difficult for you."

"Well, fortunately it was shortly after that that I met your father. But my mother was stung by the lack of success for her match, and so she rejected out of hand whomever I brought home. We had an explosive argument about it. She disliked everything about your father."

"As much as you dislike Will Riker?"

"Oh, no . . . my dear, you thought I was difficult?" Lwaxana laughed mirthlessly. "She was much worse. Much much worse.

Because to her, it was a matter of wounded pride. The notion that I could find a mate for myself where she had failed. And when I stormed out, through that very door, in fact"—she pointed to the front door—"she told me that I shouldn't bother coming back. Oh, she didn't mean it, of course. Well . . . maybe at the time, she did."

"And did you mean it when you said it to me?"

Lwaxana regarded her thoughtfully. "At the time." Then she spread her arms. "Oh, Deanna . . . I'm so sorry."

Deanna leaned forward and her mother embraced her. "Sorry for what, Mother?"

"Sorry because I know what happened when you went to see Lieutenant Riker. I mean . . . a mother knows these things."

"Especially when a mother can read minds."

"That's true. And also . . . I'm sorry because you were right about something. About how . . . things between us have changed. And we can't go back to the way they were."

"Why are you sorry about that, Mother?"

"Because I *liked* the way things were," said Lwaxana plaintively. "It was nice, simple, uncomplicated." But then she sighed and patted Deanna's hand. "But it wasn't what you wanted. I understand that. And I really am *not* an ogress, Deanna."

"I know, Mother."

"I just ask one thing. Please . . . please don't become a naked blue dancer on Zetli. It's so chilly there, I can guarantee you, you'll catch your death."

"All right, Mother." Deanna smiled. "Tell you what. Not only do I promise not to become a naked dancer of any color, but I'll stay with my psychology studies. Although . . . I don't rule out Starfleet as an eventual outlet for my career."

Lwaxana appeared about to object, but instead she simply nodded her head. "Whatever will make you happy, dear."

"Thank you, Mother."

"You know, it's so late at night, and you ran out without having dinner. You must be starving."

"I . . . am a little hungry," admitted Deanna.

"Would you like something to eat?"

"That'd be nice."

As soon as Deanna said it, she realized she'd misspoken, and she thrust her hand forward and put it gently over Lwaxana's mouth before her mother could bellow for Mr. Homn.

"Mother," she said softly, "I'll make my own dinner. In fact, if you'd like, I'll even make something for you."

Lwaxana looked thunderstruck. "Yourself?"

"Yes, Mother."

Lwaxana let out an amazed breath. "You *are* full of radical ideas today, aren't you. All right . . . let's go." She stood and looked around, momentarily confused. "Now . . . which way is the kitchen?"

Deanna took her by the elbow. "I'll show you, Mother," she said with a smile.

Lwaxana shook her head as Deanna led her off. "Children nowadays and their crazy notions. Starfleet. Cooking. I don't know what the world is coming to. . . ."

CHAPTER 31

Roper looked up as Riker walked slowly into the café. "You're late, Captain," he admonished him.

Riker just nodded . . . very slowly. He sat down and the waitress brought some black coffee over to him unasked. He was silently grateful.

"I hear," said Roper casually, "that there was something of a brouhaha last night."

"Something like that." Riker didn't even want to ask him where he'd heard it. Either it was from one of the security men describing the idiot behavior of a senior officer, or else it was from Roper's own daughter describing the aftermath of an assignation. Either way it wasn't something he wanted to dwell on.

"Planetside relationships can get somewhat tangled, eh?" said Roper. "That's the advantage of being in a ship. Hit and run, as it were."

Riker just nodded and let the coffee flow into his veins, reestablishing some measure of coherency.

"You must be happy about getting out of here."

Something about the phrasing caught Riker's attention, burrowing through the alcoholic haze. "I've . . . I've got at least another month here."

But Roper shook his head. "I thought you'd heard. *Hood* repairs finished faster than anticipated. You're out of here in twenty-four hours, Captain."

Riker felt a charge in his head as if a life-support system had come on line. "You mean . . . you mean I'm shipping out?"

"That's right. So you'd better get yourself shaped up. There's paperwork for you to finish up. Forms to be filled out, reports on the Sindareen business. Got to have everything tied off nice and neat before we kick you loose."

Riker stood quickly, tossing the coffee down his throat and trying to ignore the fact that, in so doing, he'd just burned himself. "Mark—Mark, thank you. This is great news. This is . . . ."

Mark pumped his hand and said, smiling, "When you're out carving yourself a career, just think about us poor planet-crawlers every now and then, okay?"

"I will, Mark. You can bet on that."

"Then get a move on, Captain."

Riker released Roper's hand and bolted out of the café. Mark watched him go and then sighed. "Kids."

Everything had been attended to.

Almost.

Riker told himself that he was making a final stop at the art museum to verify for himself that everything was back in place and restored to order. After all, Starfleet would want nothing to be overlooked.

But he found himself standing for an overlong time in front of one particular painting: the one Deanna had showed him, the one with all the large concentric "goopy" swirls.

He stared at it.

Then he heard the music floating from nearby. And somehow, in a way that he couldn't quite explain, the music seemed to enhance what he was looking at.

As if dancing to the notes, the colors began slowly to swirl. It bore a striking resemblance, Riker realized, to stars swimming about in a sort of galactic whirlpool. No, not just stars . . . stars and planets, and perhaps . . . perhaps that was something like what the universe had looked like in the throes of creation. Void and miasmic and filled with promise and possibilities . . .

He sensed her standing next to him. But he couldn't turn to face her.

"You're leaving," said Deanna.

"Yes."

"I wish you safe voyage."

"I wish you . . ." He stopped and found the strength to look at her. He had turned quickly, and for a moment his mind's eye superimposed the flow of the painting over her. For one insane second, she was, literally, the center of his universe. "I wish you could come with me," he said at last.

She shook her head. "You know, Imzadi . . . for a time there, I was ready to change my universe for you. But now . . . now I don't think either of us is ready for that."

He tried to say that she was wrong, but he couldn't. So instead he tried to find some way to say good-bye. But he couldn't do that either.

He turned and looked back at the painting. Such vastness that encompassed everything there was . . . and yet somehow, now, it seemed completely empty.

"Deanna." He turned back to her. "Maybe . . ."

But she was gone.

He hadn't even said good-bye. Dammit, he'd said nothing to her . . . because he hadn't been able to find the words. And so he'd blanked his mind, and now she probably thought that he didn't care all that much. If he were able to part from her with such apparent ease, without even a word . . .

He took a step in the direction he was sure she had gone . . . but then stopped. Because he knew, beyond any question, that this was the way she wanted it. And somehow, somewhere along the way, what she wanted had become more important to him than what he wanted.

CHAPTER 32

Captain's Log, Stardate 42372.5:
  Of the twenty-four hours Q allotted us to prove ourselves,
eleven have now passed without incident. And yet I cannot forget
Q's prediction that we will face here some critical test of human
worth.

As the *Enterprise* continued to orbit around Cygnus IV, Commander Riker sat across from his new captain in the ready room. Both of them were equally concerned about what they perceived as oddities on Farpoint Station, but neither was certain precisely how to proceed.

The thing that Riker was pleased about, however, was that Picard had so clearly accepted him without reservation. Once Picard had welcomed him aboard and set out the ground rules, it was as if the captain had left any sort of doubt behind him. Unlike other commanders under whom he'd served, Riker felt no pressure that he had to impress Picard. Instead Picard was clearly going to deal with him in a straightforward, no-nonsense manner. It was an attitude that Riker welcomed.

Studying his notes on Cygnus IV, Riker said, "This planet's

interior heat results in abundant geothermal energy, sir. But it's about all this world *does* offer."

Picard looked thoughtful. "And it's your belief that this is what made it possible for them to construct this base to Starfleet standards?"

"Yes, sir." Riker leaned forward. "We have to assume that they've been trading their surplus energy for the construction materials used here. According to our ship's scans, many of the materials used are not found on this world."

Picard smiled slightly. "Perhaps it's like those incidents you describe in your report as 'almost magical' attempts to please us."

From any other captain, that might have sounded patronizing. But Picard was merely stating the facts. Accordingly, Riker nodded. "Those events *did* happen, sir."

"And in time we'll discover the explanation. Meanwhile, none of it suggests anything threatening. If only *every* life-form had as much desire to please Starfleet."

Riker knew what Picard meant. With the Ferengii to contend with, not to mention the Orions, the Sindareen . . . plus the ever-present notion that the Romulans might be heard from again . . . there were certainly enough hazards for the Federation to deal with. And then this Q had shown up, whose actions Riker had reviewed earlier, just to make things even more difficult.

Picard rose. "Ready to beam down? I'm looking forward to meeting this Groppler Zorn."

Riker waited for Picard to come around the desk. After Riker's big speech earlier about being protective of the captain, he wasn't thrilled that Picard was immediately going to beam down and meet with the head of Farpoint Station. If there was some unknown danger, it would be extremely bad if that danger suddenly became known in the course of Picard's visit planetside. Still, there appeared to be no jeopardy at the moment, and so Riker kept his counsel. As Picard preceded him to the door, Riker said, "I'm convinced there's more to it than just 'pleasing us,' sir."

Picard looked thoughtful. "Like something Q is doing to trick us?"

As they stepped out toward the turbolift, Riker noticed the

turbolift door opening. His view of the occupant was momentarily blocked by Picard's raised arm as the captain gestured and said, "Over here, Counselor!" He turned to Riker and said, "I've asked her to join us in this meeting."

A ship's counselor. Riker had never served on a ship large enough, or on a long enough mission, that a counselor was required. Besides, the position was a relatively new one to Starfleet, only having been developed over the last few years. Since Riker had unbounded confidence in his own mental balance, he doubted that he'd have much need for a counselor's services, but thought a lot of people on the *Enterprise* could probably make good use of one. He just hoped that he or she wasn't going to be one of these excessively cerebral types who tried to read something into everything that was said, no matter how casual.

Now Riker had a clear view of her . . . and he felt all the blood drain from his face. Picard had turned to the woman and was saying, "May I introduce our new first officer, Comdr. William Riker. Mr. Riker, our ship's counselor, Deanna Troi."

Picard was now looking back at Riker, and his tone changed slightly as he saw the expression on his first officer's face.

Ten years it had been, but the old feelings flooded over him with the same sting as if the wound were still fresh.

She had her hair back up in that tight knot—the one that was so unflattering—that she'd worn when she wanted to discourage any advances from him. She'd known . . . *she'd known* . . . he was going to be here. Of course she would have. As a counselor, she would have reviewed the files of all the senior officers.

His mind was running riot. He was out of practice, *years* out of practice. He'd been caught completely flat-footed.

Deanna, for her part, looked utterly serene. And then there was that sensation, the one that he'd thought he'd never experience again. Her voice in his head, in his soul, as she asked, *Do you remember what I taught you, Imzadi? Can you still sense my thoughts?*

She was so smooth, so collected, that even as she thought-cast to him, she extended her hand formally. "A pleasure, Commander," she said, placing a slight emphasis on the rank.

Riker took her hand and said, "I, uh . . . likewise, Counselor."

From Riker's flustered expression, Picard now knew that something was definitely up. "Have the two of you met before?" he asked Riker.

Met? Oh, nooo . . . just had one of the most involving, intense, frustrating, and torrid relationships I've ever had with anyone. That's all. Out loud, he simply said, "We . . . we have, sir."

Riker wasn't sure whether Picard had picked up on the subtext of the statement and tumbled onto just how well Riker and Troi knew each other, or if he was simply assuming that they'd become acquainted on some previous occasion. All he said was, "Excellent. I consider it important that my key officers know each other's abilities."

Riker wasn't sure, but he thought he could hear Troi's silent laughter echoing in his brain.

"We do, sir," Troi assured him. "We do."

Picard stepped into the turbolift, and Riker and Troi followed him silently.

There was so much he wanted to say . . . so much he wanted to tell her. But his mind awhirl, and out of practice as he was, he couldn't find any way to project the thoughts to her. And now they would not have the time to speak privately before being thrust into a new and hazardous situation. A situation in which they would have to interact smoothly and professionally. But would that be possible, considering all that they had been through together? And considering the way they had parted, with so much left unsaid? Did she know he cared? Did she know the things he had wanted to say? Or had she been nursing a grudge all these years, not understanding how . . . ?

And then, there was her voice again, in his mind, carrying her thoughts to him like a dove finding its home. *I, too, would never say good-bye, Imzadi.*

Relief washed over him. He should have known better. He should have known that she would understand, and that there was indeed going to be a basis on which to build a relationship.

He wasn't sure where that relationship would go, or what its ultimate fate would be . . . but at least whatever happened in the future, they would be facing it together.

It had taken them some time to work it out. At first the impulse was to pick up where they had left off . . . but they found quickly that they couldn't. Too much time had passed, and neither of them could find some way to bridge that gap and reconcile the young people they had been with the Starfleet officers they were now.

Nor were they sure what would happen should they rekindle the passion that had burned so brightly. If things didn't work out, then it would be extremely difficult for them to work with one another without a great deal of tension. And there was a very distinct possibility it might not work out, for their predictions about each other had been remarkably on target. Riker still tended to have a roving eye. And Troi had indeed come to appreciate the pleasure of experimentation . . . so it wasn't as if she had lived like a monk in the intervening years.

With all the complications that came with becoming lovers again, they had decided simply not to rush things. Neither of them was willing to risk everything to stoke the embers of their relationship.

"Time has a way of working things out," Deanna had said to him. So they gave the relationship that time.

They did not, however, give the relationship much of anything else. And the laws of inertia tended to govern human interaction along with most other things. As their years together on the Enterprise *rolled past, their relationship, since it was at rest, tended to stay at rest.*

The only force that could have acted upon them to change it would have been the idea that they might not be able to alter the course of things anytime they felt like it. Then again . . . why should they have considered that possibility?

After all . . . they thought they had all the time in the universe. And then came the peace conference with the Sindareen . . .

CHAPTER 33

Riker lay on his back, staring up into the darkness of his quarters.

His hands were interlaced behind his head, the pillow soft under him. He had been that way for over an hour, as sleep refused to come.

Sorting out his feelings was rapidly becoming something of a royal pain. He still remembered that time a couple of years ago, in Deanna's quarters . . . Both he and Deanna had been in an extremely mellow mood, and he had also been allowing the more relaxing qualities of the Synthehol he'd consumed to have sway over his actions. A friendly good-night kiss had turned into something far more passionate, and for a moment they had been kissing each other eagerly, hungrily, and it had been just like the old days.

And then Deanna had whispered, pleaded, telling him that they shouldn't, reminding him of the difficulties of involvement while both served on the same ship. Yet even as she spoke, she would have let him . . .

But he pulled back. Her words had penetrated the Syntheholic haze on his brain and washed it away, bringing with it instant sobriety and a reminder of the line that they had drawn for themselves.

And nothing had happened.

Not that he hadn't wanted it . . . they had both wanted it . . .

But what had they wanted? Momentary gratification? Or something more . . . a rekindling of something that they had thought they'd left behind them?

Perhaps they'd been kidding themselves. Here he was someone accustomed to command situations, and here she was someone who was always in touch with feelings. So it was only natural that they would decide that they could control their feelings, dictate their relationship. Turn their emotions on and off like an old-style light switch.

How realistic was that, though? Lying there in the darkness, imagining Deanna at that moment, wrapped in the arms of Dann, laughing or saying things softly . . .

Did she say the same things to Dann that she had to Riker?

For a moment there he had actually been drifting off, his feelings about Deanna lulling his brain and convincing him that everything would seem more clear in the morning. And then something, some impulse, made him sit bolt upright in bed, moving so swiftly that he had a momentary sense of disorientation.

Someone was there. He didn't know how, he didn't know why . . . but someone was there, hiding in a corner, lurking in the darkness.

He called out, "Li—"

But he didn't get the word out.

A hand clamped over his mouth and shoved him back down onto the bed.

Riker struggled fiercely, shoving at the arm that held him down. He reached upward, grabbing at his assailant's face, feeling skin that was like parchment and a bristling beard.

And then a voice said, "Lights!"

Riker froze. Because the voice sounded insanely familiar.

The lights came up on command. He blinked against the sudden brightness and the voice amended, "Half lights." They dimmed 50 percent, and now Riker could make out the features of the intruder.

The hair and beard were thick and gray. The skin was wrinkled and timeworn. But the eyes burned fiercely with determination, and the face . . . the face was unmistakable. He was looking up at himself . . . except he was decades older.

"Shut up!" hissed the elder Riker. "We haven't much time."

Riker's eyes were wide with stupefaction. For one moment he thought he might still be sleeping, and he started to struggle again, tried to shout over the hand that was clamped on his mouth.

"Didn't you hear what I said?" snarled the old man. "Shut up, you idiot! They may be here to try and stop me at any moment! So lie still! Listen to me, and be prepared to do exactly what I tell you. Deanna's life hangs on what you do next."

THE MIDDLE

THE MIDDLE

CHAPTER **34**

The curator of the Betazed national archives shook hands with Admiral Riker and bowed slightly in acknowledgment. "Your donation of Lwaxana Troi's effects will be quite a boon to our collection, Admiral."

Riker smiled indifferently. "I'm glad I could be of service, sir. And now . . . if you'll excuse me, I believe that my transport back home is here."

"Ah, yes," said the curator. "I understand the *Enterprise* herself has come to get you."

"Just happenstance." Riker smiled evenly. "It was the closest ship. It's not as if I'm anyone particularly important."

"Oh, now, Admiral, let's not sell ourselves short. Some of us still remember your handling of the Sindareen raiders all those years ago. They stayed well clear of Betazed after that." The curator frowned. "Although it's a pity . . . they've become much more aggressive in the last decade or so. My understanding is that they've resumed many of their warlike ways. Truly a shame."

"Yes," agreed Riker, at this point anxious to just get out of there. He felt as if he would say just about anything to escape.

At that moment the air hummed a few feet away with a familiar sound, and Riker grinned openly. It was rare that he smiled these days, but when he did, it was genuine.

"Commodore Data," he said evenly. "It's a pleasure to see you again. You haven't aged a day."

Data cocked his head slightly. "Why would I, Admiral?"

Riker chuckled silently. "You may have gotten the hang of a lot of things since I first met you, Data, but humor still eludes you. Comforting to know some things don't change."

"I'm sure it is." Data turned and indicated his second officer. "You remember my science officer, Lieutenant Blair."

"Yes, of course," said Riker, and shook Blair's large, furred hand. "Well, gentlemen . . . shall we get going?"

"Whatever you say, Admiral . . . if you're done here, that is."

Riker looked at the curator questioningly.

"As far as I'm concerned, Admiral, we're finished. Oh," the curator added as an afterthought, "a woman stopped by . . . Wendy, I believe she said her name was . . . and said that you should stop by and say good-bye before you leave."

"We can wait if you wish, Admiral," offered Data.

But Riker just shook his head. "No," he said softly, and the general melancholy that routinely hovered over him these days enveloped him once more. "No, I've never been particularly good at saying good-bye on this planet."

Data didn't pretend to understand. He merely tilted his head and said, "Enterprise. Three to beam up." And a moment later, with a crackle of blue energy, they were gone.

When Riker first set foot on the ship that bore the name of that vessel he'd once served aboard, he felt a rush of pleasure. But it was quickly borne away by the realization that this wasn't really that Enterprise . . . that there would never be another one like it. It had been a unique, special time in his life, and . . . he realized bleakly . . . probably the high point. Certainly nothing since then had come close to approaching the pure joy and wonder that that particular assignment had given him.

He was more than happy to inspect the ship, examine all the various new and exciting wrinkles that had been added. Ultimately, though, once all that had been done, he was more than content to sit in his cabin, alone and comfortable with the loneliness to which he'd grown so accustomed.

It was in this state that Data found him when he came to inform Riker that they would be arriving shortly at Starbase 86.

"Thank you, Data," Riker said simply upon being given the news. He went back to staring out the viewport.

"You seem to be preoccupied, Admiral," observed Data.

"I'm watching the stars." Riker smiled thinly. "Did you know, some people believe that whatever happens to us is decided by the stars. That we have no control over our fates. I think Shakespeare even wrote that 'the fault is in the stars.'"

"Actually, Admiral, that is incorrect."

"You're going to tell me that it's ridiculous to believe that interstellar phenomenon could possibly have any sort of effect on the affairs of men?"

"No, sir. That's so self-evident it's not even worth pointing out. No, I was simply going to tell you that your endeavor to quote Shakespeare was not only imprecise, but in fact wildly wrong."

"How wildly?"

"If you're quoting the passage I believe—namely *Julius Caesar,* act one, scene two—then you have reversed it. The proper line is, 'Men at some time are masters of their fates: The fault, dear Brutus, is not in our stars, but in ourselves, that we are underlings.'"

"Really? Huh." Riker thought about that a moment. "Hell of a thing to screw up. Who said it?"

"Shakespeare, sir. You were correct about that."

"No, I mean, who in the play?"

"Cassius, in conversation with Brutus. Two of the conspirators who assassinate Julius Caesar."

"Hmm. Ironic, isn't it, Data? Men who try to decide they're going to take their fate into their own hands . . . and the only way to do that is to try and kill a man whom they admire."

"It has always been a great puzzle to me how people can do utterly immoral things in the name of morality. Certainly the philosophy of guiding your own fate is a laudable one. But how can anyone applaud the notion of murder?"

"Sometimes, Data . . . you do what you have to do. You just make a decision that something has to be done and damn the consequences."

Riker said nothing further, and even though Data simply stood there, watching him, Riker didn't feel any need to comment. "My standing immobile in this manner once bothered Captain Picard greatly," Data said after a time.

"Did it?" Riker shrugged. "Data, you'll find that nowadays, there's very little that bothers me."

"Is it because of Deanna Troi?"

Riker turned and looked up at him. "Ancient history, Data," he said in a hollow voice. "Very ancient."

Data seemed pensive, which was most unusual for him. "I am aware of something, Admiral, that—if you take it in the proper frame of mind—might serve to put much of your long-standing frustration to rest."

"Really?" Riker was more amused than anything else. "And what precisely do you know, Data?"

Data paused, and his next words were the last that Riker could possibly have expected.

"What would you say, Admiral, if I informed you that . . . somewhere . . . Deanna Troi is still alive."

The statement hung there for a moment, untouched. And then, to Data's surprise, Riker actually smiled again. "Data, you're turning philosopher on me."

"I am, sir?"

"You're about to tell me that Deanna lives on in our hearts and minds and memories, right?"

"No, sir. She lives on in an alternative time line."

Riker's smile was frozen, but the rest of his expression was an utter blank. Finally he said, "Data, what in hell are you talking about?"

Data sat down across from Riker, endeavoring to select the method of explanation that would be simplest for Riker to follow.

"Our stop right before Betazed," began Data, "was at the world of the Guardian of Forever. You're familiar with it?"

"Of course," said Riker impatiently.

"In the course of my visit there, the scientists showed me a temporal irregularity they have discovered. These irregularities are known, interchangeably, as alternative time lines or even parallel universes. There have been several encountered in Federation history. For example, the alternative universe and/or time line wherein the Klingons and Federation remained at war, from which Tasha Yar crossed over and eventually became the mother of Sela. Then there was the alternative universe and/or time line which James Kirk and several of his command crew encountered that was a 'mirror' representation of our—"

"I know all that! Dammit, Data, what does any of this have to do with Deanna?"

"It has to do, sir, with how these alternative universes and/or time lines—"

"Stop saying it that way! It's getting on my nerves! Pick a term and stick with it!"

Data blinked. Riker was showing more fire and anger in the past five minutes than he conceivably had all during the past five years. "It has to do," Data began again, "with how these time streams . . . ?" He paused on the last word, adding a slight interrogative to his intonation to see whether or not Riker approved of the terminology. The admiral nodded and gestured for him to continue. "It has to do with how these time streams are begun. No one knows how many there are; perhaps an infinite number. But apparently they key off of significant moments in time. *Focal points* was the term that then–science officer Spock coined, I believe. James Kirk's Edith Keeler, who inadvertently lived when she was supposed to have died, represented one such focal point. The constant surveying of the events that the Guardian displays will sometimes reveal one of these offshoots."

Riker swallowed hard. "And they've . . . they've found one involving Deanna?"

"That's correct, sir. Curiously, it revolves around the moment of Deanna Troi's death at the Sindareen peace conference. In the alternative time stream, Counselor Troi in fact did not die."

"How did she survive?" Riker's voice was barely above a whisper.

"They have been unable to make that determination. What they have discovered, however, is that the counselor was present at the peace conference . . . and her empathic abilities were able to discern that the Sindareen were lying about their peaceful intentions. Once she uncovered their duplicity, it was quickly learned that the entire peace conference was a scheme to use Federation resources to rebuild so that they could, years down the line, launch new and devastating forays against the Federation."

"Which they wound up doing."

"Yes, sir, in our time stream—the 'correct' one, for want of a better term. In our time stream, the Sindareen are a powerful and formidable people. In the alternative time stream, however, the Federation refused the peace initiative, pulled out, and the Sindareen economy eventually fell apart completely. At that point, the Federation then stepped in with restoration efforts, but under far more controlled and less trusting circumstances. The Sindareen were able to rebuild, but were a far more docile and chastened race."

"And Deanna lived." Riker looked to Data, his eyes sparking like flint struck together. "She lived."

"Yes, sir. So you see, Admiral . . . you can take heart. Although the counselor's death was an unfortunate and tragic thing, there is a 'cosmic justice' of sorts . . . a sense of balance. For in an alternative time stream, Deanna Troi lived and accomplished great things."

Riker was silent for a long moment . . . and then he seemed to be muttering to himself. Whispering. His voice was a low and gentle singsong, and it sounded as if he were trying to reason something out.

"Admiral?"

Riker started to get to his feet and put a hand out to Data. The android assumed that Riker needed his help getting up and so lent him support. But then Riker's hand closed on Data's shoulder with a fierceness that might have been appropriate to a man less than half his age, and he whirled Data around, galvanized by inner fires.

"Turn the ship around," Riker said hoarsely.

"Admiral?"

"You heard me. Bring us back to Betazed. Fastest possible speed."

"Sir, I'd like to be as accommodating as possible, but I don't understand why—"

With a red-hot fury, and a voice like iron pounded on a forge, Riker shouted, *"Turn the goddamn ship around, Data! That's a direct order from a superior officer. Do it now, or so help me, I'll have you relieved of command and I'll steer us back there myself!"*

CHAPTER 35

It took a day to get all the clearances from the Betazed government. But Data did it as quickly as he could because he was of the firm conviction that if he didn't get an official release for the body of Deanna Troi, then Admiral Riker might very likely go down and bring the body back himself. In the current state that he was in, he was probably single-minded enough to haul the corpse onto his back and find a way to carry it piggyback to the *Enterprise*.

Riker had lapsed into silence, but that silence was hardly benign. He fairly radiated urgency, bordering on controlled desperation. He stood there and watched as Deanna's body, still in its encasement, materialized on the cargo transporter. It floated on small, controlled waves of antigravity emanating from floater units that had been attached.

Data, Blair, and Chief Medical Officer Hauman, along with two medtechs, were all waiting there for it when it arrived. Hauman, tall and gangly with thick brown hair, looked at his commanding officer questioningly. "Sir, am I understanding this correctly? You want me to run an autopsy on a four-decade-old body?"

"That is the plan," Data said with as close to a sigh as he was capable of producing.

Riker put up a hand. "Hold it," he said as the medtechs came around to move the encasement. "Hauman . . . run a tricorder scan. Look for life signs."

Hauman stared at Riker, then at Data, and then back at Riker. "Are you expecting me to find any, sir?"

Riker looked at him coldly. "I'm expecting you to follow my order."

Hauman did as he was told, passing the small unit over Deanna's body. "Nothing. Not so much as a blip. I'm sorry, Admiral, but this is a forty-year-old corpse. Nothing more."

"It's something more than that, Doctor," said Riker. "It's a hope in hell. Now get her . . . get it . . . down to sickbay."

"What am I looking for, if I might ask."

"Cause of death."

"Sir, wouldn't that be in the autopsy performed at the time of the death?"

"Yes, it would," said Riker, sounding amazingly reasonable. "So what I want you to do is pull that autopsy from the records."

"And then?"

"And then," said Riker, "look for something that isn't there."

While the autopsy was performed, Riker stayed in his quarters. He had an inkling of what autopsies used to be like, back in the primitive days of surgical knives and catguts. Cutting up the body, studying each of the organs, searching through and running tests while a nauseating stench filled the air.

Deanna's body would not be cut or harmed. A battery of tests would be run without mussing a hair on her head. Nevertheless, Riker couldn't find it within himself to stand there while Deanna's body was treated like a large slab of meat . . . no matter how comparatively delicate that treatment might be. He'd gone through it once. Twice would be unendurable.

He stared down at Betazed, which turned under them in leisurely fashion. *Imzadi,* he whispered to someone who had not been able to respond for nearly two generations. *Imzadi . . . tell me I'm not losing my mind.*

There was a buzz at his door and he said urgently, "Come in."

Data entered with Dr. Hauman at his side. Data's face was, as always, unreadable. But Riker could immediately tell from Hauman's expression that something had happened. Something had occurred that had surprised the good doctor. That alone was enough to give Riker hope. "Well?" he demanded, waggling his fingers impatiently. "Tell me."

"It's, um . . ." Hauman looked uncomfortable. "It's . . . extremely puzzling."

"What is?"

"It would appear, Admiral," Data said, "that we have something of a paradox on our hands."

"Oh, really. Explain it to me, if you'd be so kind. No . . . better still . . . I'll explain it to you."

Riker rose from his chair and faced Hauman. "You found," he said slowly, "traces of something that didn't exist at the time of Deanna's death."

"That's . . . that's correct, sir," said Hauman. Not only did he feel foolish that his previously expressed doubts over the point of this exercise were now without foundation, but he felt even dumber over the fact that Riker was apparently one step ahead of him. "We found minute traces of Raxatocin . . . so minute that the medical equipment of the time would not have been able to detect it. It wouldn't have even shown up as an unknown substance."

"Raxatocin," said Riker slowly. "That's a poison, isn't it?"

"Yes, sir. It . . . well, it causes precisely the types of symptoms that killed Counselor Troi. Massive circulatory collapse. It was developed thirteen years ago, and as recently as five years ago it was still undetectable."

"How is the poison transmitted?"

"Any number of ways. Injection. It can be ingested. In sufficient concentration, it can even be inhaled."

"All right." Riker took a deep breath. "Has Deanna's body been returned to the proper authorities?"

"Yes, sir," said Data.

"Good. Okay, Mr. Data." Riker clapped his hands together and then rubbed them briskly. "Take us to the Guardian of Forever."

There was a dead silence in the room, and then Data turned to

Hauman. "Doctor, I thank you for your time. That will be all. And make certain the file on Deanna Troi is sealed."

Hauman nodded. Riker stared at Data and said, "What?"

Data raised a finger, indicating that they should not say anything until Hauman left. Riker waited impatiently until the doctor was out the door, and then he said, "What's the problem here, Data?"

"Admiral . . . I didn't want Dr. Hauman here because, frankly . . . I was afraid that you would say things that would be incriminating and I didn't want there to be a witness who had less loyalty to you than I do."

"Incriminating? Data," Riker said, trying to keep his anger down, "what do you mean? Isn't it obvious what's happened?"

"I blame myself, sir. I tried to tell you something I hoped would give you some measure of peace. But instead it is moving you toward thinking the unthinkable. It's obvious to me, sir, what's going to happen. You intend to try and step through the Guardian of Forever. To go back in time and save the life of Counselor Troi, and by doing so, change history."

"No, Data. Fix history. Don't you get it?" Riker started to pace the room, unable to contain his excitement. "She wasn't supposed to die! Someone went back, from right now, or maybe even years in the future. And they poisoned her!"

"We don't know that."

"We *do* know that! The poison came from the future! Maybe our future, or perhaps her future which is our past, which is . . ." His voice trailed off. "Give me a minute. I get confused sometimes when I discuss time travel."

"I understand what you're saying, sir. But I must point out that Raxatocin has been known to occur in nature, even before it was developed as a poison. It's possible that somehow she acquired it through some unique and bizarre combination of circumstances."

"Remotely possible, but not likely. I'm telling you, Data, you were absolutely right about her being a focal point in time. But it's the reverse of Edith Keeler. Deanna wasn't supposed to die. She was supposed to live. Our world, this world—it's not the 'correct' time line. It's the wrong one!"

"And your hope is that, if you're allowed to go through the Guardian of Forever, you'll have the opportunity to set things right."

"That's correct."

Although Data's expression didn't change, it was clear that a great deal was running through his mind. And all of it involved trying to determine some way to deal with this new and bizarre situation.

"Admiral . . . you cannot be allowed to do it."

"I'm giving you a direct order to—"

But Data shook his head. "No, sir. Not this time. It's not going to work, and pulling rank is going to be of no use whatsoever. Starfleet regulations in this matter are very, very specific. Ever since the first *Enterprise* slingshot back through time and proved that it could be done, a set of specific guidelines were developed regarding time travel. And the foremost of those guidelines is, no tampering."

"Dammit, Data, someone *already* tampered!"

"We can't be certain of that. What we can be certain of is Starfleet regulations—"

"The hell with regulations!" Riker stood barely two feet from Data, his fists clenched, his temper flaring beyond control. "Deanna's life is at stake!"

"Deanna has no life, Admiral. Deanna is dead." Data's calm was a striking contrast to Riker's fury. "She has been dead for four decades. Her death helped determine the universe in which we've lived all these years."

"Then I don't want to live in this universe. I want to cross over, like Tasha did."

"That's not possible, Admiral. And if you enter the Guardian, you put at risk the lives and reality of uncounted innocent people. Many things have happened since Counselor Troi died. I've evolved, both in terms of self-expression and in command ability. You have your Starbase to command."

Riker laughed bitterly.

"Wesley has his own command," Data continued. "Geordi, Worf, Alexander . . . all of them have lived their lives as the fates have determined. People have been born and died for forty years since the death of Deanna. Things have happened as they were meant to happen. You cannot now suddenly flip open the books of history, erase what's been written, and reinscribe it with a story more to your liking."

"I could go before Starfleet—"

"That's certainly your prerogative," agreed Data. "But I do not foresee any instance where Starfleet will be willing to risk sacrificing all reality for the sake of one woman."

Riker was hushed. Sensing that perhaps he was getting through to him, Data pressed on. "Have you considered something, Admiral? You say that all you wish to do is save Deanna. But have you considered the possibility that—even if you accomplish your task—you might, in the midst of doing it, make matters worse? With knowledge of forty years' worth of events, you could easily say something, do something, that has either an immediate impact or an influence further down the time stream. If knowledge is power, then knowledge of the future is the ultimate power. No one, Admiral . . . not you, nor I . . . no one has the wisdom to wield that power. The nontampering rule of time travel is in place for just as solid a reason as the Prime Directive. And as in the case of the Prime Directive, it may be something that's difficult for us to live with . . . but it is, nonetheless, necessary."

Riker stood with his back to Data. And Data could see, slowly but surely, a lot of the fire and spark slowly draining from him. His shoulders slumped, his posture drooped. His hands, which had been tightly curled around the edges of the table, slackened.

When he spoke, it was with the air of defeat that he had carried with him all these years. "She is just one woman, isn't she."

"Yes, sir. And you, sir . . . are a conscientious and ethical man. You would not put at risk an entire reality . . . for the sake of one woman."

"All right, Data," Riker said tiredly. "You've convinced me. Maybe it's . . . maybe it's time I just realized that I have to let go."

"I think, sir, it would be for the best."

Riker turned to face him, and there was the same despondency that Data had seen when he picked up Riker on Betazed.

"Take me home, Data," he said quietly. "And we'll let Deanna rest in peace."

The second return trip to Starbase 86 was uneventful. There were no more sudden outbursts from Admiral Riker, no more abrupt flurries of activity. He stayed in his cabin the entire time. Several times Data went to him, tried to engage him in casual conversation about routine matters of policy, or sought his advice on various topics that had come up in the normal course of activity.

In each instance, Riker's replies were terse and to the point. He did not try to drive away companionship, but he did not welcome it. He simply . . . existed. Data noted that Riker didn't seem interested in meeting the world on any sort of terms.

For a time, Data was concerned that Riker was making some sort of plan to head for the Guardian of Forever the moment he was dropped off at 86. Although Data hated resorting to subterfuge, he nevertheless sent his ship's counselor to try to draw out Riker on what was bothering him. The admiral was not particularly responsive, but that didn't matter. He didn't know that the counselor was a full Betazoid who, upon being told that urgent matters were at stake, forced himself to probe more deeply—albeit very gently—than he would normally have.

He reported back to Data and the account was precisely what Data had hoped to hear. "He is rather despondent, Commodore," said the counselor. "But if I had to select any single word that would most describe him at this moment, I would have to say . . . resigned."

"Resigned to what?"

"Resigned to whatever years he has left. Resigned to his life. For all intents and purposes . . . he's given up."

To a large measure, this was good news. And yet, Data could not help but feel a great sense of loss upon hearing this. As if he had somehow passed a sentence of living death upon his friend.

When he informed Riker that they had arrived at Starbase 86, the information received the merest nod of acknowledgment from him. He packed his bags quietly, and Data accompanied him to the transporter room.

"If it's all the same to you, Admiral," Data said, "I'd like to beam down with you."

Riker shrugged. "The space station is open to everyone. Why should the commander of the *Enterprise* be excluded?" It was the longest single sentence he had uttered in twenty-four hours.

Lieutenant Dexter was waiting for them at the transporter platform of the starbase and gave that customary, slightly puckered smile that he specialized in. "It's good to have you back, Admiral. I trust everything went smoothly on Betazed?"

"Fine." Riker nodded his head in Data's direction. "You know Commodore Data?"

"Actually I don't believe we've had the pleasure," said Dexter, shaking Data's hand.

Riker stepped around them and headed for his office. Dexter started to follow at his heels, but Data held him slightly back and spoke in a low undertone. "The admiral went through something of an ordeal on Betazed. I would be most appreciative if you could keep a close eye on him for the next few days."

"What?" said Dexter nervously, casting a surreptitious glance at Riker. "He's not sick or anything, is he?"

"I don't believe so. But he is quite dispirited. I would strongly suggest that you make every endeavor to proceed with business as usual. And if he should do anything out of the ordinary . . . please contact me via subspace radio."

"All right. Consider it done, Commodore."

"Thank you." In a slightly raised voice, Data now called out, "Admiral—I must return to the *Enterprise*. If I can be of further use . . ."

Riker stopped and turned, looking at Data sadly. "No, Commodore. I believe you've done more than enough." And he entered his office, the doors hissing shut behind him.

Dexter shivered slightly. "Now that is someone who is in a very bad mood."

"Yes," confirmed Data. "Unfortunately, the mood has persisted for forty years."

* * *

"And the *Chance* will be arriving by this time tomorrow," said Dexter. "We're prepared for restocking. Oh . . . and Starfleet sent another reminder about processing paperwork on time."

Riker regarded Dexter with a steady gaze. "Tell Starfleet," he said thoughtfully, "that we'll speed up the paperwork as soon as they send us paper."

Dexter blinked owlishly. "Sir . . . no one really uses paper anymore, to any great degree. It's . . . it's just a phrase, sir. Relatively speaking."

"Fine. Then tell Starfleet that we'll be processing our figurative paperwork on time . . . relatively speaking. Time, after all, is relative."

"Yes, sir," said Dexter tiredly.

"Is there anything else?"

"No, sir," said Dexter, tapping his computer padd.

"I didn't think so," said Riker slowly. "There wouldn't be, would there. Same old thing. Day in, day out. And time passes."

"Yes, sir." Now Dexter was starting to sound nervous. "Admiral, are you all right?"

"I'm fine." Riker sighed loudly. "Just fine."

Dexter nodded and then backed out of the office, taking as much time as he could to watch Riker. Riker, for his part, had his chin propped up on his hand, but spared a moment to toss off a cheery wave at Dexter before the door closed.

And then he was alone.

He swiveled in his chair and looked out at the stars. The *Enterprise* had departed orbit around the space station, off to whatever their new great adventure was. For there was still adventure out there, that much was certain. Still a big galaxy with a lot going on. Just not a lot that interested him.

He heard it behind him.

Tick.

    Tick.

        Tick.

The grandfather clock. His pride and joy.

His symbol of the passing hours.

He watched the pendulum slowly, ponderously, swing back and forth. Back and forth.

Like a large, heavy scythe. Slicing through the air, cutting through time, minute by minute, cleaving it neatly. Each second unaffected by the previous second, and uncaring of the next. Every second was the same to the pendulum.

Nothing mattered.

It just marked time.

Tick.

Tick.

Tick.

The sound grew louder in his head, louder throughout his entire being. The sound that reminded him that this was it, that time was unyielding and pointless and there was nothing to be done about it, it was just there, that's all.

The cogs of the clock irrevocably moved against each other, each tooth engaging smoothly and flawlessly, unheeding of anything except its relentless clockworks.

And he saw her.

In his mind's eye, he saw Deanna, lying there on one of the cogs. The teeth of the cogs calmly integrated, and without uttering a whimper she was mashed in between. The cogs moved on and spit her out, her remains littering the clockworks, and nothing mattered because she was just another piece of garbage to be crunched and tossed aside.

Tick.

Tick.

Tick.

With a barely controlled scream of rage, Riker grabbed the grandfather clock from behind and, with all his strength, shoved. The heavy clock toppled forward and crashed to the ground like a giant redwood, the crash virtually exploding throughout the space station. Glass shattered, wood cracked and splintered, and there was the eminently satisfying sound of clockworks screeching to a halt, cogs and wheels skittering out and across the floor and rolling in small circles before clattering to a halt.

Dexter ran in, alarmed at the racket, and saw Riker standing over the mess, his fists clenched and a crooked smile on his face. Riker looked up at him and all he said was, "Whoops."

When the surveying ship *Chance* arrived barely twelve hours later, Riker was ready.

CHAPTER 36

The *Enterprise* 1701-F was halfway to its next port of call when a subspace communication came in that immediately got Commodore Data's full attention.

"This is *Enterprise*," he said when the computer's automatic hailing program informed him of the incoming message and the point of origin. "Go ahead."

"Commodore Data?"

It was precisely the voice Data would have preferred *not* to have heard. "Yes, Lieutenant Dexter. Computer, on vid."

A three-dimensional image appeared directly in front of Data, projected there by a free-floating chip. It was Dexter, and he wiped his brow with considerable discomfort. "Commodore, we have a problem."

"Specify."

"It's the admiral."

Blair and Data exchanged glances. "Is he ill?" asked Data.

"No. He's gone."

"Do you have any idea as to where?"

"Not in the slightest," said Dexter, sounding uncharacteristically put out. "He beamed up to the *Chance,* supposedly for some sort of routine business. The next thing I knew, the *Chance* had blown out of here at warp three . . . with the admiral."

"Have you endeavored to contact them via subspace?"

"Oh, I've endeavored, all right. They don't answer. They're maintaining total radio silence."

"Yes," said Data, sounding extremely practical. "They would. The admiral would make certain of that."

"But why?" demanded Dexter. "Why? What in hell is he doing? Commodore, do you have any idea?"

"I have an excellent idea, Lieutenant. However, it is only an idea . . . one that I would prefer not to bandy about unless I have confirmation. Thank you for alerting me to the situation. I will attend to it. *Enterprise* out."

Dexter's image blinked out of existence before he could get out another word.

Data swiveled in his chair to face Blair, who said worriedly, "You know where he's going, don't you, Commodore. It's connected with what happened on Betazed, isn't it?"

Data felt the worried eyes of all his bridge crew upon him. He wished that somehow he had been able to impress on the admiral that all these people, these people right here, had something at stake in the way that things were. But Data had not been able to do so, and now the best he could do was to perform damage control.

And he would have to perform it no matter what the cost.

"The top speed of the *Chance* is warp six," Data said, accessing his thorough memory of all ships in the registry. "There is little doubt that they are heading for the Forever World. Helm, set course for the Forever World, warp eight."

"Course plotted and laid in, sir."

"Engage," said Data calmly.

The *Enterprise* leaped into warp space, and Data rose from the command chair. "Mr. Blair, come with me to the briefing room, please. We need to discuss worst-case strategy."

Blair followed his commanding officer into the ready room, and Lamont at conn looked over to Tucker at Ops. "You know," she said, "I don't know which is preferable. Not knowing what's going on . . . or finding out."

* * *

"Approaching the Forever World, Commodore."

Data had sat rigid and unmoving, staring intently at the screen, all of his considerable brainpower focused on the problem that awaited them. In an even more sedate tone than he usually used, he said, "Sensors. Is there another ship in orbit around the planet?"

"Negative," said Margolin at tactical, but then he paused and said, "No . . . wait. There's—"

The *Enterprise* was jolted slightly as they came within range of the time distortion ripples that were standard for the vicinity of the Forever World.

"—a ship in standard orbit," continued Margolin. "Markings and registry indicate that it's the *Chance*. Sorry about the confusion, sir. The time distortion ripples are especially—"

Once again the ship was knocked around, this time to a sufficient degree that automatic restraints snapped into place on the chairs of the bridge, holding the personnel firmly in their seats.

"—fierce," Margolin persevered, as if the severe buffeting were only a minor inconvenience designed to slow down the dissemination of information. "It's interfering with our sensors."

"Compensate, Mr. Margolin. Give me a hailing frequency to the *Chance*."

"You're on, Commodore."

"*Chance,* this is the USS *Enterprise,* please acknowledge."

There was no response from the smaller ship. There was, however, continued pounding from the waves of time distortion, and Data could practically sense time slipping away from him—in more than one sense of the word.

A second hail brought continued radio silence, and now Data gave an order that even he didn't quite believe. "Mr. Margolin," he said quietly, "arm phasers."

"Sir?" Margolin was thunderstruck.

They were all looking at Data with shock on their faces. Nevertheless, the commodore knew he had no choice. "Carry out my order, Mr. Margolin," he said quietly.

"Yes, sir," said Margolin hollowly. "Phasers armed and locked on target."

"Mr. Blair, inform the transporter room that you and I will be beaming down to planet surface within two minutes. Attention *Chance,"* Data continued, raising his voice and thereby activating the comm link. "Our phasers are armed and locked on you. Unless you respond immediately, we will be forced, in this state of emergency, to fire on you. Acknowledge or suffer attack. Acknowledge."

The intership radio crackled to life immediately. *"Enterprise,"* came an irritated gravelly voice, "this is Captain Tennant of the *Chance.* What in hell do you think you're playing at?"

"I believe," responded Data, "that the same could be asked of you, Captain."

"We're simply obeying orders," shot back Tennant, "as part of a confidential mission, the contents of which I am not at liberty to disclose. Not even to one of the flagship vessels of the fleet."

"Disclosing them would be pointless," Data said. "I have no doubt that they are utter fabrication. I would assume radio silence is one of those orders. One moment, please." Data turned to Margolin. "Are we within range of the Forever World yet?"

"Yes, sir."

"Raise them . . . Captain Tennant," Data continued the first conversation, "am I correct about the assumption of radio silence?"

"Yes, you are. And to be blunt, I'm jeopardizing the safety of that mission by conversing with you. But with the safety of my crew on the line, I decided to acknowledge your hail, in direct contradiction of my orders."

"Excellent judgment, Captain," said Data calmly. "Am I also correct in assuming that Admiral Riker is not there?"

"That is correct. He beamed down to the surface fifteen minutes ago. He told us to maintain orbit and radio silence."

"That does not surprise me."

"Sir," said Margolin, "we're unable to raise anyone on the surface."

"That also does not surprise me. Transporter room, can you lock on any life-forms on the surface? If so, I want them all beamed up immediately."

There was a pause as the transporter chief ran a quick scan. Then her voice came over the comm: "Negative, bridge. Readings are too sketchy. If someone is down there and gives us coordinates, that's not a problem. But as it is, I'd be afraid to try and lock on and bring something up. I might get nothing at all, or maybe a puddle of protoplasm. There's no predicting without solid confirmation."

"Very well. Mr. Blair," said Data, "with me."

Data crossed quickly to the turbolift, Blair right behind him. Almost as an afterthought, Data called out, *"Chance* . . . maintain position. We will inform you if there is anything you can do."

"Enterprise, would you mind telling us what's going on?" came the voice of Captain Tennant. "Admiral Riker said that we were being commandeered as part of a top-secret mission for Starfleet. He even had orders—"

"I'm sure he did," said Data. "I assure you, however, they were forged. You are on a mission, *Chance* . . . but it's not on behalf of Starfleet. It's on behalf of Admiral Riker."

"What? What in hell is this about, *Enterprise?"*

"Don't concern yourself about it, Captain Tennant. Whether the admiral's mission succeeds or not . . . either way, you'll never know. *Enterprise* out." And then he cut the transmission rather than waste more time.

After all, the entire conversation might end up being moot.

When Data and Blair arrived on the planet's surface, they discovered precisely what they thought they would find.

The bodies of the scientists were scattered about. A quick inspection revealed that they were alive, but clearly phaser-stunned. Riker must have secreted a small hand unit . . . perhaps several . . . on his person. He'd done it in such a way that Tennant hadn't known . . . otherwise he'd certainly have let *Enterprise* know about it.

What tissue of lies had Riker constructed? Data wondered as he and Blair quickly made their way across the compound. Sindareen scheme? Romulan incursion? Or perhaps the Ferengii were up to their old tricks? There was no end to the possibilities that an inventive mind could conjure, and Riker's mind was as inventive as anyone's.

Data scanned the entire area and came to an immediate realization. "Mary Mac is not here."

"Which means—"

"She's with him," concluded Data. "Odds are it's an unwilling accompaniment."

Above them the air swirled and crackled, and more than once lightning lanced across the sky. Data felt forces gathering around him, as if some massive, insane celestial experiment were in the works.

Quickly they ran through the compound, small bits of dirt and rock swirling around in whirlpools that moved, Data noticed, in opposite directions from one another. Somehow that seemed perfectly in keeping with the rest of the environment.

"He's crazy," Blair was muttering. "He's completely crazy."

"No, Mr. Blair," Data replied, speeding up slightly. "He's not crazy at all. He's merely determined, and certain he is doing the right thing."

The wind grew louder, and Blair raised his voice. "And what if he is? How do we know for sure?"

"We don't. But we cannot take the chance."

They raced to the top of an outcropping. Far, far in the distance, the ruins of the city were still there, as silent and unproviding of information as they had ever been. There below them was the Guardian of Forever.

The protective force field surrounding it was intact.

Riker, however, was on the inside.

So was Mary Mac. He had a firm grip on her wrist, but now she was struggling with the fierceness of her Orion heritage. Her teeth were bared, her fingernails flashing. Riker had been holding a tricorder, but it had clattered to the ground. Data saw that Riker needed both hands to keep off her savage onslaught.

She was shouting something that even Data, with his supersensitive hearing, couldn't make out over the howling of the winds. And then Data also saw, on the large screen that had been erected nearby the Guardian, events being played out that were horribly familiar. There was Deanna Troi, on the floor of her quarters, writhing and gasping, and a terrified and confused Commander Riker leaning over her, looking more helpless than he ever had in his life. On the ground nearby, the fallen tricorder continued to record the information with precision.

Data gestured for Blair to follow and the two Starfleet officers made their way quickly down toward the Guardian.

Mary Mac swung Riker's arm around and clamped down with her teeth. Riker howled in pain and slammed her in the face with as hard a punch as he could remember ever using. Mary Mac released her grip and staggered, wiping at the blood trickling down her mouth.

"You'll destroy *everything!*" she shouted.

"This 'everything' has no right to be!"

"You're not the one to make that decision!"

"Wrong! I'm the only one!"

She leaped at him again, a feral snarl ripping from her throat. Riker ducked and she sailed over him, and he stood quickly, catching her in midlunge. Before she could make a countermove, he deliberately threw himself backward and body-slammed her to the ground. He twisted quickly around while she was stunned and, giving it everything he had, slugged her on the side of the head. The green-skinned woman's eyes rolled up into the back of her head, and she went limp.

Quickly Riker felt under her chin and checked her pulse. He wasn't entirely sure what was normal for an Orion, but this felt strong and firm. Good enough.

He grabbed his fallen tricorder and forced himself to be dispassionate as he programmed it. Carefully, he began to calibrate the tricorder to the enlarged screen designed specifically to display the Guardian's readouts. The tricorder would be able to measure the speed of the Guardian's actual display against the time-delayed playback of specific moments as depicted on the screen. Once it was all fed in and cross-programmed, the tricorder would be able to tell him exactly when to jump through the portal.

There would still be no guarantee of 100 percent accuracy. But it was the only shot that Riker had. His determination was to try to leap through as close to the actual event as possible. He knew that the longer he was back in the *Enterprise* 1701-D, the more chance he had of affecting things he wanted to leave alone. So he had to bring himself as near to Deanna's death as he could without missing it . . . while leaving himself enough time to do something about it.

His fingers flew over the tricorder's controls, cross-referencing the two displays. He programmed in, basically, a countdown. When the correct moment was approaching, a small green light on the tricorder would snap on. The moment that happened, Riker had to leap through precisely five seconds later . . . a built-in delay factor, as he had calculated how long the actual, physical act of taking two steps forward and jumping through would require.

"Guardian!" he shouted. "The display I just witnessed—on my mark, begin again. Three . . . two . . . one . . . now!"

Images began to coruscate across the face of the Guardian of Forever. The same dizzying blur that Riker had seen before. The primary command had been simple: Riker had asked to see the history of the *Enterprise*. The Guardian had proceeded to show it—except that the display had begun with the first event that the Guardian had considered to be instrumental to the creation of the mighty starship. Unfortunately for Riker, that event had been the invention of fire. Images of beings that were barely recognizable as ancestors of humanity, clustered around a small pile of sparking wood, was hardly what Riker needed.

Fortunately enough, the Guardian was renowned for its speed. In an eyeblink Riker witnessed the creation of the wheel, the development of tools. They were wonders that, under other circumstances, Riker would have been spellbound to witness. As it was, he was merely impatient to get past them.

The tricorder's programming had brought it on line as soon as the Guardian began the playback. It hummed along silently, matching and timing the display. Inside its circuitry, the countdown had begun.

Riker patted the vial that he had hidden in his jacket.

"Admiral!" came the shout from behind him.

Riker spun, and he saw Blair and Data approaching. For a moment he was startled and even frightened that they would stop him when he was so near to his goal . . . and that he would never get another opportunity. But then he remembered the force screen that was serenely in place. "It won't do any good, Data!" Riker called. "My mind's made up!"

Data and Blair came to a halt just on the other side of the force field. Blair's thick fur was blown this way and that in the fierce windstorm that surrounded them. Data called out, "Is Mary Mac all right?"

Riker checked the Guardian. Leonardo da Vinci was stroking his chin thoughtfully, studying his designs for a primitive flying machine.

"She's fine, Data! She was less than cooperative when I forced her, at phaser point, to open up the forcefield. I told her I'd just stun her and used her handprint and retina pattern even if she was semiconscious. She chose to remain conscious, hoping that she could talk me out of this. And when she realized she couldn't, she seized a moment when I was distracted and tried to take me out. Damn near did, too," he said, rubbing the back of his neck ruefully.

"Admiral, you must turn away from this destructive course."

Riker glanced back at the Guardian. Alexander Graham Bell was just informing Watson that he needed him, and in an overlapping image, Thomas Edison was staring in wonderment at the glowing light in front of him.

"I'm going to save her, Data! For forty years, I've been eaten up by the thought that I should have done something! She begged me to . . . I promised that I would, and then all I did was stand there and watch her die!"

"She wouldn't have wanted this, Admiral! You're risking everything!"

"Don't you remember, Data?" called back Riker. "The name of James Kirk's autobiography?"

Data needed only a moment to recall it. "It was entitled *Risk Is Our Business.*"

"Damn right! I owe Deanna nothing less than to try everything! You hear me, Data? Nothing less!"

"Admiral, if you do not come out of there immediately, I shall order the *Enterprise* to open fire and use ship's phasers to penetrate the force field! You may very well be destroyed if that happens!"

"And the Guardian might be as well!" shouted back Riker. He took a step toward the time gate. Seconds before, a Saturn V rocket had been lifting off. Now Zephram Cochrane was about to activate the first warp drive unit. "Would you do that, Data? Would you risk destroying the Guardian? Don't you see, Data? You've longed to understand humanity! You've longed for a soul! Well, Mr. Data— the Guardian is the resting place of all the souls, throughout all time! It's God's window on eternity! Who are you to destroy it?"

And with icy calm, Data replied, "I have already contacted Starfleet, Admiral. Their orders were very specific. Protect the time stream, no matter what. Deanna Troi must die . . . and if it takes the destruction of God's window, then who better, Admiral, to assume that responsibility? After all . . . I am not one of God's creatures." And Data angled his head upward and said, *"Enterprise . . . target the shielding directly in front of me. On my command . . . fire."*

"Don't do it, Mr. Data!" called Riker with genuine pleading in his voice. "Don't kill Deanna!"

"I did not kill her, Admiral. But if maintaining the integrity of the space-time continuum were at stake, I would take her life with my own hands. I would derive no satisfaction from it. Indeed, the counselor was as dear to me in my own way as she is to you in yours. But I am prepared to accept that her death is a requirement in the natural order of things, and to preserve that order, I will do whatever I have to do."

Data had spoken with certainty and a sense of implacable decision. And Riker knew that lines had been drawn. "So will I, Mr. Data."

"Enterprise," said Data tonelessly. "Fire."

From orbit, the mighty phasers of the *Enterprise* cut loose. They struck the force field directly above Riker's head. The force field sparked and shimmered under the barrage, resisting the power of the weapons.

It was the strongest force field that Federation technology had to offer . . . on par with the deflector shields of the *Enterprise* herself. Furthermore, the Forever World had been equipped with its own heavy-duty defense array, protected by similar shields. If a hostile vessel had shown up, the scientists below could very easily have given a very formidable accounting of themselves—in all likelihood, blowing the attacking ship out of orbit.

But the *Chance* had not been a hostile vessel, and the renowned and esteemed Adm. William T. Riker was hardly considered to be a malevolent presence. It had been the scientists' error to take Riker's word that there was urgent Starfleet business to discuss.

By the time they had realized their mistake, it had been too late.

Data was trying to make up for that mistake now. He watched, stone faced, as the *Enterprise* pitted her phasers against the force field. That they would eventually penetrate, he had no doubt whatsoever. The question was whether they would break through in time.

Riker took a step back, watching the phasers with a sense of grim desperation. There was nothing he could do. He was trapped inside, and besides, getting out would simply put him farther from the Guardian. He heard a low moan behind him—Mary Mac was coming around. Perfect—that was all he needed.

The field began to buckle. He could see the power reserves straining, the field integrity collapsing. How incredibly ironic that here he was at the gateway to all time, and time was the one thing he did not have.

He glanced down at the tricorder.

The green light was glowing.

He emitted a horrified yell. He should have been standing in front of the Guardian the whole time, watching, monitoring, waiting for the signal to flash to life. Had it just come on? Had it been on for a few seconds?

Too far! his mind screamed. *Too far from the Guardian!*

He spun and charged at the gateway. The sand crunched beneath his boots. On the display face of the Guardian, he saw a brief image of Q dancing with Lwaxana Troi, and then Locutus threatening the ship, and it was all merging and blending together . . .

"Admiral, we will stop you!" came Data's voice, rising above the wind and the screaming of the *Enterprise* phasers, and he heard Blair's voice shouting something as well.

No time! No time!

Help me, Imzadi . . . the voice seemed to reach back through the years.

Riker leaped.

And then he was out of time.

Literally.

CHAPTER 37

Lieutenant Barclay stood in the holodeck of the USS *Enterprise* 1701-D and cracked his knuckles.

He knew that he shouldn't. He knew he might get caught. But the odds were slim. Captain Picard, Commander Riker, all the senior officers had been involved with a major diplomatic bash that evening. So the chances were that they wouldn't be anywhere near the holodeck that night.

Besides, he was off duty now. And he had pared down his holodeck activity to once a week. It wasn't interfering with anything important. And if he had his own ways of entertaining himself, well—as long as he didn't hurt anyone, and as long as he wasn't overdependent on it . . . well, where was the harm in that?

He had already informed the computer precisely what he wanted. Now he said simply, "Run program."

A moment later he was standing on a vast, grassy plain. Far in the distance, ancient Rome stood in all its glory. But right in front of him was a small temple, circular with tall pillars.

Standing in the middle of the temple was Deanna Troi. She was scantily clad in gauze, flowing robes. She extended her arms to him and in a musical lilt said, "I am the goddess of the mind."

Barclay started toward her, his voice robust and deep. "And I am the one who worships you . . . and whom you will worship in return."

And at that precise moment, something else appeared on the holodeck—seemed to just step right out of nowhere.

Barclay stopped, utterly confused. It was a man in what appeared to be some sort of uniform. It even looked vaguely like a Starfleet uniform, but the coloring was different and—

Then Barclay took a close look at the face.

"What the hell . . . ?" he breathed.

The new holodeck image, which appeared for all the world to be an older version of Riker, looked around in what seemed to be momentary disorientation. Then "Riker" turned, looked at Barclay, then to the image of Deanna, and back to Barclay. Riker put his hands on his hips and addressed Barclay with a voice of utter authority. "So . . . I should have known. Still at it, Lieutenant?"

In total confusion, Barclay called out, "Computer. Remove image of . . ." He wasn't sure what to call it. "Remove new image and run a systems check."

Riker merely stood there, showing no signs of disappearing. "I," he said, "am a holodeck failsafe, built in to monitor the types of programs you're engaging in, Mr. Barclay. I am *very* disappointed to see you still perpetrating such . . . bizarre . . . scenarios. I want it halted immediately." He pointed at Barclay sternly. "Is that clear?"

"Y-yes sir!" stammered Barclay uncomprehendingly. "Computer! Cancel this program! In fact . . . in fact, cancel all programs that I've created. As a matter of fact—cancel all my future participation in holodeck activities!"

Rome, its environs, and the image of Deanna Troi, all vanished back into the nothingness they had come from. The only things remaining in the room were the glowing yellow grids, Barclay, and Riker.

"Very good, Lieutenant," said Riker approvingly.

"Are . . . are you going to go now, too?" asked Barclay hopefully. He had no idea why, of all images, an older Riker had been chosen. But whatever the reason, it was a damned effective selection. He was totally unnerved by it.

"Yes, I'm going to go, too," said Riker. "And I'll tell you what. If you don't mention this incident to anyone, then I won't, either. We'll keep it just between us."

"Th-thank you, sir," Barclay said.

The image of Riker headed for the door. Barclay waited for it to vanish, as all holodeck creations did if they tried to leave the holodeck. Instead the doors hissed open obediently, and the elder Riker walked out, turned left, and headed down a corridor. The doors hissed shut behind him.

Barclay stood there for a long time. And then he went out, turned right, and returned to his cabin.

He didn't go near the holodeck for the rest of his stay on the *Enterprise*.

Admiral Riker walked quickly down the corridor, looking neither right nor left. He passed a couple of crewmen, some of whom did double takes upon spotting him. Perhaps they would assume that some uncle of Riker's had come to visit the ship, or maybe the commander was coming from some sort of costume function. He didn't slow down enough for anyone to get a really clear look at him, and he certainly didn't stop to answer any questions.

He had to get his bearings. Figure out precisely when he was. He could have asked Barclay, but he hadn't wanted the lieutenant to question his existence as anything other than some sort of confusing holodeck manifestation. It had saved him time—and he didn't know how much time he had.

He ducked into a room to his left that he knew was going to be vacant because it was one of the guest quarters. Once inside, he called out, "Computer! Tell me the stardate and time."

There were few moments in Riker's life that he could precisely remember down to the second of their occurrence. But the day and time of Deanna Troi's death was certainly one of those. He was able to recall the exact sound of Beverly Crusher's voice as she had labored to bring Deanna back to life. And when she had failed . . . when she had finally realized that nothing was going to help, and her best friend on the ship was forever gone . . . she had said, in a voice that sounded choked with dirt from a grave, "Record the time and date of death." The computer had obediently, and uncaringly, said it out loud for the record.

Riker had been standing there and had heard it—heard it punctuated by a choked sob from Beverly Crusher. There had been no noise from Riker himself—already the cloud was settling over him. The cloud that would cloak him for forty years.

Now, in the vacant guest quarters, the computer informed him of the day and time.

He felt his breath catch in his throat, the blood pounding in his temple.

He had hoped to arrive a day or two beforehand. Somehow, cautiously, make contact with Deanna. Inform her of what was to happen. Convince her, put her on guard. And even more importantly—give her the antidote for the poison that he had brought back with him, securely stored in his jacket.

He had known that it would be dangerous. Somewhere, somehow, Data might have sent people back, anticipating his moves. Trying to block his plans. But Data would have to be judicious—he didn't want to upset the applecart of time, and he would be very, very careful as to what he did and how he did it. Riker had anticipated that there would be something of a chess match of strategy, played out through the corridors of the *Enterprise* 1701-D.

But he had been wrong.

He didn't have time for subtlety. He didn't have time for finesse. What he had was twenty-three minutes.

Twenty-three minutes from right now, until the point where Deanna Troi would be lying on Beverly Crusher's medtable, a lifeless bundle of flesh.

"Damn!" he snarled.

He charged out into the hallway, resetting his chronometer, and bolted down the corridor, running full-tilt toward Deanna's quarters.

His arms pumped furiously, and as he turned a corner, his pounding footsteps alerted a security guard. The guard turned, and Riker didn't recognize him. That, in and of itself, didn't mean anything. Even when he was the second-in-command, he didn't necessarily know every single crewman on sight—particularly if it was a relatively new arrival. And he wasn't even the contemporary Riker—forty years had passed, and faces blurred with the years.

Then again—it might be someone sent back by Data.

The security guard frowned and started to reach for his phaser. "Hold it!" he called out.

Again, Riker had no way of knowing for sure. Certainly, with so many dignitaries presently on board the *Enterprise,* it would be standard operating procedure for guards to be on alert to anyone who didn't seem to belong there. And Riker certainly seemed out of place.

Then again—the "guard" might know precisely who the gray-haired man was, and what his mission was.

Riker raised an arm in front of his face to block the guard's view and slammed into him, knocking the younger man back before he could bring his phaser up. "Security alert, deck fourteen!" shouted the guard, and then Riker grabbed him up, pivoted, and slammed him headfirst into the wall. The guard went down, unconscious, and Riker scooped up his phaser.

Riker knew security would be all over the place within a minute. If Riker were to be captured, dragged down to the brig, interrogated . . . by the time he got everything straightened out, it would be too late.

There was only one person he could think to trust.

More to the point—there was only one person he could trust whose cabin was close enough.

The thoughts had gone through his mind so quickly that he was already dashing down a side corridor before the guard had even completely slumped to the ground.

A right, then another left, and he was standing in front of the cabin. He took a deep breath. The door was locked, which was not unusual when someone had retired for the evening. But his voice was still his voice, and he said briskly, "Computer, override lock and open for William Riker."

The computer checked that this was indeed the voice of William T. Riker, authorized occupant of the cabin, and consequently, the doors hissed open. The admiral stepped inside.

He heard soft breathing in the bed. He squinted, his eyes adjusting quickly to the darkness as the doors slid shut behind him.

He hadn't been quite sure how he would react upon seeing his younger self. He was pleased to discover that, for the most part, he didn't really care. His younger version was simply a means to an end.

Perhaps, when all this was over, he would get a massive case of the shakes. Just as Deanna had those many, many years ago.

For the briefest of moments he was distracted by the mental image of Deanna from their steamy encounter in the jungle, and then he was immediately snapped back to business when his younger self suddenly sat up in bed.

Commander Riker squinted into the darkness, looking straight at his older self, but wasn't able to make out anything clearly. He started to say, "Lights."

But the admiral moved quickly, moving with assurance in the darkness since, after all, it was his old quarters and he remembered where everything was. He dropped onto the bed next to his younger self and clamped his hand over Will Riker's mouth.

The commander struggled fiercely, shoving at the arm that held him down, grabbing upward at his face. The elder Riker, for his part, felt nothing but impatience and quickly called out, "Lights!"

He felt the younger man freeze in momentary confusion at the no-doubt familiarity of the voice. The lights came up, too bright for Will, and the admiral snapped, "Half lights," bringing the illumination to a more bearable level.

Commander Riker stared up in shock at his future self. The latter hissed, "Shut up! We haven't much time!"

Momentarily startled, Will began to struggle again, trying to make some sort of noise. The admiral, losing what little patience he had, and aware of the rapidly passing time, snapped, "Didn't you hear what I said? Shut up, you idiot! They may be here to try and stop me at any moment! So lie still! Listen to me, and be prepared to do exactly what I tell you. Deanna's life hangs on what you do next."

That was more than enough to get Will's attention. He stopped struggling, slowly realizing that he was not under direct attack; that he was not dreaming; and that there was more to this than he was going to be able to discern upon first exposure.

"I'm going to let go of your mouth now," said the admiral. "So help me, if you shout or try to get attention, I'll knock you cold and take care of this myself. And if I have to do that and get nailed because I'm easily spotted, then you will quite literally have no one but yourself to blame for the rest of your life."

Will nodded, indicating he understood, and the admiral slowly released his hand. He stepped back off the bed as Will sat up. There was still confusion in his eyes, but also amazement. "Who . . . *are* you?"

"The Easter bunny," snapped the admiral. "Who in hell do you *think* I am. We're wasting time . . . time we haven't got. Get dressed. Move. *Move!*"

Will rolled off the bed, never taking his eyes off the senior Riker, even as he started to pull on his uniform. "You're from the future, aren't you?"

"That's right. You don't sound surprised."

"After the time that Captain Picard ran into himself, I swore that nothing would surprise me."

"Oh, yes," said the admiral. "I did swear that, didn't I." Then he turned deadly serious. "Listen to me and don't interrupt. Deanna's life is in mortal danger."

"Then why in hell am I taking the time to get dressed?"

"Because they may be watching for anything unusual—and you running down the corridor in your nightclothes would qualify."

"Who is 'they'?"

"I said don't interrupt. Just listen: Deanna is going to be poisoned." He pushed on despite Will's expression of astonishment and held up the vial from his jacket. "This will counteract it. You've got to get to her quarters and get her to drink it. And you've got"—he glanced at his chronometer—"just over fifteen minutes to do it."

At that moment, Will's communicator beeped.

"You don't have time!" hissed the admiral.

But Will, never taking his eyes off the admiral, tapped it. "Riker here."

"Security alert, sir," came the deep voice of Worf. "An intruder was reported in your general vicinity. Have you seen him?"

Will Riker stared at his future self.

The admiral realized that everything was hinging on this moment. A word from Commander Riker would bring Worf and his people charging to the rescue. And the admiral had not had enough time to convince his younger self of the truth of his words.

Words.

His own words.

And in a very low voice, he said, "The future holds such promise . . . and just as I cannot imagine how I survived the past . . . without you . . ."

Will's eyes widened in shock, even as over his communicator Worf said, "Commander . . . what did you say?"

"Nothing," was the firm reply. "I haven't seen him. I'll meet you in a few minutes. I just . . . have to get dressed. Riker out."

There was a silence that, to both of them, seemed to stretch on for eternity. And then Will said, with slow understanding, "She died. In your past . . . my future . . . she died. And you've come back somehow to try and prevent it. You're . . . you're tampering with time . . . and the 'they' you're worried about are the people from your time—maybe scientists or, my God, Starfleet personnel— who might try and stop you."

"She wasn't supposed to die," said the admiral. "It was wrong. Wrong for her. Wrong for me, for everyone. And I'm here to prevent that wrong, and I don't give a damn what regulations say, and if you love her . . . if you're truly *Imzadi* . . . you won't give a damn either."

"But . . . but how am I supposed to believe you? How am I supposed to just . . . just take the future into my own hands. *Our* own hands?"

The admiral took a step toward him. "We do it every moment of our lives, kid. Every day we make our own future. But someone came back and decided to remake the future in their own image . . . and now I'm here to stop it."

"Unless someone stops you. Which means that someone isn't certain."

Admiral Riker grabbed Will Riker by his uniform front. Despite his age, his strength was almost undiminished and was fueled by anger. "Damn you, you sanctimonious clod! You think you know everything? You don't know a damn thing! You want certainty? This is a certainty, then—Deanna is going to die! She's going to writhe on the floor and beg you to do something, and all you're going to do is watch her suffer massive circulatory collapse and die! And it's not going to be until that moment, you purblind idiot, that you realize that she's the better part of you!"

"You're . . . it's wrong," Will said, but there was tremendous conflict in his eyes. "It's wrong to tamper with the past. . . . I can't believe that there's any circumstance under which I'd . . . I'd knowingly . . ."

"You think you can judge *me!*" said the admiral. "Remember what we wrote? 'And just as I cannot imagine how I survived the past without you . . . I cannot imagine a future without you.' Remember? Well, *I'm* the future without her, buddy boy, and I can tell you right now that it's not something you're going to relish." He shoved the vial into Will's palm. "It's going to happen, Riker! In just a few minutes now! Her life is going to end. You can save it! You have the power, right here, right now! Now are you going to stand there debating philosophies and moralities and rights and wrongs? Or are you going to deal with the genuine, real, here-and-now fact that Deanna's life is at stake and only you have a hope in hell of saving her. And if you don't save her, then hell is where you're going to be—forty years of hell! Of might-have-beens and what-ifs.

"Except for me, there was just the frustration that I should have done something, but didn't know what. For you, it's going to be the knowledge that you could have done something, but didn't. How much worse for you, Riker? When you call out with your mind, 'Imzadi,' and there's no one to respond, no part of your soul that acknowledges that the word has any meaning to anyone else, what will happen to you then? *God damn you,* Riker! When your heart's been cut out, how's it going to feel knowing that *you're the one who wielded the knife?*"

Will ripped away from him, his face ashen, his heart pounding.

"Deanna!" he screamed, and charged from his quarters.

CHAPTER 38

Dann nibbled at Deanna's neck and began to work his way down. She sighed, a slow, languorous sigh. She was on the bed, wearing only the flimsiest of shifts. She started to push it down off her shoulders so that Dann's downward course would be unobstructed.

But still, something bothered her. "Dann . . . are you all right?"

He raised his head slightly. "Of course I am," he said reasonably. "Why wouldn't I be?"

"I don't know. I just sense . . . I mean . . ."

And suddenly she sat up, confused, a voice echoing in her head. "Will?" she said in bewilderment.

"What's wrong?" asked Dann, sitting up as well.

"It's . . . it's Will. Something's wrong . . . I sense . . . total panic. It's . . . something directed towards me, I don't . . ."

"Deanna, calm down," said Dann firmly, taking her by the shoulders. "He's probably just, well, jealous about us. That's what's giving him anxiety. He's probably even asleep and you're just . . . just tuning in to his dreams somehow. I know you two are close, but—"

"No!" She pushed him aside. "Something *is* wrong."

"Deanna . . ."

She got out of bed, adjusting the shift around her, and went over to her uniform, which was neatly hung nearby. She tapped the communicator on it and said, "Troi to Riker."

"Deanna!" came Riker's desperate shout. "Stay there! Don't move! I'll be there in a few seconds!"

She spun and faced Dann. "Did you hear that? He's terrified!"

"Yes," said Dann sadly. "Yes . . . I can't say I'm surprised."

Will hurtled down the corridor at warp speed. He skidded once and, to his panic, almost bobbled the vial and dropped it. But he recovered quickly and turned a corner.

His mind was racing furiously. He didn't know how or why any of this was happening, but there were two things of which he was completely, instinctively convinced—that he had confronted his future self, and that Deanna was going to die in the next few minutes.

He skidded to a halt outside her quarters and charged in. Deanna was seated on the bed, arguing with Dann, but when she saw Riker, she rose to her feet. "Will . . . ?"

He thrust the vial outward. "Drink this! Quickly!"

Dann came off the bed and stood between them. "What are you, crazy? She's not just going to drink some vial of unknown liquid because you told her to. Get out of here!"

"Deanna, you have to," said Riker. "Your life depends on it."

Deanna knew, of course, that Riker believed every word of what he was saying. But it didn't make her any less befuddled. "My *life?*"

"Out of my way!" Riker said to Dann, trying to push him aside.

"Like hell! Deanna, don't listen to him! He's trying to hurt you! He's jealous of me!"

Dann moved once again to block Riker, and this time Will grabbed him by the shoulders and tried to push him to one side. To his shock, Dann didn't budge. He was a head shorter and considerably slimmer than Riker, but he held his ground. Instead he grabbed Riker by the forearms and held him in a grip of iron.

"Deanna!" shouted Riker, and somehow, in his head, he heard a slow, steady ticking, like time slipping away from him, spiraling out of control. Everything seemed to slow down and distort as he twisted in Dann's grasp and flipped the vial onto the bed. It landed on the sheets, bounced once, and started to tumble to the floor. But Deanna's hand snatched out and grabbed it. She stared at it, trying to understand.

"Give me that!" shouted Dann, and her head snapped around in amazement at the desperation in his tone. With his free hand he lunged for the vial, but now Will Riker shifted his grip and spun on the ball of his foot. Dann was thrown across the room, crashing into furniture.

"Drink it!" Riker yelled at Deanna. "If you ever trusted me, if you ever loved me, *drink it!*"

Deanna needed no further urging. She pulled at the stopper.

It was stuck.

Dann came to his feet and with an animalistic roar sprang toward Deanna. Riker met his charge, braced himself, and the two of them went down in a tumble of arms and legs.

Riker rolled over, gaining the advantage, and pounded furiously on Dann's head. The blows didn't seem to have any effect, and Dann drove a knee up, shoving Riker off. But Riker didn't lose his grip on one of Dann's arms, and the Starfleet officer, even off balance, managed to send Dann crashing into the wall.

Deanna worked desperately at the stopper, kneading it with her fingers. It worked its way upward.

Dann began to transform.

He became larger, his body covered with thick brown fur, his hands shaping into claws.

Riker recognized his species immediately. It was a Chameloid. Shape-shifters, incredibly powerful, incredibly dangerous.

Deanna, her fingers still pushing on the stopper, stared at the man she had thought was Dann, her dark eyes registering her utter shock. And then, somewhere deep within her, she felt some sort of distant, burning sensation.

At that moment, the stopper popped off, rolling onto the bed.

"NO!" roared "Dann," and he made one final, desperate lunge. He shoved Riker aside, his fingers reaching for the vial, and then

Riker snared his long, matted fur from behind and leaped on, wrapping his arms down and around the Chameloid's arms, and up around the creature's neck.

Deanna drank down the contents of the vial in one gulp.

The Chameloid howled in fury, trying to bat Riker off his back. "You idiot! Do you have any idea what you've done! *Do you?*"

Riker said nothing. Instead, all of his energy was being used to shove the creature's neck forward.

The Chameloid broke the grip, slamming Riker to the floor. Towering over him, the creature roared, "You selfish bastard! You've risked everything!"

"I've risked everything for Deanna before," Riker said defiantly, "and I'd do it again!"

"Well, I don't have that choice!" snapped the Chameloid.

He started toward Deanna, his hands outstretched . . .

And a phaser blast from behind sent the Chameloid to his knees.

Worf stood in the doorway, his phaser leveled. "One side, Commander," he said calmly. Immediately Riker leaped out of the way and Worf fired again. The phaser beam enveloped the Chameloid once again. He wailed in frustration, and then consciousness slipped from him and he pitched forward, right on top of Riker.

Worf helped roll the Chameloid off Riker, who sat up, rubbing his chest in pain. Then he looked to Deanna, who was making a similar motion of her own. "Deanna," he said urgently, "are you all right? Are—"

"I . . . I felt something. Some sort of . . . of burning pain in my chest . . . but now it's gone. Will . . . what's happened here? Who is . . . is that?" She pointed distastefully at the unconscious Chameloid. "Where did this vial come from? How did you know . . . ?"

Riker patted her hand with all the reassurance that he could muster at that moment. Then he said, "Worf . . . get our 'friend' here to the brig. Alert the captain, tell him to meet me outside my quarters. Emphasize that. *Outside* my quarters."

"Very well," said Worf, hauling the Chameloid over his shoulder.

Two other security men had shown up by this point, but Worf clearly had matters in hand. "Am I correct in assuming that this is our intruder?"

Will looked up at him bleakly. "Worf, you don't know the half of it."

Worf grunted and headed off to the brig with the Chameloid. When he was gone, Riker rotated his arm, which had been banged up as he'd wrestled with the Chameloid.

Troi, for her part, merely looked at him with awe. "You saved my life, Will," she said quietly. "I was in danger, and you came charging in here—risked your life—and you saved me."

"Actually," said Riker, "not to sound boastful or anything—but it appears I went to even greater lengths than that to save you. You'd better get dressed and come with me. I don't think you're going to believe this unless you see it. I'll . . ." He cleared his throat, chucking a thumb toward the hallway. "I'll wait out here for you to put some clothes on."

"That's very decent of you, Commander."

She slid off the bed, stood on her toes, and kissed him.

"Thank you for saving me," she whispered in his ear.

He smiled tiredly. "All part of the service."

CHAPTER 39

When Will and Deanna returned to his cabin, Picard was standing there looking extremely annoyed.

"All right, Number One," he said stiffly, arms folded. "I have complied with your wishes and stood here outside your cabin. I cannot say I like to be kept waiting."

"The counselor was just making herself look presentable," said Will.

"Presentable for whom?" demanded Picard.

"Yes, Commander," chimed in Troi. With the danger past, she was all business. "Whom exactly am I being made presentable for?"

For answer, Will walked into his cabin, hoping his future self had stayed put. It had potential to be a very embarrassing situation if—

He was gone.

Will stood in the middle of the cabin, looking around dismally. Troi and Picard followed him in, staring uncomprehendingly at the officer's obvious discomfiture.

"He was right here!" said Riker desperately.

"Number One," Picard told him, speaking slowly and deliberately, "who . . . *precisely* . . . was here?"

"Me."

It had been Will Riker's voice that had replied, but it was not the

Will Riker that Picard was looking at. For an instant Picard thought that Riker was practicing ventriloquism or some such nonsense. But then, slowly, Picard realized that the voice had come from behind them.

He turned in time to see a gray-haired version of his second-in-command emerging from the bathroom. "I was here," he said. "Still am, actually. Which makes me con—"

He caught a glimpse of Deanna, who was standing just behind the younger Will Riker. Will stepped aside and gestured to her. "I did it," he said quietly, "or rather . . . we did it."

Picard had not yet fathomed what to say, much less what to make of the situation. At that precise moment, however, Picard could have been a million light-years away and Adm. William Riker would not have noticed.

Instead Riker was staring at Deanna Troi with a mixture of disbelief and shock. "Deanna . . . ," he whispered.

She took a step toward him, stunned. "Will—?"

It was the fastest shift in emotion that Deanna had ever felt. An air of despair and doom had hung like a shroud over the man facing her . . . until he had set eyes on her. And suddenly it had been ripped away, just like that. How was it possible that one person—*one person*—could make that much difference in someone's life?

He approached her, reaching out to her. Picard and his Number One made no move, but merely watched in pure amazement.

The admiral brought his hands up to her face, hovered over it for an instant as if afraid to touch her. As if afraid that if he made any such movement, she would burst like a soap bubble and all of it, all of this moment, would just vanish.

But then he did touch her. Riker put his hands to her face, and they were shaking. "Oh . . . my God," he breathed.

It was like that moment in the Jalara Jungle, except now he was the one who was trembling. Deanna, for her part, reacted entirely on instinct, putting her arms around him and pulling him tightly against her.

His chest began to heave with pent-up emotion, and the old man began to sob. He no longer cared where he was, or who was watching. The ethics of his actions did not weigh on him. All that mattered was that she was there, and she was alive, and in his arms. Years of agony and guilt and second-guessing, washed away by the hot tears and first real emotion besides grief that he had experienced for decades.

And she heard his thoughts, and it was as startling as that first time had been. *Oh, God . . . Imzadi . . . I'm whole again,* echoed in her mind, the prayer of thanksgiving from a man who had given up on everything, especially himself. *I never knew . . . what I had until you were gone.*

"It's all right," she murmured, stroking his back. "It's all right."

He drew back from her to look her in the eyes, those eyes that had been closed in death for years. They were as bright and transcendent as he had remembered, and both of their faces were wet with tears. Whether hers was wet from his or she had generated her own, he couldn't tell. He also couldn't care.

Standing to one side, Comdr. Will Riker watched the reunion of two lovers and realized—insanely—that he was jealous.

"Worf to Riker."

Riker the elder had to rein in his impulse to answer, but instead nodded in the direction of Will. "I think it's for you."

Will tapped his communicator. "Yes?"

"We checked the cabin to which Ambassador Dann had been assigned and found him unconscious. Apparently the Chameloid had accosted Dann at some point earlier this evening and taken his place."

The admiral's head now turned, his attention switching to the matters at hand. He released his hold on Deanna and turned to Will, making a throat-cutting gesture. Will said, "Thank you, Mr. Worf. Make sure the Chameloid is secure. Riker out." Then he turned to his future self and said, "This Chameloid is one of 'them,' isn't he."

"I believe so," said the admiral. "You sure he's a Chameloid? Large? Brown hair and furry?" When Will nodded, Admiral Riker continued, "Well, unless I miss my guess, he's an officer named Blair. There was only one Chameloid on . . . on the ship, and

Lieutenant Blair was it. I doubt . . . they could have gotten another one so quickly. It figures that he would assume the appearance of someone close to Deanna. If they anticipated my trying to save her, then the logical thing was to take on the aspect of whoever was with her at the key moment in time. Simplest way to keep an eye on her and make sure things progress smoothly."

"For all you knew," Will now said, "*I* could have been one of *them.* When you came here, you might have been walking into a trap."

"I know. That's why I mentioned the lines of poetry to you. I watched your reaction very carefully. That wasn't just to convince you that I'm you. It was also to convince me that you're me."

"I hate to break this up," Picard now said, stepping forward, "but I, who am unquestionably me, would be most grateful if either of you cared to tell either of me *what in hell is going on?*"

"Watch your tone with me, Captain," said the elder Riker with a half-serious smirk. "I have seniority, *and* I outrank you."

Picard was not someone who was easily flustered, but now he turned to his second-in-command with utter perplexity. "Number One—?" And there was a distinct tone of warning to his voice.

"Simply put, Captain," said Will, stepping forward and gesturing to the gray-haired man, "this is myself, from the future."

"I surmised that, Number One," said Picard tightly. "Now what the blazes is he doing here?"

"All right, Captain," the admiral told him. "To put this as succinctly, and as noncommittally, as possible—Deanna's life was in danger. I came back through time to see her through that danger. And there are some people who would prefer that I didn't."

"Will . . . ," began Picard.

Two Rikers said, "Yes?"

Despite the seriousness of the situation, Deanna had to make an effort not to laugh.

"Admiral," Picard started again, "Counselor Troi has been in danger before. We all have. Why was this threat so significant that it warranted your taking the extremely dangerous step of coming back through time?"

"She died," said the admiral, trying not to look at her. "But now she hasn't . . . except that I haven't returned to my own time. Which means . . ." And his voice darkened. "It means the danger to her isn't over yet."

Picard leaned against a bureau. "How . . . how did you come here?"

The admiral gave Riker a long, hard look. There seemed to be a great deal going through his mind, as if he were coming to a variety of decisions. "I can't tell you," he said finally.

Picard blinked. "Well, then . . . tell us why Counselor Troi was"—he found he couldn't say the word and settled for—"attacked. What happened as a consequence of it?"

"I can't tell you that, either."

"Oh, for God's sake!" said Picard in exasperation. "It seems just yesterday we went through this with Rasmussen—and he turned out to be from the past, for that matter!"

"I know," the admiral reminded him. "I was there."

"Well, then?"

The admiral placed the palms of his hands together. "Jean-Luc," he began, and noted the surprised expression of the *Enterprise* captain upon hearing his first name spoken by the man he still thought of as a subordinate. "Jean-Luc . . . you understand the tremendous risk I've taken by coming back here. You know, as well as I, the Starfleet regulations against any sort of interference with the time stream."

"Of course. But since you are here, and since you've already interfered . . ."

"In for a penny, in for a pound? Is that it?" The admiral smiled humorlessly. "I wish it were that simple. I came here for one reason and one reason only: to save Deanna. Violating those regulations—taking the responsibility for a universe on my shoulders—was the second most difficult thing I've ever done . . . the first being when I had to leave you behind to be killed by the Romulans."

The last time Will had seen Picard as white as he was now was back when he'd been transformed into a Borg. "I'm . . ." His voice was barely above a whisper. "I'm killed by the Romulans?"

"No, Jean-Luc. I made that up."

"You . . ." Picard looked at Will and Deanna, and then back to Riker. "You made that up? *Why?* Why would you joke about such a thing?"

"It wasn't a joke. It was to make a point. If I start talking about events—*any* events—beyond my immediate goal of saving Deanna, then I run the risk of saying the wrong thing. The slightest slip could end up changing the time stream beyond what I've already committed to. Making the initial decision was already enough of playing God for me. I'm not prepared, under any circumstance, to expand on it. What if I accidentally talk about someone on this ship—you, Worf, Beverly—in the past tense? Let slip that people I know now aren't around forty years from now. Then they get to spend the next forty years, every time they run into any sort of difficult situation, wondering, 'Is this it? Is this what results in my death?' Or the other way around. What if I tell you, Jean-Luc, that in my time, you're running Starfleet? That could result in your becoming overly confident. You could go into dangerous scenarios thinking that you'll definitely get out of them because, hell, you know you'll be around four decades hence. And as a result, you can get yourself, and everyone else, killed. Time is very malleable, Jean-Luc. And I'm just not going to mold the clay any further. I'm really very sorry."

The three younger officers looked at each other, and then Picard—drumming his fingers on the table—said, "If you don't tell us the bare facts we need to know in order to handle the situation . . . then Deanna could still die."

Riker looked up at her grimly. "I know that, Jean-Luc; but the first time, there was no warning. Now . . . forewarned is forearmed. That will have to do for you. And I still have a few tricks up my sleeve. I just can't show them to you, that's all."

Riker sat down and folded his arms in a manner that made it quite clear he was not going to say anything further.

Picard sighed. "Very well. I can't say that I'm overly pleased with the situation. On the other hand . . . thanks to you . . . Counselor Troi is still alive. It would seem that I am going to have to hope that the instincts of the man whom I presently trust to be my second-in-command . . . are still present in the man who is also—at this moment in time—my superior officer."

Picard rose, and Riker stood with him. "I'll need some sort of modern-day Starfleet uniform . . . and preferably some sort of disguise, so I can move about."

"What you will need, Admiral, is some reading material to keep you busy. I have no interest in marching you around the ship—I think the fewer people who see you, the better. These quarters are going to serve as your personal brig. The doors will be sealed with an override that only I can command, and guards will be posted outside. You are going nowhere, Admiral."

"You can't do that!" said the admiral angrily. "There are things I can do that you can't! Things I know to watch out for."

"Maybe," said Picard. "Then again, maybe not. As you have made clear, time has already slipped into another stream. From here on in we are all of us improvising, Admiral, and to be blunt, I can tap-dance as well as you. You will stay safe and secure here so that I don't have to worry about a random time factor running about my ship. You, Counselor," he said to Deanna, "will go nowhere without Lieutenant Worf as a security escort."

"Won't he question why you've given him that full-time assignment if, as far as he knows, the danger is past?" said the admiral.

Picard, Will, and Troi looked at him in surprise.

He grimaced in chagrin. "What was I thinking? Of course he won't question: he's a Klingon. Forgive me. It's been a while since I dealt with . . ." He stopped. "Well . . . it's been a while. Captain . . . believe me, you're not pursuing the right course here. You've got to give me freedom to move."

"Number One," said Picard calmly, "kindly check him for weapons."

The first officer went to Riker, who stood absolutely still, glowering at Picard. Will took off him the phaser he'd taken from the guard, as well as another, much more diminutive phaser that he found hidden in his jacket. Will held it up and whistled. "Small. What'll they think of next?"

"You'll find out," the admiral informed him dryly. "Jean-Luc . . ."

"Save it, Admiral." Picard tapped his communicator and summoned two security guards to be stationed outside Riker's cabin. As they waited for the guards to arrive, no words were exchanged between the four of them . . . until finally Picard broke the silence and said, "Can you at least tell me . . . is there still a vessel named *Enterprise?*"

At that, Riker smiled slightly. "Is it important for you to know that?"

"I would like to."

"All right. The answer is yes," said Riker quietly. "And she carries the name as nobly as her forebearers did. You . . ." He paused and then said, "You see? I was either going to say that you *will* be proud of her, or that you *would* have been proud of her. Very easy to make mistakes. Like the one you're making by cooping me up in here."

"As with all mistakes, Admiral, we learn to live with them."

Riker looked at Deanna, his dry skin crinkling around the eyes. "Some of us never learn," he said in a bittersweet voice. "And some of us will move heaven and earth to change things for the better."

She looked down, her cheeks reddening slightly. The admiral picked up on it immediately. "I'm sorry. I'm embarrassing you . . . because I'm being so overt about how I feel for you, and you've gotten used to the nice, easy, comfortable relationship we developed while on the ship."

She bobbed her head. "Yes," she admitted.

The admiral turned and slapped Will on the chest. "You idiot," he admonished the surprised younger man. "You're choosing the tidy, easy path instead of the more difficult but ultimately more rewarding path. You aren't even smart enough to know when you have a good thing." The admiral made a noise of utter disgust and dropped down into a chair.

Picard, Will, and Troi slowly backed out of the quarters, leaving the sullen admiral to himself. Once in the corridor, they received the security guards, whom Picard instructed to stand outside and listen for signs of problems. If there were problems, they were to summon Captain Picard at once. They were not to enter under any circumstance. The guards nodded in obedience, if not in understanding, and then Picard issued an order to the computer to keep the doors sealed unless he himself should order them unsealed.

They moved away from the guards, who had taken up their position outside the doors. "I apologize, Captain," said Will. "And to you, too, Counselor."

Picard looked at him in surprise, as did Deanna. "Good heavens, Number One, why?"

"Because of his attitude."

"Yes, but he's not y—well, he *is* you, I suppose. But there are significant differences, Number One, not the least of which is years and experience. You shouldn't feel badly."

"Well . . . I do. Seeing someone who is, to all intents and purposes, *me,* acting that way . . ."

"I don't know," said Deanna with a shrug. "He didn't seem so bad to me."

"You're kidding," said Will. "I don't know . . . I mean . . . I know how much I owe him"—he looked at her—"for everything. But there was still something about him that just . . . just rubbed me the wrong way."

"But he's what you'll become, Number One," pointed out Picard. "You must have seen something of yourself in him."

"No," said Riker firmly. "Very, very little. To be honest, he reminded me of . . ." Then he stopped.

"Of who, Number One?"

Riker sighed. "He reminded me of my father."

Deanna chuckled, and Riker shot her a look.

"Yes, well," said Picard, trying to hide his own smile, "be that as it may . . . due to the delicate situation that we're in, we're going to keep this on a need-to-know basis. However . . . there is someone whom I feel that it's important to consult. Someone who should be able to afford some unique insight into our situation."

On the bridge, Data answered the signal on his communicator. "Commander Data here."

Over the comm unit came the familiar, clipped tone of Picard.

"Mr. Data . . . I have a matter of some urgency to discuss with you. Please report to your quarters immediately."

"My quarters?" Data tilted his head in curiosity. "That is a rather unusual procedure, Captain."

"We're in a rather unusual situation, Mr. Data."

"Very well, Captain," said Data, standing. "I will be there directly."

Lieutenant Barclay was walking down the corridor, feeling disoriented, and he bumped shoulders with Data just as he passed the android officer's cabin. Data looked at him curiously. "Lieutenant . . . are you quite all right?"

"I'm . . . I'm fine, sir," said Barclay hollowly.

"Very well." Data turned and walked into his cabin.

Barclay sighed. He still didn't know what to make of his holodeck experience. Perhaps . . . perhaps he simply needed some regular, normal R&R. Not something holodeck-generated. Some real experience instead. Otherwise . . .

Well . . . was it possible that he was having difficulty separating fantasy from reality? Was he, in fact, totally losing touch with the world around him?

No, he thought. It couldn't be. It simply couldn't . . .

He turned a corner and bumped shoulders with Data.

Barclay stepped back, gasping in confusion. "But . . . but . . ."

Data stared at him, his yellow eyes glittering in curiosity. "Lieutenant, are you quite all right?"

With an insane sense of déjà vu, Barclay stammered out, "I'm . . . I'm fine, sir."

"Very well," said Data, taking him at his word and continuing on his way toward his cabin.

Barclay's head snapped back and forth like a yo-yo. Then he sagged against a wall and whimpered like a lost child.

Data entered his cabin and said, "Captain?"

The door closed behind him, but there was no sign of Picard. "Captain?" he said again.

He sensed a presence behind himself and he spun . . .

And a hand was already at his off-switch. He did not even manage to get a look at his assailant before he went limp.

The gold-skinned intruder lowered the insensate android onto the bed and then stepped back. Then he turned and studied his reflection in the mirror.

Perfect, of course. But then again, why shouldn't he be? He was, after all, the same individual. He hadn't aged a day. His body was the same, his brainpower undiminished. And his ability to mimic voices—in this case, Picard's—had been invaluable.

He tilted his head as a thought hit him. He had no recollection of this event ever occurring. But it had just happened in, effectively, his own past. How was it possible for something to have happened to him without his remembering it?

For that matter, how could Admiral Riker be acting as if the entire notion of saving Deanna Troi was just occurring to him? If he had gone back in time to his own past, then he should be aware of everything that had already happened. But unless he was engaging in a massive subterfuge for Data's benefit . . .

No. Data didn't think that was what was happening. The only thing that he could conceive of was that neither he nor Admiral Riker had any memory of the events because, to all intents and purposes, they hadn't happened yet. Right here, right now, was where they were shaping all that was to come.

Except all that was to come had already been shaped. Riker was trying to remold it to his own image. Data, on the other hand, had to try to preserve it.

Deanna Troi could not live to affect the peace conference . . . no matter what was required.

He removed the communicator from the unconscious Data's uniform, removed the one that he had taken from the same supplies room that he had stolen the uniform from that he was now wearing, and affixed Data's actual communicator to his uniform front. No point in leaving anything to chance.

He tapped the communicator. "Computer," he said briskly, "locate Counselor Deanna Troi."

For one moment he hoped that the computer would say, "Deanna Troi is in the morgue." That would have simplified things immensely.

Instead the computer said, "Deanna Troi is in her quarters."

Data nodded. Then he went to the unmoving form of Lieutenant Commander Data, made one small change to it as a safety precaution, and headed off to kill the ship's counselor.

CHAPTER 40

Picard had gone straight from Riker's cabin to the Ten-Forward, and now he said in soft tones to Guinan, after telling her as much as he knew, "What do you think?"

"What do I think? I think it's possible," Guinan allowed.

"Would you know?" asked Picard. "If time had shifted around us . . . one way or the other . . . would you be aware of it? You've intimated in the past that you have a sensitivity for such things."

"A sensitivity, yes, but I'm not omniscient." She had just poured Picard a drink and slid it over to him. Now she stared at her reflection in the glass. "Look . . . I live day to day, same as you, Captain. Same as anyone. Now if there's a large enough disturbance in the space-time continuum . . . particularly when it has its origins in the past . . . I might be aware of it and be able to tell you that something's wrong. But if it's happening right here, right now"— she shook her head—"then I'm on the same roller coaster as you are, Captain. And all we can do is hold on."

He nodded. "For a moment I toyed with the notion of canceling the peace conference. After all, it would logically appear that an attempt on her life would be connected with the conference. Or I could have all the delegates questioned, or . . ." Then he shook his head in exasperation. "But now we enter the realm of temporal second-guessing. How far do I go, beyond guarding Deanna? If none of this had happened, then I would have no reason to take extraordinary measures. Which means that I really don't have any reason now."

"Best to let matters proceed then," said Guinan.

Again Picard nodded.

At that moment Data walked into the Ten-Forward. He looked around thoughtfully, then glanced up as Picard gestured for him to come over. Data took a place next to the captain, and politely nodded to Guinan.

"A question, Captain," said Data. "Why are Lieutenant Worf and three other security guards stationed around Counselor Troi's quarters?"

Picard glanced at Guinan and then lowered his glass. "I will tell *you,* Data, and will inform Commander Riker that you have been brought into our little circle of secrecy. But it is to go no further. Now the *official* reason is that an unknown assailant, presently in the brig, made an attempt on the counselor's life. That much is, in fact, true. However, it's quite a bit more involved than that . . ."

Data, naturally, knew precisely how involved it was.

He had gone to Troi's quarters, and when he had seen the guards there . . . including a scowling Worf studying every passerby with intense scrutiny . . . he knew he had a problem. It was, of course, perfectly likely that he could force his way past Worf and the others. They were not expecting a friendly face to turn on them, and he could probably down them before they could mount a serious defense. Deanna would have been dead before any help could have been summoned, and once that happened, the currents of time would have pulled him—and presumably, Riker and Blair—back to their own time.

But to attack her so overtly would have exposed that there was more than one Data waltzing around on the *Enterprise.* Or even worse . . . what if the present Data were unable to convince the others that he had not, in fact, simply gone berserk? In one scenario, they would have come to the realization that Data still existed in the future . . . and that knowledge could have serious consequences. On the other hand, if they simply decided that their own Data had become unreliable, or even dangerous, they might conclude that the only reasonable course of action was to deactivate or dismantle him. If they did that . . .

Then what?

Would he, the Data of the future, then cease to exist? And if he didn't exist, then who would go back to stop Admiral Riker? But if he didn't exist to come back to try to stop Admiral Riker, then how could he possibly kill Deanna Troi and set in motion the events that could get himself shut off? And who . . . ?

It was this sort of self-involving confusion that had once prompted Geordi LaForge to declare, during one such discussion of a theoretical paradox, "This is precisely why time travel gives me nosebleeds."

Data didn't have a nosebleed. Data had a situation.

But one way to remedy that situation was to get himself "officially" brought into the information loop. Which was precisely what he was doing now.

And once he had that information, it was just a matter of determining the most effective way to proceed.

CHAPTER 41

There had been one change of security guards since the captain ordered the guard. Worf, however, had remained. This did not surprise anyone. In similar situations, Worf had displayed stamina that was, quite simply, inhuman.

As a result, when Will Riker approached, Worf turned to him with just as fierce a protective glare as he had possessed since he'd first taken his post.

"No one has seen or spoken to Counselor Troi," Worf said, "except for a carefully supervised visit by Dr. Crusher."

Riker nodded approvingly. "Good. Despite everything that happened last night, she wanted to be fresh for the peace conference." He tapped his communicator. "Riker to Counselor Troi. Are you awake, Deanna?"

"Yes, Commander. Awake and ready to go."

"Good." He gestured for Worf and the others to follow, and they entered behind him. Worf observed that Riker was wearing a phaser. Silently he approved.

Deanna was standing there, looking radiant.

"How are you feeling today, Counselor?"

"Well," she said, extending her neck. "Actually I wound up sleeping in a slightly awkward position. My neck is a little stiff."

"Need me to get the kink out?"

"No." She smiled. "Actually . . . the pain isn't so bad. It reminds me that I'm alive."

Riker returned the smile. "I can think of more pleasurable ways to be reminded of being alive."

"Yes, Commander," she said dryly. "I'm sure you can. Well"—she slapped her thighs and rose—"to the peace conference, then."

They started down the hallway—Deanna, Worf, Riker, and the guards. They attracted curious glances as others walked past them in the corridor, and in a low voice Deanna asked, "Do I really require an entire entourage?"

"Just until we get to the conference room," said Riker. "We've shifted the location, however, to the high-security conference room. We've set up a low-level null field that will detect any sort of weapons. Once you're there you'll be safe, and Worf and the others can return to their duties."

"My duty," said Worf firmly, "is to ascertain the safety of all personnel."

"And you've done an excellent job, Worf," Deanna told him.

The Klingon merely grunted.

"Are you sure you're all right?" Riker asked her.

Deanna nodded. "Right after you posted the guards, Beverly came down to check me over."

"Yes, so I heard. 'Carefully supervised.'"

"Her instruments didn't detect anything wrong with me. And yet I felt something . . . or at least, for a few moments, I had. That burning sensation I mentioned. But then it vanished. I can only assume that whatever was in that vial did whatever it was supposed to do. I truly owe a great debt to . . . both of you."

"I know," said Will. "We both do. I was thinking about it last night . . . and maybe I was a little hard on him. I mean, it took real guts to do what he did. I don't know if I could have done it."

She patted him on the arm. "Don't worry, Commander. I suspect the answer is yes . . . but hopefully you'll never have to find out."

In the quarters of Commander Riker, Adm. William Riker crouched in a corner and pulled at the heel of his boot.

He had kept a careful eye on his chronometer and now said, "Computer . . . locate Deanna Troi."

The communications function for the cabin had been deliberately disabled by Commander Riker. Wisely, he had anticipated the possibility that his older self might try to take advantage of their natural voice similarities and use that function to summon help from some unknowing individual. But the locator function still worked just fine.

"Deanna Troi is on deck twenty-three," replied the computer.

"Probable destination?"

The computer did not hesitate. "The Sindareen peace conference is scheduled for conference room twenty-three-D. Deanna Troi is among the personnel scheduled to attend the conference. She is presently one hundred and fifty meters from the conference room and moving towards it. The likelihood that her destination is the conference room is approximately—"

"Never mind. I get the idea."

He twisted the heel of his boot and it came clean off. Holding his palm under it, he upended it.

A miniature phaser fell into his palm.

He nodded approvingly and snapped the heel back in place.

As he did so, he prayed that he had done the right thing in withholding the information that he had. He could have told them so easily that the Sindareen were being duplicitous. Flushing that knowledge out into the open might have ended all of this . . . especially if it was, in fact, the Sindareen who were somehow behind the whole thing.

But he had spoken the truth to Picard. He was indeed treading on very shaky ground and was not at all sure just how far he should go in giving them information. Should he tell them about the Sindareen? Should he tell them about the fact that perhaps Data himself—Data from the future—might be wandering the ship? Certainly if he had been Data, that's what he would have done: gone back himself. Who knew the ship better? Who could blend in more effectively than someone who was already supposed to be there?

He couldn't just tell them all these things. Where would it end? Worse . . . what would it begin?

But he could take action himself . . . actions without explaining them. Be Deanna's guardian angel. Her knight, her cowboy riding to the rescue.

Her Imzadi.

First, though . . . he had to get out of there.

He went over to the far wall. He knew that the officer in the adjoining cabin was already on duty, so this was definitely the preferred exit route.

He held the phaser close up to the wall and set it for as low and quiet a setting as he could. He couldn't risk giving the guards any sort of warning at all.

He pressed down on the trigger device and a pencil-thin beam of light emerged from the miniature phaser. Forcing himself to be patient, Riker proceeded to cut a hole in the wall.

The ship's security system, programmed to recognize 398 different weapons, did not recognize the futuristic phaser for what it was. Therefore, it identified the weapon as the closest analogue in its system, a hand-held arc welder—just as the admiral knew the computer would do. Hardly a weapon, the welder was not something that required any sort of security alert. Riker continued his work undisturbed.

When Will and Deanna entered the conference room, they saw that Picard and the delegates from the Cordians, the Luss, and the Byfrexians were already there. Only the Sindareen had yet to arrive.

Dann was sitting next to the Luss ambassador, and he had a profoundly befuddled expression on his face. His inquiries as to how in hell he had come to be unconscious in his cabin had not really been answered by anyone. When he saw Deanna, he started to rise, his entire face a question. But Deanna silently gestured for him to sit back down, somehow putting across that she'd speak to him later about it.

Will turned to Worf and the other guards and said in a low voice, "All right . . . we'll be okay for now."

"If you are certain," said Worf slowly.

"Yes," said Riker, and he patted his phaser. "I have the only working weapon in the room—it's keyed into the safe code of the null field. I'll sit next to her and make sure no one gets near her. All this attention . . . it's disconcerting to her. We'll be fine."

"Very well," Worf said. "But summon me instantly at the first sign of trouble."

It sounded remarkably like an order, which was not particularly appropriate for a lieutenant to issue a commander. But Will took it in stride. "Yes, sir."

If Worf picked up on the amused sarcasm, he gave no sign. Instead he grunted again and then turned and exited the room.

"I see the Sindareen are not yet with us," observed Picard as Riker and Troi settled into their seats.

"Perhaps we should start without them," suggested the Cordian ambassador. "After all, the Sindareen peace initiative will probably go far more smoothly without the Sindareen actually being involved." This produced a small chuckle from around the table.

"I think we'll wait for them," said Picard good-humoredly. "After all . . . it would be the polite thing to do."

Data sat on the bridge, watching the home planet of the Sindareen turning beneath them.

The turbolift door opened and Worf emerged. Data waited until the Klingon had taken his station before rising and saying, "I have something I must attend to, Mr. Worf. You have the conn."

He walked out before Worf could say anything. Mentally, the Klingon shrugged. Whatever Data had to take care of, certainly it was none of his concern.

Lieutenant Barclay, deciding that the entire previous night had been one, long bad dream—overstimulation of the imagination— stepped out of the shower, dried himself off, and got dressed for duty.

The two security guards outside Riker's quarters took no notice when the door to the adjoining quarters hissed open.

As a result, they never had a chance to react before the phaser beam, now set to stun, cut loose from the miniature weapon in the hand of Admiral Riker. Instantly, they both fell to the ground, unconscious.

Riker bent over them, glancing around quickly and breathing a sigh of relief that no one was coming. He grabbed each of them by one wrist and, moving as quickly as he could and cursing the achiness of his aging muscles, backed up and dragged them into the cabin from which he'd just exited.

He left them lying on the floor, next to the large piece of wall that he had cut out and pushed through into this cabin. He knew that the phaser blast would have knocked them both out for at least an hour.

When he reemerged from the cabin, he was wearing the uniform of one of the guards. Although there was nothing he could do about his obvious resemblance to the *Enterprise*'s second-in-command, at least he could make himself a bit less noticeable as he moved through the corridors.

He had a little bit of time. He hoped that would be all he needed.

Data, he thought desperately, *if you are here . . . where would you be? What would you be up to? Would you really be so coldhearted as to kill Deanna . . . and if so, how would you go about it?*

Data stood on the turbolift as it whisked him to his destination. He had worked out what needed to be done and was reasonably certain that he could succeed.

He would leave some confusion in his wake. But confusion could easily be dealt with. There would be nothing absolutely incriminating.

And Deanna would be dead.

The Sindareen entered the conference room. "Our apologies," said Ambassador Nici. "We were unaware that the switch had been made to this conference room."

Eza was staring at Troi with a most peculiar expression on his face. And Deanna started to feel the first tickle to her mind of something . . . something that she was starting to place . . .

That vague feeling that she had encountered once before . . . when she had been the captive, years ago, of a Sindareen raider.

*　　*　　*

In the corridor, Admiral Riker suddenly skidded to a halt.

"Of course," he whispered.

He turned and barreled down the corridor.

Data stepped off the turbolift and abruptly a voice called, "Data!"

Geordi LaForge came up to him quickly. "I'm glad I happened to run into you. We've been getting some weird variants in the warp field fluctuations."

"Now is not a good time, Geordi." Data started down the hallway.

Geordi stopped him, looking at him with concern. "Data, are you okay?"

"Functioning perfectly. We can discuss the field fluctuations at a later date, Geordi. For the moment, I have other things to attend to."

"But it's really odd. The time-space capacitors seem to be reacting to . . . well, to nothing that I can detect."

"Later." Data's voice was firm. He turned and walked off, leaving a very puzzled chief engineer behind him.

Will Riker studied the ambassadors around the table. Everyone seemed perfectly calm. Everything seemed friendly . . . or at least polite.

He looked to Deanna. A faint, puzzled expression was on her face that he knew quite well. She was concentrating, trying to pick the threads of emotions out of the air and weave them into something that she could examine and make pronouncements on.

He thought of giving her a gentle nudge, to ask her what was happening . . . but then decided against it. When she was ready to tell him, she would.

Lieutenant Barclay checked his morning duty log, saw nothing particularly unusual, glanced in the mirror once more, approved of his hairstyle, and walked out of his quarters whistling and ready for a far more sane day.

He walked past Lieutenant Commander Data, who barely afforded him a glance. "Good morning, sir."

"Good morning, Barclay. You look much more relaxed today," said Data, and kept on going. Barclay, still whistling aimlessly, headed for the turbolift.

Admiral Riker dashed into Data's quarters and moaned softly.

Data was lying, unmoving, on the bed. From his skewed position, it was clear that he had been shut off and tossed there like a sack of wheat.

And to make matters worse . . . his head was gone.

Riker allotted sixty seconds to locate it before he went after the future Data himself. It would have been nice to have the strength of the present Data as backup . . . but he would make do if he had to.

He always had in the past . . .

. . . or future . . .

. . . or whatever.

The door to the conference room hissed open, and Data stepped in. Picard looked up at Data questioningly.

"A private matter, sir, for Counselor Troi."

"Very well," said a slightly puzzled Picard.

Troi rose, as did Will. With Data, they stepped over to one of the corners of the room.

"You are aware that the captain has filled me in on the present situation," Data said softly. When Riker and Troi nodded, he continued, "I have some rather bad news. Admiral Riker . . . your future self . . . seems to have suffered some sort of massive heart attack. Dr. Crusher says he's barely stabilized and"—he turned to Troi—"he's calling for you, Counselor."

Deanna frowned. "I . . . I don't feel him in that sort of distress."

"He's barely conscious, Counselor. Perhaps that affects your empathic abilities . . . or perhaps the proximity of our own Commander Riker deters your ability to focus on the other. I took the liberty of coming in person, rather than using communicators. In the event that unauthorized individuals are somehow tapping into our comm systems . . ."

"Yes, good thinking, Mr. Data," said Riker.

"I'd better go to him," Deanna said worriedly.

"I'll go, too," Riker added.

"Are you certain you wish to do that, Commander?" Data asked. "Watching yourself die . . . I'd think it would be difficult for you."

Deanna turned to Riker. "He's right, Will. Please . . . I don't want to put you through that. Data's with me. I'll be fine. Honestly . . . if you ask me, I think you're being overconcerned. The danger is probably over."

Data nodded in agreement.

CHAPTER 42

With three seconds to spare in his self-imposed countdown, Admiral Riker found Data's head. It had been wrapped carefully in a sheet and shoved into the back of the closet . . . just inconvenient enough to serve as a delay, but not so dangerous that it would actually endanger the future existence of the android called Data.

Riker activated the head as soon as he had pulled it free from the cloth. Data blinked and looked around. Then he stared up into the face of his liberator.

"I assume you are not the person who put me into this predicament."

"No, Data. You did this all to yourself."

"You appear to be Commander Riker . . . but significantly aged."

"Come on," said Riker, getting to his feet. "Can you operate your body from here?"

With a cybernetic impulse from Data's positronic brain, his body lurched off the bed like something from an old horror film.

"Good," Riker snapped. "I'll fill you in on the way. Come on, let's go!"

"Be certain to face me forward so that I can see where I am going," Data cautioned him.

Riker bolted into the corridor and started down the hallway, Data's head tucked under one arm. Behind him at a rapid jog came Data's body.

"Would you care to apprise me of what is happening?" asked Data.

Riker was ready for this. He knew that if he told Data the truth, or even part of the truth, he might have a bigger problem than when he started. If this Data decided that the future Data's mission was a sound one, then he might very well have two androids trying to kill Deanna. That he did not need.

So he lied through his teeth.

"I'm Will Riker, all right, but from another dimension. We're pursuing the individual you know as Lore. He crossed over into our universe, killed Deanna Troi there for reasons that we do not know, and now has returned to this dimension and is intent on performing the same murderous act. We have no idea why he's doing these things."

"Neither do I," Data said, "but Lore has been known to behave in an irrational manner. He must be stopped. Shall we warn Counselor Troi via communicator?"

"No. Lore might be monitoring the frequencies. Our best hope is to catch him by surprise."

Commander Will Riker sat down again as Data and Troi walked out of the conference room together. Picard leaned over to him and said, "Number One?"

In a low voice, Will said, "My future self is . . . very ill. Data says he's calling for Deanna. She's going to him."

Picard studied Riker to make sure that his second-in-command was dealing with this news. But Riker's face was inscrutable . . . in fact, he seemed lost in thought.

Deanna Troi looked worriedly at Data as he stepped to one side when they emerged from the conference room and said, "After you, Counselor." She started down the corridor, Data a foot or two behind her.

* * *

Barclay stepped out of the turbolift . . . and stopped breathing.

The Riker from the holodeck pushed past him and onto the lift . . . which was impossible. Under his arm he'd tucked the head of Lieutenant Commander Data . . . which was also impossible since Barclay had just left Data on another deck. He turned, staring at the bizarre sight in utter shock, and then was rudely shoved out of the way by what appeared to be a headless body, which joined the other two . . . or maybe it was one and a half . . . in the turbolift.

"Hope you're keeping your nose clean, Barclay," Riker warned him.

"Good morning, Barclay," said Data's head. "You look much more relaxed today."

Then the turbolift hissed shut.

"Thank you, sir," was all Barclay managed to say, before he mercifully passed out.

Deanna Troi and her escort started down the hallway. Data had already determined how he would pin the blame on Lore, thus leaving his own time line unaffected. Now he studied her long neck, trying to decide what would be the most painless method of disposing of her. For some reason, now that the moment would shortly be at hand . . . he felt . . .

Reluctant.

But his duty was clear.

In the conference room, Riker suddenly jumped as if someone had jammed a rod into his back.

He had done so right as Nici began to make her opening remarks, and she looked at him with stern disapproval.

"Commander?" said Picard.

"Data said he's calling for her." He turned to face Picard and looked as if he'd seen a ghost.

Picard was at a loss, but he saw the consternation of his first officer. "I know, Number One. You told me th—"

Riker's voice became louder. "You don't understand, Captain! That's *exactly* what Data said. 'He's calling.' He said 'he's.' Several times! *He used contractions!*"

"But Data doesn't use—"

Immediately both officers were on their feet, but Riker was nearer the exit. The ambassadors were babbling in utter confusion as Riker bolted out the door.

He saw them, just turning the corner of the corridor.

As if from a separation of years, he shouted, *"Deanna! It's a trap!"*

Troi spun, his words and his mind reaching out to her and warning her.

Data, aware that he had been found out, drew back his fist, and Troi saw it just as she turned. He stepped forward and drove his fist straight toward her face.

With a cry of alarm, Deanna dropped back. Data's fist whistled bare inches from her face and smashed into a wall, going in with such force that his arm penetrated up to his elbow.

Deanna tried to run, but Data lashed out with one of his feet and tripped her up. She fell with a cry, and Will charged forward, bringing his phaser up.

With the hand that had already entered the wall, Data ripped out a huge chunk and hurled it directly at Riker. Riker dodged it, and as the twisted metal thudded to the ground in back of him, Riker fired the phaser.

Data moved with blinding speed and grabbed at the phaser that Riker was holding. Taking a desperate gamble, knowing that he couldn't match Data's superior strength, Riker relaxed his grip and instead shot his hand out toward Data's off-switch.

It wasn't there.

"I had it disconnected, Commander," said Data, sounding almost apologetic. "It became a nuisance." Data's fingers wrapped around the phaser and squeezed, and Riker had to release his grip or risk his hand getting crushed along with it.

Data dropped the twisted metal to the ground, then picked up Riker and hurled him against the far wall. Riker crashed into it and slumped to the ground, dazed.

Picard came from nowhere, hurtling through the air and grabbing Data from behind. Data reached around, grabbing the captain's arm and twisting it around and back. Picard cried out, but that didn't stop him from slamming his free hand up into Data's face. The resulting injury was severe . . . but not for Data. Picard, however, sprained his hand.

"I'm doing this for you, Captain," said Data, sounding almost remorseful. "If I had any choice, I'd do anything else." And he lifted Picard completely off his feet, about to hurl him into the ambassadors who were flooding into the hallway. They fell back, trying to get out of the way.

And Will Riker, pushing off from the wall, charged and tackled Data around the legs. It knocked the android off balance, and he lost his grip on Picard, who tumbled down on top of him.

"Stop it!" Deanna was shouting. *"Stop it!"*

Picard and Riker each grabbed an arm, trying to pin Data. It didn't work. With his superior strength, Data twisted around, lifting Riker clear and crushing him against Picard. Data started to get to his feet.

All the ambassadors were shouting at once.

Data was turning his attention to Deanna.

Riker, indomitable, was grabbing at Data's leg, trying to slow him down. Picard, using the wall for support, was pulling himself to his feet.

Everywhere there was confusion, chaos, raw emotions running rampant . . .

And that was when Deanna Troi pointed at the Sindareen delegation.

"They're deceiving us!" she cried out.

Time froze.

"It's a lie!" said Nici with amazing calm.

"No," said Deanna, her voice building in intensity. "No, it's not a lie."

"Shut up," Eza now said, looking to Nici. "Make her shut up."

"I sense that you want him"—she pointed at Data—"to succeed. You . . . you did not come here in good faith. I sense duplicity . . . lies, cheats, anything to stall for time for the Sindareen."

"This is madness," Nici snarled, louder and angrier.

But Deanna ignored her, whirling on Eza. "And you! You want me dead! You'd do anything to see me dead. You . . . you tried! You tried to kill me! Put something in the drink . . . I sense your emotions, homicidal, murderous."

The air around them seemed to be shifting, coming to life somehow. There was a crackling of energy that seemed to come from nowhere . . .

And Eza howled, *"You empathic bitch! You've ruined everything!"*

From his sleeve he produced a small phaser, smaller than almost anyone had ever seen.

He had a clear shot at Deanna. He wasn't going to miss.

And suddenly, arcing through the air over Deanna's head, came a tumbling, golden object. It struck Eza squarely in the chest, knocking him backward. The phaser fired but the shot went wide, striking the ceiling over Deanna's head.

The golden object skittered across the floor and rolled up to Deanna's feet. She looked down in astonishment at Data's face. "I suggest you drop to the floor, Counselor."

Deanna was still staring in confusion at Data's head, presenting a perfect target. A split second later, Data's body slammed into her from behind, knocking her to the floor next to Data's profusely apologizing head. However, his apologies were drowned out by the phaser beam that crackled over them. It enveloped Eza, staggering him, and he screeched in protest.

Adm. William T. Riker advanced on him slowly, inexorably, the power blasting out of his phaser. "Stay down, Deanna. It still takes a lot of phaser power to put these bastards down for the count."

"Bastards!" shrieked Nici in indignation. "Captain Picard, I object to being described in—"

"Be quiet!" snapped Picard.

Eza writhed in the power of the phaser. He lost his grip on his own phaser and it tumbled to the floor, but so consumed with fury was he that he still tried to make headway against the blast.

"You're from my time, aren't you," said the admiral, progressing relentlessly. "That's the only place you could have gotten that weapon. You're from the time stream that was . . . and will be again. You decided that this point in time was the turning point for your people—was the downfall of your race—and you decided to come back and change it to your liking. Kill the woman who blew the whistle on your people. And in one reality, you got away with it. But not in my reality, you murderer. Not in *my* reality! Because you picked the *wrong focal point!*"

Around Eza the scream of the phaser merged with the howling of the air, and he was knocked completely off his feet, thrown against the wall like a straw in a hurricane. He sagged to the floor, unconscious and helpless.

And then the air around them was roaring. Roaring with far-off winds that seemed to call from another time and place, from an infinity of maybes. A coruscating, sparkling whirlpool of color and light.

Eza was starting to dematerialize, his very molecules being drawn into the vortex around them.

And Will Riker suddenly lost his grip on Data. For a panicked moment he thought that the android had slipped loose and was going to make one final, desperate lunge for Deanna. But he realized his error immediately. Data was starting to fade. Will's hands were passing through him.

Deanna whirled to face the admiral.

He, too, was being drawn off. The color seemed to be fading from him, as if being yanked away.

"Deanna!" he called to her, reaching out.

Heedless of the danger to herself, Deanna Troi stretched out her hand to the man who had crossed decades, remodeled the universe, all for her.

Her hand passed right through him, as if he were a ghost. The ghost of things yet to come.

His body started to flatten out, twisting from three dimensions to two and then one.

"I'm sorry!" she cried out to him. "I tried . . . to touch you one last time."

He smiled, his body disappearing like the Cheshire cat's. His voice sounded distant as he said, "Don't be. Maybe it won't be the

PETER DAVID

last time. Besides . . . who really cares about all this physical touching. Not young Deanna Troi. It's the spiritual that's important . . . that's forever . . ."

And then, with a final roar and burst of wind that swept over everyone in the corridor . . .

He was gone.

332

CHAPTER 43

"**C**ome in," said Deanna as the tone at her door chimed.

Riker entered, his hands behind his back. He stopped as the door closed behind him. "Are you okay?"

She shut off the computer screen she was studying, folded her hands, and said, "Why shouldn't I be okay?"

"Well . . . you went through a lot."

"We both did," she reminded him. "But that was twenty-four hours ago. I bounce back quickly, given time."

"Given time."

He walked slowly toward her. "I thought you'd be interested . . . the Chameloid disappeared about the same time as . . . the others."

"I assumed as much," she said quietly.

"The Sindareen ambassador has been sent packing. She's not particularly happy about it. The peace initiative has fallen apart, and the experts predict that it's just a matter of time now before the entire Sindareen civilization collapses. There's already talk about how the Federation might come in to pick up the pieces if that happens."

"That would be very humane."

"Oh, and Data has his head together . . . so to speak. It turns out that I . . . that the admiral told him that this other Data—the one who tried to kill you—was actually Lore."

"And was it?"

Riker paused. "I don't know," he said slowly. "I know Data believes it to be. I think he is far more . . . satisfied . . . with the notion that it was Lore than he would be with the concept that there would be a circumstance in which he'd try to murder you."

"We have no idea what influences will shape Data over the next forty years," she said slowly. "For all we know, given a set of circumstances where the life of one woman is weighed against the reality that he knows . . . he might very well decide that that woman is dispensable."

"Even if the woman is you?"

"Even if. And frankly . . . I'd understand his decision."

"Yes . . . but maybe he wouldn't understand. That's a hell of a thing for him to have to live with. So maybe it would be better if we . . ."

"Kept it between ourselves?"

He nodded.

"Consider it kept." She leaned back. "So . . . did you come here to discuss everything except what you really want to discuss?"

"And what might that be?"

"Us."

He let out a slow breath. She waited for him to speak.

"I don't know what's going to happen with us," he said. "I saw what my life was like without you . . . saw what I developed into. I can't say I like it very much. But . . . that was when you had been pulled from my life completely. We could continue in the way that we are now, and as long as you're there to be friend, confidant . . . soul mate . . . things could work out well for both of us."

"I see what you're saying," Deanna said slowly. "Of course, on the other hand, if we become . . . or go back to being . . . lovers . . . things could work out even better for us."

"Or worse," he pointed out.

"Or worse," she acknowledged.

He shook his head. "I feel so ridiculous. Do we really have to wait forty years until we're ready to take a chance on the two of us?"

"No, Will"—she smiled—"we just have to wait until we're ready. It might take forty years. Or who knows? It might take forty days. We have to wait and see. But at least we have a chance. It's up to us how we use it."

He nodded and then said, "Oh . . . by the way . . . I made something for you. It's only an approximation, of course, based on my memories . . . memories which were filled, at the time, with the sight of a particularly nubile young maid of honor and her magnificent figure."

Her face colored slightly. "Will, what are you talking about?"

He brought his hand from behind his back. In it was a thin, white, gauze headband.

She stared at it, uncomprehendingly at first. But then she understood. "That's . . . that's like the one Chandra wore!"

"So I *did* make it close enough so that it's recognizable. Good. Um . . . if you wouldn't mind turning your head . . ."

She angled her head around and he looped it around and back, pulling her hair through. She stood and presented herself for inspection. "How does it look?"

"As beautiful as the woman wearing it."

She felt her emotions turning to melted butter, and she went to him. He enveloped her in his arms, and their lips came together. . . .

And for a long moment, all the confusion and complexity of their lives fell away, and they were once again the young man and woman hungering for each other; the couple shyly learning about one another and exploring the things that each of them lacked and each of them provided; the new lovers in the jungle, intoxicated with their environment and each other; she was the woman whose life he'd saved, and he was the man whose life she had made.

And they had all the time in the universe. . . .

THE BEGINNING
OF THE
END

CHAPTER 44

Mary Mac watched in astonishment as four people emerged from the swirling vortex of the Guardian of Forever: Admiral Riker, Commodore Data, Lieutenant Blair, and one more form that tumbled forward, clearly unconscious.

She went to them, rolling the body over to get a better look and confirm what she had thought. "This . . . this is Mar Loc!"

Data looked at her, his head tilted. "The scientist whom you said had departed?"

She nodded in silent amazement.

And then the Guardian spoke, in that vast and all-encompassing way that it had: "All is . . . as it was."

Data turned to face the Guardian. "You mean that Admiral Riker did indeed restore the time line to its original form?"

"All is as it was," repeated the portal.

And now Blair stepped forward, his long fur swirling. "For crying out loud," he shouted, "if you knew that time had been tampered with in the first place, and you knew that the admiral's actions were correct . . . then why in hell didn't you *tell* us that?!"

With utter serenity, the Guardian replied, **"You did not ask."**

There was dead silence, except for the howling of the wind, for about ten seconds. And then Blair managed to get out, "We didn't *ask?*"

Riker started to laugh.

"We didn't ask!" Blair sounded positively outraged. "You mean everything we went through, all the difficult decisions we had to make, all the . . . *we didn't ask!"*

"We didn't," said Data in quiet amazement. "That was very foolish of me. In my determination to uphold the Starfleet imperative of noninterference with time, I . . ."

And Riker, who had managed to calm himself down sufficiently, said, "What you did, Data, is forget the very first *duty* of Starfleet . . . something that I started thinking about when I was spending time with Capt. Wesley Crusher, and remembering the hard lesson he learned back in his Academy days. The duty that supersedes all the imperatives and directives . . ."

"That we must always seek the truth," said Data.

"Right. And the truth," said Riker, hauling the unconscious Mar Loc, a.k.a. Eza, to his feet, "is that this little sleaze decided to make his people's life better. Mary Mac . . . have you had any unexplained bruises in recent weeks?"

"Why . . . why yes," she said, looking at Data. "Remember, Commodore? I had a round bruise on my upper arm."

"A spray-hypo mark," said Riker. "Press down too hard, you leave one. One night while you were asleep, he must have shot you up with something to make sure you stayed asleep—or perhaps even something that induced sleepwalking. He brought you out to the Guardian, used you in your sleeping state to open the force field, returned you to where you were sleeping, stepped into the Guardian . . ."

"And the rest is history," said Blair.

Riker smiled. "Not anymore."

Moments later, Mary Mac had enlisted Blair's aid in dragging the unconscious Mar Loc away, vowing that when she got through with her report to the Federation science council, Mar Loc was going to be sent somewhere where time could truly be appreciated . . . an Orion prison (for his crimes against Mary Mac), where life was so difficult that days tended to pass like years.

"I want you to understand, Admiral," Data said slowly as they stared into the glowing arch of the Guardian of Forever, "that I am truly sorry for my actions."

"It's all right, Data. On the face of it . . . what you did, or tried to do, was correct."

"Curious . . . in my efforts to kill Deanna Troi, I made several mistakes. I did not intend to, but I did. They were almost *clumsy* in nature."

"Perhaps, Data, you did it on purpose. Perhaps you wanted to be stopped."

Data looked at Riker with curiosity. "Is that possible?"

"Of course it's possible. One of the key things about being human, Data . . . is that you don't always know why you do the things you do."

"How very odd. I must admit . . . I did feel somewhat like Brutus."

"Ah, but Brutus, remember, was an honorable man," pointed out Riker. "The important thing is that it's all worked out for the best."

"Has it?"

Riker looked at Data speculatively. "What do you mean?"

Data gestured around them. "While we are on this planet, Admiral, in the heart of the temporal vortex . . . we are untouched by whatever changes might have been made by your reparations. When Mar Loc originally altered time, we—and our memories— were simply altered with it. We had no awareness that anything was different. Now, however, we were at the center of the change. Although you were the architect of the restoration, the actual changes were made without us being a part of them in the here and now. When we leave this world . . . there is no certainty as to what will happen to us. Our memories may shift to accommodate the new time stream. Or we may retain our memories, but find ourselves in a strange new environment. There is even a remote possibility that we may simply blink out of existence, if we do not exist as entities in this time stream."

"I don't think that's going to happen. And you know why, Data? Because I meant what I said earlier. I think that this thing"—Riker pointed to the Guardian—"is God's window. And I don't think that God would have let us in through his window if he didn't intend for us to live in his house."

"That's very spiritual, Admiral."

"I didn't use to be a spiritual person, but I had a good teacher."

Riker gazed up at the swirling skies, the vast colored streaks and the miasma of temporal rifts that formed the heavens above the Forever World.

Distracted, he said, "I really don't know what else there is to say, Data, except . . ."

"Let's get the hell out of here?" suggested Data.

Not looking away from the skies, Riker simply nodded. "I think that probably covers it," he said, but he wasn't paying attention.

And he realized that in the sky's swirling and whirlpool shape, he saw a painting he'd seen a lifetime ago. . . .

"We're going to face a new and different universe, Admiral. Are you not at all afraid?"

There were reds and purples, and then, in the midst of that vast mixture of cosmic existence, Riker saw a face. . . .

"No, Data," he said quietly. "I'm not afraid at all. I think it's going to work out just fine."

And he called out, as he had called out in hopelessness and despair for year upon year of desolation.

And the answer came.

Whether it was from within him, or whether it came from somewhere out there in the galaxy, from someone who was the better part of all that he was, he couldn't be sure.

But it was there just the same. Tears came to his eyes as he heard, in his head, the words that he had waited half a lifetime to hear. Sweet and musical, in a voice filled with promise.

And the words were:

Welcome home . . . Imzadi . . .